W9-BQK-870

# THE RIDER OF
# THE RUBY HILLS

# THE RIDER OF THE RUBY HILLS

## LOUIS L'AMOUR

BANTAM BOOKS

TORONTO • NEW YORK • LONDON • SYDNEY • AUCKLAND

THE RIDER OF THE RUBY HILLS
*A Bantam Book / published by arrangement with
the author*
*Bantam edition / September 1986*
*The Louis L'Amour Collection / May 1987*

*All rights reserved.*
*Book Design by Reneé Gelman.*
*Copyright © 1986 by Louis L'Amour.*
*This book may not be reproduced in whole or in part, by
mimeograph or any other means, without permission.*
*For information address: Bantam Books, Inc.*

*If you would be interested in receiving bookends for The
Louis L'Amour Collection, please write to this address
for information:*

> The Louis L'Amour Collection
> Bantam Books
> P.O. Box 956
> Hicksville, New York 11802

ISBN 0-553-06308-1

*Published simultaneously in the United States and Canada*

*Bantam Books are published by Bantam Books, Inc. Its trade-
mark, consisting of the words "Bantam Books" and the por-
trayal of a rooster, is Registered in U.S. Patent and Trademark
Office and in other countries. Marca Registrada. Bantam
Books, Inc., 666 Fifth Avenue, New York, New York 10103.*

PRINTED IN THE UNITED STATES OF AMERICA

0   9   8   7   6   5   4   3   2   1

# Contents

# FOREWORD

The stories presented in this volume are more bits of history from my early days as a writer when my work was being published exclusively in magazines. The life of a young writer is never easy, and at the time these stories were written it was a struggle to eat more than occasionally. The book and movie sales did not come until much later.

When World War II came along I was just beginning to see my work on the magazine stands. But during the four years I was first in the Army, then the Tank Destroyers, and later the Transportation Corps, I rarely found time to write. Returning home from overseas duty, I found all had changed at the magazines. I literally had to begin again by convincing a new crop of editors that I could write.

The stories I published back then were classified by their length. The "short-short," often with a surprise ending, had been made popular by O. Henry and usually ran to 1,500 words, more or less. A "short story" rarely was more than 6,000 words. A "novelette," or "novella," usually amounted to 9,000 to 15,000 words. A "novel," which the stories collected here are, rarely consisted of more than 40,000 words. By comparison, a novel published as a book is usually at least 60,000 words, but there's no upward length limit.

The editors of the magazines in which these stories originally appeared, affectionately known then and now as "pulps," demanded I stress action—swift and hard hitting. Little time was to be devoted to atmosphere, characterization, or background. Yet a good writer knows that action always derives from character and situation, so some of us tried to push on to tell a better story in a more complete fashion. Yet some stories need development, time and space, and the "pulps" gave neither.

Often a writer will live so closely with a character he has created that he cannot leave him alone but must return to relate more of his story. Once accepted as a novelist I was able to realize my long-held wish to redo my "magazine novels" for publication as books. Over the years, the works herein were revised and slightly expanded, often with new characters and additional plot lines, into novels I published as full-length paperbacks under other titles.

These particular early magazine versions of my books seem to be a source of considerable speculation and curiosity among fans who have requested the opportunity to read all the stories I have written. So much so is this the case of late, that I've decided to bring four of my "magazine novels" back into print in this book.

The title story of this volume, "The Rider of the Ruby Hills," was my first telling of the novel *Where the Long Grass Blows*. It was also once filmed as *The Treasure of Ruby Hills*, a movie with Zachary Scott, Carole Matthews, and Raymond Hatton among the players. "Showdown Trail," the original version of *The Tall Stranger*, was the basis for a movie with the latter title, starring Joel McCrea and Virginia Mayo.

"A Man Called Trent" became *The Mountain Valley War* and is the second in a trilogy of stories about Lance Kilkenny. "The Trail to Peach Meadow Canyon" was the original version of *Son of a Wanted Man*. In it, I was able to follow in more detail what happened to the various groups of outlaws operating out of their canyon hideout and bring them into contact with two law officers of the time and area, Tyrel Sackett and Borden Chantry, neither of whom is aware that they are distantly related. (Nor did I tell the reader, for that is Another Story!)

I do not think of the protagonists of these or any of my stories as heroes. They are simply people living their lives within the circumstances of their time. Most stories cover only a few hours, days, or weeks in the life of a character. The characters in my stories are *people*. They are born, they live, and they die. Much happens in the lives of the people you'll meet in the following pages that I haven't told you. Perhaps I'll do that in future books.

# AUTHOR'S NOTE
# The Rider of the Ruby Hills

*Often the most beautiful parts of western states are only to be found far from the highways; a casual traveler can pass through, say, Arizona or Nevada, without being able to see much of what the areas have to offer. For example, in Arizona the great pine forests of the White Mountain area, their running, rushing streams and wild game, lie hidden away from major highways, although the roads through them are usually excellent.*

*Monument Valley, the San Francisco Mountains, and other places, also lie off the highways.*

*In Nevada, the beautiful Ruby Mountains lie somewhat to the south of Elko and its highway. The Rubies soar up to 11,000 feet, with several beautiful lakes and the waterfalls of Lamoille Canyon. It is lovely, inspiring country, and every pass and every canyon has its story of Indians, mining, and cattle, of lost mines, buried treasure, and gun battles.*

# THE RIDER OF THE RUBY HILLS

## Chapter I
### *Losing Bet*

There was a lonely place where the trail ran up to the sky. It turned sharply left on the very point of a lofty promontory overlooking the long sweep of the valley below. Here the trail offered to the passerby a vision at this hour. Rosy-tipped peaks and distant purple mountains could be seen, beyond the far reach of the tall grass range.

Upon the very lip of the rocky shelf sat a solitary horseman. He was a man tall in the saddle, astride a strangely marked horse. Its head was held high; its ears were pricked forward with attention riveted upon the valley, as though in tune with the thoughts of its rider—thoughts that said there lay a new country, with new dangers, new rewards, and new trails.

The rider was a tall man, narrow hipped and powerful of chest and shoulder. His features were blunt and rugged, so that a watcher might have said, "Here is a man who is not handsome, but a fighter." Yet he was good-looking in his own hard, confident way. He looked now upon this valley as Cortez might have looked upon the Valley of Mexico.

He came alone and penniless, but he did not come as one seeking favors. He did not come hunting a job. He came as a conqueror.

For Ross Haney had made his decision. At twenty-seven he was broke. He sat in the middle of all he owned, a splendid Appaloosa gelding, a fine California saddle, a .44 Winchester rifle, and two walnut-stocked Colt .44 pistols. These were his all. Behind him was a life that had taken him from a cradle in a covered wagon to the hurricane deck of many a hardheaded bronc.

It was a life that had left him rich in experience but poor in goods of the world. The experience was the hardfisted experience of hard winters, dry ranges, and the dusty bitterness of cattle drives. He had

3

fought Comanches and rustlers, hunted buffalo and horse thieves. Now he had decided that it all had brought him nothing but grief and more riding. Now he was going to ride for himself, to fight for himself.

His keen dark eyes from under the flat black brim of his hat studied the country below with a speculative glint. His judgment of terrain would have done credit to a general, and in his own way Ross Haney was a general. His arrival in the Ruby Valley country was, in its way, an invasion.

He was a young man with a purpose. He did not want wealth but a ranch, a well-watered ranch in a good stock country. That his pockets were empty did not worry him, for he had made up his mind, and as men had discovered before this, Ross Haney with his mind made up was a force to be reckoned with.

Nor was he riding blind into a strange land. Like a good tactician he had gathered his information carefully, judged the situation, the terrain, and the enemy before he began his move.

This was new country to him, but he knew the landmarks and the personalities. He knew the strength and the weakness of its rulers, knew the economic factors of their existence, knew the stresses and the strains within it. He knew that he rode into a valley at war—that blood had been shed and that armed men rode its trails day and night. Into this land he rode a man alone, determined to have his own from the country, come what may, letting the chips fall where they might.

With a movement of his body he turned the gelding left down the trail into the pines, a trail where at this late hour it would soon be dark, a trail somber, majestic in its stillness under the columned trees.

As he moved under the trees, he removed his hat and rode slowly. It was a good country, a country where a man could live and grow, and where if he was lucky, he might have sons to grow tall and straight beside him. This he wanted. He wanted no longer the far horizons. He wanted his own hearth fire, the creak of his own pump, the heads of his own horses looking over the gate bars for his hand to feed them. He wanted peace, and for it he came to a land at war.

A flicker of light caught his eye, and the faint smell of wood smoke. He turned the gelding toward the fire, and when he was near, he swung down. The sun's last rays lay bright through the pines upon this spot. The earth was trampled by hoofs, and in the fire itself the ashes were gray but for one tiny flame that thrust a bright spear upward from the end of a stick.

Studying the scene, his eyes held for an instant on one place where the parched grass had been blackened in a perfect ring.

His eyes glinted with hard humor. "A cinch ring artist. Dropped her there to cool and she singed the grass. A pretty smooth gent, I'd say."

Not slick enough, of course. A smarter man or a less confident one would have pulled up that handful of blackened grass and tossed it into the flames.

There had been two men here, his eyes told him. Two men and two horses. One of the men had been a big man with small feet. The impressions of his feet were deeper and he had mounted the larger horse.

Curiously, he studied the scene. This was a new country for him and it behooved a man to know the local customs. He grinned at the thought. If cinch ring branding was one of the local customs, it was a strange one. In most sections of the country the activity was frowned upon, to say the least. If an artist was caught pursuing his calling, he was likely to find himself at the wrong end of a hair rope with nothing under his feet.

The procedure was simple enough. One took a cinch ring from his own saddle gear and holding it between a couple of sticks, used it when red hot like any other branding iron. A good hand with a cinch ring could easily duplicate any known brand, depending only upon his degree of skill.

Ross rolled and lighted a smoke. If he were found on the spot it would require explaining, and at the moment he had no intention of explaining anything. He swung his leg over the saddle and turned the gelding down trail once more.

Not three miles away lay the cow town known as Soledad. To his right and about six miles away was an imposing cluster of buildings shaded beneath a splendid grove of old cottonwoods. Somewhat nearer, and also well shaded, was a smaller ranch.

Beyond the rocky ridge that stretched an anxious finger into the lush valley was Walt Pogue's Box N spread.

The farther ranch belonged to Chalk Reynolds, his RR outfit being easily the biggest in the Ruby Hills country. The nearer ranch belonged to Bob and Sherry Vernon.

"When thieves fall out," Ross muttered aloud, "honest men get their dues. Or that's what they say. Now I'm not laying any claim to being so completely honest, but there's trouble brewing in this valley. When the battle smoke blows away, Ross Haney is going to be top dog on one of these ranches.

"They've got it all down there. They have range, money, power. They have gunhands riding for them, but you and me, Rio, we've only got each other."

He was a lone wolf on the prowl. Down there they ran in packs, and he would circle the packs, alone. When the moment came, he would close in.

"There's an old law, Rio, that only the strong survive," he said. "Those ranches belong to men who were strong, and some of them still are. They were strong enough to take them from other men, from smaller men, weaker men. That's the story of Reynolds and Pogue. They rustled cows until they grew big, and now they sit on the housetops and crow. Or they did, until they began fightin' one another."

"Your reasoning," the cool, quiet voice was feminine, "is logical, but dangerous. I might suggest that when you talk to your horse, you should be sure his are the only ears!"

She sat well in the saddle, poised and alert. There was a quirk of humor at the corners of her mouth and nothing of coyness or fear in her manner. Every inch of her showed beauty, care, and consideration of appearances that was new to him, but beneath it there was both fire and steel—and quality.

"That's good advice," he agreed, measuring her with his eyes. "Very good advice."

"Now that you've looked me over," she suggested coolly, "would you like to examine my teeth for age?"

He grinned, unabashed. "No, but now that I've looked you over I'd say you are pretty much of a woman. The kind that's made for a man!"

She returned his glance and then smiled as if the remark had pleased her. So she changed the subject. "Just which ranch do you plan to be top dog on when the fighting is over?"

"I haven't decided," he said frankly. "I'm a right choosy sort of man when it comes to horses, ranches, and women!"

"Yes?" She glanced at the gelding. "I'd say your judgment of horses isn't obvious by that one. Not that he isn't well shaped, and I imagine he could run, but you could do better."

"I doubt it." He glanced at her fine, clean-limbed Thoroughbred. "I'd bet a little money he can outrun that beauty of yours, here to Soledad."

Her eyes flashed. "Why, you idiot! Flame is the fastest horse in this country. He comes of racing stock!"

"I don't doubt it," Haney agreed. "He's a fine horse. But I'll bet my saddle against a hundred dollars that this Appaloosa will kick dust in his face before we get to Soledad!"

She laughed scornfully, and her head came up. "You're on!" she cried, and her red horse gave a great bound and hit the trail running. That jump gave the bay the start, but Ross knew his gelding.

Leaning over he yelled into the horse's ear as they charged after the bay. "Come on, boy! We've got to beat that bay! We need the money!" And Rio, seeming to understand, stretched his legs and ran like a scared rabbit.

As they swept into the main road and in full sight of Soledad, the bay was leading by three lengths, but despite the miles behind it, the Appaloosa loved to run, and he was running now.

The gelding had the blood of Arabians in his veins, and he was used to offhand, cow camp style racing. The road took a small jog, but Ross did not swing the gelding around it, but took the desert and mountain bred horse across the stones and through the mesquite, hitting the road scarcely a length behind the big red horse.

Men were gathering in the street and on the edge of town now and shouting about the racing horses. With a half mile to go the big red horse was slowing. He was a sprinter, but he had been living too well with too little running. The gelding was just beginning to run. Neck stretched, Ross leaning far forward to cut the wind resistance and lend impetus with his weight, the mustang thundered alongside the bay horse, and neck and neck they raced up to the town. Then, with the nearest building only a short jump ahead, Ross Haney spoke to the Appaloosa:

"Now, Rio! Now!"

With a lunge, the spotted horse was past and went racing into the street leading by a length.

Ross eased back on the reins and let the horse run on down the street abreast of the big red horse. They slowed to a canter, then a walk. The girl's eyes were wide and angry.

"You cheated! You cut across that bend!"

Ross chuckled. "You could have, ma'am! And you got off to a running start. Left me standing still!"

"I thought you wanted a race!" she protested scornfully. "You cheated me!"

Ross Haney drew up sharply, and his eyes went hard. "I reckon, ma'am," he said, "you come from a long line of sportsmen! You can forget the bet!"

The sarcasm in his voice cut like a whip. She opened her mouth to speak, but he had turned the Appaloosa away and was walking it back toward the center of town.

For an instant, she started to follow, and then with a toss of her head, she let him go.

## Chapter II
### *Hunting Trouble*

Several men were standing in front of the livery stable when he rode up. They looked at his horse and then at him. "That's a runner you got there, stranger! I reckon Sherry Vernon didn't relish getting beat! She sets great store by the Flame horse!"

Haney swung down and led the horse into the stable, where he rubbed him down and fed him. As he worked, he thought over what he had just learned. The girl was Sherry Vernon, one of the owners of the Twin V spread, and she had overheard his meditations on his plans. How seriously she would take them would be something else again. Well, it did not matter. He was planning no subterfuge. He had come to Ruby Valley on the prod, and they could find it out now as well as later.

The girl had been beautiful. That stuck in his mind after he thought of all the rest. It was the feeling that hung over his thinking with a certain aura that disturbed him. He had known few women who affected him, and those few had been in New Orleans or Kansas City on his rare trips there. Yet, this one touched a chord that had answered to none of the others.

Suddenly he was conscious of a looming figure beside him. For a moment he continued to work. Then he looked around into a broad, handsome face. The man was smiling.

"My name's Pogue," he said, thrusting out a hand. "Walt Pogue. I own the Box N. Is that horse for sale?"

"No, he's not."

"I'd not figured you'd be willing to sell. If you get that idea, come look me up. I'll give you five hundred for him."

Five hundred? That was a lot of money in a country full of ten-dollar mustangs or where a horse was often traded for a quart of whiskey.

"No," Haney repeated, "he's not for sale."

"Lookin' for a job? I could use a hand."

Ross Haney drew erect and looked over the horse's back. He noticed, and the thought somehow irritated him, that Pogue was even bigger than himself. The rancher was all of three inches taller and forty pounds heavier. And he did not look fat.

"Gunhand? Or cowhand?"

Walt Pogue's eyes hardened a shade, and then he smiled, a grim knowing smile. "Why, man," he said softly, "that would depend on you. But if you hire on as a warrior, you've got to be good!"

"I'm good. As good as any you've got."

"As good as Bob Streeter or Repp Hanson?"

Ross Haney's expression made no change, but within him he felt something tighten up and turn hard and wary. If Pogue had hired Streeter and Hanson, this was going to be ugly. Both men were killers, and not particular how they worked or how they killed.

"As good as Streeter or Hanson?" Haney shrugged. "A couple of cheap killers. Blood hunters. They aren't fighting men."

His dark eyes met that searching stare of Walt Pogue's again. "Who does Reynolds have?"

Pogue's face seemed to lower, and he stared back at Haney. "He's got Emmett Chubb."

*Emmett Chubb!*

So? And after all these years? "He won't have him long," Haney said, "because I'm going to kill him!"

Triumph leaped in Pogue's eyes. Swiftly, he moved around the horse. "Haney," he said, "that job could get you an even thousand dollars!"

"I don't take money for killing snakes."

"You do that job within three days and you'll get a thousand dollars!" Pogue said flatly.

Ross Haney pushed by the big man without replying and walked into the street. Three men sat on the rail by the stable door. Had they heard what was said inside? He doubted it, and yet?

Across the street and three doors down was the Trail Emporium. For a long moment his eyes held their look at the one light gleaming in the back of the store. It was after hours and the place was closed, but at the back door there might be a chance. Deliberately, he stepped into the street and crossed toward the light.

Behind him Walt Pogue moved into the doorway and stared after him, his brow furrowed with thought. His eyes went down the lean, powerful figure of the strange rider with a puzzled expression. Who was he? Where had he come from? Why was he here?

He wore two well-worn, tied-down guns. He had the still, remote face and the careful eyes typical of a man who had lived much with danger, and typical of so many of the gunfighters of the West. He had refused, or avoided the offer of, a job, yet he had seemed well aware of conditions in the valley.

Had Reynolds sent for him? Or Bob Vernon? He had ridden into town racing with Sherry. Had they met on the trail or come from the VV? That Pogue must know and at once. If Bob Vernon was hiring gunhands it would mean trouble, and that he did not want. One thing at a time.

Where was he going now? Resisting an instinct to follow Haney, Pogue turned and walked up the street toward the Bit and Bridle Saloon.

Haney walked up to the back door of the store building, hesitated an instant, and then tapped lightly.

Footsteps sounded within, and he heard the sound of a gun being drawn from a scabbard. "Who's there?"

Haney spoke softly. "A rider from the Pecos."

The door opened at once, and Ross slid through the opening. The man who faced him was round and white haired. Yet the eyes that took Haney in from head to heel were not old eyes. They were shrewd, hard, and knowing.

"Coffee?"

"Sure. Food, if you got some ready."

"About to eat myself." The man placed the gun on a sideboard and lifted the coffeepot from the stove. He filled the cup as Ross dropped into a chair. "Who sent you here?"

Haney glanced up and then tipped back in his chair. "Don't get on the prod, old-timer. I'm friendly. When an old friend of yours heard I was headed this way and might need a smart man to give me a word of advice, he told me to look you up. And he told me what to say."

"My days on that trail are over."

"Mine never started. This is a business trip. I'm planning to locate in the valley."

"Locate? *Here?*" The older man stared at him. He filled his own cup, and dishing up a platter of food and slapping bread on a plate, he sat down. "You came to me for advice. All right, you'll get it. Get on your horse and ride out of here as fast as you can. This is no country for strangers, and there have been too many of them around. Things are due to bust wide open and there will be a sight of killin' before it's over."

"You're right, of course."

"Sure. An' after it's over, what's left for a gunhand? You can go on the owlhoot, that's all. The very man who hired you and paid you warrior's wages won't want you when the fighting is over. There's revolution coming in this country. If you know the history of revolutions you'll know that as soon as one is over the first thing they do is liquidate the revolutionists. You ride out of here."

Ross Haney ate in silence. The older man was right, of course. To ride out would be the intelligent, sensible, and safe course, and he had absolutely no intention of doing it.

"Scott, I didn't come here to hire on as a gunhand. In fact, I have already had an offer. I came into this country because I've sized it up and I know what it's like. This country can use a good man, a strong man. There's a place for me here, and I mean to take it. Also, I want a good ranch. I aim to settle down, and I plan to get my ranch the same way Pogue, Reynolds, and the rest of them got theirs."

"Force? You mean with a gun?" Scott was incredulous. "Listen, young fellow, Pogue has fifty riders on his range, and most of them are ready to fight at the drop of a hat. Reynolds has just as many, and maybe more. And you come in here alone—or are you alone?"

The storekeeper bent a piercing gaze upon the young man, who smiled. "I'm alone." Haney shrugged. "Scotty, I've been fighting for existence ever since I was big enough to walk. I've fought to hold other people's cattle, fought for other men's homes, fought for the lives of other men. I've worked and bled and sweated my heart out in rain, dust, and storm. Now I want something for myself.

"Maybe I came too late. Maybe I'm way off the trail. But it seems to me that when trouble starts a man might stand on the sidelines and when the time comes, he might move in. You see, I know how Walt Pogue got his ranch. Vin Carter was a friend of mine until Emmett Chubb killed him. He told me how Pogue forced his old man off his range and took over. Well, I happen to know that none of this range is legally held. It's been preempted, which gives them a claim, of course. Well, I've got a few ideas myself. And I'm moving in."

"Son," Scott leaned across the table, "listen to me. Pogue's the sort of man who would hire killers by the hundreds if he had to. He did force Carter off his range. He did take it by force, and he has held it by force. Now he and Chalk are in a battle over who is to keep it and which one is to come out on top. The Vernons are the joker in the deck, of course. What both Reynolds and Pogue want is the Vernon place, because whoever holds it has a grip on this country. But both of them are taking the Vernons too lightly. They have something up their sleeve, or somebody has."

"What do you mean?"

"There's this Star Levitt, for one. He's no soft touch, that one! And then he's got some riders around there, and I'd say they do more work for him than for the Vernon spread—and not all honest work, by any means!"

"Levitt a western man?"

"He could be. Probably is. But whoever he is, he knows his way around an' he's one sharp hombre. Holds his cards close to his chest, an' plays 'em that way. He's the one you've got to watch in this deal, not Reynolds an' Pogue!"

Ross Haney leaned back in his chair and smiled at Scott. "That meal sure tasted good!" he acknowledged. "Now comes the rough point. I want to borrow some money—military funds," he added, grinning.

Scott shook his white head. "You sure beat all! You come into this country huntin' trouble, all alone an' without money! You've got nerve! I only hope you've got the gun savvy and the brains to back it up."

The blue eyes squinted from his leather-brown face and he smiled. He was beginning to like Haney. The tall young man had humor, and the nerve of the project excited and amused the old outlaw.

"How much do you want?"

"A hundred dollars."

"That all? You won't get far in this country on that."

"No, but along with it I want some advice." Haney hitched himself forward and took a bit of paper from his pocket and then a stub of pencil. Then from a leather folder he took a larger sheet which he unfolded carefully. It was a beautifully tanned piece of calfskin, and on it was drawn a map. Carefully, he moved the dishes aside and placed it on the table facing the older man.

"Look that over, and if you see any mistakes, correct me."

Scott stared at the map, and then he leaned forward, his eyes indicating his amazed interest. It was a map, drawn to scale and in amazing detail, of the Ruby Hills country. Every line camp, every waterhole, every ranch, and every stand of trees was indicated plainly. Distances were marked on straight lines between the various places, and heights of land were also marked. Lookout points were noted and canyons indicated. Studying the map, Scott could find nothing it had missed.

Slowly, he leaned back in his chair. When he looked up his expression was halfway between respect and worry. "Son, where did you get that map?"

"Get it? I made it. I drew it myself, Scotty. For three years I've talked to every puncher or other man I've met from this country. As they told me stuff, I checked with others and built this map. You know how western men are. Most of them are pretty good at description. A man down in the Live Oak country who never left it knows how the sheriff looks in Julesburg and exactly where the corrals are in Dodge."

Haney took a deep breath and then continued his story.

"Well, I've been studying this situation quite a spell," he said. "An old buffalo hunter and occasional trapper was in this country once, and he told me about it when I was a kid. It struck me as a place I'd like to live, so I planned accordingly. I learned all I could about it, rode for outfits oftentimes just because some puncher on the spread had worked over here. Then I ran into Vin Carter. He was born here. He told me all about it, and I got more from him than from any of them. While I was riding north with a herd of cattle, Emmett Chubb moved in, picked a fight with the kid, and killed him. And I think Walt Pogue paid him to do it!

"So it goes further than the fact that I'm range hungry, and I'll admit I am. I want my own spread. But Vin rode with me and we fought sandstorms and blizzards together from Texas to Montana and back. So I'm a man on the prod. Before I get through I'll own me a ranch in this country, a nice ranch with nice buildings, and then I'll get a wife and settle down."

Scott's eyes glinted. "It's a big order, son! Gosh, if I was twenty years younger, I'd throw in with you! I sure would!"

"There's no man I'd want more, Scotty, but this is my fight, and I'll make it alone. You can stake me to eating money, if you want, and I'll need some forty-fours."

The older man nodded assent. "You can have them, an' willin'. Have you got a plan?"

Haney nodded. "It's already started. I've filed on Thousand Springs."

Scott came off his chair, his face a mask of incredulity. "You *what?*"

"I filed a claim, an' I've staked her out and started to prove up." Ross was smiling over his coffee, enjoying Scott's astonishment.

"But, man! That's sheer suicide! That's right in the middle of Chalk's best range! That waterhole is worth a fortune! A dozen fortunes! That's what half the fighting is about!"

"I know it." Haney was calm. "I knew that before I came in here. That palouse of mine never moved a step until I had my plan of action all staked out. And I bought the Bullhorn."

This time astonishment was beyond the storekeeper. "How could you buy it? Gov'ment land, ain't it?"

"No. That's what they all seem to think. Even Vin Carter thought so, but it was part of a Spanish grant. I found that out by checking through some old records. So I hunted up a Mexican down in the Big Bend country who owned it. I bought it from him, bought three hundred acres, taking in the whole Bullhorn headquarters spread, the waterhole, and the cliffs in back of it. That includes most of that valley where Pogue cuts his meadow hay."

"Well, I'm forever bushed! If that don't beat all!" Scott tapped thoughtfully with his pipe bowl. Then he looked up. "What about Hitson Spring?"

"That's another thing I want to talk to you about. You own it."

"I do, eh? How did you come to think that?"

"Met an old sidewinder down in Laredo named Smite Emmons. He was pretty drunk one night, and he told me how foolish you were to file claim on that land. Said you could have bought it from the Indians just as cheap."

Scott chuckled. "I did. I bought it from the Indians, too. Believe me, son, nobody around here knows that. It would be a death sentence!"

"Then sell it to me. I'll give you my note for five thousand right now."

"Your note, eh?" Scott chuckled. "Son, you'd better get killed. It will be cheaper to bury you than pay up." He tapped his pipe bowl again. "Tell you what I'll do. I'll take your note for five hundred and the fun of watching what happens."

Solemnly, Ross Haney wrote out a note and handed it to Scott. The old man chuckled as he read it.

I hereby agree to pay on or before the 15th of March, 1877, to Westbrook Scott, the sum of five hundred dollars and the fun of watching what happens for the 160 acres of land known as Hitson Spring.

"All right, son! Sign her up! I'll get you the deed!"

## Chapter III
### Uneasy Town

When Ross had pocketed the two papers—the deed from the government to Scott and deeded over to him, and the skin deed from the Comanches—the old man sat up and reached for the coffeepot.

"You know what you've done? You've now got a claim on the three best sources of water in Ruby Valley, the only three that are surefire all the year around. And what will they do when they find out? They'll kill you!"

"They won't find out for a while. I'm not talking until the fight's been taken out of them."

"What about your claim stakes at Thousand Springs?"

"Buried. Iron stakes, and driven deep into the ground. There's sod and grass over the top."

"What about proving up?"

"That, too. You know how that spring operates? Actually, it is one great big spring back inside the mountain flowing out through the rocky face of the cliff in hundreds of tiny rivulets. Well, atop the mesa there is a good piece of land that falls into my claim, and back in the woods there is some land I can plow. I've already broken that land, smoothed her out, and put in a crop. I've got a trail to the top of that mesa, and a stone house built up there. I'm in business, Scotty!"

Scott looked at him and shook his head. Then he pushed back from the table and getting up, went into the store. When he returned he had several boxes of shells.

"In the mornin' come around and stock up," he suggested. "You better make you a cache or two with an extra gun here and there and some extra ammunition. Maybe a little grub. Be good insurance, and son, you'll need it."

"That's good advice. I'll do it, an' you keep track of the expense. I'll settle every cent of it when this is over."

With money in his pocket he walked around the store and crossed the street to the Bit and Bridle. The bartender glanced at him and then put a bottle and a glass in front of him. He was a short man, very thick and fat, but after a glance at the corded forearms, Ross was very doubtful about it all being fat.

A couple of lazy-talking cowhands held down the opposite end of the bar, and there was a poker game in progress at a table. Several other men sat around on chairs. They were the usual nondescript crowd of the cow trails.

He poured his drink and had just taken it between his thumb and fingers when the batwing doors thrust open and he heard the click of heels behind him. He neither turned nor looked around. The amber liquid in the glass held his attention. He had never been a drinking man, taking only occasional shots, and he was not going to drink much tonight.

The footsteps halted abreast of him, and a quick, clipped voice said in very precise words, "Are you the chap who owns that fast horse, the one with the black forequarters and the white over the loin and hips?"

He glanced around, turning his head without moving his body. There was no need for anyone to tell him that this was Bob Vernon. He was a tall, clean-limbed young man who was like her in that imperious lift to his chin, unlike her in his quick, decisive manner.

"There's spots, egg-shaped black spots over the white," said Haney. "That the one you mean?"

"My sister is outside. She wants to speak to you."

"I don't want to speak to her. You can tell her that." He turned his attention to his drink.

What happened then happened so fast it caught him off balance. A hand grasped him by the shoulder and spun him around in a grip of iron, and he was conscious of being surprised at the strength in that slim hand. Bob Vernon was staring at him, his eyes blazing.

"I said my sister wanted to speak to you!"

"And I said I didn't want to speak to her." Ross Haney's voice was slow paced and even. "Now take your hand off me, and don't ever lay a hand on me again!"

Bob Vernon was a man who had never backed down for anyone. From the East he had come into the cow country of Ruby Valley and made a place for himself by energy, decision, and his own youthful strength. Yet he had never met a man such as he faced now. As he looked into the hazel eyes of the stranger he felt something turn over away deep inside him. It was as though he had parted the brush and looked into the face of a lion.

Vernon dropped his hand. "I'm sorry. I'm afraid your manner made me forgetful. My sister can't come into a place like this."

The two men measured each other, and the suddenly alert audience in the Bit and Bridle let their eyes go from Vernon to the stranger. Bob Vernon they knew well enough to know he was afraid of nothing that walked. They also knew his normal manner was polite to a degree rarely encountered in the West, where manners were inclined to be brusque, friendly, and lacking in formality. Yet there was something else between these two now. As one man they seemed to sense the same intangible something that had touched Bob Vernon.

The batwing doors parted suddenly, and Sherry Vernon stepped into the room.

First, Haney was aware of a shock that such a girl could come into such a place, and second, of shame that he had been the cause. Then he felt admiration sweep over him at her courage.

Beautiful in a gray tailored riding habit, her head lifted proudly, she walked up to Ross Haney. Her face was set and her eyes were bright.

Ross was suddenly conscious that never in all his life had he looked into eyes so fine, so filled with feeling.

"Sir," and her voice could be heard in every corner of the room, "I do not know what your name may be, but I have come to pay you your money. Your horse beat Flame today, and beat him fairly. I regret the way I acted, but it was such a shock to have Flame beaten that I allowed you to get away without being paid. I am very sorry.

"However," she added quickly, "if you would like to run against Flame again, I'll double the bet!"

"Thank you, Miss Vernon!" He bowed slightly, from the hips. "It was only that remark about my horse that made me run him at all. You see, ma'am, as you no doubt know, horses have feelin's. I couldn't let you run down my horse to his face, thataway!"

Her eyes were on his, and suddenly they crinkled at the corners and her lips rippled with a little smile.

"Now, if you'll allow me—" He took her arm and escorted her from the room. Inside they heard a sudden burst of applause, and he smiled as he offered her his hands for her foot. She stepped into them and then swung into her position on the horse.

"I'm sorry you had to come in there, but your brother was kind of abrupt."

"That's quite all right," she replied quickly, almost too quickly.

He stepped back and watched them ride away into the darkness of early evening. Then he turned back to the saloon. He almost ran into a tall, carefully dressed man who had walked up behind him. A man as large as Pogue.

Pale blue eyes looked from a handsome, perfectly cut face of city white. He was trim, neat, and precise. Only the guns at his hips looked deadly with their polished butts and worn holsters.

"That," said the tall man, gesturing after Sherry Vernon, "is a staked claim!"

Ross Haney was getting angry. Men who were bigger than him always irritated him, anyway. "It is?" His voice was cutting. "If you think you can stake a claim on any woman you've got a lot to learn!"

He shoved by toward the door, but behind him the voice said, "But that one's staked. You hear me?"

Soledad by night was a tiny scattering of lights along the dark river of the street. Music from the tinny piano in the Bit and Bridle drifted down the street, and with it the lazy voice of someone singing a cow camp song. Ross Haney turned up the street toward the two-story frame hotel, his mind unable to free itself from the vision that was Sherry Vernon.

For the first time, the wife who was to share that ranch had a face. Until now there had been in his thoughts the vague shadow of a personality and a character, but there had been no definite features, nothing that could be recognized. Now, after seeing Sherry, he knew there could be but one woman in the ranch house he planned to build.

He smiled wryly as he thought of her sharing his life. What would she think of a cowhand, a drifting gunhand? And what would she say when it became known that he was Ross Haney? Not that the name meant very much, for it did not. Only in certain quarters where fighting men gather had he acquired something of a reputation. The stories about him had drifted across the country as such stories will, and while he had little notoriety as a gunfighter, he was known as a hard, capable man who would and could fight.

He was keenly aware of his situation in Soledad and the Ruby Hills country. As yet, he was an outsider. They were considering him, and Pogue had already sensed enough of what he was to offer a job, gun or saddle job. When his intentions became known he would be facing trouble and plenty of it. When they discovered that he had actually moved in and taken possession of the best water in the valley, they would have no choice but to buy him out, run him out, or kill him.

Or they could move out themselves, and neither Walt Pogue nor Chalk Reynolds was the man for that.

In their fight Ross had no plan to take sides. He was a not-too-innocent bystander as far as they were concerned. When Bob and Sherry Vernon were considered, he wasn't too sure. He scowled, realizing suddenly that sentiment had no place in such dealings as his. Until he saw Sherry Vernon he had been a free agent, and now, for better or worse, he was no longer quite so free.

He could not now move with such cold indifference to the tides of war in the Ruby Hills. Now he had an interest, and his strength was lowered to just the degree of that interest. He was fully aware of the fact. It nettled him even as it amused him, for he was always conscious of himself and viewed his motives with a certain wry, ironic humor, seeing himself always with much more clarity than others saw him.

Yet, despite that, something had been accomplished. He had staked his claim at Thousand Springs and started his cabin. He had talked with Scott, and won an ally there, for he knew the old man was with him, at least to a point. He had met and measured Walt Pogue, and he knew that Emmett Chubb was now with Reynolds. That would take some investigation, for from all he had learned, he had been sure that Pogue had hired Chubb to kill Vin Carter, but now Chubb worked for Reynolds.

Well, the allegiance of such men was tied to a dollar sign, and their loyalty went no further than their next payday. There might have been trouble between Pogue and Chubb, and that might be the reason Pogue was so eager to have him killed.

He directed his thoughts toward the Vernons. Bob was all man. Whatever Reynolds and Pogue planned for him he would not take. He would have his own ideas, and he was a fighter.

What of the other hands whom Scott had implied were loyal to Levitt rather than Vernon? These men he must consider, too, and must plan carefully for them, for in such an action as he planned, he must be aware of all the conflicting elements in the valley.

The big man in the white hat he had placed at once. Carter had mentioned him with uncertainty, for when Carter left the valley Star Levitt had just arrived and was an unknown quantity.

With that instinctive awareness that the widely experienced man has for such things, Ross Haney knew that he and Star Levitt were slated to be enemies. They were two men who simply could not be friends, for there was a definite clash of personalities and character that made a physical clash inevitable. And Haney was fully aware that Star Levitt was not the soft touch some might believe. He was a dangerous man, a very dangerous man.

## Chapter IV
### *Bold Challenge*

Ross Haney found that the hotel was a long building with thirty rooms, a large empty lobby, and off to one side, a restaurant open for business. Feeling suddenly hungry he turned to the desk for a room, his eyes straying toward the restaurant door.

When Haney dropped his war bag a young man standing in the doorway turned and walked to the desk. "Room?" he smiled as he spoke, and his face was pleasant.

"The best you've got." Ross grinned at him.

The clerk grinned back. "Sorry, but they are all equally bad, even if reasonably clean. Take fifteen, at the end of the hall. You'll be closer to the well."

"Pump?"

The clerk chuckled. "What do you think this is, New York? It's a rope-and-bucket well. It's been almost a year since we hauled a dead man out of it. The water should be good by now."

"Sure." Ross studied him for a moment. "Where you from? New York?"

"Yes, and Philadelphia, Boston, Richmond, London, and San Francisco, and now—Soledad."

"You've been around." Ross rolled a smoke and dropped the sack on the desk for the clerk. "How's the food?"

"Good. Very good—and the prettiest waitress west of the Mississippi."

Ross smiled. "Well, if she's like the other girls around here, she's probably a staked claim. I had a big hombre with a white hat tell me tonight that one girl was staked out for him."

The clerk looked at him quickly, shrewdly. "Star Levitt?"

"I guess."

"If he meant the lady you had the race with today, I'd say he was doing more hoping than otherwise. Sherry Vernon," the clerk spoke carefully, "is not an easy claim to stake!"

Ross pulled the register around, hesitated an instant, and then wrote, "Ross Haney, El Paso."

The clerk glanced at it and then looked up. "Glad to meet you, Ross. My name is Allan Kinney." He looked down at the name again. "Ross Haney. I've heard that name from somewhere.

"It's funny," he added musingly, "about a name and a town. Ross Haney, from El Paso. Now you might not be from El Paso at all. You might be from Del Rio or Sanderson or Uvalde. You might even be from Cheyenne or from Fort Sumner or White Oaks.

"What happened to you in El Paso or wherever you came from?

And why did you come here? Men drift without reason sometimes, but usually, there is something. Sometimes the law is behind them, or an outlaw ahead of them. Sometimes they just want new horizons or a change of scene, and sometimes they are hunting for something. You, now. I'd say you came to Soledad for a reason—a reason that could mean trouble."

"Let's drink some coffee," Haney suggested, "and see if that waitress is as pretty as you say."

"You won't think so," Kinney said, shaking his head, "you won't think so at all. You've just seen Sherry Vernon. After her, all women look washed out—until you get over her."

"I don't plan on it."

Kinney dropped into a chair. "That, my friend, is a large order. Miss Vernon usually handles such situations with neatness and dispatch. She is always pleasant, never familiar."

"This is different." Ross looked up, and suddenly he knew with a queer excitement just what he was going to say. He said it. "I'm going to marry her."

Allan Kinney gulped and put his cup down carefully. "Have you told her? Does she know your intentions are honorable? Does she even know you have intentions?" He grinned. "You know, friend, that is a large order you have laid out for yourself."

The waitress came up. She was a slender, very pretty girl with red hair, a few freckles, and a sort of bubbling good humor that was contagious.

"May," Kinney said, "I want you to meet Ross Haney. He is going to marry Sherry Vernon."

At this, Ross felt his ears getting red and cursed himself for a thickheaded fool for ever saying such a thing. It may have been startled from him by the sudden realization that he intended to do just that.

"What?" May said quickly, looking at him. "Another one?"

Haney glanced up, and suddenly he put his hand over hers and said gently, "No, May. *The* one!"

Her eyes held his for a moment, and the laughter faded from them. "You know," she said seriously, "I think you might!"

She went for their coffee. Kinney looked at Ross with care. "Friend Haney," he said, "you have made an impression. I really think the lady believed you! Now if you can do as well with Miss Vernon, you'll be doing all right."

The door opened suddenly from the street, and two men stepped in. Ross glanced up, and his dark eyes held on the two men who stood there.

One of the men was a big man with sloping shoulders, and his eyes caught Haney's and narrowed as if at sudden recognition. The other man was shorter and thicker, but obviously a hard case. With a queer sort of premonition, Ross guessed that these men were from the Vernon ranch—or they could be. At least, they knew about Ross Haney and were more than casually interested.

These could be the men who worked for Star Levitt, and as such they merited study, yet their type was not an unfamiliar one to Ross Haney or to any man who rode the borderlands or the wild country. While many a puncher has branded a few mavericks or rustled a few cows when he needed drinking money or wanted a new saddle, there was a certain intangible yet very real difference that marked those who held to the outlaw trail, and both of these men had it.

They were men with guns for hire, men who rode for trouble and for the ready cash they could get for crooked work. He knew their type. He had faced such men before, and he knew they recognized him. These men were a type who never fought a battle for anyone but themselves.

Without warning, the door pushed open and two more men came into the room. Ross glanced around and caught the eye of a short, stocky man who walked with a quick, jerky lift of his knees. He walked now—right over to Haney.

"You're Ross Haney?" he said abruptly. "I've got a job for you! Start tomorrow morning! A hundred a month an' found. Plenty of horses! I'm Chalk Reynolds an' my place is just out of town in that big clump of cottonwoods. Old place. You won't have any trouble finding it."

Ross smiled. "Sorry, I'm not hunting a job."

Reynolds had been turning away, but he whipped back quickly. "What do you mean? Not looking for a job? At a hundred a month? When the range is covered with top hands gettin' forty?"

"I said I didn't want a job."

"Ah?" The genial light left the older man's face, and his blue eyes hardened and narrowed. "So that's it! You've gone to work for Walt Pogue!"

"No, I don't work for Pogue. I don't work for anybody. I'm my own man, Mr. Reynolds!"

Chalk Reynolds stared at him. "Listen, my friend, and listen well. In the Ruby Hills today there are but two factions, those for Reynolds and those against him. If you don't work for me, I shall regard you as an enemy."

Haney shrugged. "That's your funeral. From all I hear you have enemies enough without choosing any more. Also, from all I hear, you deserve them."

"*What?*" Reynolds's eyes blazed. "Don't sass me, stranger!"

The lean, whip-bodied man beside him touched his arm. "Let me handle this, Uncle Chalk," he said gently. "Let me talk to this man."

Ross shifted his eyes. The younger man had a lantern jaw and unusually long gray eyes. The eyes had a flatness about them that puzzled and warned him.

"My name is Sydney Berdue. I am foreman for Mr. Reynolds." He stepped closer to where Haney sat in his chair, one elbow on the table. "Maybe you would like to tell me why he deserves his enemies."

Haney glanced up at him, his blunt features composed, faintly curious, his eyes steady and aware. "Sure," he said quietly, "I'd be glad to.

"Chalk Reynolds came west from Missouri right after the war with Mexico. For a time he was located in Santa Fe, but as the wagon trains started to come west, he went north and began selling guns to the Indians."

Reynolds's face went white and his eyes blazed. "That's not true!"

Haney's glance cut his words short. "Don't make me kill you!" Ross said sharply. "Every word I say is true! You took part in wagon train raids yourself. I expect you collected your portion of white scalps. Then you got out of there with a good deal of loot and met a man in Julesburg who wanted to come out here. He knew nothing of your crooked background, and—"

Berdue's hand was a streak for his gun, but Haney had expected it. When the Reynolds foreman had stepped toward him, he had come beyond Haney's outstretched feet, and Ross whipped his toe up behind the foreman's knee and jerked hard just as he shoved with his open hand. Berdue hit the floor with a crash and his gun went off with a roar, the shot plowing into the ceiling. From the room overhead came an angry shout and the sound of bare feet hitting the floor.

Ross moved swiftly. He stepped over and kicked the gun from Berdue's hand and then swept it up.

"Get up! Reynolds, get over there against the wall, pronto!"

White-faced, Reynolds backed to the wall, hatred burning deep in his eyes. Slowly, Sydney Berdue got to his feet, his eyes clinging to his gun in Ross Haney's hand.

"Lift your hands, both of you. Now push them higher. Hold it."

He stared at the two men. Behind him, the room was slowly filling with curious onlookers. "Now," Ross Haney said coolly, "I'm going to finish what I started. You asked me why you deserved to have enemies. I started by telling you about the white people you murdered and about the guns you sold, and now I'll tell you about the man you met in Julesburg."

Reynolds's face was ashen. "Forget that," he said. "You don't need to talk so much. Berdue was huntin' trouble. You forget it. I need a good man."

"To murder, like you did your partner? You made a deal with him, and he came down here and worked hard. He planted those trees. He built that house. Then three of you went out and stumbled into a band of Indians, and somehow, although wounded, you were the only one who got back. And naturally, the ranch was all yours.

"Who were those Indians, Chalk? Or was there only *one* Indian? Only one, who was the last man of three riding single file?

"You wanted to know why I wouldn't work for you and why you should have enemies. I've told you. And now I'll tell you something more: I've come to the Ruby Hills to stay. I'm not leavin'."

Deliberately, he handed the gun back to Berdue, and as he held it out to him their eyes met and fastened, and it was Sydney Berdue's eyes that shifted first. He took the gun, reversed it, and started it into his holster, and then his hand stopped, and his lips drew tight.

Ross Haney was smiling. "Careful, Berdue!" he said softly. "I wouldn't try it, if I were you!"

Berdue stared, and then with an oath he shoved the gun hard into its holster, and turning out the door, walked rapidly away. Behind him went Chalk Reynolds, his neck and ears red with the bitterness of the fury that throbbed in his veins.

Slowly, in a babble of talk, the room cleared, and then Ross Haney seated himself again. "May," he said, "you've let my coffee get cold. Fill it up, will you?"

## Chapter V
### *A Look at the Country*

Persons who lived in the town of Soledad were not unaccustomed to sensation, but the calling of Chalk Reynolds and his supposedly gunslick foreman in the Cattleman's Cafe was a subject that had the old maids of both sexes licking their lips with anticipation and excitement. Little had been known of the background of Chalk Reynolds. He was the oldest settler, the owner of the biggest and oldest ranch, and he was a hard character when pushed. Yet now they saw him in a new light, and the story went from mouth to mouth.

Not the last to hear it was Walt Pogue, who chuckled and slapped his heavy thigh. "Wouldn't you know it? That old four-flusher! Crooked as a dog's hind leg!"

The next thing that occurred to anyone, occurred to him. How did Ross Haney know?

The thought drew Pogue up to a standstill. Haney knew too much. Who was Haney? If he knew that, he might— But no! That didn't necessarily follow. Still, Ross Haney was going to be a good friend to have, and a bad enemy.

Not the least of the talk concerned Haney's confidence, the way he had stood there and dared Berdue to draw. Overnight, Haney had become the most talked about man in the Ruby Hills.

When gathering his information about the Ruby Hills country, Ross Haney had gleaned some other information that was of great interest. That information was what occupied his mind on his first morning in Soledad.

So far, in his meandering around the country, and he had done more of it than anyone believed, he had had no opportunity to verify this final fragment of information. But now he intended to do it. From what he had overheard, the country north and west of the mountains was a badlands that was avoided by all. It was a lava country, broken and jagged, and there was much evidence of prehistoric volcanic action, so much so that riding there was a danger always, and walking was the surest way to ruin a pair of boots.

Yet at one time there had been a man who knew the lava beds and all of that badlands country that occupied some three hundred square miles stretching north and west across the state line. That man had been Jim Burge.

It had been Jim Burge who had told Charlie Hastings, Reynolds's ill-fated partner, about the Ruby Hills country, and it had been Jim Burge who had first driven a herd of Spanish cattle into the Ruby Hills. But Burge had tired of ranching and headed north, leaving his ranch and turning his horses loose. His cattle had already been gone.

Gone, that is, into the badlands. Burge knew where they were, but cattle were of no use without a market, and there was no market anywhere near. Burge decided he wanted to move and he wanted quick money, so he left the country, taking only a few of the best horses with him.

He had talked to Charlie Hastings, and Hastings talked to Chalk Reynolds, but Jim Burge was already gone. Gone east into the Texas Panhandle and a lone hand fight with Comanches that ended with four warriors dead and with Jim Burge's scalp hanging from the belt of another. But Jim Burge had talked to other people in Santa Fe, and the others did not forget, either. One of these had talked to Ross Haney, and Ross was a curious man.

When he threw his saddle on the Appaloosa, he was planning to satisfy that curiosity. He was going to find out what had become of those cattle.

Nine years had passed since Burge had left them to shift for themselves. In nine years several hundred cattle can do pretty well for themselves.

"There's water in those badlands if you know where to look," Burge had told the man in Sante Fe, "an' there's grass, but you've got to find it." Knowing range cattle, Ross was not worried about them finding it, and if he could find it, he would find them—unless someone else had.

So he rode out of Soledad down the main trail, and there were many eyes that followed him out. One pair of these belonged to Sherry Vernon, already out and on her horse, drifting over the range, inspecting her cattle and seeing where they fed. She noted the tall rider on the queerly marked horse, and there was a strange leap in her heart as she watched him heading down the trail.

Was he leaving? For always? The thought gave her a pang, even though remembering the oddly intent look in his eyes and the hard set in his jaw, she knew he would be back.

Of course, she had heard the story of his meeting with Chalk Reynolds and Sydney Berdue. Berdue had always frightened her, for wherever she turned, his eyes were upon her. They gave her a crawling sensation, not at all like the excitement she drew from the quick, amused eyes of Ross Haney.

The palouse was a good mountain horse, and ears pricked forward, he stepped out eagerly. The sights and smells were what he knew best and he quickened his step, sure he was coming home.

Ross Haney knew that with his action of the previous night he was in the center of things whether he liked it or not, and he liked it. From now on he would move fast and with boldness, but not too definitely, for it would pay to keep them puzzled for a few days longer. Things would break between Pogue and Reynolds, especially now that his needling of Reynolds would scare the man into aggressive action.

Chalk was no fool. He would know how fast talk would spread. It might not be long before embarrassing questions might be asked. The only escape from those questions lay in power. He must put himself beyond questions. Eyes squinted against the glare, Haney thought about that, trying to calculate just what Reynolds would do. It was up to him to strike, and he would strike, or Haney knew nothing of men under pressure.

The trail he sought showed itself suddenly, just a faint track off to the right through the piñons, and he took it, letting Rio set his own gait.

It was midafternoon before Ross reached the edge of the lava beds. The great black, tumbled masses seemed without trails or any sign of vegetation. He skirted the lava, searching for some evidence of a trail. It was miserably hot, and the sun threw heat back from the blazing rocks until he felt like he was in an oven. When he was on a direct line between the lava beds and Thousand Springs, he rode back up the mountain, halted, and swung down to give his horse a rest.

From his saddlebags he took a telescope, a glass he had bought in New Orleans several years before. Sitting down on a boulder while the palouse cropped casually at the dry grass, he began a systematic, inch-by-inch study of the lava beds.

Only the vaguest sort of plan had formed in his mind for his next step. Everything had been worked out carefully to this point, but from now on his actions depended much upon the actions of Pogue and Reynolds. Yet he did have the beginnings of a plan. If the cattle he sought were still in the lava beds, he intended to brand them one by one and shove bunches of them out into the valley. He was going to use that method to make his bid for the valley range.

After a half hour of careful study he got up, thrust the glass in his belt, and rode slowly along the hillside, stopping at intervals to continue his examination of the beds. It was almost dusk when he raised up in the stirrups and pointed the glass toward a tall finger of rock that thrust itself high from the beds. At the base of it was a cow, and it was walking slowly toward the northwest!

Try as he might, Ross could find no trail into the lava beds, so as dusk was near, he turned the palouse and started back toward Thousand Springs. He would try again. At least he knew he was not shooting in the dark. There was at least one cow in that labyrinth of lava, and if there was one, there would certainly be more.

The trail he had chosen led him up the mesa at Thousand Springs from a little-known route. He wound around through the clumps of piñon until the flat top was reached. Then he rode along slowly, drinking in this beauty that he had chosen for the site of his home. The purple haze had thickened over the hills and darkened among the trees, and deep shadows gathered in the forested notches of the hills while the pines made a dark fringe against a sky still red with the last rose of the sinking sun.

Below him the mesa broke sharply off and fell for over a hundred feet of sheer rock. Thirty feet from the bottom of the cliff the springs trickled from the fractured rock and covered the rock below with a silver sheen from many small cascades that fell away into the pool.

Beyond the far edge of the pool, fringed with aspens, the valley was a long sweep of tall grass range, rolling into a dark distance against the mystery of the hills. Ross Haney sat his horse in a place rarely seen by man, for he was doubtful if anyone in many years had mounted the mesa. That he was not the first man here, he knew, for there were Indian relics and the remains of stone houses, ages old. These seemed to have no connection with any cliff dwellings or pueblos he had seen in the past. The building was more ancient and more massive than in Acoma, the Sky City.

The range below him was the upper end of Ruby Valley and was supposedly under the control of Chalk Reynolds. Actually, Reynolds rarely visited the place, nor did his men. It was far and away at the end of the range he claimed, and the water was available for the cattle when they wished to come to it. Yet here on the rim of the mesa, or slightly back from the rim, Haney had begun to build a ranch house, using the old foundations of the prehistoric builders and many of their stones.

The floor itself was intact, and he had availed himself of it, sweeping it clean over a wide expanse. He had paced it off and planned his house accordingly, and he had large ideas. Yet for the moment he was intent only on repairing a part of the house to use as his claim shanty.

There was water here. Water that bubbled from the same source as that of the Thousand Springs. He knew that his water was the same water. Several times he had tried dropping sticks or leaves into the water outside his door, only to find them later in the pool below.

From where he sat he could with his glass see several miles of trail and watch all who approached him. The trail up the back way was unknown so far as he could find out. Certainly it indicated no signs of use but that of wild game, although it had evidently been used in bygone years.

To the east and south his view was unobstructed. Below him lay all the dark distance of the valley and the range for which he was fighting. To the north, the mesa broke sharply off and fell away into a deep canyon with a dry wash at its bottom. The side of the canyon across from him was almost as sheer as this and at least a quarter of a mile away.

The trail led up from the west and through a broken country of tumbled rock, long fingers of lava, and clumps of piñon giving way to aspen and pine. The top of the mesa was at least two hundred acres in extent and absolutely impossible to reach by any known route but the approach he used.

Returning through the trees to a secluded hollow, Ross swung down and stripped the saddle and bridle from the palouse, then turning it loose. He rarely hobbled or tied the horse, for Rio would come at a call or whistle and never failed to respond at once. But a horse in most cases will not wander far from a campfire, feeding away from it and then slowly feeding back toward it, seeming to like the feeling of comfort as well as a man.

He built his fire of dry wood and built it with plenty of cover, keeping it small. Even at this height there was danger of its being seen and causing wonder. The last thing he wanted now was for any of the people from the valley to find him out.

After he had eaten he strolled back to the open ground where the house was taking shape. Part of the ancient rock floor he was keeping for a terrace from which the whole valley could be seen.

For a long time he stood there, looking off into the darkness and enjoying the cool night air. Then he turned and walked back into the deep shadows of the house. He was standing there, trying to see it as it would appear when complete when he heard a low, distant rumble.

Suddenly anxious, he listened intently. It seemed to come from within the very rock on which he stood. He waited, listening for the sound to grow. But after a moment it died away to a vague rumble and then disappeared altogether. Puzzled, he walked around for several minutes, waiting and listening, but there was no further sound.

It was a strange thing, and it disturbed him and left him uneasy as he walked back to his camp. Long after he had rolled in his blankets he lay there puzzling over it. He noted with an odd sense of disquiet that Rio stayed close to him, closer than usual. Of course, there could be another reason for that. There were cougars on the mesa and in the breaks behind it. He had seen their tracks. There were also elk and deer, and twice he had seen bear.

The country he had chosen was wildly beautiful, a strange, lost corner of the land, somehow cut off from the valley by the rampart of Thousand Springs Mesa.

He awakened suddenly as the sky was growing gray and found himself sitting bolt upright. And then he heard it again, that low, mounting rumble, far down in the rock beneath him, as though the very spirit of the mountain were rolling over in his sleep. Only now the sound was not so plain, it was fainter, farther away.

## Chapter VI
### *Hidden Range*

At daybreak Ross rolled out of his blankets, built a fire, and made coffee. While eating, he puzzled over the strange sound he had heard the night before. The only solution that seemed logical was that it came somehow from the springs. It was obvious that forces of some sort were at work deep in the rock of the mesa.

Obviously, these forces had made no recent change in the contour of the rock itself and so must be insufficient for the purpose. Haney continued with his building, working the morning through.

Unlike many cowhands, he had always enjoyed working with his hands. Now he had the pleasure of doing something for himself, with the feeling that he was building to last. By noon he had another wall of heavy stone constructed and the house was beginning to take shape.

He stopped briefly to eat and slipped on his shirt before sitting down. As he buttoned it up, he saw a faint movement far down the Soledad trail. Going to his saddlebags he dug out his glass and took his position in a lookout post among the rocks on the rim. First making sure the sunlight would not reflect from the glass and give him away, he dropped flat among the rocks and pointed the glass down trail.

The rider's face was still indistinct, but there was something vaguely familiar about him. And then as he drew nearer, Ross saw it was Sydney Berdue.

What was the Reynolds foreman doing here? Of course, as this was considered RR range, he might be checking the grass or the stock. He rode swiftly, however, and paid no attention to anything around him. When he reached the pool below, he swung down, seated himself on a rock, and lighted a cigarette.

Waiting for someone.

The sun felt warm and comfortable on his back after the hard work of the morning, and Ross settled himself comfortably into the warm sand behind the rocks. Thoughtfully, he turned his glass down the trail, but saw no one else. Then he began scanning the country and after a few minutes, picked up another rider. The man rode a sorrel horse with three white stockings and must have approached through the timber as he was not in sight until the last minute. He rode swiftly up to the pool and swung down. The two men shook hands. Puzzled, Ross shifted his glass to the brand.

The sorrel carried a VV on his shoulder! A Vernon rider at what was apparently a secret meeting with the foreman of the RR! The two seated themselves, and Haney waited, studying them and then the trail. And now he saw two more horsemen, and these were riding up the trail together. One was a big, slope-shouldered man whom he had seen in Soledad, and he rode a Box N horse. The last man rode a gray mustang with the Three Diamonds of Star Levitt on his hip.

Here was something of real interest. The four brands, two of them outwardly at war, the others on the verge of it, meeting in secret. Haney cursed his luck that he could not hear what was said, but so far as he could see, Berdue seemed to be laying down the law.

Then he saw something else.

At first it was a vague suggestion of disturbance in the grass and brush near the foot of the cliff, and then he saw a slight figure. His heart leaped as he saw Sherry Vernon, crawling nearer!

Sherry Vernon!

Whatever the meeting of the four men meant, it was at least plain that they intended no one to overhear what they had to say. If the girl was seen, she would be in great danger. Sliding back from his lookout point, he ran in a crouching run toward the house and got his Winchester.

By the time he was back, the brief meeting was breaking up. The girl lay still below him, and the men mounted one by one and rode away. The last to go was Sydney Berdue.

After several minutes had passed, Sherry got to her feet and walked out in the open. She went to the spring and drank and then stood looking around, obviously in profound thought.

Ross debated the possibility of getting his horse, but dismissed his idea as impossible. It would require a couple of hours at least to ride from here to the spring, although he was within a few hundred feet of it.

The girl walked away toward the woods finally, evidently for her horse. After some minutes she rode out of the trees on Flame and started down the trail toward the VV Ranch, distant against the far hills.

There had been a meeting of the four brands, but not of the leaders. Sherry Vernon had probably overheard what was said. He scowled thoughtfully. The girl had moved with care and skill, and her actions showed she was no mean woodsman when it came to playing the Indian. None of the four below had been a tenderfoot, yet she had approached them and listened without giving herself away. Sherry Vernon, he decided, would bear some watching herself.

Saddling Rio, Ross rode back through the aspens and down the lonely and dangerous trail to the rim of the badlands. He still had found no way to enter the lava beds, and if he was to take the next step in his program of conquest, he must find the cattle that he was sure still roamed among those remote and lost waterholes in the lava.

The afternoon was well along before he found himself skirting the rim of the canyon that opened near the lava beds, and when he reached them it was already late. There would be little time for a search, but despite that, he turned north, planning to cut back around the mesa and return to Soledad by way of the springs.

A slight movement among the trees ahead caused him to halt, and then he saw several elk drifting slowly down a narrow glade toward the lava. His eyes narrowed suddenly. There was no water of which he knew closer than the Thousand Springs pool, and these elk were drifting away from it rather than toward it. As they usually watered at sundown or before daybreak, they must be headed for water elsewhere, and that could be in the lava.

Dismounting, he ground hitched his horse and watched the elk as they drifted along until they had almost vanished in the trees; then he mounted and followed them down. When the trail he was following turned down and joined theirs, he continued along it. In a few minutes he grunted with satisfaction, for the hoof marks led him right up to the lava and into a narrow cleft between two great folds of the black rocks.

Riding carefully, for the trail was very narrow and the lava on both sides black and rough, he kept on, following the elk. It was easy to see how such a trail might exist for years and never be found, for at times he was forced to draw one leg up and lift the stirrup out of the way, as it was too narrow otherwise.

The trail wound around and around, covering much distance without penetrating very far, and then it dipped down suddenly through a jagged and dangerous-looking cleft. Ross hesitated, studying the loosely hanging crags above with misgiving. They looked too shaky and insecure for comfort. He well knew that if a man was ever trapped or hurt in this lava bed, he might as well give up. There would be no help for him.

Yet, with many an upward glance at the great, poorly balanced chunks of rock, many of them weighing many tons, he rode down into the cleft on the trail of the elk.

For over a half mile the cleft led him steadily downward, much of the going very steep, and he realized that he was soon going to be well below the level of the surrounding country. He rode on, however, despite the growing darkness, already great in the dark bottom of the cleft. Then the trail opened out, and he stopped with a gasp of amazement.

Before him lay a great circular valley, an enormous valley surrounded by gigantic black cliffs that in many places shelved out over the edge, but the bottom was almost level and was covered with rich green grass. There were a few scattered clumps of trees, and from somewhere he heard the sound of water.

Drifting on, he looked up and around him, overcome with astonishment. The depth of the valley, at least a thousand feet lower than the surrounding country, and the unending sameness of the view of the beds from above safely concealed its existence. It was without doubt an ancient volcanic crater, long extinct, and probably the source of the miles of lava beds that had been spewed forth in some bygone age.

The green fields below were dotted with cattle, most of them seemingly in excellent shape. Here and there among them he noticed small groups of horses. Without doubt, these were the cattle and horses, or their descendants, left by Jim Burge.

Despite the lateness of the hour, he pushed on, marveling at the mighty walls around him, at the green grass and the white-trunked aspens. Twice he found springs of water, in both cases bubbling from the ground. Later, he found a spring that ran from a cleft in the rock and trickled down over the worn face of the cliff for some thirty feet to sink into the ground below.

None of the cattle seemed in the least frightened of him, although they moved back as he approached, and several lifted their noses at him curiously.

When he had ridden for well over two miles he drew up in a small glade near a spring, and stripping the saddle from his horse, he made camp. This would end his rations, and tomorrow he must start back. Obviously, this would be a good place to start such a cache of supplies as Scott had advised.

Night brought a strange coolness to the valley. He built a fire and fixed his coffee, talking to Rio meanwhile. After a moment he became conscious of movement. He looked up and saw that a dozen or more cows and a bull had moved up. They were staring at the fire and at him with their amazed bovine eyes. Apparently they had never seen a man before.

From all appearances, the crater was a large one, several miles across and carpeted with this rich grass. The cattle were all in good shape. Twice during the night he heard the cry of a cougar and once the howl of a wolf.

With daylight he was in the saddle once more, but by day the crater proved to be smaller than he had at first believed; there were probably some two thousand acres in the bottom. But it was all level ground with rich grass and a good bit of timber.

Twice, when skirting the edges of the crater, he found ice caves. These he knew were caused by the lava mass's cooling so unevenly that when the surface had become cold and hard the material below was still molten. As the fluid drained away, caves were formed under the solid crust. Because lava is a poor heat conductor, the cold air of the caves was protected. Ice formed there, and no matter how warm it might be on the surface, there was always snow in the caves. At places, pools of clear, cold water had formed. He could see that some of these had been used as watering places by the deer, elk, and wild horses.

When at last he started back toward the cleft through which he had gained entrance to the crater, he was sure there were several hundred, perhaps as many as six hundred, head of wild cattle in the bottom of the crater.

He rode out, but not with any feeling of comfort. Some day he would scale those cliffs and have a look at the craggy boulders on the rim. If they ever fell into the cleft, whoever or whatever was in the bottom would never come out.

It was dusk of another evening before the palouse cantered down the one street of Soledad and drew up at the livery stable. A Mexican came to the door, glanced at him, and then accepted his horse. He looked doubtfully at the strange brand.

"You ride for Señor Pogue or Señor Reynolds?" he asked hesitantly.

"For myself," Ross said. "What's the matter? The town seems quiet."

"Sí, Señor. There has been a killing. Rolly Burt of the RR was in a shooting with two hands from the Box N. One of them was killed and the other wounded, and Señor Burt has disappeared."

"Left the country?"

"Who knows? He was wounded, they say, and I am sorry for that. He was a good man, Señor Burt." The Mexican lighted a smoke, glancing at Haney. "Perhaps he was no longer wanted on the RR, either."

"Why do you say that?" Ross asked quickly. "Have you any reason for it?"

"Sí. He has told me himself that he has trouble with Señor Berdue."

Berdue had trouble with Burt, yet Burt had been attacked by two Box N hands? That didn't seem to tie in—or did it? Could there be any connection between this shooting and the meeting at the springs? In any event, this would probably serve to start hostilities again.

## Chapter VII
### *Manhunt*

Leaving his horse to be cared for, Ross returned to his room in the Cattleman's Hotel. Kinney was not in the lobby when he crossed it, and he found no one on the stairs. He knew how precarious was his own position, for while the house he was building was reasonably safe from discovery, there was no reason to believe that someone would not soon discover that the ground had been plowed back under the trees. It wasn't much, but enough to indicate he was working on the place.

Uneasily, he surveyed the situation. So far everything was proceeding according to plan, and almost too well. He had his water rights under control. He had found the cattle. He had in the crater and on the mesa two bases of action that were reasonably safe from attack, yet the situation was due to blow up at almost any moment.

Berdue seemed to be playing a deep game. It might be with the connivance of his uncle, but he might be on his own. Perhaps someone else had the same idea he had, that from the fighting of Pogree and Reynolds would come a new system of things in the Ruby Hills country. Perhaps Berdue, or some other person or group planned to be top dog.

Berdue's part in it puzzled Haney, but at least he knew by sight the men he had met today and would be able to keep a closer watch on them. Also, there were still the three strange men, of whom he had seen but two, who lived on the VV. Somehow they did not seem to fit with what he had seen of the Vernons. "The next order of business," he told himself, "is a visit to the VV."

A dozen people were eating in the saloon when he entered. He stopped at one side of the door and surveyed the groups with care. It would not do to walk into Berdue or Reynolds unawares, for Berdue would not, and Reynolds dared not, ignore him. He had stepped onto the scene in Soledad in no uncertain terms.

Suddenly he saw Sherry Vernon at a small table alone. On an impulse, he walked over to her, his spurs jingling. She glanced up at him, momentarily surprised.

"Oh, it's you again? I thought you had left town."

"You knew better than that." He indicated the chair opposite her. "May I sit down?"

"Surely." She looked at him thoughtfully. "You know, Ross Haney, you're not an entirely unhandsome sort of man, but I've a feeling you're still pretty savage."

"I live in a country that is savage," he said simply. "It is a country that is untamed. The last court of appeal is a six-shooter."

"From all I hear, you gave Sydney Berdue some uncomfortable moments without one. You're quite an unusual man. Sometimes your language sounds like any cowboy, and sometimes it doesn't, and sometimes your ideas are different."

"You find men of all kinds in the West. The town drunk in Julesburg, when I was there, could quote Shakespeare and had two degrees. I punched cows on the range in Texas with the brother of an English lord."

"Are you suggesting that you are a duke in disguise?"

"Me?" he grinned. "No, I'm pretty much what I seem. I'm a cowhand, a drifter. Only I've a few ideas and I've read a few books. I spent a winter once snowed up in the mountains in Montana with two other cowhands. All we had for entertainment was a couple of decks of cards, some checkers, and a half dozen books. Some Englishman left them there, and I expect before spring we all knew those books by heart, an' we'd argued every point in them."

"What were they?" she asked curiously.

"Plutarch's *Lives*, the plays and sonnets of Shakespeare, some history—oh, a lot of stuff. And good reading. We had a lot of fun with those books. When we'd played cards and checkers until we were black in the face, we'd ask each other questions on the books, for by the time we'd been there half the winter we'd read them several times over."

He ate in silence for a few minutes, and then she asked, "Do you know anything about the shooting?"

"Heard about it. What sort of man is Rolly Burt?"

"One of the best. You'd like him, I think. Hard as nails, and no youngster. He's more than forty, I'd say. But he says what he thinks, and he thinks a good deal."

Ross hesitated a few moments and then said, "By the way, I saw one of your hands in town yesterday. A tall, slope-shouldered fellow in a checkered shirt. You know the one I mean?"

She looked up at him, her eyes cool and direct. He had an uncomfortable feeling that she knew more than she was letting on. Of course, this was the man she had watched from hiding as he had met Berdue. Probably she had overheard their talk.

"Oh, you mean Kerb Dahl! Yes, he's one of our hands. Why do you ask?"

"Wondering about him. I'm trying to get folks placed around here."

"There are a lot of them trying to get you placed, too."

He laughed. "Sure! I expected that. Are you one of them?"

"Yes, I think I am. You remember I overheard your talk on the trail, and I'm still wondering where you plan to be top dog?"

He flushed. "You shouldn't have heard that. However, I back down on none of it. I know how Chalk Reynolds got his ranch. I know how Walt Pogue got his, and neither of them have any moral or other claim to them aside from possession, if that is a right.

"You probably heard what I told Chalk in here the other night. I could tell him more. I haven't started on Pogue yet, and I'd as soon you didn't tell anyone I plan to. However, in good time I shall. You see, he ran old man Carter off his place, and he had Emmett Chubb kill Vin Carter. That's one of the things that drew me here."

"Revenge?"

"Call it that if you like. I have a different name." He leaned toward her, suddenly eager for her to understand. "You see, you can't judge the West by any ordered land you know. It is a wild, hard land, and the men that came west and survived were tough stern men. They fought Indians and white men who were worse than Indians. They fought winter, flood, storm, drouth, and starvation.

"We have a sheriff here in town who was practically appointed by Chalk Reynolds. We have a jail that stands on his land. The nearest court is two hundred miles away, over poor roads and through Indian country. North of us there is one of the wildest and most remote lands in North America, where a criminal could hide for years.

"The only law we have here is the law of strength. The only justice we have must live in the hearts and minds of men. The land is hard, and so the men are hard. We make mistakes, of course, but when there is a case of murder, we try to handle the murderer so he will not kill again.

"Someday we will have law, we will have order. Then we can let the courts decide, but now we have none of those things. If we find a mad dog, we kill him, for there is no dogcatcher or law to do it. If we find a man who kills unfairly, we punish him. If two men fight and all is equal, regardless of which cause is right, we let the killing stand. But if a man is shot in the back, without a gun or a fair chance, then the people or sometimes one man must act.

"I agree that it is not right. I agree that it should be different, but this is yet a raw, hard land, and we must have our killers, not punished, but prevented from killing again.

"Vin Carter was my friend. Of that I can say nothing, only that because he was my friend, I must act for him. He was not a gunfighter. He was a brave young man, a fair shot, and on the night he was killed, he was so drunk he could scarcely see. He did not even know what was happening. It was murder.

"So I have come here. It so happens that I am like some of these men. Perhaps I am ruthless. Perhaps in the long run I shall lose, and perhaps I shall gain. No man is perfect. No man is altogether right or altogether wrong. Pogue and Reynolds got their ranches and power through violence. They are now in a dog-eat-dog feud of their own. When that war is over, I expect to have a good ranch. If it leaves them both alive and in power, I shall have my ranch, anyway."

She looked at him thoughtfully. "Where, Ross?"

His pulse leaped at the use of his first name, and he smiled suddenly. "Does it matter now? Let's wait, and then I'll tell you."

The smile left his face. "By the way, as you left me the other evening, a man told me you were a staked claim and to stay away."

"What did you do?" she looked at him gravely, curiously.

"I told him he was a fool to believe any woman was a staked claim unless she wanted it so. And he said nevertheless, you were staked. If it is of interest, you might as well know that I don't believe him. Also, I wouldn't pay any attention if I did."

She smiled. "I would be surprised if you did. Nevertheless," her chin lifted a little, "what he said is true."

Ross Haney's heart seemed to stop. For a full minute he stared at her, amazed and wordless. "You mean—what?"

"I mean that I am engaged to marry Star Levitt. I have been engaged to him for three months."

She arose swiftly. "I must be going now." Her hand dropped suddenly to his with a gentle pressure, and then she was gone.

He stared after her. His thoughts refused to order themselves, for of all the things she might have said or that he might have expected, this was the last. Sherry Vernon was engaged to Star Levitt.

"Some hot coffee?" It was May, smiling down at him.

"Sure." She cleaned up the table and then left him alone. "Sure," he said again, speaking softly into empty air. "That's the way it would be. I meet a girl worth having and she belongs to somebody else!"

"Mind if I sit down?"

He looked up to see Allan Kinney, the hotel clerk, standing by the table. "Go ahead," he suggested, "and have some coffee."

May delivered the coffee, and for a few minutes there was silence. Then Kinney said, "Ross, you'd do a lot for a friend, wouldn't you?"

Surprised, he glanced up, and something in Kinney's eyes told him what was coming. "Why, sure!" But even as he said it he was thinking it over, thinking over what he knew Kinney had on his mind.

Of course, he should have guessed it right away. There was no other place. This was a Walt Pogue, Chalk Reynolds town.

"Do you regard me as a friend? Of course, I haven't known you long, but you seem like a regular fellow. You haven't any local ties that I can see."

"That's right! I just cut the last one. Or had it cut. What do you want me to do? Get him out of town?"

Kinney jerked sharply. "You mean—you know?"

"I guessed. Where else would he go? Is Burt hurt bad?"

"He can ride. He's a good man, Ross. One of the best. I had no idea what to do about him because I know they will think of the hotel soon."

"You've got him *here*?" Haney was incredulous. "We'd best get him out tonight. That Box N crowd will be in hunting him, and I've a hunch the RR outfit won't back him the least bit."

"He's in the potato cellar. In a box under the potatoes."

"Whatever made you ask me?" Ross demanded.

Kinney shrugged. "Well, like I said, you hadn't any ties here, and seemed on the prod, as they say in Soledad. Then, May suggested it. May did, and Sherry."

"She knows?"

"I thought of her first. The VV is out of this fight so far, and it seemed the only place, but she told me she would like to, but there were reasons why it was the very worst place for him. Then she suggested you."

"She did?"

"Uh-huh. She said if you liked Burt, she knew you would do it, and you might do it just as a slap at Reynolds and Pogue. She didn't seem to believe Reynolds would help, either."

Haney digested that thoughtfully. Apparently Sherry had a pretty good idea of just what undercurrents were moving the pawns about in the Soledad chess game. Of course, she would have heard at least part of Berdue's meeting with Kerb Dahl and the others.

"We can't wait," Haney said. "It will have to be done now. The Box N hands should be getting to town within the hour. Have you got a spare horse?"

"Not that we can get without everybody knowing, but May has one at her place," Kinney answered. "She lives on the edge of town. The problem is to get him there."

"I'll get him there," Haney promised. "But I'd best get mounted myself. I know where to take him, too. However, you'd best throw us together a sack of grub from the restaurant supplies so there won't be too many questions asked. After I come back again, I can arrange to get some stuff."

Ross Haney got to his feet. "Get him ready to move. I'll get my horse down to May's and come back." He listened while Kinney gave him directions about finding her house, and then hurried to the door.

It was too late.

A dozen hard-riding horsemen came charging up the street and swung down at the hotel. Two men stepped up on the boardwalk and strode into the hotel. Haney knew one by his size. It was Walt Pogue himself, and the man at his right was the man who had been with Berdue at the springs!

Pogue confronted Kinney. "Kinney! I want to search your place! That killer Rolly Burt is somewhere in town, an' by the Lord Harry we'll have him hangin' from a cottonwood limb before midnight!"

"What makes you think he'd be here?" Kinney demanded. He was pale and taut, but completely self-possessed. He might have been addressing a class in history, or reading a paper before a literary group. "I know Burt, but I haven't seen him."

## Chapter VIII
## *Help Needed*

Unobtrusively, Ross Haney was lounging against the door to the kitchen, his mind working swiftly. They would find him, and there was no earthly way to prevent it. The only chance would be to avert the hanging, to delay it. He knew suddenly that he was not going to see Rolly Burt hang. He didn't know the man, but Burt had won his sympathy by winning a fair fight against two men.

"What are you so all-fired wrought up about, Pogue?" he drawled.

Walt Pogue turned square around to face him. "It's you! What part have you got in this?"

Ross shrugged. "None at all! Just wonderin'. Everywhere I been, if a man is attacked an' kills two men against his one, he's figured to be quite a man, not a lynchin' job."

"He killed a Box N man!"

"Sure!" Ross smiled. "Box N men can die as well as any others. It was a fair shake from all I hear. All three had guns, all three did some shootin'. I haven't heard any Reynolds men kickin' because it was two against one. Kind of curious, that. I'm wonderin' why all the RR men are suddenly out of town?"

"You wonder too much!" It was the man from the springs. "This is none of your deal! Keep out of it!"

Ross Haney still leaned against the door, but his eyes turned to the man from the springs. Slowly, carefully, contemptuously he looked the rider over from head to heel, then back again. Then he said softly:

"Pogue, you've got a taste for knickknacks. If you want to take this boy home with you, keep him out of trouble."

The rider took a quick step forward. "You're not running any bluff on me, Haney!"

"Forget it, Voyle! You get to huntin' for Burt. I'll talk to Haney." Pogue's voice was curt.

Voyle hesitated, his right hand hovering over his gun, but Ross did not move, lounging carelessly against the door-post, a queer half smile on his face.

With an abrupt movement then, Voyle turned away, speaking quickly over his shoulder. "We'll talk about it later, Haney!"

"Sure," Ross Haney said, and then as a parting he called softly, "Want to bring Dahl with you?"

Voyle caught himself in midstride, and Voyle's shoulders hunched as if against a blow. He stopped and stared back, shock, confusion, and puzzlement struggling for expression.

Haney looked back at Pogue. "You carry some characters," he said. "That Voyle now. He's touchy, ain't he?"

"What did you mean about Dahl? He's not one of my riders!"

"Is that right? I thought maybe he was, although I'll admit I didn't know."

Walt Pogue stared at him, annoyed and angry, yet puzzled, too. The big man walked back to the table and poured a cup of coffee from the big pot on the stove. He put sugar in it and then cream. He glanced once over his shoulder at Ross.

Haney felt a slight touch on his shoulder and glanced around and found May at his shoulder.

"He's gone!" she whispered. "He's not there!"

There was dust on her dress and he slapped at it, and she hurriedly brushed it away. "Where was he shot?" he asked, under his breath.

"In the leg. He couldn't go far, I know."

Pogue turned around. "What are you two talking about?" he demanded. "Why the whispering?"

"Is it any of your business?" Haney said sharply.

Walt Pogue stiffened and put his cup down hard. "You'll go too far, Haney! Don't try getting rough with me! I won't take it!"

"I'm not askin' you to!" Ross replied roughly. He straightened away from the doorpost. "I don't care how you take it. You're not running me or any part of me, and you might as well learn that right now. If I choose to whisper to a girl, I'm doin' it on my own time, so keep out of it!"

Pogue stared at him and then at the girl, and there was meanness in his eyes. He shrugged. "It's a small matter. With all this trouble I'm gettin' jumpy."

Voyle came back into the room accompanied by two other men. "No sign of him, boss. We've been all over the hotel. Simmons an' Clatt went through the vegetable cellar, too, but there ain't a sign of him. There was an empty box under those spuds, though, big enough to hide a man."

Allan Kinney had come back into the room. "What about that, Kinney?"

"Probably somethin' to keep the spuds off the damp ground, much as possible," Haney suggested carelessly. "Seems simple enough."

Pogue's jaw set and he turned swiftly. "You, Haney! Keep out of this! I was askin' Kinney, not you!"

This time Voyle had nothing to say; once Ross glanced at him, and the man looked hastily away. "He's scared," Ross told himself mentally. "He's mixed in some deal an' don't want his boss to know it. He's afraid I'll say too much."

Pogue turned and strode from the restaurant, going out through the hotel lobby, his men trooping after him. When the last man was gone, May turned to Kinney. "Allan, where can he be? He was there, you know he was there!"

Kinney nodded. "I know." He twisted his hands together. "He must have heard them and got out somehow. But where could he go?"

Ross Haney was already far ahead of them. He was thinking rapidly. The searchers would probably stop for a drink, but they would not stop long. Voyle was apparently in on the plot to have Burt killed, for he had been at the springs, and this had happened too swiftly. Too little noise had come from the RR for it to be anything but a plot among them. Or so it seemed to Haney. For some reason Rolly Burt had become dangerous to them, and he was intended to die in the gunfight the previous night, but had survived and killed one of their men and wounded another. Now he must be killed, and soon.

Yet Haney was thinking further than that. His mind was going outside into the darkness, thinking of where he would go if he were a wounded man with little ammunition and no time to get away.

He would have to hobble or to drag himself. He would be quickly noticed by anyone and quickly investigated. He would not dare go far without shelter, for there was some light outside even though it was night.

Yet Haney was recalling the stone wall. It started not far from the hotel stables and went around an orchard planted long ago. Some of the stones had fallen, but much of it was intact. A man might make a fair defense from behind that wall, and he could drag himself all of a hundred yards behind it.

Ross walked swiftly out of the hotel through the back door. There in the darkness he stood stock-still at the side of the door letting his eyes become accustomed to the night. After a minute or two he could pick out the stable, the orchard, and the white of the stones in the wall.

Walking to the stable, he took the path along its side and then put a hand on the stone wall and dropped over it with a quick vault. Then he stood still once more. If he approached Burt too suddenly the wounded man might mistake him for an enemy and shoot. Nor did he know Burt, or Burt him.

Moving silently, Haney worked his way along the stone wall. It was no more than three feet high, and along much of it there was a hedge of weeds and brambles. He ripped a scratch on his hand and then swore. Softly, he moved ahead, and he was almost to the corner when a voice spoke, very low.

"All right, mister, you've made a good guess but a bad one. Let one peep out of you an' you can die."

"Burt?"

"Naw!" the cowhand was disgusted. "This is King Solomon an' I'm huntin' the Queen of Sheba! Who did you think it would be?"

"Listen, an' get this straight the first time. I'm your friend, and a friend of May and Kinney from the hotel. I've been huntin' you to help you out of here. There's a horse at May's shack, an' we've got to get you there just as fast as we can make it. You hear?"

"How do I know who you are?"

"I'd have yelled, wouldn't I? If I found you?"

"Once, maybe. No more than once though. This Colt carries a kick. Who are you? I can't see your face."

"I'm Ross Haney. Just blew in."

"The hombre that backed Syd Berdue up? Sure thing, I know you. Heard all about it. It was a good job."

"Can you walk?"

"I can take a stab at it if you give me a shoulder."

"Let's go, then."

With an arm around Burt's waist, Haney got him over the fence and then down the dark alleyway between it and the stone house next to it. They came out in an open space, and beyond it there was the trail and then the woods. Once in the shelter of the trees they would have ample concealment all the way to May's house.

Yet once they were started across that open space, any door opened along the backs of the buildings facing them from across the street would reveal them, and they would be caught in the open. There would be nothing for it then but to shoot it out.

"All right, Burt. Here we go! If any door opens, freeze where you are!"

"Where you takin' me?" Supporting himself with a hand on Haney's shoulder, and Haney's arm around his waist, he made a fair shift at hobbling along.

"May's shack. If anything delays me, get there. Take her horse an' light out. You know that old trail to the badlands?"

"Sure, but it ain't no good unless you circle around to Thousand Springs. No water. An' that's one mighty rough ride."

"Don't worry. I'll handle that. You get over there and find a spot to watch the trail until you see me. But with luck we'll make it together."

Burt's grip on Haney's shoulder tightened. "Watch it! Somebody openin' that door!"

They stopped, standing stock-still. Ross felt Burt's off arm moving carefully, and then he saw the cowhand had drawn a gun. He was holding it across his stomach, covering the man who stood in the light of the open door. It was the bartender.

Somebody loomed over the bartender's shoulder. "Hey! Who's that out there?"

"Go on back to your drinks," the bartender said. "I'll go see." He came down the steps and stalked out toward them, and Haney slid his hand down for his left gun.

The fat man walked steadily toward them until he was close by. He glanced from one face to the other. "Pat," Burt said softly, "you'd make a soft bunk for this lead."

"Don't fret yourself," he said. "If I hadn't come, one of those drunken Box N riders would have, an' then what? You shoot me, an' you have them all out here. Go on, beat it. I'm not huntin' trouble with any side." He looked up at Haney. "Nor with you, Ross. You don't remember me, but I remember you right well from your fuss with King Fisher. Get goin' now."

He turned and strode back to the door. "What is it?" A drunken voice called. "If it's that Rolly Burt, I'll fix him!"

"It ain't. Just a Mexican kid with a horse. Some stray he picked up, an old crowbait. Forget it!" The door closed.

Ross heaved a sigh. Without further talk, they moved on, hobbling across the open, then into the trees. There they rested. They heard a door slam open. Men came out into the street and started up the path away from them. They had been drinking and were angry. The town of Soledad would be an unpleasant place on this night.

When Haney had the mare saddled, he helped Rolly up. "Start down the trail," he said. "If you hear anybody comin', get out of sight. When I come, I'll be ridin' that palouse of mine. You've seen it?"

"Sure. I'll know it. I keep goin' until you catch up, right?"

"Right. Keep out of sight of anybody else, and I mean anybody. That goes for your RR hands as well. Hear me?"

"Yeah, an' I guess you're right at that. They sure haven't been much help. But I'll not forget what you've done, a stranger, too."

"You ride. Forget about me. I've got to get back into Soledad an' get my horse out without excitin' comment. Once I get you where I'm takin' you, nobody will find you."

He watched the mare start up the road at a fast walk, and then he turned back toward the town.

He heard shouts and yells, and then a drunken cowhand blasted three shots into the air.

Ross Haney hitched his guns into place and started down the road for Soledad. He was walking fast.

## Chapter IX
### *Baited Trap*

The disappearance of Rolly Burt was a nine-day wonder in the town of Soledad and the Ruby Hills. Ross Haney, riding in and out of town, heard the question discussed and argued from every standpoint. Burt had not been seen in Rico or in Pie Town. Nor had any evidence of him been found on the trails.

No horses were accounted missing, and the search of the Box N cowhands had been fruitless, if intensive. Neither Allan Kinney nor May asked any questions of Ross, although several times he recognized their curiosity.

The shooting and the frenzied search that followed had left the town abnormally quiet. Yet the rumor was going around that with the end of the coming roundup, the whole trouble would break open once more and be settled, once and for all. For the time being, with the roundup in the offing, both ranches seemed disposed to ignore the feud and settle first things first.

Second only to the disappearance of Rolly Burt was Ross Haney himself as a topic of conversation. He spent money occasionally, and he came and went around Soledad, but no one seemed to have any idea what he was doing, or what his plans were. Curiosity was growing, and the three most curious men were Walt Pogue, Chalk Reynolds, and Star Levitt. There was another man even more curious, and that one was Emmett Chubb.

It was after the disappearance of Burt that Chubb first heard of Haney's presence in the Ruby Hills. The RR hands ate at one long table presided over by Chalk himself, and Syd Berdue sat always at his right hand.

"Heard Walt Pogue an' his man Voyle had some words with that Haney," Reynolds said to Berdue. "Looks like he's gettin' this country buffaloed."

Berdue went white to the lips and had started to make an angry reply when he was cut off by a sudden movement down the table. Emmett Chubb had lunged to his feet. The stocky, hard-faced gunman leaned across the table. "Did you say *Haney?*" he rasped. "Would that be Ross Haney?"

"That's right." Reynolds looked up sharply. "Know him?"

Chubb sat back in his chair with a thud. "I should smile I know him! He's huntin' me!"

"You?" Reynolds stared. "Why?"

Chubb shrugged. "Me an' a friend of his had a run-in. You knew him. Vin Carter."

"Ah? Carter was a friend of Haney's?" Reynolds chewed in silence. "How good is this Haney?"

"He thinks he's plumb salty. I wouldn't be for knowin', however. Down thataway they sure set store by him."

A slim, dark-faced cowhand looked up and drawled softly, "I know him, Emmett, an' when you tangle with him, be ready. He's the hombre who went into King Fisher's hideout in Mexico after a horse one of Fisher's boys stole off him. He rode the horse out, too, an' the story is that he made Fisher take water. He killed the hombre who stole his horse. The fellow was a fool halfbreed who went for his gun."

"So he's chasin' you, Emmett?" Reynolds muttered. "Maybe that accounts for his bein' here."

"An' maybe he's here because of Vin Carter," Berdue said. "If he is, that spells trouble for Pogue. That won't hurt us any."

In the days that had followed the escape of Rolly Burt, Haney had not been idle. He had thrown and branded several of the wild cattle and had pushed a few of them out into the open valley below Thousand Springs. There would be plenty of time later to bring more of them; all he wanted was for the brand to show up when the roundup was under way.

Astride the palouse, he headed for the VV. The morning was warm but pleasant, and he rode down into the shade under the giant old cottonwoods feeling very fit and very happy. Several of the hands were in sight, and one of them was the slope-shouldered Dahl, mending a saddle girth.

Bob Vernon saw him, and his brow puckered in a slight frown. He turned and walked toward Ross Haney. "Get down, won't you? Sherry has been telling me something about you."

"Thanks, I will. Is she here?" His purpose had been to verify, if he could, some of his ideas about that conversation he had seen and she had overheard at the spring. Also, he was curious about the setup at the VV. It was the one place he had not catalogued in his long rides.

"Yes," Vernon hesitated, "she's here." He made no move to get her. Suddenly he seemed to make a decision. "I say, Haney. You're not coming with the idea of courting my sister, are you? You know she's spoken for."

"That idea," Haney said grimly, "seems to be one everyone wants to sell me. First heard it from Star Levitt."

Vernon's lips tightened. "You mean Star talked to you about Sherry?"

"He did. And Sherry told me she was to marry him."

Bob Vernon appeared relieved. He relaxed. "Well, then you understand how things are. I wouldn't want any trouble over her. Star's pretty touchy."

"Understand this." Haney turned sharply around and faced Bob. "I was told that by Levitt and by Sherry. Frankly, the fact that she is engaged to him doesn't make a bit of difference to me. I haven't told that to her, but you're her brother, and I'm tellin' you. You don't need any long-winded explanations about how I feel about her. When I'm sure she's in love with him, I'll keep away. Until then, I'm in to stay!"

Surprisingly, Vernon did not get angry. He appeared more frightened and worried. "I was afraid of that!" he muttered. "I should have known!"

"Now, if you won't get her for me, I'll go to the house after her!"

"After whom?" They turned swiftly to see Sherry walking toward them, smiling. "Hello, Ross. Who were you coming after? Who could ever make your voice sound like that?"

"You," he said bluntly. "Nobody but you."

Her smile vanished, but there was warmth in her eyes. "That's nice," she said. "You say it as if you mean it."

"I do."

"Boss?" A tall, lean, and red-headed cowhand had walked up to them, and when they turned, he asked, "Who has the Gallows Frame brand?"

"Gallows Frame?" Vernon shrugged. "Never heard of it. Where did you see it?"

"Up toward Thousand Springs. Seen several mighty fine lookin' bulls an' a few cows up thataway an' all wearin' that brand, a gallows frame with a ready noose hangin' from it. An' them cows, why they are wilder'n all get-out. Couldn't get nowhere near 'em."

"That's something new," Vernon commented. "Have you seen any of them, Sherry?"

She shook her head, but there was a strange expression in her eyes. She glanced over at Ross Haney, who listened with an innocence combined with humor that would have been a perfect giveaway to anyone who knew him.

"No, I haven't seen any of them, Bob." She looked at the redhead again. "Mabry, have you met Ross Haney? He's new around here, but I imagine he's interested in brands."

Mabry turned to Haney and grinned. "Heard somethin' about you," he said. "Seems you had a run-in with Syd Berdue."

Ross noted that Kerb Dahl's fingers had almost ceased to move in their work on the girth.

Mabry walked away with Bob Vernon, and Sherry turned to Ross, her eyes cool but friendly. "I thought you might be interested in knowing Bill Mabry. He was always a good friend of that cowhand they were looking for in town—Rolly Burt."

Haney's eyes shifted to her thoughtfully. There seemed to be very little this girl did not know. She would be good to have for a friend, and not at all good as an enemy. She was as intelligent as she was beautiful. Her eyes never seemed asleep; she seemed to see every-thing and to comprehend what she was seeing. Was that a lucky guess about Burt? Or did she know? Would Kinney have told her?

Of course, he recalled, Kinney had said she had suggested him. That might be it. She was guessing.

Dahl's ears were obviously tuned to catch every word, so he turned. "Shall we walk over and sit down?" He took her elbow and guided her to a seat under one of the huge cottonwoods.

"Sherry," he said suddenly, "I told Bob I didn't intend to pay no attention to this engagement of yours unless I found out you were in love with Levitt. Are you?"

She looked away quickly, her face suddenly pale and her lips tight. Finally, she spoke. "Why else would a girl be engaged to a man?"

"I haven't an idea. There might be reasons." He stared at her, and then his eyes strayed to Dahl. "Until you tell me you do, and look me in the eye when you say it, I'm goin' ahead. I want you, Sherry. I want you like I never wanted anything in this world, an' I mean to have you if you could care for me. I'm not askin' you now. Just tellin' you. When I came into this valley I came expectin' trouble, an' I thought I knew all the angles. Well, I've found out there's somethin' more goin' on here than I expected, an' it's somethin' you know about.

"Maybe you don't know it all. I'm bankin' you don't. You heard me talkin' to myself. Well, what I said then goes. I'm here alone, an' I'm ridin' for my own brand, an' you've guessed right, for that Gallows Frame is mine, an' the noose is for anybody who wants to hang on it.

"The RR spread an' the Box N are controlled by a couple of range pirates. They whipped and murdered smaller, weaker men to get what they've got. If they keep it, they'll know they've been in a fight."

Sherry had listened intently. Her face had become serious. "You can't do anything alone, Ross! You must have help!" She put her hand on his arm. "Ross, is Rolly safe? Understand, I am not asking you where he is, just if he is safe. He did me a good turn once, and he's an honest man."

"He's safe. For your own information, and not to be repeated, he's workin' for me now. But he can't do much for another ten days or more, an' by that time it may be too late. Can I rely on Mabry?"

"You can. If he will work for you, he'll die for you and kill for you if it's in the right kind of fight. He was Burt's best friend."

"Then if I can talk to him, you'll lose a hand." He looked down at her. "Sherry, what's goin' on here? Who is Star Levitt? Who are those men I saw in town? Who's this Kerb Dahl, and Voyle? I know there's some connection."

She got up quickly. "I can't talk about that. Star Levitt is going to be my husband."

Ross got up, too. Roughly, he picked up his hat and jerked it on his head; then he stood there, hands on hips, staring at her.

"Not Levitt!" he said harshly. "Well, if you won't tell me, I'll find out anyway!"

He turned abruptly and saw the two men he had seen in town at the restaurant. Kerb Dahl and the shorter, hard-faced man.

In that single instant he became aware of many things. Bob Vernon stood in the door, white as death. Kerb Dahl, a hard gleam in his eyes, was on the right and he walked with elbows bent, hands swinging at his gun butts. Behind them Haney could see the big, old tree with a bench around it and a rusty horseshoe nailed to the trunk. Two saddled horses stood near the corral, and the sunlight through the leaves dappled the earth with shadow.

Behind him there was a low moan of fear from Sherry, but he did not move, but waited and watched the two men coming toward him. It could be here. It could be now. It could be at this moment.

Dahl spoke first, his lean, cadaverous face hard and with a curiously set expression. The shorter man had moved apart from him a little. Haney remembered the girl behind him, and knew he dare not fight—but some sixth sense warned him that somewhere else would be a third man, probably with a rifle. The difference.

Kerb Dahl spoke. "You're Ross Haney. I reckon you know me. I'm Dahl, an' this here is the first time you've come to the VV an' this is goin' to be the last. You come on this place again an' you get killed. We don't aim to have no troublemakers around."

Ross Haney held very still, weighing his next words carefully. This could break into a shooting match in one instant. "Then have your artillery ready when I come back," he warned them. "Because when I'm ready, I'll come back."

"We told you."

Ross looked them over coldly, knowing they had expected to find him as tough and ready for a fight as he had been with Chalk Reynolds and Berdue. Yet there was a queer sense of relief in their eyes, too. Haney guessed that while there must be a hidden rifle-man, these men were afraid for their skins.

Mabry stood nearby as Ross swung into the saddle. "I've a job for you if you can get to town within the next twelve hours. At the saloon. You might run into a friend of yours."

Mabry did not reply, so Haney rode away leaving the cowhand standing there. He had spoken softly enough, so he knew he was not overheard. Yet Haney knew he was no closer to a solution than before.

There was danger here. An odd situation existed in the Ruby Hills. Scowling, he considered it. On the one hand was Walt Pogue with Bob Streeter and Repp Hanson, two notorious killers. On the other was Chalk Reynolds with Syd Berdue and Emmett Chubb.

Here at the VV was a stranger situation. Bob and Sherry Vernon, who owned the ranch, seemed completely dominated by Levitt and their own hands. Also Levitt had a strong claim of some kind on Sherry herself. What could be behind that? Scowling, Ross consid-ered it. Whatever it was, it could mean everything to him, not only for his plans in the valley, but because of his love for Sherry.

Somewhere in this patchwork of conflicting interests, there was another grouping, that small band who had gathered at the springs with Syd Berdue. The band was made up of at least one man from each ranch. Of Kerb Dahl of the VV, Voyle of the Box N, and Tolman of the Three Diamonds.

Where did this last group stand? Voyle, from his actions, wanted Pogue to know nothing of his tie-up with Dahl. Did Reynolds know about Berdue's meeting at the springs? Who was behind it?

## Chapter X
## *Narrow Squeak*

Quiet reigned at the Bit and Bridle when Ross Haney rode into town in the late afternoon. He left his horse at the rail and strolled through the half doors to the cool interior.

Only Pat the bartender was present. The room was dusky and still. Pat idly polished glasses as he came in, glanced up at him, and then put a bottle and a glass on the bar. Ross leaned an elbow on the hardwood and dug out the makings. He built a smoke without speaking, liking the restfulness and coolness after his hot ride, and thinking over what he had seen at the VV.

"You've lived here a long time, Pat?"

"Uh-huh. Before Carter was killed."

"Lots of changes?"

"Lots."

"There's goin' to be more, Pat."

"Room for 'em."

"Where do you stand?"

Pat turned abruptly and fixed his eyes on Haney. "Not in the middle. Not with Reynolds or Pogue. As for you, I'm neither for you nor against you."

"That's plain enough." Haney didn't know whether to be pleased or angry. After Pat's attitude in regard to Burt, he had hoped he might be an ally. "But you don't sound like much help."

"That's right. No help at all. I've got my saloon. I'm doin' all right. I was here before Reynolds and Pogue. I'll be here after they are gone."

"And after I'm gone?"

"Maybe that, too." Pat suddenly turned again and rested his big hands on the bar. "You fool around with Pogue all you want. With Reynolds, too. But you lay off of Star Levitt an' his crowd, you hear? They ain't human. They'll kill you. They'll eat you like a cat does a mouse, when they get ready."

"Maybe." Ross struck a match with his left hand. "Who are his crowd?"

Pat looked disgusted. "You've been to the VV. He runs that spread. Don't you be too friendly with that girl, either. She's poison."

Haney let that one ride. Maybe she was poison. Maybe feeling the way he did about her was the thing that would break him. He was a strong man. He had not lived that long under the conditions he knew without knowing his own strength and knowing how it compared with the strength of others. He knew that when he was sure he would push his luck to any degree, but as yet, he was not pushing it; as yet, no one in the valley knew his real intentions.

Pogue believed he had come looking for Chubb. Reynolds and Berdue, despite their hatred for him, believed he was after Pogue. Each was prepared to keep hands off in hopes he would injure the other. Yet the roundup was going to blow the lid off, for the roundup was going to show that he had cattle on the range and had pitched his hat into the ring. Then he would be in the middle of the fight, with every man's hand against him.

Pat's warning was right. Pogue and Reynolds were dangerous, but nothing to Levitt's crowd. Lifting his glass, Ross studied his reflection in the mirror, the reflection of a tall, wide-shouldered young man with blunt, bronzed features and a smile that came easily to eyes that were half cynical, half amused.

He was a tall young man with a flat-brimmed, flat-crowned black hat and a gray shield-chested shirt and a black knotted kerchief, black crossed belts, supporting the worn holsters and walnut-stocked guns.

He was a fool, he decided, to think as he did about Sherry. What could he offer such a girl?

On the other hand, what could Star Levitt offer her?

Regardless, he was here to stay. When he rode the palouse into the street of Soledad he had come to remain. If he had to back it with gunfire, he would do just that. Carefully, he considered the state of his plans. There was no fault to find there. In fact, he had progressed beyond where he had expected in that he had a friend, an ally, a man who would stay with him to the last ditch.

He had Rolly Burt.

Camping on the mesa, the wounded man was rapidly knitting. They had talked much, and Burt had told him what to expect of the roundup. He knew the characters and personalities of the people of the Ruby Hills, and he knew something more of Pogue and Reynolds. Over nights beside the campfire they had yarned and argued and talked. Both of them had ridden for Goodnight, both for John Chisum. They knew the same saloons in Tascosa and El Paso. Both had been over the trail to Dodge and to Cheyenne.

Both had been in Uvalde and Laredo, and they talked the nights away of cattle and horses, of rustling and gunfighters, until they knew each other and knew they spoke the same language. Rolly had talked much of Mabry. He was a good man. While Mabry liked both Bob and Sherry Vernon, he had confided to Burt that he must leave the VV or be killed.

"Why were the Box N boys gunnin' for you, Rolly?"

A frown gathered between Rolly Burt's eyes. He looked up at Ross over the fire. His blue eyes were puzzled and disturbed. "You know, I can't figure that. It was a set deal. I saw that right away. They'd been sent to murder me."

"How'd you happen to be in town?"

"Berdue sent me in for a message."

"I see." Ross told him then about the meeting below the mesa, everything but Sherry's part in it. "There's a tie-up there somewhere. I think Berdue sent you in on purpose, an' he had those Box N boys primed to kill you."

"But why?"

"Something you know, probably. The way I have it figured is that Syd Berdue is in some kind of a double-cross that he don't want Chalk to know about. Maybe he figured he'd tipped his hand somehow, and you knew too much. Voyle is in the deal with him, and I figured from the way he acted the other night in front of Pogue that he's double-crossing Walt. And I think Star Levitt is the man behind the whole thing!"

"You mean a deal between Berdue and Levitt? But they are supposed to be on the outs."

"Sure, and what better coverup? You keep an eye on the springs. They may meet again."

"Say!" Burt glanced up. "Something I've been meaning to ask you. Several times I've heard a funny kind of rumbling, sounds like it comes out of the rock under me. You heard it?"

"Uh-huh. Don't reckon it amounts to much, but someday we'll do some prowling. Kind of gives an hombre the shivers."

Standing now at the Bit and Bridle bar, Ross Haney went over that conversation. Yes, he was ahead of his plans in having such an ally as Rolly Burt.

He leaned his forearms on the hardwood and turned his head to glance out into the street. The rose of the setting sun had tinted the dusty, unpainted boards of the old building opposite with a dull glow, and beyond it, in the space between the buildings, a deep shadow had already gathered. At the rail, Rio stamped his feet against a vagrant fly and blew contentedly.

It was a quiet evening. Suddenly, he felt a vague nostalgia, a longing for a home he had never known, the deep, inner desire for peace, his children about him, the quiet evening rest on a wide porch after a hard day on the range, and the sound of a voice inside, a voice singing.

Yet when he straightened and filled his glass again, the guns felt heavy against his legs.

Someday, with luck, things would be different.

Then the half doors pushed open, and Star Levitt stood there, tall and handsome against the fading light. He looked for an instant at Ross and then came on into the room.

He wore the same splendid white hat, a white buckskin vest, and perfectly creased gray trousers tucked into polished boots.

As always, the worn guns struck the only incongruous note. His voice was easy, confident.

"Thanks. I've got one." In the mirror his eyes caught the difference between them, his battered shabbiness against the cool magnificence of Levitt.

Levitt's smile was pleasant, his voice ordinary and casual. "Planning to leave soon?"

"No." Haney's voice was flat. "I'm never going to leave."

"That's what the country needs, they tell me. Permanent settlers, somebody to build on. It's a nice thought, if you can stick it."

"That's right. How about you, Levitt? Do you think you'll be able to stick it when Reynolds and Pogue get to checking brands?"

He heard a glass rattle in Pat's suddenly nervous fingers. He knew he had taken the play away from Levitt with that remark, and he followed it up. "I've been over the range lately, and there's a lot of steers out there with VV's made over into Three Diamonds, an' Box N's to Triple Box A's, an' I understand that brand happens to be yours, too."

Levitt had straightened and was looking at him, all the smile gone from his face. "You understand too much, Haney! You're getting into water that's too deep for you, or for any drifting cowhand!"

"Am I? Let me judge. I've waded through some bad water a few times, an' where I couldn't wade, I could swim."

Star Levitt's eyes had widened, and the bones seemed to stretch the skin of his face taut and hard. He was not a man used to being talked back to, and he wasn't used to being thwarted. He was shrewd, a planner, but in that instant, Ross learned something else of him.

He had a temper, and when pushed, he got angry. Such a man was apt to be hasty. All right, Ross told himself, let's see.

"Another thing: you spoke the other day about a staked claim. I'm curious to see how deep your stakes are driven, so I'm going to find out for myself, Levitt. I don't think that claim is very secure. I think a little bit of bad weather an' all your stakes would shake loose. You're a big boy, Levitt, but you're not cutting the wide swath you think you are. Now you know where I stand, so don't try running any bluffs on me. I won't take a pushing around!"

"Stand aside, Star, an' let me have him!" The voice rang in an almost empty room, and Haney's hair prickled along his scalp as he saw Emmett Chubb standing just inside the door. "I want him, anyway, Star!"

Ross Haney stood, his feet wide apart, facing them, and he knew he was in the tightest spot of his life. Two of the deadliest gunmen in the country were facing him, and he was alone. Cold and still he waited, and the air was so tense he could hear the hoarse breathing of the bartender beside him and across the bar.

So still was the air in the room that Bill Mabry's voice, low as it was, could be heard by all.

"If they want it, Haney, I'll take Star for you. He's right here under my gun."

Levitt's eyes did not waver. Haney saw the quick calculation in the big man's eyes and then saw decision. Levitt was sharp, and this situation offered nothing for anybody. It was two and two, and Mabry's position at the window from which he spoke, commanded the situation perfectly, as he was just slightly behind both Levitt and Chubb.

It was Pat who broke the stalemate. "Nobody does any shootin' here unless it's me!" he said flatly. "Mabry, you stand where you are. Chubb, you take your hand away from that gun an' get out of that door, face first. Star, you foller him. I ain't aimin' to put clean sawdust on this here floor again today. Now git!"

He enforced his command with the twin barrels of a shotgun over the edge of the bar, and nobody had any argument with a shotgun at close quarters. A six-gun warrants a gamble, but there is no gamble with a sawed-off scattergun.

Chubb turned on his heel and strode from the room, and Star smiled suddenly, but his eyes were cold as they turned to Haney. "You talk a good fight," he said. "We'll have to see what you're holding!"

"All right," Ross replied shortly. "I'll help you check brands at the roundup!"

Levitt walked out, and then Bill Mabry put a foot through the open window and stepped into the bar. He grinned.

"That job open?"

Haney laughed.

"Friend, you've been working for me for the last three minutes!" he declared warmly.

"You two finish your drinks and pull out," Pat said dryly. "Powder smoke gives me a headache!"

# Chapter XI
## *Sinister Signs*

Gathered over the fire in the hollow atop the mesa crouched three men, not daring to use the partly constructed house, as the glow of the fire might attract attention. Here, in a more sheltered position far back from the rim, they could talk in quiet and without fear of the fire attracting attention.

Burt, whose leg was much better, was cooking. "It ain't all clear, Ross, but I think you've got the right idea. It looks like Levitt is engineerin' some kind of a steal if Voyle, Dahl, an' Berdue are in it with him. I do know this: there's been a passel of hard cases comin' into the valley here lately. They ain't all tied in with the Box N or the RR by any means."

"Sure, look at Streeter an' Hanson. They are with Pogue, but how far can he count on 'em? I think Streeter an' Hanson will stay out of things if Levitt says to. I think he's cut the ground from under the feet of both men."

"Those brands I've looked at aren't intended to fool anybody, it seems to me," Haney commented. "I think Levitt plans to start trouble. It's my opinion that he'll blow the lid off things just when the rest of them are standin' by for the roundup. How many reliable hands has Vernon got?"

"Three or four. Dahl and his partner ran several off. A man sure don't feel comfortable workin' around a ranch with two hombres on the prod like that."

"What goes on around there?" Haney asked Mabry. "You've lived on that spread an' should know."

Mabry shrugged. "I sure don't know," he said honestly. "Seems to be a lot of movin' around at night on that spread, but Dahl or his partner are usually by the door, an' they go out to see what it's all about. Several times at night riders have showed up there, leavin' hard-ridden horses behind when they take off. No familiar brands but one. That I think I've seen down Mexico way."

Ross took the plate he was handed and dished up some frijoles and then accepted the coffee Burt poured for him. There seemed to be but one answer. He would have to do some night riding and look around a little. Maybe he could figure it out. After all, there couldn't be many possibilities.

"Well," Burt suggested at last, "the roundup starts tomorrow. Before it has gone very far, we'll know a lot of things."

From the rim of the mesa they watched all the following morning. Reynolds's hands were rounding up cattle, driving them out of the timber and down into the flat. Some of the Box N riders were part of the group.

The weather was hot and dry, and dust arose in clouds. The cattle moved from the shade and ample water of the springs with reluctance. As always, it gave Ross a thrill to watch the cattle gathered and to see a big herd moving. He kept back and out of sight but took turns with Mabry at watching the work.

Regardless of their sympathies, there were good cattlemen on both sides. The riders got the cattle out of the brakes and started them down valley to the accompaniment of many yells, much shouting back and forth, and the usual good-natured persiflage and joking that is part of any roundup crew. As far as his glass was able to see, the same thing was happening. There would be several thousand head of stock to work in this roundup, and it would move on down the range for many miles before completed.

Mabry slid up alongside of him at noon on the second day. "You want me to rep for you, or will you tackle it your own self?"

Haney thought a minute. "We'll both go down, but we'll go loaded for bear. I think hell is going to break loose down there before many days."

"If they start to fight, what do we do?" Mabry asked keenly.

"Pull out. We don't have a battle with any of them. Not yet, we don't, but almost any of them might take a shot at us. When they see what's happened, that I've got cattle on this range, they aren't going to be too happy about it."

"Have you seen Scott?"

"Only for a minute or two. He's advisin' me to get more hands, but I don't want anybody killed, neither of you nor myself, either. If there's only three of us we'll play our cards the way we should, close to our belt. If there were more we might take chances and get somebody killed. If they start a battle, pull out."

"Don't you rate that Levitt too low, Haney." Mabry shook his head seriously. "He's cold-blooded, and he'll do whatever he's a mind to, to get his way on this range. He hasn't any use for either Pogue or Reynolds, but he's a sight worse than either of them."

It was good advice, and the following day when the two drifted down off the mesa toward the roundup, Ross Haney was thinking about it.

"Remember one thing," he advised Mabry. "We may not be together all the time. Don't let yourself get sucked in. Hold to the outer edge all the time, and keep an eye on the hands we've talked about whom we believe to be tied in with Levitt. I wouldn't be surprised at anything. If they start scattering out and seem to be taking up any definite positions, ease out of there quick!"

Walt Pogue looked unhappy when he saw the two riding up. Then he brightened noticeably. "You two hunting work? I need some men."

"No." Haney noted that Chalk Reynolds was riding over. "I've come to rep for my brand."

Pogue's head came down and his eyes squinted. He leaned toward them, and his somewhat thick lips parted. "Did you say—*your* brand?"

"That's right—the Gallows Frame."

The big rancher's face went white and then darkened with a surge of blood. He reined his horse around violently. "Who said you could run cattle on this range?"

Ross Haney shrugged. Chalk Reynolds looked as astonished and angry as Pogue. "Does anybody have to say so? Strikes me this here is government land, and my stock has as much right to run on it as yours, an' maybe more right."

"You'll find there's a difference of opinion on that!" Chalk Reynolds put in violently. "This range is overcrowded now."

"Tell that to Star Levitt. He's on it, with two brands."

This was obviously no news to either of them, but neither had anything to say for a minute, and then Reynolds said coldly, "Well, he'll be told! From what I hear somebody's doin' some mighty smooth work with a cinch ring!"

Ross hooked his leg around the saddle horn and began to dig for the makings. "Reynolds, if you an' Pogue will take a look at those altered brands, you'll see that whoever altered them doesn't give a hoot whether you know it or not. He's throwin' it right in your face an' askin' what you intend to do!"

"I'll do plenty!" Chalk bellowed. "There's goin' to be a new setup on this range after this roundup is over!"

"You throwin' that at me?" Pogue demanded. Fury was building in the man, and he was staring at Reynolds with an ugly light in his eye.

"Why don't you two either go to it or cut it out?" Haney drawled. "Or are you both afraid of Levitt? He's the hombre who's cuttin' in on you. He doesn't even bother to bring his own cows, he brands yours!"

Ross chuckled, and Reynolds's face went white. He turned and spoke flatly, the rage trembling behind his even tones. "We might get together, Walt an' I, long enough to get shut of you!"

"Take first things first," Ross said. "An' you'd better learn this right now, Chalk. An' you, too, Pogue. I came here to stay. If you fellows stay here, it will be with me alongside of you. If you go, I'll still be here. I didn't come to this valley by chance. I came here on purpose and with a definite idea in mind. Any bet you make, I'll double and raise. So anytime you want to get into the game with me, just start the ball rolling, anyway you like!"

He struck a match and lighted his smoke, then dropped his leg back and kicked his foot into the stirrup. Coolly and without a backward glance, he rode away.

Bill Mabry sat quietly for a minute or two, watching him ride.

Pogue glared at him. "What's in this, Bill? You've always been a good man."

"You listen to him," Mabry advised dryly. "He's mucho malo hombre, if you get what I mean. But only when he's crossed. He's got no reason to like either of you, but he's got other things on his mind now. But in case either of you wonder where I stand. Me an' my six-gun, we stand right alongside of Ross Haney. And that's where you'll find Rolly Burt, too!"

"Burt?" Pogue's face flamed. "Where is that murderin' son?"

Bill Mabry turned, his hand on the cantle of the saddle: "Listen, why don't you find out why two of your men were gunning for him,

Pogue? I'll bet a paint pony you don't know! An' why don't you, Chalk Reynolds, find out why none of your boys were in town that night to side Burt? Why did your nephew send him into town with a message?"

Mabry turned and cantered his horse over to Ross. "I gave 'em some more," he said briefly, and explained.

Haney chuckled. "Their ears will be buzzing for a week if they live that long. Some nice stock here, Bill, at that."

"How many head have you got out here?"

"Not many. Couple of dozen head is all. Just something to make them unhappy."

"Suppose they start to get sore? Reynolds an' Pogue both can be mighty mean."

"We'll get meaner. I've got them cold-decked, Bill. Someday I'll tell you about it. I've got them all cold-decked. The only way they can beat me in the long run is with hot lead."

"Maybe. But that Star Levitt is poison."

"You think Pogue and Reynolds will get through the roundup without a fight?"

"No. There's too much hard feelin' amongst the boys. Somebody will blow his top, and then the whole thing will bust up in a shootin' match."

Ross Haney looked across the valley, watching the familiar scene with a little of the old lift within him. This was the roundup, the hardest work in a cowhand's life, and in many ways, the highest point. They cussed the roundup and loved it. It was hot, dusty, full of danger from kicking hoofs and menacing horns, but filled with good fellowship and comradely fun.

The waving sea of horns tossed and rolled and fell as the cattle milled, or the herd, starting to line out for somewhere, anywhere, was turned back on itself by some cowhand quick to stop the movement. At such times the horns would send a long ripple of movement across the herd.

Wild-eyed steers lunged for a getaway, but were quickly harried back into the herd. At the branding pens men were gathered, the sharp line of demarcation between the RR and Box N a little broken here by the business of the day. Elsewhere, the men from the two big outfits drew off to themselves, worked together, and avoided contact with the rival ranch hands.

Star Levitt, astride a magnificent white horse, was everywhere to be seen. For a time he was at the branding pens, and then he was circling the herd. Finally, sighting Ross Haney and Mabry, he walked his horse toward them. Ross saw Mabry stiffen and saw the cowhand's face tighten and grow cold. Certainly, there was no love lost here.

"How are you, Haney?" Levitt was easy, casual. He seemed to have forgotten completely the events of the day in the Bit and Bridle. He was clean shaven as always, and as always he was immaculate. The dust of the roundup seemed scarcely to have touched him.

Mabry, glancing at the two, was struck for the first time at something strikingly similar in the two men; only there was a subtle difference that drew the cowhand inexorably to Ross Haney.

Both were big men, Levitt the taller and heavier and probably somewhat softer. Ross was lean and hard, his rugged build seeming so lean as to belie his actual weight, which was some two hundred pounds. Yet in the faces of both men there was strength, and in the faces of both men there was the look of command. Haney's manner was easy and careless, yet there was something solid about him, something rocklike that was lacking in the brittle sharpness of Star Levitt.

These two were shaped by nature to be enemies, two strong men with their faces turned in the same direction, yet backed by wholly varied thinking. The one ruthless and relentless, willing to take any advantage, willing to stop at nothing. The other, hard, toughened by range wars and fighting, with the rough-handed fair play of the western plains, yet equally relentless. It could be something, Mabry thought, if they ever came together in physical combat.

Ross began building a smoke. "Looks like a good herd. You got many cows here?"

"Quite a few." Levitt glanced at him sharply. "I hear you have some, too. That you're running the Gallows Frame brand."

"That's right." Ross lighted his smoke and eased his seat on the palouse. "It's a good brand."

"Seems so. Strange that I hadn't heard of any cattle coming into the country lately. Did you pick yours up on the range?"

At many times in many places such a remark would have meant shooting. After Haney's equally insulting remarks in the Bit and Bridle they were not important. These two knew their time was coming, and neither was in a rush. Levitt was completely, superbly confident. Ross hard and determined, his hackles raised by this man, his manner always verging on the outrightly aggressive.

"No, I didn't need to. Your pattern suits you, mine suits me." He inhaled deeply and let the smoke trickle out through his nostrils. "My cattle were already here."

The remark drew the response he wanted. It was a quick, nervous, and irritable scowl from Levitt. "That's impossible!" he said. "Only three brands ran on this range until I moved in!"

Haney smiled, knowing his enigmatic smile and manner would infuriate Levitt.

"Star," he drawled, "you're an hombre that figures he's right smart, an' you might be if you didn't figure the other fellow was so all-fired dumb.

"A man like you ain't got a chance to win for long in any game for that reason. You take everybody for bein' loco or dumb as a month-old calf. You ride into everything full of confidence an' sneers. You're like most crooks. You think everything will turn out right for you. Why, you're so wrong it don't need any argument!

"You came into this country big an' strong. You were goin' to be the boss. You saw Reynolds an' Pogue, an' you figured them for easy marks. You maybe had something on the Vernons, I haven't figured that out yet, but like so many crooks you overlooked the obvious.

"Let me tell you something, my cutthroat friend, an' get it straight: you lost this fight before you started. You might win with bullets, that's still anybody's guess, but you'll lose. You're smart in a lot of ways, an' if you were really smart you'd turn that horse of yours and start out of this country an' never stop until you're five hundred miles east of Tascosa."

Levitt smiled, but the smile was forced. For the first time the big man was uneasy, yet it was only for a moment. "I may not be as smart as I think, Haney, but no four-bit cowhand is going to out-smart me."

Ross turned slightly. "Bill, let's drift down toward the pens. I want to see what Reynolds an' Pogue think of those altered brands."

## Chapter XII
### Roundup Massacre

Nonchalantly Haney turned his back on Levitt and started away. Mabry rode beside him, occasionally stealing a glance his way. "Boss, you're sure turnin' the knife in that hombre. What you aimin' to do, force his hand?"

"Somethin' like that. It does me good just to goad him. But you keep your eyes open, because he's got something cookin' now. I only wish," his brow creased with worry, "I knew what he had on the Vernons. You don't suppose she really cares for that hombre, do you?"

Mabry shrugged. "I can guess what a fool cow will do, an' I can outguess a bronc, but keep me away from women. I never could read the sign right to foller their trail. Just when you think you can read the brand, they turn the other way an' it looks altogether different."

Despite the growing sense of danger, the roundup was moving very well, yet the tenseness of the riders for all the brands was becoming increasingly evident. Several times Ross saw Sherry, but she avoided him. Bob Vernon was there, working like any of his men and showing himself to be a fair hand and a very willing one. Yet as his eyes roved the herd and searched the faces of the riders, Ross could see that under the heat, the irritating confusing dust, and the hard labor, tempers were growing short.

On the third day, when the roundup had moved to the vicinity of Soledad, the break came. He had been trying to find a chance to talk to Sherry, and suddenly he saw it. The girl had been talking with Levitt. She had started away from him, riding toward the cottonwoods that marked the VV ranch house.

Ross started after her and noticed Kerb Dahl, his hard, lupine face set grimly, staring after him. Dahl had drawn aside from the crowd and was building a smoke. Mabry, who had been working hard all morning, was still in the center of things, but Voyle was saddling a fresh horse.

Haney overtook Sherry, and she looked up at him. He noticed for the first time how thin she had grown and how white her face was.

"Sherry?" Surprisingly, his voice was unsteady. "Wait a minute."

She drew up, waiting for him, but he thought she waited without any desire for conversation. She said nothing as he rode alongside. "Leaving so soon?"

She nodded. "Star said the men were getting pretty rough in their talk, and they'd be more comfortable if I went in."

"I've been hoping I'd have a chance to talk to you. You've been avoiding me." His eyes were accusing, but bantering.

She looked at him directly then. "Yes, Ross, I have. We must not see each other again. I'm going to marry Star, and seeing you won't do."

"You don't love him." The statement was flat and level, but she avoided his glance and made no response.

Then suddenly she said, "Ross, I've got to go. Star insisted I leave right away."

Haney's eyes hardened. "Do you take orders from him? What is this, anyway? Are you a slave? Haven't you a chance to make up your own mind?"

Her face reddened, and she was about to make a quick and probably angry retort when her remark hit him. He seized her wrist. "Sherry, you say Star *insisted*? That you leave *now*?"

"Yes." She was astonished and puzzled by his expression. "He said—"

The remark trailed off, for Ross Haney had turned sharply in his saddle. Kerb Dahl had finished his cigarette. Voyle was fumbling with his saddle girth, and for the first time, Haney noticed that he carried a rifle in his saddle scabbard, a rifle within inches of his hands. Ross's eyes strayed for the white horse and found it on the far side.

He turned quickly. "Sherry, he's right. Get back to that ranch as fast as you can, and don't leave it!"

He wheeled his horse and started back toward the branding pens at a rapid canter, hoping he would be in time. A small herd of cattle was drifting down toward the pens, and behind it was Streeter and Repp Hanson.

As he drew up on the edge of the branding, Mabry was just straightening up from slapping a brand on a steer. "Bill!" Haney had to speak three times before Mabry heard him, and then the red-headed cowhand turned and walked toward him. "Look out, Bill! It's coming!"

His remark might have been a signal, for Emmett Chubb, sitting his horse near the corral on the outside of the pole fence, spoke up and pointed his remark at Riggs, a Box N rider. "You all feet or just nat'rally dumb?"

Riggs looked up sharply. "What's the matter with you, Chubb? I haven't seen you down here doin' any work!"

Riggs was a slim, hard-faced youngster and a top hand. His anger was justifiable, and he was not thinking or caring who or what Chubb was. Riggs had worked while the gunman lounged in his saddle, carrying his perpetual sneer.

"Shucks!" Chubb said. "You Box N hands done enough work afore the roundup, slappin' brands on everythin' in sight! Bunch of tinhorn cow thieves!"

"You're a liar!" Riggs snapped, and Chubb's hand flashed for his gun. At that, Riggs almost made it. His gun was coming up when Chubb's first shot smashed him in the middle. He staggered back, gasping fiercely, struggling to get his gun up.

Instantly, the branding pens were bursting with gunfire. Mabry swung into the saddle and whipped his horse around the corner of the stock pens, and he and Ross Haney headed for the timber. "It's their fight," Mabry said bitterly. "Let them have it!"

"Look!" Haney was pointing.

Mabry glanced over his shoulder as the firing burst out, and his face went hard and cold.

Streeter and Hanson, from their saddles, had opened up on Reynolds and Pogue. Voyle was firing over the saddle of his horse, and cattle were scattering in every direction. Dust arose in a thick cloud.

From it came the scream of a man in agony and then another burst of firing.

Mabry gasped out an oath. The freckles were standing out against the dead white of his face. "Pogue's own men turned on him!"

"Yeah," Ross Haney hurled his cigarette into the dust. "We'd better light a shuck. I think they intended to get us, too!"

The crash of guns stopped suddenly, but the scene was obscured by dust from the crazed cattle and excited horses. Ross saw a riderless horse, stirrups flopping, come from the dust cloud, head high and reins trailing. Behind them there was a single shot, then another.

Finally, with miles behind them, Mabry looked over at Ross. "I feel like a coyote ridin' away from a fight, like that, but it sure wasn't none of ours."

Haney nodded grimly. "I saw it comin' but never guessed it would break out just like that. It couldn't be stopped without killin' Levitt."

"You think he engineered it?"

"Sure." Haney explained how Levitt had started Sherry home, and how his riders had moved out of the working men's group to good firing positions. "Chubb had his orders. He deliberately started that fight when he got the signal."

"I'll get him if it's the last thing I do!" Mabry said, bitterly. "That Riggs was a good hand. We hunted strays together."

"There was nothing we could have done but stay there an' die. We've got other things to do, Bill. We've got to see that Levitt's plans go haywire an' that he gets his deserts. We've got to get the Vernons out from under. Star will have this country sewed up now, with no one able to buck him but us. He'll rave when he finds we got away."

"As far as Reynolds an' Pogue," Mabry said, "I can't feel no sorrow. They were a couple of murderin' wolves, but they had some good men ridin' for 'em."

Mabry scowled. "Wonder what Levitt will do now? He's got the range sewed up with them two out of the way an' the Vernons knucklin' under to him."

Ross frowned. He had thought that over and believed he knew the answer. "That we'll have to wait an' see," Haney said. "I'm right curious, myself. He'll hunt us, an' we'll have to lay low. He'll blame the whole thing on the feud between the two big outfits an' claim he was just an innocent bystander."

"What about the riders?" Mabry protested. "Some of them will tell the truth!"

"Bill," Haney said, "I'd lay a good bet none of them know. We knew pretty well what was comin', an' moreover we got off to one side with a clear view. Down there among the stampedin' cows, the dust an' shootin', I'll bet the ones who are alive won't know. Moreover, I'll bet most of them drift out of the country.

"If they don't drift," Haney added, "Levitt will probably see that they do. From his standpoint it's foolproof. Remember, too, that Levitt's gunmen were men from both outfits."

"If he kills like that," Mabry asked, "what chance have three men got?"

"The best chance, Bill. We're still honest men, even if the only law is gun law. We'll wait an' see what Levitt does, but I imagine the first thing he'll do will be to clean up the loose ends. He may even call in the law from outside so he'll be in the clear with a clean bill of health."

Rolly Burt was waiting for them when they rode in. "What happened?" he demanded. "Did the lid blow off? I heard shootin'."

Briefly, Haney explained. "The fight would have come, I expect, even if Levitt hadn't planned it."

"How many were killed?"

"No tellin'. I doubt if so many. Enough to warrant Levitt playin' the big, honest man who wants to keep the peace. Down there in the dust, I doubt if anybody scored many good shots. Too much confusion and too many running cattle. Riggs is probably dead."

"Murderin' coyotes!" Burt limped to the fire. "Set an' eat. I've got the grub ready."

He dished up the food and then straightened, fork in hand. "Ross, what happened to Chalk?"

Haney did not look up. "He's sure to be dead. So's Pogue. Even Syd Berdue was shootin' at them. Killed his own uncle, or lent a hand."

"Chalk was no good, but no man deserves that."

Burt looked up suddenly. "Boss, while you two were gone I done some stumpin' around to loosen the muscles in this here game leg, an' guess what I found?"

"What?" Haney dished up a forkful of beans and then looked over it at Rolly, struck by something in his tone.

"That rumblin' in the rock. I found what causes it!" he said. "An' man, when you see it, your hair'll stand on end, I'm a-tellin' you!"

## Chapter XIII
### *Cavern of Terror*

Yawning, Ross Haney opened his eyes to look through the aspen leaves at a cloudless sky. The vast expanse of blue stretched above them as yet unfired by the blazing heat of the summer sun. He rolled out of his soogan and dressed, trying to keep his feet out of the dew covering the grass.

Bill Mabry stuck a head bristling with red hair, all standing on end, out of his blankets and stared unhappily at Haney.

"Rolly," he complained, "what can a man do when his boss gets up early? It ain't neither fittin' nor right, I say."

"Pull your head back in then, you sorrel-topped bronc!" Haney growled. "I'm goin' to have a look at the valley, an' then Rolly can roll out an' scare up some chuck."

"How about this all-fired rumblin'?" Mabry sat up. "I heard it again last night. Gives a man the creeps."

Burt sat up and looked around for his boots. He rubbed his unshaven jowls as he did every morning and muttered: "Dang it, I need a shave!"

"Never seen you when you didn't." Mabry thrust his thumb through a hole in his sock, swore, and then pulled it on. "You need a haircut, too, you durned Siwash. Ugly, that's what you are! What a thing to see when you first wake up! Lucky you never hitched up with no girl. She sure would have had you curried and combed to a fare-thee-well!"

Ross left them arguing and, picking up his glass, walked to the nest of boulders he used for a lookout. Settling down on his stomach in the sand, he pointed the glass down valley.

At first, all seemed serene and beautiful. The morning sunlight sparkled on the pool below, and the sound of the running water came to his ears. Somewhere, far off, a cow bawled. He swept the edge of the trees close at hand, studied the terrain below, and then bit by bit eased his line of quest up until he was looking well down range toward the Soledad trail.

The sun felt good on his back, and he squirmed to shift his position a little; he leveled the glass and then froze.

A group of horsemen was coming up the trail toward Thousand Springs, riding slowly. Star Levitt, he made out, was not among them. As they drew nearer, he picked out first one and then another. They were led by Syd Berdue, and Kerb Dahl and Voyle were with him. Also, Emmett Chubb and a half dozen other riders. As they drew rein below him and let their horses drink, their words drifted up to him.

This time they were making no secret of their conversation, and in the bright morning air, their words were, for the most part, plain enough.

"Beats all where he got to!" Voyle complained. "One minute both of them were there, an' then they were gone."

"We'd better find 'em," Dahl replied. "I never did see Star so wrought up about anythin' as when he found they'd got away. He must have turned over everything in the flat, a-huntin' 'em. Refused to believe they'd got away. Golly, was he mad!"

"He's a bad man to cross," Streeter commented. "I never seen him mad before. He goes crazy."

Chubb hung at one edge of the group, taking no part in their talking. His eyes strayed toward Berdue from time to time. Finally, he swung down and walked to one of the springs for a drink, and when he came back, wiping his mouth, his eyes shifted from one to the other. "Some things about this I don't like," he said.

There was no reply. Watching, Ross had the feeling that Chubb expressed the view of more than one of them. Syd idly flicked his quirt at a mesquite.

"Well, you can't say he ain't thorough!" he said grimly.

Chubb looked around. "Yeah," he agreed sarcastically. "But how thorough? Where does his bein' thorough stop? You ever start to figure like that? He had me primed to start the play by gunnin' Riggs, as he had Riggs pegged as a hothead who would go for a gun if pushed. Well, I hadn't no use for Riggs, my own self, but he never told me what was to come after. It was pure luck I didn't get killed!"

"Where do you reckon Haney went?" Dahl demanded, changing the subject.

"Where did Rolly Burt go?" Voyle asked. "You ask me, that Ross Haney is nobody's fool. He an' Mabry sure got shut of those brandin' pens in a hurry! They lit out like who flunk the chunk. Maybe left the country."

"He shore didn't!" Chubb said bitterly. "He wants my scalp! He'll not leave if I read his tracks right."

"He called the boss a couple of times," Voyle said. "Pogue, too. Don't seem to take no water for anybody."

Syd Berdue's eyes shifted from face to face, waiting for somebody to mention his own fuss with Haney, but they avoided his eyes. "I'd say the thing to do would be to stop chasin' over the country an' keep an eye on that Kinney feller. He was right friendly with Haney, they tell me."

"Or Sherry Vernon!" Berdue sneered. "I think the boss is buckin' a stacked deck with her."

Watching from the mesa and listening to the faint sound of their voices, Ross could see Kerb's eyes shifting from man to man. He shook his own head, disgusted.

"They talk too much," he told himself, "that Dahl will tell Levitt every word or I miss my guess. He wasn't planted on the VV for nothing."

Long after the group rode away, he lay there restlessly, hoping for some sight of Sherry, but there was none. More than he cared to admit, he was worried about her. Star Levitt had been revealed as a much more ruthless man and a more cruel man than he had believed.

Perhaps of them all, Emmett Chubb was the nearest to correct in his estimation of Levitt's character.

There was small chance he would ever allow any of the group below to escape the valley and repeat what they knew over too many glasses of whiskey. He was thorough, and he would be thorough enough and hard enough to carry out what he had started.

Yet there was little Haney could do until Levitt's next move was revealed. Reynolds and Pogue were gone, and the Ruby Hills country lay in the big man's palm.

Haney longed for a talk with Scott, for the old storekeeper was a shrewd judge of men, and he listened much and heard everything.

Returning to the fire, he joined Burt and Mabry in eating a quick breakfast. "Now," he said as he finished his last cup of coffee, "we'll see what you've got to show us. Then Mabry an' me will go down into the lava an' push out some more cows. We've got to keep Levitt sweatin'."

Burt, whose leg was rapidly returning to normal, led them through the aspens to the open mesa, and then along its top toward the jumbled maze of boulders that blocked off any approach from the northwest except by the narrow trail Haney used in coming and going.

The way Burt took followed a dim pathway into the boulders and ended at a great leaning slab of granite under which there was a dark, chill-looking opening.

"Come on," he said. "We're going down here!" He had brought with him several bits of candle, and now he passed one to each of them. They stooped and crept into the hole. The air felt damp inside, and there was a vast, cavernous feeling as of a dark, empty space. Holding their candles high, they saw they were on a steep floor that led away ahead of them, going down and down into an abysmal darkness from which came the faint sound of falling water.

Burt hobbled along ahead of them, and they had descended seventy or eighty feet below the level of the mesa above, when he paused on the rim of a black hole. Leaning forward, Ross Haney saw a bottomless blackness from which there came at intervals a strange sighing and then a low rumble.

"We got maybe ten minutes, the way I figure it," Burt said. "And then to be on the safe side, we've got to get out." He knelt and touched the rock at the edge of the hole. "Look how smooth! Water done that, water falling on it for years an' years!

"I tried to time it yesterday, an' it seems to come about every three hours. Pressure must build away down inside the mountain somehow, an' then she blows a cork an' water comes a-spoutin' an' a-spumin' out of this hole. She shoots clear up, nigh to the roof, and she keeps a-spoutin' for maybe three, four minutes. Then it dies away, an' that's the end."

"Well, I'm doggoned!" Mabry exclaimed. "I've heard about this place! Injuns used to call it the Talkin' Mountain. Heard the Navajos speak of it afore I ever came over here."

"Stones come up on that water, too, an' water fills this whole room, just boilin' an' roarin', but that ain't all. Look up there!" He stepped back and pointed, and moving away from the rim, they looked up.

High above them, in the vaulted top of the cave, were several ragged holes. "Back in the trees, too! A man could walk right into them if he wasn't careful, an' he'd go right on through into that, or else break a leg an' lie on the rim until the water came."

"Ugly lookin'," Ross said. "Let's get out of here!"

They turned and started out, and then from behind them came a dull, mounting rumble!

"Run!" Burt's face was suddenly panic-stricken. "Here it comes!"

He lunged forward, and stumbling, fell full length on the steep trail. Haney stooped and grabbed the man, but he was a big man and powerful, and if Bill Mabry had not grabbed the other arm he never would have gotten him up the steep hole in time.

They scrambled out into the sunlight, their faces pale, and below and behind them they heard the pound and rumble of boulders and the roar of water tumbling in the vast and empty cavern.

"That," Mabry said dryly, "is a good place to keep out of!"

When they returned to the camp, Burt started for his horse. "I'll saddle up," he said, "an' help you hombres. I've been loafin' long enough."

"You stay here." Ross turned around and grinned at him. "You keep an eye on the springs, as I've a hunch we'll have more visitors. This is a two-man job. Tomorrow, if we need help, you can go an' we'll leave Bill behind, or I'll stay."

Mabry had little to say on the ride into the lava beds, and Haney was just as pleased, for his thoughts were busy with Sherry and the situation in the valley and at Soledad. He made up his mind he would take a chance and slip into town.

Then he could talk to Scott or Kinney and would be able to find out just what was taking place.

He had no idea what had happened beyond the words he could catch from the conversation of the posse searching for him, but Scott would know all that had happened. On second thought, it would be wiser to see only Scott, for the chances were that Kinney would be watched. Already, the connection with him would be formed in Star Levitt's mind.

The work in the lava beds was hot and tiring. The wild cattle fought like devils, and branding them was a slow task and a hazardous one for the two men.

Yet by nightfall they had branded enough of them to warrant their work. They camped that night in the canyon, and the following morning they started the cattle out through the deep crevasse toward open range. Once they had them started toward Thousand Springs, they returned to the mesa where Rolly was waiting for them.

"Took a ride in last night," he volunteered. "Been goin' stale layin' around. I talked to Kinney a little, but they are watchin' him."

"What's happened?" Haney's irritation at Burt's gamble was lost in his eagerness for news.

"Well, Levitt seems to be havin' everythin' his own way. He made Emmett Chubb sheriff and says it's goin' to be necessary to be strict until they rid themselves of the 'lawless elements,' which probably means us.

"I talked to Scott, an' he sure wants to see you. Sherry Vernon ain't been seen in town since the fight, an' Bob only once, an' then he came an' hightailed it out of there. Levitt, he sent for outside law."

"He did *what?*"

"Sent for some outside law. He says he aims to have this Reynolds an' Pogue feud cleared up, an' he wants you caught. Says you're a rustler an' may have had more than a little hand in the killin' at the stock pens. He wants the blame fixed, he says. Also, the story's around," Burt cleared his throat and avoided Haney's eyes, "that there will be a weddin' out at the VV pretty soon."

Ross stared at the fire. So that was it? Now he would marry Sherry Vernon and the VV would be his in name as well as in appearances, for once they were married he would know how to handle Bob. If Haney was to do anything, it must be done soon. It must be done now.

"Howsoever, there seems to be some talk around. Syd Berdue ain't happy with the new setup. Kerb Dahl is foreman at the VV, an' Chubb is sheriff. Bob Streeter is foreman on the RR, an' they say Berdue fair raised mischief over that, but Levitt told him he would be taken care of."

"I reckon that's what he's scared of," Mabry said dryly. "I know what I'd do if Star Levitt said I was to be taken care of. I'd either get me a shot at Star or a fast horse out of the country."

"Well, Berdue ain't leavin'. Not willin', anyway. I reckon Star is anxious to have everything looking shipshape for the law when it comes up. They'll be glad to get shut of the trouble anyway, an' if things look pretty, they'll leave them as they be."

Ross pondered the news. Certainly, Levitt's position was good. He was a smooth-talking man with a good outward appearance, and if everything looked settled and calm, the outsiders would go away.

The valley would be safely in Levitt's hands, and Ross Haney would be declared an outlaw and hunted by the forces of the law wherever he happened to appear.

It was, apparently, time to come off the mesa and enter the game once more. Suddenly, he knew just exactly what he was going to do!

"Somethin' else," Burt added, "there's a lot of talk around about those steers of yours. Seems to be a lot of difference of view as to where they come from. No other brands on 'em, but full-growed steers. There's a rumor around that you've had a herd in the hills for some time."

"Rolly," Ross said thoughtfully, "there's been some talk about another man on the VV spread. And when I was out there I saw a small cabin off across the wash. You know anything about that?"

"No, I don't know anything at all. There's somethin' mighty peculiar about that cabin, an' none of us ever went near it but Star or Kerb Dahl."

Mabry leaned back against a tree and built a smoke. "Dahl, he acted mighty skittish around that cabin, his own self."

When morning came again to the Ruby Hills, Ross Haney mounted the Appaloosa and started by a winding route toward Soledad. He had no intention of getting there before dark unless it could be managed without his being seen.

After Soledad, he planned to go to the VV and bring Sherry away.

While he was about it, he would investigate that mysterious cabin and learn once and for all if it had anything to do with Sherry and her attitude toward Levitt.

The trail he was using was the same used on the previous trips. A trail that lay along a concealed route through the timber, mountain, and chaparral. It was the trail of which he had learned from the same source as had provided the story of the cattle, the lava beds, and the mesa.

This might well be the last time he would travel it, for he needed no additional warning to let him know that every man's hand would be against him in Soledad.

His own position in the valley was a good one, but must be backed by gun power, and he could not match Levitt as to numbers. However, Levitt himself was bringing the law in, and the law outweighed the brute force of any outlaw or the tricks of any criminal working beyond it.

## Chapter XIV
### *Quick on the Draw*

Circling around Soledad he cut down through the chaparral to a position on the point of the ragged hills that overlooked the VV. Then, glass in hand, he took a comfortable position where he could watch all movement on the ranch and began a systematic survey of the entire area below.

The isolated cabin he located without trouble. He studied it for a long time, watching for any evidence of life, but found none. The cabin looked bare and lonely, and no smoke came from its small chimney, nor did anyone approach it. Obviously, the cabin held something or someone of great importance to Levitt, or it would not be kept so secret.

After a careful survey of the ranch buildings, he decided the door of the cabin was not actually in view of the ranch house, for that view was cut off by the stable and several large stacks of hay for feeding saddle stock through the winter months.

Kerb Dahl was loitering around the ranch yard, and he was wearing two guns, but no one else was in view. Once, as dusk drew nearer, he saw Bob Vernon come to the door of the house and stare off toward town, but he turned then without coming outside and walked back. But in that moment when he had stood in the door, Dahl had walked hastily forward and stood facing him, for all the world like a prison guard.

The evening faded and the stars came out. From away on the desert a soft wind picked up and began to blow gently. Back over the mountains lay a dark curtain of cloud, black and somber. As he glanced that way, Haney saw its bulging billows darting with sudden lightning, and once, like the whimper of far-off trumpets, he heard the distant sound of thunder.

He waited there, his ears attuned to every sound, his eyes roving over the ranch and all its approaches. On what he saw and heard now his life might depend, for in a matter of minutes he was going down there. Yet aside from the restless roving of Kerb Dahl, there was no evidence of life about the ranch until a light came on. And when that light brightened the windows, Ross got to his feet, brushed the sand from his clothes and stretched.

Then, leading his horse, he came off the hill, concealed from the ranch by the point of the ridge on which he had waited. He took a winding route up a sandy wash toward the ranch, stopping from time to time to listen once more, then moving on. In the shadows back of the stable, he let the horse stand, reins trailing, with a light touch on the shoulder and a whisper of warning. Nothing now but Haney's own shrill whistle would move him from the spot.

Loosening his guns in their holsters, Ross Haney took a deep breath and turned his eyes on the lonely cabin. Then he went down into the gully and started for the cabin door.

Stark and alone on the knoll it stood, a gloomy little building that seemed somehow ominous and strange. Nearby, he crouched in the darkness listening for any sound of movement that might warn him of a possible occupant. Wind whispered around the eaves and from the ranch house itself there came a rattle of dishes, the sound made plain by that cool night air. Here at the cabin, all was silence. The only window was covered with a fragment of sacking, so after a long minute, he moved to the door.

His heart pounded against his ribs, and his mouth felt dry. He paused, flattened against the building, and listened once more. Only the wind made a sound to be heard, a soft soughing that seemed to whisper of the impending rain. The clouds towered in the sky now, higher and closer, and the rumble of thunder was close, like a lonely lion, growling in his chest as he paced his cage.

Carefully, his hand went to the knob. In the darkness the metal seemed strangely chill. His right hand moved back to his gun butt, and then, ever so carefully, he turned the knob.

It was locked.

Gently he released the knob. The pause irritated him. He had built himself to a crisis that was frustration in this most obvious of ways, and the piling up of suspense made him reckless. A glance toward the ranch assured him he was unobserved and probably could not be seen against the blackness along the cabin wall.

This was a puzzle he must solve, and now was the time. There might never be another. Behind this locked door might lie the answer to the mystery, and he moved forward suddenly and placed his shoulder against the flimsy panel.

*     *     *

Light streamed from the bunkhouse windows, too. From the ranch, there came only the continuing rattle of dishes and once a loud splash as someone threw water out onto the ground. Taking the knob in his hand he turned it, and then putting his shoulder to the door and digging his feet into the earth, he began to push.

The construction was flimsy. Evidently, whatever was kept here was guarded enough by Dahl and his partner. Haney relaxed and took a deep breath, and then putting his shoulder to the door again, he shoved hard. Something cracked sharply, and he drew back, hand on his gun, waiting and listening.

From within there came no sound. From the ranch, all was normal. He put his shoulder again to the door and heaved, but this time the damage had been done and the door came open so suddenly that he sprawled on hands and knees inside!

Catlike, he wheeled, back to the door and gun in hand. His eyes wide for the darkness, he stared about. The light wind caught the sacking with a ghostly hand and stirred it faintly. Lightning flashed, and the room lay bare before him for an instant.

A wooden chair on its side, a worn table with an empty basin, a cot covered with odorous blankets, and against the wall, several stacks of boxes.

Puzzled, Haney crossed to them. They were not heavy. He hesitated to risk the screech of a drawn nail, but by that time he was almost beyond caring. With his fingers, he got a grip on one of the boards that made up the box, and pulled hard. It held, and then as he strained, it came loose. If it made any sound it was lost in the convenient rumble of thunder.

Inside the box there was more sacking and, when that was parted, several round cans, slightly larger and not unlike snuff cans. Lifting one to his nostrils, he sniffed curiously, and from the box came a strange, pungent odor.

"So that's it?" he said. Then he scowled into the darkness. It did not clarify the position of Sherry or her brother. And yet—his heart seemed to go empty within him—maybe it did!

Pocketing several of the boxes, he replaced the boards as well as he could and turned the box so as to conceal the more obvious damage. Then he slipped outside and pulled the door to behind him.

Confused by the unexpected turn of events, he returned to his horse, whispered reassuringly, and then went around the stable toward the house.

Nearby was a window, and he moved up under the trees and looked through into what was the dining room of the ranch house. Three people sat at the table: Bob and Sherry Vernon and, at the head of the table, Star Levitt!

The window was slightly open, and he could hear their voices.

Levitt was speaking: "Yes, I think that's the only solution, my dear." His tone was suave, cruel, and decisive. "We shall be married in this house on Monday. You understand?"

"You can't get away with this!" Bob burst out angrily, but the undercurrent of hopelessness in his voice was plain. "It's a devil of a thing! Sherry hates you! What sort of a mind can you have?"

"Sherry will change!" Levitt smiled across the table at her. "I promise you both, she will change. Also, it will be convenient for her to be my wife. She cannot be made to testify against me, and I scarcely believe that with her as my wife you'll care to bring any charges, Bob. Also, I'll have control of this ranch, and as the others are in my hands, the situation is excellent."

"I've a good notion to—" Bob's voice trailed off into sullenness.

"Have you?" Levitt glanced up, his eyes ugly. "Listen, Vernon! Don't give me any trouble! You're in this deeper than I am! You've got murder against you, as well as smuggling! If I'm ever exposed, you know that you and Sherry will both go down with me! What will your precious father think then, with his fine family pride and his bad heart?"

"Shut up!" Bob cried angrily. He leaped to his feet. "If it weren't for Dad, I'd kill you with my bare hands!"

"Really, Bob," Sherry said quietly, "perhaps we should talk this over. I'm not so sure that prison for both of us wouldn't be preferable to being married to Star!"

Levitt's face went white and dangerous. "You're flattering!" he said dryly, striving to retain his composure. "What, I might ask, would have happened to Bob if I hadn't gotten him away from that mess and brought him here? The killing of Clyde Aubury was not any ordinary killing."

*Aubury?* Ross Haney's brows drew together, and he strained his ears to hear more.

"Yes, I think I should have earned your gratitude," Levitt continued. "Instead, I find you falling for that drifting cowhand."

Sherry Vernon's eyes lifted from her plate. "Star," she said coolly, "you could never understand through that vast ego of yours that Ross Haney is several times the man you could ever have been, even if you hadn't become a thief and a blackmailer of women."

Haney's heart leaped, and his lips tightened. In that instant, he would cheerfully have gone through the window, glass and all, and cheerfully given his life if it would have helped. Yet even in his elation at her praise of him, he could not but admire her coolness and composure. Her manner was quiet, poised. He stared into the window, his heart pounding. Then she lifted her eyes and looked straight into his!

For an instant that seemed an eternity, their eyes held. In hers he saw hope leap into being and then saw her eyes suddenly masked, and she turned her head, passing something to her brother with an idle comment that ignored Levitt completely.

"Well," she said after a minute, her voice sounding just a tone louder, "everything is all right for the time. At least I have until Monday!"

He drew back. That message was for him, and between now and Monday was a lifetime—three whole days!

Three days in which many things might be done, in which she might be taken from here—in which he might even kill Star Levitt.

For he knew now that was what he would do if the worst came to the worst. He had never yet actually hunted a man down for the purpose of killing him, but he knew that was just what he would do if there were no other way out.

Tiptoeing to the corner of the house, Ross started for the stable and his horse, and then as he stepped past the last tree, a huge cottonwood, a man stepped out. "Say, you got a match?"

It was Kerb Dahl!

Recognition came to them at the same instant, and the man let out a startled yelp and grabbed for his gun.

There was no time to grapple with the man, no chance for a quick, soundless battle. Too much space intervened, so there was only one chance. Even as Dahl's hand grasped his gun, Haney plucked out his own gun and fired!

Flame stabbed from the muzzle, and then came a second stab of fire. Dahl took a hesitant step forward, his gun half out. Then his gun belched flame, shooting a hole through the bottom of the holster, and Dahl toppled forward on his face.

Behind Dahl the bunkhouse door burst open, and there was a shout from the ranch house itself. As quickly, Ross ducked around the stable and hit the saddle running.

The palouse knew an emergency when he felt one, and he lit out, running like a scared rabbit. A gun barked and then another, but nothing in that part of the country could catch the palouse when he started going places in a hurry, and that was just what he was doing.

On the outskirts of Soledad, with the pounding hoofs of the pursuit far behind, Haney leaped the horse over a gully and took to the desert, weaving a pattern of tangled tracks into a trail where cattle had been driven and then cutting back into the scattered back alleys of Soledad, leaving town a few minutes later, crossing a shale slide and swinging around a butte to hit his old trail for Thousand Springs Mesa.

"Rio, you saved my neck tonight, an' we took a scalp. I'd as soon never take another, but if we have to, let 'em all be hombres like Dahl!"

Yet what was all this about a murder charge against Bob Vernon? And what was their connection with the smuggling and the cans of opium he had found in the cabin? He had known the smell the instant he lifted the can to his nostrils, for it is a smell one does not soon forget. He remembered it from a visit, a few years before, to some of the dives along the Barbary Coast.

And now he must think. Somehow, some way, he must free Sherry from this entanglement, and as a last resort, he would do it, if he must, by facing Star Levitt with a gun!

# Chapter XV
## *Captured*

Haney's course was clear. Whatever other plans he might have had must be shelved and the whole situation brought into the open by Monday. Studying the situation carefully, he could see little hope, unless the sheriff and the investigating officers from the outside arrived on Monday. Then, if he could present his case—but Levitt would take every measure to avoid that, and his only chance would be to get into town before time.

On Sunday night, in absolute blackness, the three rode down the back trail toward Soledad. Outside of town they slackened pace. Ross turned in his saddle as Burt and Mabry came up beside him.

He gestured toward the town. "It looks quiet enough. You two leave your horses at May's. Put them in the stable, and I'll leave mine there, too. Then you two either hide out in the stable or get down to the hotel and see Kinney. I'm going direct to Scott, and he'll see Allan for me.

"If the worst comes to the worst, and there is no other way, I'm going gunning for Star. I'd rather die myself than see that girl forced to marry him, or to see him win after all this murder and deceit.

"However, I may give myself up when the sheriff gets here."

Mabry nodded thoughtfully. "Who are these hombres Levitt's bringin' in, Ross? Are they really the law?"

"Yeah. You see, he calls Chubb the sheriff; actually, he's only a town marshal. The county seat is over a hundred miles away by trail, an' there's no deputy up here. Star Levitt is shrewd. He knows that sooner or later some word of this scrap will get out. Somebody, on a stage or somewhere, will talk. The chances are they already have.

"Well, so he sends to the governor for an investigating officer, wanting the whole thing cleared up. That puts him on the map as a responsible citizen. He'll do the talking, and the men he selects will back him up. The whole situation will be smoothed over. The chances are, one of his men will be made a deputy sheriff.

"Then the investigatin' officers will go back to the capital, and Levitt's in a nice spot. If any trouble comes up, they will always remember him, apparently rich, a stable citizen, a man who called on the law. They wouldn't believe a thing against him. His skirts will be clear, an' we three will be outlawed.

"Somehow, we've got to block that an' expose the true state of affairs."

"What is this joker you said you had?" Mabry asked.

"Wait. That will do for the showdown. Nobody knows about that but myself an' Scott. We'll have this whole show well sewed up."

He was the first to move forward, walking the palouse through the encircling trees to May Ashton's cabin on the edge of Soledad. There was no one in sight, but a light glowed in the cabin. He moved up and led his horse into the stable and left it there. Then he slipped along the wall of the house until he could glance into a window. The waitress was inside, and alone.

She opened the door at his tap, and he slipped inside. "You!" she gasped. "We were wondering how to get word to you! Star Levitt is marrying Sherry tomorrow!"

"I know. What about the officers from the capital?"

"They'll be in tomorrow, too. In the morning. The sheriff is coming up from the county seat, and some attorney from the capital named Ward Clymer. Two state rangers are coming with them. I've heard it all discussed in the restaurant."

"They will have a hearing? Where?"

"In the lobby of the hotel. It's the only place large enough, aside from the Bit and Bridle. I heard Voyle talking with Syd Berdue about it. Incidentally," she added quickly, "there's a warrant out for your arrest. Emmett Chubb has it. They want you for killing Kerb Dahl. Was that you?"

"Uh-huh, but it was a fair shake. In fact, he went for his gun first. I had no choice but to shoot."

"Well, the order is out to shoot on sight, and they have reward posters ready to go out tomorrow morning. They will be all over town for the officers to see when they come in. You're wanted for murder, dead or alive, and they are offering a thousand dollars."

Ross smiled wryly. "That will make it worse! A thousand dollars is money enough to start the blood hunters out.

"Now listen: I'm going to Scott, and I'm going now. Mabry and Burt will be in soon, and they'll hide either here or close to here. They will be standing by in case of emergency; I'll try to communicate with you in case of really serious trouble, and then you can get word to them. If the worst comes to the worst, I'll give myself up to the state officials and make them hold a preliminary hearing right here. I can talk them into that, I think. Then we can get facts in front of them."

"Ross, don't plan on anybody siding you," May said quickly. "Chubb has been around town with Hanson, and they have frightened everybody. You can't depend on a soul. I don't even know whether I'd have nerve enough to back you up, but I'm afraid Allan will. He's that kind."

The street was dark when Ross Haney stepped out of May's cabin. He did not try to keep out of sight, realizing that such an attempt, if seen, would be even more suspicious. He walked rapidly down the street, staying in the deep shadows, but walking briskly along. Old man Scott was the man he must see. He must get to him at once, and he would know what to do. Also, it would be a place to hide.

Glancing across the street, he saw a half dozen horses standing at the hitch rail in front of the Bit and Bridle. There was light flooding from the windows, and the sound of loud laughter from within.

A man opened the door and stumbled drunkenly into the street, and for a moment, Ross hesitated, feeling uneasy. The street was altogether too quiet, there was too little movement. He turned at right angles and went between a couple of buildings, starting for the back door of Scott's place. Once he thought he glimpsed a movement in the shadows and hesitated, but after watching and seeing nothing more, he went on up to the back door and tapped gently. The door opened, and he stepped in.

Scott glanced at him, and alarm sprang into his eyes.

"Set down!" he said. "Set down! You've sure been stirrin' up a pile of trouble, Haney!"

He poured a cup of coffee and placed it on the table. "Drink that," he said quietly. "It will do you good."

Scott stared at him as he lifted the cup. "Big trouble's goin' to break loose, Scott," Haney said. "I hope I can handle it."

His ears caught a subtle whisper of movement outside, and his eyes lifted, and then his face went to a dead, sickly white.

Old man Scott had a shotgun, and its twin barrels were pointed right at his stomach.

"Sit tight, son," he said sternly. "A move an' I'll cut you in two!"

He lifted his voice. "All right, out there! Come on in! I've got him!"

The door burst open and Emmett Chubb sprang into the room, and with him were Voyle, Tolman, and Allan Kinney!

Chubb's eyes gleamed, and his pistol lifted. "Well, Mr. Ross Haney, who's top dog now?"

"Hold it!" Scott's shotgun made a sharp movement. "You take her easy, Emmett Chubb! This man's my prisoner. I'm claimin' the reward, right now. Moreover, I'm holdin' him alive for Levitt!"

"You will not!" Chubb snarled. "I'll kill the dirty dog!"

"Not unless you want a blast from this shotgun!" Scott snapped. The old outlaw's blue eyes sparked. "Nobody's beatin' me out of my money! Kinney here, he has a finger in it, maybe, because he tipped me off, but you take him away from me over my dead body."

Baffled, Chubb stared from one to the other. "He's right, Emmett," Kinney agreed. "He got him first."

Ross Haney stood flat-footed, staring from Kinney to Scott. "Sold out!" he sneered. "I might have suspected it!"

Kinney flushed, but Scott shrugged.

"A thousand dollars is a lot of money, boy. I've seen men killed for a sight less."

"Let's take him off to jail then," Chubb said. "This ain't no place for him!"

"He stays right here!" Scott said harshly. "He's my prisoner until Levitt gets him, an' then Levitt can do what he's a might to. Nobody's beatin' me out of that money! Stay here an' help guard if you want, but don't you forget for one minute that he's my prisoner! This shotgun won't forget it!"

Kinney slipped around behind Haney and lifted his guns. Reluctantly, Haney backed into a corner and was tied to a chair. Shocked by the betrayal, he could only stare from Allan to Scott, appalled by the sudden turn of fortune.

From the high, if desperate, hopes of the day, he was suddenly smashed back into hopelessness, a prisoner, betrayed by the men he had had most confidence in. How could they have known he was in town? There was only one way. May must have betrayed him! She and Allan must have planned together, and when he left her house, she must have gotten word to him at once.

Chubb dropped into a chair and pulled one of his guns over into his lap. "I'd like to blast his heart out," he said sullenly. "What you frettin' so about, Scott? You get the money, dead or alive."

"Sure!" Scott said. "And if you kill him you'll lay claim to it. I wouldn't trust you across the street where that much money was concerned! Nor any of you!"

He chuckled, his eyes sneering at Haney. "Anyway, Levitt's top dog around here from now on, an' he's the boy I do business with! I'm too old to be shoved out in the cold at my time of life! I ain't figurin' on it! I'll work with Star, an' he'll work with me!"

"I never heard of you bein' so thick with him!" Chubb's irritation was obvious.

Scott chuckled. "Who got him into this country, do you suppose? I've knowed him for years! Who told him this place was right for a smart man? I did! That's who!

"Haney, here, he figured on the same thing. He figured on takin' over when Reynolds an' Pogue were out of it, but he was leavin' too much to chance. Star doesn't leave anything to chance."

Bitterly, Ross Haney stared at the floor. This time he was finished. If Mabry and Burt had gone to May's they would have been sold out, too. He listened, straining his ears for shots, hoping at least one of them would manage to fight it out and go down with a gun in his hand.

The situation was all Levitt's now. The man was a front rider, and these others were with him. He stared at Kinney, and the young man's eyes wavered and looked away. How could he have guessed that such a man would sell him out? And Scott? Of course, the old man was an admitted outlaw, or had been. Still, he had felt very close to the old man and liked him very much.

There was no chance for Sherry now—unless . . . His eyes narrowed with thought.

What would they do with him? Would they get word to Star that he was a prisoner and then smuggle him out of town to be killed? Or would they bring him out in the open with evidence arrayed against him, or kill him "trying to escape"?

If only there would be some break, some chance to talk to Ward Clymer or the sheriff! Of course, held as a prisoner, with reward posters out and the stories Star and his men would tell, he would find himself in a bad position even before they talked to him, for they would be prejudiced against him and everything he might say. And what evidence had he? Star Levitt would have plenty, and as May had told him, no one in town would testify for him against Star.

They were frightened, or they were getting on the band wagon.

He was through.

Unless—there was a vague hope—Mabry and Burt had not come in. If they could somehow free him. Knowing the manner of men they were, he knew they would not hesitate to make the attempt.

## Chapter XVI
## *Back to the Wall*

In the back room of the store the night slid slowly by and crawled into the gray of day, slowly, reluctantly. The rising sun found the sky overcast, with no opening in the clouds through which it could shine down on the clustered false-fronted frame buildings and adobes of Soledad. A lone Mexican, a burro piled twice its own height with sticks, wandered sleepily down the town's dusty street.

Pat walked out of the Bit and Bridle, stared at the sky, and then turned and walked back within. A pump rattled somewhere and then began a rhythmical speaking.

Half asleep in his bonds, Ross Haney heard the water gushing into the pail in spouts of sound. He stirred restlessly, and his chair creaked. He opened his eyes to see four pairs of eyes leveled at him. Emmett Chubb, Voyle, Allan Kinney, and Scott all sat ready and watchful. His lids fluttered and closed. Behind them his mind began to plan, to contrive.

No man is so desperate as a prisoner. No man so ready to plan, to try to think his way out. If only his hands were free! In a few minutes, an hour at most, the stage would rattle down the street and halt in front of the Cattleman's Hotel, and the passengers would go into the cafe to eat. Later they might go upstairs to sleep. During that interval, he would know his fate. He touched a tongue to dry lips.

"Al," Scott said suddenly, "you take this here shotgun. I'll throw together a few ham an' eggs. I'm hungry as a hibernatin' bear in the springtime!"

Tolman, who had left earlier, returned now and stuck his head in the door. "Stage a-comin'!" he said. "An' Syd Berdue just blowed in!"

"That VV bunch in yet?" Chubb asked, without turning his head. "When Dolph Turner gets in, you tell him about this. He'll see that Levitt knows first of all!"

Scott was working around the room, and soon it was filled with the pleasant breakfast smell of frying ham and eggs and the smell of coffee. Despite his worry, Haney realized he had been hungry, and for the first time recalled he had eaten nothing the night before.

Emmett Chubb got up. He was a stocky, swarthy man with a square jaw and a stubble of beard. His hair was unkempt, and when he crossed the room to splash water on his face and hands, Ross noted the worn guns had notches carved in them, three on one gun, five on the other. Eight men.

"The only thing I'm sorry for," Chubb said as he dried his hands, his eyes on Haney, "is that I didn't get the chance to shoot it out with you in the street!"

His black eyes were sneering and cold. "I'd like to put you in the dust," he said. "I'd like to see you die!"

"Well," Haney said dryly, "my hands are tied, so you're safe enough to try.

"You're a lot of yellow-backed double-crossers. You, Chubb, are a cheap murderer. You blew town fast enough after killin' Vin Carter or you'd have had a chance to draw on me—or run."

Chubb walked across the room and stopped, his feet apart, in front of Haney. Lifting his open palm, he slapped Ross three times across the mouth. Scott did not turn, and Kinney shuffled his feet on the floor.

"Maybe Levitt will give me the job," he said harshly. "I hope he does!"

The door opened suddenly and three men stood there. Ross Haney's head jerked up as he saw Levitt. Star Levitt glanced from Chubb to Scott and then indicated the men with him.

"Neal an' Baker, of the rangers. They want the prisoner!"

Chubb stared, disappointment and resentment struggling for place in his eyes. "Here he is! Scott's been holdin' him."

Neal bent over Haney and cut the ropes that tied his arms. "You come with us. We're havin' the hearin' right now."

Haney turned and as he started toward the door, he saw Scott smiling. The old outlaw looked right into his eyes and winked, deliberately.

What did that mean? Scowling, Haney walked across the street toward the hotel. Neal glanced at him a couple of times. "You know a man named Mabry?"

"Bill Mabry?" Ross turned to Neal, astonished. "Why, sure. He works for me, an' a mighty good man!"

"When Clymer asks the questions," Neal said, "give him the information you have straight, honest, and without prejudice."

Puzzled by the suggestion, Ross Haney walked into the room and was shown to a chair.

A big man with a capable, shrewd-looking face glanced at him sharply and then went back to examining some documents on a table. Several other men trooped in, and then Sherry and Bob Vernon walked into the room. More and more astonished, Ross stared from one to the other, trying to see what must have happened.

He had never believed that Levitt would allow Clymer to confront the Vernons or himself, if it could be avoided. Yet here they all were, and it looked like a showdown. Allan Kinney was there, and

May. The pretty waitress glanced at him, and he averted his eyes. Scott had come over, and Star Levitt was one of the last to come into the room.

From the dark expression on Levitt's face, he decided all could not be going well for the big man, and the thought cheered him. Anything that was bad news for Levitt was sure to be good news for him.

Ward Clymer sat back in his chair and looked over the room, his eyes noncommittal. "Now, friends," he said briskly, "this is an entirely informal hearing to try to clarify the events leading up to the battle between the Reynolds and Pogue factions and to ascertain the guilt, if any, of those who are here with us.

"Also," he glanced at Haney, "I am informed that Ross Haney, the cattleman, is held on a charge of murder for the slaying of one Kerb Dahl, a cowhand from the VV. If such is the truth, and if the evidence warrants it, Ross Haney will be taken south to the county seat for trial. In the meantime, let us examine the evidence."

"Mr. Levitt, will you tell us the events that preceded the fight between Reynolds and Pogue?"

Star Levitt got to his feet, very smooth, very polished. He glanced around, smiled a little, and began. "It seems that before I arrived in the Ruby Hills country there had been considerable trouble over water and range rights, with sporadic fighting between the two big outfits. The VV, owned by the Vernons, was not involved in this feud, although there seemed to be some desire on the part of both outfits to possess the VV holdings and water. On the day the fight started, there was some minor altercation over branding, and it led to a shooting which quickly spread until most of the hands on both sides were involved, with resulting deaths."

"What was your part in the fight?" Clymer asked shrewdly.

"None at all, sir. I saw trouble coming and withdrew my men and got out of the way myself. After it was over, we did what we could for the wounded."

"There are no witnesses present from the other outfits?"

"Oh, yes! Emmett Chubb, now the town marshal, survived the fight. Also Voyle, of the Box N, is here. Kerb Dahl, of the VV, who was in the middle of things was later murdered by the prisoner, Ross Haney."

"Sir?" Haney asked suddenly.

Clymer's eyes shifted to him, hesitated, and then asked, "Did you have a question?"

"Yes, I'd like to ask Star Levitt where his range holdings were."

"I don't see that the question has any bearing on the matter," Levitt replied coolly.

"It's a fair question," Clymer admitted. "It may have some later bearing on it. I understand you were running cattle. Where was your headquarters?"

Levitt hesitated. "On the VV," he said. "You see, I am soon to marry Miss Vernon."

Clymer glanced curiously at Haney. "Does that answer your question?"

"Sure, it answers it for now. Only I want it plain to everybody that Star Levitt had no holdings on the range other than cattle and the use of the VV headquarters."

Levitt stared at Haney and shrugged in a bored manner. The attorney then asked Chubb and Voyle a few questions about the killing, and through Scott, Pat the bartender, and others brought out the facts of the long-standing feud between the Reynolds and Pogue outfits. Every story served to bolster Levitt's position. Bob Vernon offered his evidence in short, clipped sentences, and then Sherry hers.

As she started to return to her chair, Haney spoke up. "Another question: Sherry, did anyone warn you away from the roundup, telling you to leave at once, that there might be trouble?"

She hesitated. "Why, yes. Star Levitt did."

"I could see some of the men were spoiling for a fight," Star said quietly. "It seemed a bad place for a woman, due to the impending trouble and the profanity attending the work of the men."

"May I ask a few questions?" Ross asked.

"Mr. Clymer," Levitt interrupted, "this man Haney is a trouble-maker! His questions can do no good except to try to incriminate others and to put himself in a better light. The man is a murderer!"

Clymer shrugged. "We're here to ascertain the facts. However, the prisoner should be examined in connection with the killing of Kerb Dahl. What have you to say to that, Haney?"

"That it is impossible to divide the killing of Dahl from the other sides of the case. Nor is it going to be of any use to talk of it until the events leading up to that point are made plain."

"Well, that's reasonable enough," Clymer said. "Go ahead."

Levitt's lips tightened and his nostrils flared. Voyle had walked into the back of the room with Syd Berdue, and they stood there, surveying the crowd. With them was the silent man who had been Dahl's partner.

"I want to ask Levitt how many hands he had when he came into this country," Ross said evenly.

Star was puzzled and wary. "Why, not many. What difference does it make?"

"How many? You used the VV spread, how many hands did *you* have?"

"Why, one that actually came with me." The question puzzled Levitt and disturbed him. He couldn't see where it pointed.

"The one man was that short, dark man at the back of the room, wasn't it? The man called Turner?"

"That's right."

Haney turned suddenly in his chair and fired a question at Dahl's partner. "Turner, what's a piggin string?"

"What?" The man looked puzzled and frightened. The question had startled him, and he was irritated at being suddenly noticed.

"I asked what a piggin string was. I'd also like to know what a grulla is."

Turner turned his head from side to side, eager for a way out, but there was none. He wet his lips with his tongue and swallowed.

"I don't know," he said.

"These questions make no sense at all!" Levitt said irritably. "Let's get on with the murder hearing!"

"They make sense to me," Ross replied. Then, turning to Clymer, he added, "You, sir, were raised on a cow ranch, so you know that a piggin string is a short piece of rope used to tie a critter when it's throwed—thrown. You also know that a grulla is a mouse color, a sort of gray, an' usually applied to horses.

"The point I'm gettin' at is that Levitt came into this country with one man, who wasn't a cowhand. Turner doesn't know the first thing about a ranch or about cattle."

"What's that got to do with it?" Levitt demanded.

Clymer was looking at Ross Haney thoughtfully. He began to smile as he anticipated the reply.

"Why, just this, Levitt. How many cattle did you bring into this country?" Haney demanded sharply. He leaned forward. "An' how many have you got now?"

Somebody out in the room grunted, and Scott was grinning from ear to ear. The question had caught Levitt flat-footed. Clymer turned on him, his eyes bright with interest. "A good question, Mr. Levitt. On the way here you told me you ran a thousand head. Where did you get them?"

"That's got nothing to do with it!" Levitt shouted angrily. For the first time he was out in the open, and Ross Haney had led him there, led him by the nose into a trap. As Haney knew, Levitt grew angry when pushed, and it was that he was playing for.

"Mr. Clymer," Ross interrupted, "I think it has a lot to do with it! This man, claimin' to be a representative rancher, admits comin' into this country with one man who wasn't a cowhand, even if he may be fairly good with a gun. No two men like that are bringin' a thousand head of cattle into this country an' brandin' 'em.

"But I'll show you that Levitt does have a thousand head, or near to it, an' every one with a worked-over brand!"

"That's a lie!" Levitt shouted, leaping to his feet.

Ross settled back in his chair, smiling. "Now ask me about the killin' of Kerb Dahl," he said gently.

Star Levitt sagged back in his chair, flushed and angry. He had let go of his temper. Despite his burning rage, he knew he was in an ugly position, where Haney, by his fool questions, had led him. The killing led away from the cattle, so he jumped at the chance.

Before he could speak, Clymer asked Haney, "If he has the branded cattle now, who branded them?"

"Kerb Dahl, the man I killed on the VV, Voyle of the Box N, Tolman, who hired on after Levitt got here, an' Emmett Chubb, among others."

"That's absurd!" Levitt said contemptuously.

"Sherry, name the men you heard talking at Thousand Springs!" Ross asked quickly.

The sudden question startled her, and before Levitt could catch her eye, she glanced up and replied, "Why, Dahl was there, and Voyle, Tolman, and Sydney Berdue."

"What did they talk about?"

Levitt was leaning forward in his chair, his eyes upon her. Sherry glanced at him, and her eyes wavered. "Why, I—" Her voice trailed off.

"Before you answer," Ross told her, "let me tell you that you've been the victims, you and your brother, of the foulest trick ever played."

Haney turned to Clymer: "Sir, Miss Vernon was concealed near the springs, and overheard some of the plotting between the men mentioned. These were the same men who altered the brands for Levitt. Through them, Levitt engineered and planned the whole fight, forcing an issue between Reynolds and Pogue deliberately, and in the battle, killing the two men who opposed him in the Ruby Hills country. It will no doubt strike you that among the survivors of that battle were *all* the men seen by Miss Vernon at the springs.

"Also," he added, "Levitt was blackmailing the Vernons, using their ranch as a storage depot and transfer point for his deals in the opium trade!"

# Chapter XVII
## *Desperate Chance*

Knocked off balance by these public revelations, Star Levitt struggled to his feet, his face ashen. The carefully planned coup was tumbling about his ears, and he who had come into the valley as a leader in a dope ring and planned to become the legitimate owner of a great ranch, suddenly saw the whole thing reduced to chaos.

"Furthermore," Ross got to his feet, and the ringing sound of his voice reduced to silence the stir in the room, "I think this is the proper time to make a few points clear." Opening his shirt, he drew a leather wallet from inside it and from the wallet drew a handful of papers, which he passed to Clymer. "Will you tell Mr. Levitt," he said, "what you have there?"

Clymer glanced at them and then looked up in amazement. "Why, these are deeds!" he exclaimed, glancing from Haney to Levitt. "These indicate that you are the owner of both Hitson Springs and the Bullhorn ranch headquarters, including the water right. Also, here are papers that show Haney has filed on the Thousand Springs area!"

"*What?*" Star Levitt's fingers gripped the arms of his chair, and his brow creased. Before his eyes came the whole plan he had made, all his planning, his actions—all were rendered perfectly futile. Who controlled the water in those three sources controlled the Ruby Hills, and there was no way of circumventing it. From the beginning he had been beaten and now he had been made ridiculous.

"I told you," Haney said quietly, looking at Levitt, "that you had overlooked the obvious. Somehow, a crook always does."

"Now, sir," Ross said to Clymer, "with the cattle brands I can show you, the evidence we can produce, I'd say that you have a strong case for robbery and murder against Star Levitt!"

There was a slight stir in the back of the room, and Haney's eyes shifted. Emmett Chubb was slipping from the room to the street.

As the accusation rang in the silent room, Star Levitt held himself taut. The crashing of his plans meant less to him now than the fact that he had been shown up for a fool by the cowhand he despised and hated. Suddenly, the rage that was building within him burst into a fury that was almost madness. His face went white, his eyes glassy and staring, and letting out a choking cry, he sprang for Haney.

Warned by Sherry's scream, Ross jerked his eyes back from the vanishing Chubb and lunged from his chair swinging two brain-jarring blows to the head. They rocked Levitt, but nothing could stop his insane rush, and Haney gave ground before the onslaught.

Levitt swung wildly with both hands, beside himself with hate and fury.

But Ross lunged at him, burying a right in the bigger man's stomach and then hooking a powerful, jarring left to the chin. Levitt staggered, and Ross, eager for battle, bulled into him, bringing his head down on Levitt's shoulder and smashing away with both hands in a wicked body attack. He threw the punches with all the power built into his shoulders by years of bulldogging steers and hard range work.

He caught Levitt with a wicked overhand right and battered him back into the chairs. The crowd scattered. From somewhere outside Ross heard the sharp rap of a shot and then another. Then quiet. His right smashed Levitt over a chair, and the big man came up with a lunge, grabbing for the chair itself.

Ross rushed him and Star tried to straighten, but Haney clubbed him with a fist on the kidney and the big man went to his knees. Ross stepped back, panting. "Get up!" Ross said. "Get up an' take it!"

Levitt lunged to his feet, and Ross smashed his lips with a sweeping left. He ripped a gash in Levitt's cheek with a right. Star tottered back, his eyes glazed. He straightened then and shook his head, some measure of cunning returning to him. Suddenly he turned and hurled himself through the glass of the window!

Ross sprang to the window after him and caught a fleeting glimpse of Emmett Chubb as a bullet whirred within a hair of his cheek and buried itself in the window frame.

There was a clatter of horses' hoofs and then silence.

Haney's hands fell helplessly. Scott moved up beside him, handing him his guns. "Sorry I couldn't get 'em to you sooner," he said, "but you did plenty without 'em!"

Clymer caught his arm. "You've loyal friends, Haney. Burt and Mabry stopped the stage outside of town. Levitt had ridden on ahead, and they took time to tell me a lot of things and asked that I get you and the Vernons together with Levitt and withhold judgment until you had talked and I had listened.

"As it happens," he added, "Neal and I had both been reared on ranches where Mabry worked. We knew him for a good man and an honest one. From the first we had doubts that all Levitt had told us was the truth. Mabry also had a cowhide with him, and any western man could see the brand had been altered from a VV to Three Diamonds."

Ross shoved his guns into his holsters and pushed his way to Sherry who was standing white and still near the door, waiting for him. He said gently: "Sherry, we can talk about it some other time, but I think I can make a rough guess at most of it. Why don't you go in and get some coffee? I'll join you in a minute."

Mabry and Burt were waiting outside, and they had the palouse. "We can chase 'em, boss," Rolly said, "but they've got quite a start."

"Later, I head some shooting. What was it?"

"That *was* Voyle," Mabry said grimly. "He made a rush for his horse an' met Rolly halfway. He made a grab for his gun an' I guess he wasn't as gunslick as he figured."

"Tolman?"

"Roped an' hogtied. He'll go south with the rangers, an' unless I miss my guess, he'll talk all the way. We've got Turner, too."

"Incidentally," Mabry added, "don't you jump to no conclusions about Kinney an' Scott. I ain't had much time to talk to Scott, but we moved down to May's like you said, an' all three of us seen you follered to Scott's by some of Levitt's crowd.

"They had us way outnumbered, an' Kinney came up and said if he butted in he might keep you from gettin' killed."

"That was my idea," Scott put in. "I thought I seen somethin' in the shadows when I let you in, an' then I heard a step outside, an' I knowed I either had to get you as my prisoner or we'd both be in a trap. Chubb would kill you sure as shootin' if he got a chance, but with you as my prisoner I'd have the right to interfere."

"So then Levitt, Chubb, an' Berdue are the only ones who got away?" Ross mused.

"Uh-huh," Mabry agreed, and then running his fingers through his coarse red hair, he commented: "That ain't good! I know that sort, an' you can take my word for it, they'll be back!"

Yet as the days found their way down the year and the summer faded toward autumn, there was no further sign of the three missing men. The mornings became chill, but the sun still lay bright and golden upon the long valley and the view from the growing house upon the mesa top changed from green to green and gold shot through with streaks of russet and deep red. The aspen leaves began to change, and sometimes in the early morning the countryside was white with the touch of frost.

Rumors came occasionally to their ears. There had been a bank held up at Weaver, a stage had been looted and two men killed at Canyon Pass, and one of the three bandits had been recognized by a passenger as Emmett Chubb. Then the town marshal in Pie Town was shot down when he attempted to question a big, handsome man with a beard.

When Sherry rode the valley or over into the Ruby Hills, Ross Haney was constantly at her side. The Appaloosa and Flame became constant companions. Despite the fact that no reports came of any of the three men being seen nearby, Haney was worried.

"Ross," Sherry said suddenly, "you've promised to take me to the crater in the lava beds. Why not today?"

He hesitated uneasily. "That place has me buffaloed!" he said after a while. "I never go into it myself without wishing I was safely out. The way those big rocks hang over the trail scares a man. If they ever fell while we were in there, we'd never get out, never in this world!"

She smiled. "At least we'd be together!"

He grinned and shoved his hat back with a quick, familiar gesture. His eyes twinkled. "That sure would be something, but I'd not like to have you confined in that place all your life. You might get tired of me. This way you can see a few folks once in a while an' maybe I'll wear better."

"But you've been there so many times, Ross, and Rolly tells me it's perfectly beautiful. I want to see the ice caves, too!"

Below them, there was a faint rumbling and stirring within the mountain, and they exchanged a glance. "I'm getting used to it now," he admitted, "but when I first heard it that rumbling gave me the chills. When we move into the house we'll have those holes fenced off. They are really dangerous."

"I know. Ever since you took me down there and showed me that awful hole, I've been frightened of it. Suppose someone was trapped down there, with a foot caught or something? It would be frightful!"

"It would be the end!" Ross replied grimly. "When that geyser shoots up there it brings rocks with it that weigh fifty or sixty pounds, and they rattle around in that cave like seeds in a gourd. You wouldn't have to have a foot caught, either. All you would have to do would be to get far enough away from the mouth of that cave so you couldn't make it in a few steps. A man wouldn't have a chance!"

They were riding down the mesa through the slender aspens, the graceful white trunks like slender alabaster columns. The trail was carpeted with the scarlet and gold of autumn leaves.

"Somehow it all seems like some dreadful dream!" she said suddenly. "We'd been so happy, Bob and I. It was fun on the ranch, working with the men, building our own place, learning all the new things about the West. Bob loved handling the horses and working with cattle, and then when we were happiest, Star Levitt came out to the ranch.

"You can't imagine what a shock it was to us, for we thought all that had been left behind and forgotten. Our brother, the oldest one in the family, had gone down to Mexico and got mixed up with a girl down there and started using dope. He'd always been Father's favorite and we all loved him, but Ralph was weak and easily led. Levitt got hold of him and used his name for a front to peddle dope in the States.

"Father has been ill for a long time with a heart condition that has become steadily worse. He has just two great prides, two things to live for. One is his family reputation and the other his children. Principally, that meant Ralph.

"We knew about it, but we kept it from Dad, and later when Ralph was killed down there, we managed to keep the whole truth of the story from him. We knew the shock and the disgrace would kill him, and if by some chance he lived, he would feel the shame and the disgrace so much that his last years would be nothing but sorrow.

"Star told us that he needed our ranch. It was the proper working base for him, not too far from Mexico, yet in easy reach of a number of cities. He said he wanted to use the ranch for a headquarters for two months, and then he would leave. If we did not consent, he threatened to expose the whole disgraceful affair and see that my father heard it all.

"We were foolish, of course, but it is so hard to know what to do. And Levitt didn't give us time; he just started moving in. The next thing we knew he had his own men on the ranch, and we were almost helpless. Reynolds and Pogue were outlaws or as bad, and we could not turn to them. There was nobody, until you came."

Ross nodded grimly. "Don't I know it? When I started digging into the background of this country I found fewer good people here than anywhere I ever knew. And the best folks were all little people."

"It was after he had been here a few weeks," Sherry continued, "that he decided to stay. He was shrewd enough to know he couldn't keep on like that forever, and here was a good chance to have power, wealth, and an honest income. He saw that the fighting between the Box N and RR was his chance."

The two rode on in silence, their horses' hoofs making little sound on the leaf-covered trail. Suddenly, before Ross realized how they were riding, they were at the entrance to the lava bed trail.

Sherry laughed mischievously. "All right, now! As long as we're here, why don't we go in? We can be back before dark, you told me so yourself!"

He shrugged. "All right, have it your way."

## Chapter XVIII
### *Thirst for Vengeance*

Very reluctantly the Appaloosa turned in to the trail between the great black rolls of lava, leading the way. Once started, there was no turning back, for until a rider was well within the great cleft itself there was insufficient room for any turning of the horses.

When they reached the deepest part of the crevasse, where in some bygone age an earthquake or volcanic eruption had split the rim of the crater deep into the bedrock, Ross pointed out the great crags suspended over the trail.

"This place will be inaccessible someday," he told her. "There will be an earthquake or some kind of a jar, and those rocks will fill the cleft so there will be no trail or place for one.

"From the look of them, a man might get them started with a bar or lever of some kind. I never ride in here without getting the creeps at the thought. They are just lying up there, and all they need is the slightest start and they would come roaring and tumbling down."

Tilting her head back, Sherry could see what he meant, and for the first time she understood something of the fear that Ross had for this place. One enormous slab that must have weighed hundreds of tons seemed to be hanging, ready to slide at the slightest touch.

It was an awesome feeling to be riding down here, with no sound but the click of their horses' hoofs, and to have those enormous rocks poised above them.

Yet once within the crater itself she forgot her momentary fears in excitement over the long level of green grass, the running water, and the towering cliffs of the crater that seemed to soar endlessly toward the vast blue vault of the sky. Great clouds piled up in an enormous mass in the east and north, seeming to add their great height to the height of the cliffs.

It was warm and pleasant in the sunlight, and they rode along without talking, listening to the lazy sound of the running water and watching the movements of the few remaining great red and brindle cattle, which were becoming more tame as a result of the frequency of their visits.

"There must have been more than six hundred down here and probably would have been more, but there are a good many varmints around. I've seen cougars down here, an' heard 'em."

"Where are the ice caves?" Sherry demanded. "I want to see them. Rolly was telling me about the crystals!"

For two hours they rambled over the great crater and in and out of the caves. They found several where cattle and horses had been drinking, and whatever cattle they found they started back toward the trail. Then suddenly, as they were about to leave, Sherry caught Haney's arm. "Ross!" There was sudden fear in her voice. "Look!"

It was a boot track, small and quite deep.

Her breath caught. "It might be—Rolly?" Her voice was tight, her fear mounting.

"No, it wasn't Rolly." Mentally, he cursed himself for ever bringing her here. "That foot is smaller than either Mabry's or Burt's, an' a heavy man made it. Let's get out of here."

When they were outside, he could see the pallor of her face in the last of the sunlight. He glanced at the sky, surprised at the sudden shadows, although it was drawing on toward evening. Great gray thunderheads loomed over the crater, piling up in great, bulging, ominous clouds. It was going to rain, and rain hard.

Leading the way, he started for the horses, every sense alert and wary, yet he saw no one. His movements started the cattle drifting again, and as they reached the horses, he told her, glancing at the sky:

"You go ahead. I think I'll start the rest of the cattle out of here while I'm at it."

"You can't do it alone!" she protested.

"I'll try. You head for home now. You'll get soaked."

"Nonsense! I have my slicker, and—" her voice faded and her eyes fastened on something beyond Ross's shoulder, widening with fear and horror.

He knew instantly what it was she saw, and for a fleeting moment he considered making his draw as he turned, but he realized the girl was directly in the line of fire.

"And so, after so long a time, we meet again!" The voice was that of Star Levitt. But there was a strange tone in it now, less self-assurance, something that sounded weirdly like madness.

Carefully, Ross Haney turned and met the eyes that told him the worst.

All the neatness and glamour of the man was gone. The white hat was soiled, his shirt was dirty, and his face was unshaven. His eyes were still large and magnificent, but now the light of insanity was in them. Haney realized the line between sanity and something less had always been finely drawn in this man. Defeat and frustration had been all that were needed to break that shadow line.

"Oh, this is great!" Levitt chortled. "Today we make a clean sweep! I get you, and later, Sherry! And while I am doing that,

Chubb and Berdue will finish off Mabry and Burt. They are up on the mesa now, waiting for them!"

"On the mesa?" Haney shrugged. "They'll never surprise the boys there. Whenever one of us has not been on the mesa all day, we are very careful. We've been watching for you, Levitt."

Star smiled. "Oh, have you? But we found our own hiding place! We found a cave there, an ideal spot, and that's where they'll wait until they can catch Mabry and Burt without warning them!"

"A cave?" Ross repeated. Horror welled up within him, and he felt the hackles rising along his neck and his scalp prickled at the thought. "A cave? You mean you've been in that cave on the mesa?"

Levitt smiled. "Only to look, enough to know that it was an ideal hiding place. At first, I planned to stay, too, but then when I saw you two leaving the mesa and heading for the lava beds, I decided this was a better chance. Besides," he glanced at Sherry, "I want her for a while—alone. She needs to be taught a lesson."

Ross Haney stared at him. "Levitt, you're mad! That cave where those men are hiding is a death trap! If they aren't within a few feet of the opening, they won't have a chance to get out of there alive! Did you see that black hole in the center? That's a geyser! Those men will be trapped and drowned!"

Levitt's smile vanished. "That's a lie, of course. If it isn't, it won't matter. I was through with them, anyway. And Mabry and Burt are small fry. It is you two that I wanted."

Ross Haney had shifted his position slightly now and he was facing Levitt. His heart was pounding, for he knew there was only one chance for them. He must draw, and he must take a chance on beating Levitt to the shot. He would be hit, he was almost sure, but regardless of that, he must kill Star Levitt.

Wes Hardin had beaten men to the shot several times when actually covered with a gun. There were others who had done it, but he was no fool, and he knew how tremendously the odds weighed against him. Thunder rumbled and a few spatters of rain fell.

"Better get your slicker, Sherry," he said calmly. "You'll get wet!"

His eyes were riveted upon Star Levitt, and what he waited for happened. As the girl started to move, Levitt's eyes flickered for a fraction of an instant, and Ross Haney went for his guns.

Levitt's gun flamed, but he swung his eyes back and shot too fast, for the bullet ripped by Haney's head just as Ross flipped the hammer of his gun.

Once! Twice! And then he walked in on the bigger man, his heart pounding, Levitt's gun flaming in his face, intent only upon getting in as many shots as possible before he was killed.

A bullet creased his arm, and his hand dropped. Awkwardly, he fired with his left-hand gun and knew the shot had missed; yet Star Levitt, his shirt dark with blood, was wilting before his eyes, his body fairly riddled with the bullets from Haney's first, accurate shots.

Ross held his gun carefully and then fired again, and the shot ripped away the bridge of Star's nose, smashing a blue hole in his head at the corner of his eye.

Yet he wouldn't go down. The guns wavered in his hands as his knees slowly gave 'way, but some reflex action brought the guns up again. Both men bellowed their defiance into the pouring rain, their flames stabbing and then winking out. As the echoes of the gunfire died, there was only the rain, pouring down into the crater like a great deluge as Levitt lay still forever.

Sherry rushed to him. "Oh, Ross! You're hurt! Did he hit you?"

He turned dazedly. He didn't feel hurt. "Get into that slicker!" he yelled above the roar of the rain. "We've got to pull out of here! Think of those rocks in this rain and lightning! Let's go!"

Fighting his way into his slicker, he saw the girl mount, and then he crawled into the saddle. The cattle moved when he started his horse toward them. Suddenly, he made a resolution. He was taking them out—now.

Surprisingly, the big steer who took the lead seemed to head into the cleft of his own choice—possibly because it seemed to offer partial shelter from the sweep of the rain, perhaps because he had seen so many of his fellows go that way in the weeks past.

Waving the girl ahead of him, Ross followed on into the cleft, casting scared glances aloft at the huge rocks. "Get on!" he yelled. "Get going!"

He glanced up again as they neared the narrowest part. Horror filled him, for the great, hanging slab seemed to move!

"Hurry!" he yelled. "For heaven's sake, hurry!" He grabbed a stone and hurled it at a loitering steer, and the animal sprang ahead.

Sherry cast a frightened look upward, and her eyes widened with horror. Her face went stark white, as though she had been struck.

A thin trickle of stones fell, splashing into the cleft. A steer ahead stopped and bawled complainingly, and Ross grabbed a chunk of rock from the bank and hurled it, and the steer, hit hard, struggled madly to get ahead.

Sherry moved suddenly, closing up the gap between her horse and the nearest cattle, harrying them onward with stones and shouts. Ross looked up again, and caught as in a trance, he saw the great slab stir ponderously, almost majestically. Its tablelike top inclined, and then slowly, but with gathering impetus, it began to slide!

Shale and gravel rattled down the banks, and Ross touched spurs to his horse. The startled palouse sprang ahead, forcing Flame into the steers, who began to trot, and then as the two horses crowded up into the folds of lava, but out of the cleft in the crater wall, the air behind them was suddenly filled with a tremendous sound, a great, reverberating roar that seemed to last forever.

The rain forgotten, they sat riveted in place, listening to the sound that was closing the crater forever and leaving the body of Star Levitt as the only thing that would ever tell of human movement or habitation.

Yet as they remembered what Star Levitt had said about Berdue and Emmett Chubb, they unconsciously moved faster, and once out of the lava beds they left the cattle to shift for themselves and turned toward the mesa trail.

There was no letup to the rain. It roared down in an unceasing flood. They bowed their heads and hunched their slickers around them. The red of Flame's coat turned black with wet. Under his slicker, Ross rode with one hand on his gun, hoping for no trouble, but searching every clump of brush, every tree.

Rolly Burt ran from the cabin and grabbed their horses when they swung down. "Hustle inside an' get dry!" he yelled. "We've been worried as all get-out!"

When they got inside and had their slickers off, Mabry looked up, rolling a smoke. "Burt thought he saw Chubb today. We were worried about you."

"You haven't seen them?" Ross turned on him sharply.

Burt came in, overhearing the question. "No, an' I'm just as well satisfied. Say!" he looked up at them. "That danged geyser sure gives off some funny noises! I was over close when it sounded off the last time this afternoon, and I'd of swore I heard a human voice a-screechin'! That's one reason we have been worried about you two, although Bill did say you rode off the mesa!"

Sherry's face blanched, and she turned quickly toward an inner room.

Rolly stared after her. "Hey, what's the matter? Did I say something wrong?"

"No. Just forget about it. And don't mention that geyser again!" Then he explained, telling all that had happened during the long, wet afternoon, the end of Star Levitt and the closing of the great cleft.

Sherry came out as they finished speaking. "Ross, those poor men! I hated them, but to think of anything human being caught in that awful place!"

"Forget about it. They asked for it, and now it is all over. Look at that fire! It's our fire, in our own fireplace! Smell that coffee Mabry has on? And listen to the rain! That means the grass will be growin' tall an' green next year, honey, green on our hills an' for our cattle!"

She put her hand on his shoulder and they stood there together, watching the flames dance, listening to the fire chuckling over the secrets locked in the wood, and hearing the great drops hiss out their anguish as they drowned themselves in the flames. A stick fell, and the blaze crept along it, feeling hungrily for good places to burn. From the kitchen they heard the rattle of dishes and the smell of bacon frying, and Rolly was pouring the coffee.

# AUTHOR'S NOTE
# Showdown Trail

*Stories are rarely conceived in one piece. Often, just one situation appears, with perhaps a character in that situation. If not, one tries to find a character or characters whose presence would contribute to the drama. Fictionalized events may be chosen in the same way. For example, the trip across the mountain during the terrible thunderstorm like the one in this book happened to me. Not in just that way or at that same place, but I lived through the experience, so when I had to put it on paper I knew what I was writing about.*

*Men and women in the West were nearly always from somewhere else. The West in its beginning at least was not old enough to have bred grown men. Yet wherever they came from, they brought with them their previous experience, whatever it happened to be, and when a man or woman reacted to an event, the reaction would have developed from previous training, experience, and temperament.*

*These people who came west were largely from small towns or farms. Only a few came from cities. Many of the men had already ventured into a wilderness somewhere or had taken part in wars and were accustomed to hardship. They adapted very quickly to new styles of living and to the customs of the people among whom they were to live.*

*What I have sought from the very beginning was to understand the thinking of the people of the West, to know how they worked and lived. I wished to understand the background against which dramas would be played. One cannot judge the actions of a man on the frontier in Texas by the same measure as one would a man living in New Jersey or Virginia. The thinking of the man on the frontier would be altered by the demands made upon him, as well as by the freedom from society's restrictions. Yet always there was the desire on the part of most westerners for the amenities of the more civilized life they had formerly led.*

*Unfortunately, perhaps, stories deal with drama, and great drama is always found at the cutting edge, and one is inclined to forget the churches, schools, square dances, sewing circles, box suppers, and other aspects of social living on the frontier. For instance, Dodge City had gunfighters and gunfights, but it also had band concerts and a baseball team.*

# SHOWDOWN TRAIL

## I

**W**ith slow, ponderously rhythmical steps, the oxen moved, each step a pause and an effort, each movement a deadening drag. Fine white dust hung in a sifting cloud above the wagon train, caking the nostrils of animals and men, blanketing the lean sides of oxen and horses, dusting with a thin film the clothing of men and women.

Red-rimmed and bloodshot eyes stared with dazed weariness into the limitless distance before them, seeing nothing, knowing nothing. Long since all had been forgotten but heat, dust, and aching muscles. Each succeeding step lifted a powdery dust, stifling and irritating. It lay a foot deep on the endless plain, drowning the sparse grass and sage.

Rock Bannon, riding away from the train and alone, drew in his steel-dust stallion and turned in the saddle, looking back over the covered wagons, sixteen of them in a long line with some lead horses and a few outriders, yet not one who rode so far out as himself.

From where he sat he could not see their faces, but in the days just past he had seen them many times, and the expression of each was engraved in his mind. Haggard, worn, hungry for rest and cool water, he knew that in the secret heart of each was a longing to stop.

The vision was in them yet, the golden promise of the distant hills, offering a land of milk and honey, the fair and flowering land sought by all wandering peoples of whatever time and whatever place. No hardship could seem too great, no trail too long, no mountains impassable when the vision was upon them.

It was always and forever the same when men saw the future opening beyond the hills where the sun slept; yet this time the vision must hold meaning, this time the end of the trail must bring realization, for they had brought their women and children along.

\*     \*     \*

All had done so but Rock Bannon. He had neither woman nor child, nor anyone, anywhere. He had a horse and a saddle, a ready gun, and a mind filled with lore of the trail, and eyes ever fixed on something he wanted, something faint and indistinct in outline, ever distant, yet ever real.

Only of late as he rode alone on the far flank of the wagon train had that something begun to take shape and outline, and the shape was that of Sharon Crockett.

His somber green eyes slanted back now to the last wagon but one, where the red gold hair of Sharon on the driver's seat was a flame no dust could dim. In the back of that heavily loaded wagon was Tom Crockett, her father, stirring, restless with fever and hurt, nursing a bullet wound in his thigh, a memento of the battle with Buffalo Hide's warriors.

From the head of the train came a long, melodious halloo, and Cap Mulholland swung his arm in a great circle and the lead oxen turned ponderously to swing in the beginning of the circle. Rock touched the gray with his heels and rode slowly toward the wagon train. He was never sure these days as to his reception.

Cap's beard was white with dust as he looked up. Weariness and worry showed in his face. "Rock," he said, "we could sure use a little fresh meat. We're all a mite short on rations, and you seem to be the best hunter amongst us."

"All right," Rock said, "I'll see what I can do after I get Crockett's wagon in place."

Mulholland's head turned sharply. "Bannon, I'd let that girl alone if I were you. No offense intended, but she ain't your kind. I ain't denyin' you've been a sight of help to us. In fact, I don't know what we'd have done without you, and we're glad you came along, but Sharon Crockett's another story. Her pa's bedded down now, and in no shape to speak."

Bannon turned the steel dust sharply. His face was grim and his jaw hard. "Did he ask you to speak to me? Or did she?"

"Well, no—not exactly," Mulholland said uncomfortably. "But I'm headin' this train."

"Then I'll thank you to mind your own business! Headin' this wagon train is job enough for any man! Any time the Crocketts ask me to stay away, I'll stay, but that's their affair!"

Mulholland's face flushed and his eyes darkened with anger. "She ain't your kind," he persisted, "you bein' a killer and all."

Rock Bannon stared at him. "You didn't seem to mind my killing Indians!" he said sarcastically. "In fact, you killed a few yourself!"

"Don't get me wrong!" Cap persisted. "I ain't gainsayin' you ain't helped us! Without you I don't know if we could have beat off those

Indians or not, but killin' Indians and killin' our own kind is a lot different thing!"

"You're new to the West, Cap." Bannon's voice was rough. "In a short time you'll find there's men out here that need killin' a sight worse than Indians. In fact, I'm not so sure those Indians jumped us without help!"

"What do you mean?" Mulholland demanded.

"I mean," Bannon said, "that Morton Harper told you there'd be no hostile Indians on this route! I warned you of Buffalo Hide then, but he told you he ranged further north. You took his advice on this trail, not mine!"

Pagones and Pike Purcell were coming up to join them. Pike heard the last remark, and his lean, lantern-jawed face flushed with anger.

"You ridin' Harper again?" he harshly demanded of Bannon. "He said this was a better trail, and it is. We ain't had no high passes, and we had six days of the best travel we've had since we left Council Bluffs, with plenty of water and plenty of grass. Now we get a few bad days and a brush with Indians, but that ain't much!"

He glared at Rock. "I'm sick of your whinin' about this trail and Harper! I figure he's a durned good man. He was sure a help to me when I needed it. Out of supplies, no medicine for the wife, and he staked me."

"I wasn't talking to you," Rock replied shortly, "and I don't like your tone. As far as your loan from Harper, remember that you haven't heard from him on it yet. I've a hunch he'll collect, and plenty!"

"I don't need no killer to tell me my business!" Pike snapped, reining his horse around to face Rock. "And I ain't afeerd of no reputation for killin', neither. You don't bluff me none."

"Here, here!" Cap protested. "We can't afford to have trouble in camp. You'll have to admit, Pike, that we'd have been in bad shape a couple of times in that fight if it hadn't been for Bannon. He's been a help. I don't agree with him on Mort Harper, either, but every man to his own idea."

Rock swung the steel dust and cantered off toward the hills. Inwardly, he was seething. He was a fool to stay on with the wagon train—he understood that perfectly well. Not a man here liked him; not a man here talked to him except on business. He was not even a member of their train except by accident.

They had found him at the crossing of the Platte. Riding, half dead, with two bullet wounds in his body, his horse ready to drop with fatigue, he had run up to the wagon train. Sharon Crockett had bedded him down in her wagon and cared for him, and he had ridden on in the same place where her father rode now.

He had offered no explanation of his wounds, had talked but little. A grim and lonely man, gentle words came hard, and he could only look up into Sharon's face and wonder at her beauty, tongue-tied and helpless. Yet his hard, tough, trail-battered body was too used to pain to remain helpless for long. He had recovered rapidly, and afterward he had ridden along with the wagons, hunting for fresh meat and helping when he could.

He was not a man who made friends easily, yet gradually the ice was melting, and the clannishness of the wagon train was breaking down. Twice he had even talked with Sharon, riding beside her wagon, speaking of the mountains and his own wild and lonely life. All that had ended abruptly that night beside the campfire at the fort.

They had been seated around the fire eating supper, listening to the bustle of life around the fort, when a tall, handsome man rode up on a beautiful black mare.

Perfectly groomed, his wide, white hat topping coal-black hair that hung to his shoulders, a drooping black mustache and a black broadcloth suit, the trousers tucked into hand-tooled boots, Morton Harper had been a picture to take any eye.

Swinging down, he had walked up to the fire. "Howdy, folks!" His voice was genial, his manner warm and pleasant. In an instant his personality and voice had done what Rock Bannon's could not do in two weeks. He had broken down their reserve and become one of the group. "Headin' for California?"

"Reckon we are," Mulholland had agreed. "We ain't rightly decided whether to stay on the Humboldt Trail or to swing north and go to Oregon."

"Why go either way?" Harper asked. "There's a southern route I could recommend that would be much easier going for your womenfolks." His alert eyes had already found and appraised Sharon Crockett. "More water, plenty of grass, and no high mountain passes."

Cap Mulholland looked up interestedly. "We ain't heard of no such pass, nor no such trail," he admitted. "How does she go?"

"Man named Hastings scouted some of it, and I scouted the rest myself. It is a more southerly route, and within another few months all the travel will be going that way. Right now," he winked, "the trains that go that way are going to have a mighty fine trip of it. Very little dust except in one stretch, fine grass, lots of water. Also, the hostile Indians are all raiding far north of there along the traveled routes.

"But," he added, "I can see you're well led, and you'll no doubt learn about this trail yourselves. From the look of your teams I'd say you were lucky in your choice of a leader."

Leaning against the hub of a wagon wheel, Rock Bannon ate in silence. The even, smooth flow of the stranger's language had an enchanting quality, but his own hard-grained, cynical character was impervious to mere talk.

As the hours flowed by, Harper sat among them, pleasing the men with subtle flattery, the women with smiles. The reserve of the group thawed under his easy manner, and before long they began to discuss his trail and its possibilities, considering themselves fortunate to know of it first.

There was some talk of putting it to a vote, but it was morning before it came to that. Until then, Rock was silent. "You'd do better," he interposed suddenly, "to stick to the regular trail."

Harper's head came up sharply, and his eyes leveled at Bannon. "Have you ever been over the trail I suggest, my friend?"

"Part way," Rock replied. "Only part of it."

"And was that part easy going for oxen and horses? Was there a good trail? Grass? Water?"

"Yes, I reckon it has all that, but I wouldn't advise it."

"You say it is a better trail but you wouldn't advise it." Harper glanced around at the others, smiling tolerantly. "That doesn't make much sense, does it? I've been over the entire trail and found it very good going. Moreover, I can give you a map of the trail showing the waterholes, everything. Of course, it's nothing to me what route you take, but if you want to avoid Indians—" He shrugged.

"What about Buffalo Hide?"

Morton Harper's face tightened, and his eyes strained to pry Rock Bannon's face from the shadows in which he sat. "He's a Blackfoot. He ranges further north."

Harper's eyes shifted to Mulholland. "Who is this man? I'm surprised he should ask about Buffalo Hide, as he isn't known to most white men other than renegades. I can't understand why he should try to persuade you to neglect an easier route for a more dangerous one. Is he one of your regular train?"

Pike Purcell was abrupt. From the first day he had disliked and been suspicious of Bannon. "No, he ain't none of our crowd, just a feller what tied up with us back yonder a ways. He ain't got no wagon, nothin' but the horse he's ridin'."

"I see." Morton Harper's face became grave with implied doubt. "No offense, friend, but would you mind telling me your name? I know most of the men along this trail, and Colonel Warren was asking about some of them only tonight. You'll admit it is safer to be careful, for there are so many renegades who work with the Indians."

"My name's Rock Bannon."

Morton Harper's lips tightened and his eyes grew wary. For a moment he seemed taken aback. Then as he perceived where his own interests lay, his eyes lighted with triumph.

"Ah? Bannon, eh? I've heard of you. Killed a man in Laramie a month or so back, didn't you?"

"He drew on me."

Rock was acutely conscious of the sudden chill in the atmosphere, and he could see Sharon's shocked gaze directed at him. The people of the wagon train were fresh from the East. Only Cap had been as far west as the Platte before, and he only once. They were peace-loving men, quiet and asking no trouble.

Morton Harper was quick to sense his advantage. "Sorry to have brought it up, Bannon," he said smoothly, "but when a man advises a wagon train against their best interests, it is well to inquire into the source of the advice."

Bannon got up. He was a tall man, lean hipped and broad shouldered, his flat-brimmed hat shadowing his face, his eyes glowing with piercing light as he spoke.

"I still say that route's a darned fool way to go. This ain't no country to go wanderin' around in, and that route lays through Hardy Bishop's country. You spoke of Hastings. He was the man who advised the Donner party."

As his footsteps died away in the darkness, the members of the wagon train sat very still, their enthusiasm suddenly dampened by that ill-fated name. They all knew the story. The horror of it still blanketed the trail with its bloody shadow of the party caught by snows in the high passes and starving until they resorted to cannibalism as a way out.

Morton Harper shrugged. "Of course. They started on Hastings's trail, but left it too soon, and the route I suggest avoids all the higher passes." His eyes swung around the group, gathering their attention like the reins of a six-horse team, and he led them on with promises and suggestions, an easy flow of calm, quiet talk, stilling their fears, quieting their doubts, offering them grass and water instead of dust and desert.

In the morning when they moved out, they took the trail Harper had advised, turning off an hour after they left the fort. He glanced back, and smiled when he saw he was unobserved. Then he wished them luck and promised to overtake them when a message came for which he waited. Turning, he galloped back to the fort.

Rock Bannon was with them. He rode close to Sharon's wagon, and after a time she looked up. He had watched her the night before, had seen her fascinated eyes on Harper's face.

"You don't approve, do you?"

He shook his head. Then he smiled, somewhat grimly. He was a dark, good-looking man with a tinge of recklessness in his green eyes.

"My views aren't important," he said. "I don't belong."

"Pike shouldn't have said that," she said. "He's a strange man. A good man, but very stubborn and suspicious."

"Not suspicious of the right folks, maybe."

Her eyes flashed. "You mean Mr. Harper? Why should we be suspicious of him? He was only trying to help."

"I wonder."

"I think," Sharon said sharply, "you'd do better to be a little less suspicious yourself! You admitted this was a good trail!"

"You haven't met Hardy Bishop yet. Nor Buffalo Hide."

"Mr. Harper said that Indian was farther north." She looked at him. "Who is Hardy Bishop? You mentioned him before?"

"He's a man who is trying to run cattle at Indian Writing. They said he's insane to try it, but he's claimed seventy miles of range, and he has cattle there. We have to cross his range."

"What's wrong with that?"

"If you cross it, maybe nothing, but Bishop's a funny man. He doesn't like strangers very much. He's going to wonder why you're so far south. He's going to be suspicious."

"Well, let him be suspicious then!" Sharon said, her eyes bright and her chin lifting. "We don't care, and we won't bother him any. Does he think he owns the whole country?"

"Uh-huh," Rock said. "I'm afraid he does. With some reason as far as that valley goes. He made it what it is today."

"How could any man make a valley?" Sharon protested. "This is all free country. Anyway, we're just going through."

The conversation had dwindled and died, and after a while he rode off to the far flank of the wagon train. Sharon's manner was distinctly stiff and he could see she was remembering that story of the killing in Laramie. After a few rebuffs he avoided her. Nobody talked to him. He rode alone and camped alone.

## II

It had remained like that for six days. They were six days during which Morton Harper's name became one to reckon with. The long green valley down which they moved was unrutted by wagon trains, the grass was green and waving, and water was plentiful. Harper's map showed an accurate knowledge of the country and was a great help. On the sixth day after leaving the fort, the Indians hit them.

The attack came at daybreak. Rock Bannon, camping near a spring a half mile from the wagons, awoke with a start. It was scarcely light, yet he felt uneasy, and getting to his knees, he saw the steel dust staring, ears pricked, at a distant pile of rocks. Then he noticed the movement.

Swiftly and silently he saddled the stallion, bridled it, and stowed his gear in the saddlebags. Then, rifle in hand, he skirted the trees along the tiny stream and headed back for the wagons. He rode up to them, and the man on guard got up, stretching. It was the short, heavyset Pagones. A good man and a sharp one. He smiled at Bannon.

"Guess Harper had it more right than you when he said there were no hostiles here," he said. "Ain't that right?"

"No," Bannon said sharply. "Get everybody up and ready. We'll be attacked within a few minutes!"

Pagones stared. "Are you crazy?"

"Get busy, man!" Bannon snapped at Pagones. He wheeled and running from wagon to wagon, slapped the canvas and said, "On your feet! Indians!"

Men boiled from the wagons, crawling into their clothes and grabbing at rifles. "Get around the whole circle!" he told them. "They are in those rocks and a draw that runs along south of us."

Mulholland rushed out and halted, glaring around. The sky was gray in the east, and everything lay in a vague, indistinct light. Not a movement showed in all the dark width of the prairie. He started for Bannon to protest, when he heard a startled exclamation. Wheeling, he saw a long line of Indian horsemen not over two hundred yards away and coming at a dead run!

Even as his eyes touched them, the nearest Indian broke into a wild, shrill whoop! Then the whole charging line broke into yells.

Rock Bannon, leaning against the Crockett wagon, lifted his Henry rifle and fired. A horse stumbled and went down. He fired again, and an Indian threw up his arms and vanished in the turmoil of oncoming horses and men, and then the other men of the wagon train opened up.

Firing steadily, Bannon emptied his rifle before the Indians reached the edge of the circle. One brave, his wild-eyed horse at a dead run, leaned low and shot a blazing arrow into the canvas of the Crockett wagon. Rock fired his right-hand pistol and the Indian hit the dirt in a tumbling heap, just as a second arrow knocked off Rock's hat. Reaching up with his left hand, Rock jerked the burning arrow from the canvas. The fire had not yet caught. Then he opened up, firing his pistol, shifting guns, and firing again. The attack broke as suddenly as it had begun.

Tom Crockett was kneeling behind a water barrel, his face gray. A good shot, he was not accustomed to killing. He glanced up at Rock, a sickened expression on his face.

"I never killed nothing human before!" he said weakly.

"You'll get used to it out here!" Rock said coldly. His eyes lifted to Sharon.

"You saved our wagon!" she said.

"It might have been anybody's wagon," he said brutally, and turned away. He counted seven dead Indians on the prairie. There were probably one or two more hidden in the tall grass. He could see several dead ponies. The Indian who had shot the flaming arrow lay not more than a dozen feet away. The bullet had gone through his stomach and broken his spine.

Rock walked around. He had eyes only for the men. Cap looked frightened, but determined. Pagones had fired steadily and with skill. Bannon nodded at the short man.

"You'll do," he said grimly.

Pagones started to speak, started after him, and scowled a little. He was ashamed of himself when he realized he was pleased at the compliment.

They were good men, Rock decided. Purcell was reloading his rifle, and he looked up as Bannon passed, but said nothing. Rock walked back to the Crockett wagon. Cap was standing there, his rifle in the hollow of his arm.

"Will they come again?" he asked.

Bannon nodded. "Probably several times. This is Buffalo Hide. Those were his warriors."

"But Morton said—" Crockett started to protest.

Bannon looked around, and then he pointed at the dead Indian. "You goin' to believe Morton Harper or that?" he demanded. "That Indian's a Blackfoot. I know by the moccasins."

This time they came in a circle, going around and around the wagon train. A volley of flaming arrows set two wagon tops afire. Rock stood at the end of the wagon and fired steadily, carefully, making every shot count.

Dawn came with a red, weird light flaming in the east and turned the wagon colors to flame. Guns crashed, and the air was filled with wild Indian yells and the acrid smell of gunpowder and burned canvas. Three times more they attacked, and Bannon was everywhere. Firing, firing, firing. Crockett went down with a bullet through his thigh. Bjornsen was shot through the head, and a warrior leaped from a horse into Greaves's wagon and the two men fought there until the Indian thrust a knife into Greaves's side. Bannon shot the brave with a snapped pistol shot, almost from the hip.

The last attack broke, and the sun lifted into the sky. As if by magic the Indians were gone. Rock Bannon wiped the sweat from his forehead and stared out over the plain. Buffalo Hide had lost men in this fight. At least twenty of his braves were dead, and there would be wailing and the death chant in the Blackfoot villages tonight.

Two horses and an ox had been killed. They gathered around, buried the two dead men and butchered the ox. Rock sat on a wagon tongue alone. Cap walked over to him. The man's face was round and uncomfortable.

"Reckon you saved us, Rock," he said. "Don't rightly know how to thank you!"

Bannon got up. He had been cleaning his rifle and reloading it while the men were buried. "Don't try," he said.

Bob Sprague walked over and held out his hand. "Guess we haven't been very friendly," he said, "but you were right about the Indians."

Suddenly, boyishly, Bannon grinned. "Forget it, Bob! You did a right good job with that rifle of yours!"

They were the only two who mentioned it. Rock helped lift Crockett into the back of the wagon and then harnessed the oxen. He was gone, riding out on the flank on the steel dust when Sharon came to thank him. She looked after him, and her heart felt suddenly lost and alone.

It was late that day when they reached the dry country. The settlers did not realize the change until the dust began to rise, for in the distance it had looked much the same, only the grass was darker and there was less of it. Within a mile they were suffused in a cloud of powdery, sifting dust, stifling and irritating in the heat.

This was no desert. Merely long miles of plain where the hills receded and there was no subirrigation to keep the grass green and rich. All the following day the dust cloud hung over the wagon train, and from Mulholland's place in the van the last wagons could not even be distinguished.

Mulholland looked up at Bannon, who was riding beside him. "Harper said there was one bad stretch," he said, almost apologetically.

Bannon did not reply. He alone of all the party knew what lay ahead. He alone knew how brutal the passage would be. Let them find out.

Days later, when Cap asked him to go for game, they all knew. They were still in that desert of dust and dirty brown brush. They had camped in it five days now. Their water barrels were empty, the wagons so hard to pull in the thick dust that they made only a few miles each day. It was the worst kind of tough going.

When he had killed two antelope in the hills, Rock rode back to join the party. Pagones, hunting on the other side, had killed one.

Rock turned toward Sharon's wagon and swung down from the saddle. She looked up at him from over a fire of greasewood.

"Hello," she said. "We haven't seen much of you?"

He took off his black, flat-brimmed hat. His dark, curly hair was plastered to his brow with sweat.

"There are some here who don't want me talking to you," he said dryly. "Figure I'm a bad influence, I guess."

"I haven't said that!" she protested. She brushed a strand of hair from her eyes. "I like to have you riding close. It—it makes me feel safer."

He looked at her an instant and then looked away. "How's your dad?"

"Better, I think. But this heat! It's so awful! How long before we get out of this dust?"

"Tomorrow night, at this rate. This bad stretch is over."

"Then we're free of that. Morton said there was only one."

He noticed that she had called Harper, "Morton." "He was wrong. You'll strike another near Salt Lake that's much worse than this. You'll never get across unless you swing back and take the old trail for Pilot Peak."

"But he said—" Sharon protested.

Rock Bannon looked up at her from where he squatted on his haunches. "I know he did. I heard everything he said, and I'm still wondering what he has to gain by it. Nobody takes this route. Crossing the Salt Desert by this route is suicide—with wagons, at least. You've all placed a lot of faith in a stranger!"

"He was right, Rock. Those first six days were heaven, and from now on it should be good."

"From now on it will be good until you hit the desert," he admitted, "unless you stop."

"Unless we stop?" Sharon dished up a plate and handed it to him, and then poured the coffee. "Why?"

"Tomorrow we get into Hardy Bishop's country." Rock Bannon's face was somber.

"You always refer to him as if he were an outlaw or something awful!"

"No," he said. "Bishop isn't any of those things. If you are his friend or a guest, he's one of the finest men alive. If you are an enemy or try to take something that's his, he is absolutely ruthless."

When she returned from feeding her father, she sat down beside him on the wagon tongue. The sun was down, and the dust had settled. Near a fire on the far side of the circle, Dud Kitchen was singing softly over his mandolin.

The air was cool now, and the soft music mingled in the air with the scent of wood smoke, the low champing of the horses, and the mumbling of the oxen. In the distance they could see the hills, purple with the last shadows before darkness, and shadowed with a promise of coolness after the long days of heat and dust and bitterness.

He stared away at the hills, remembering so much, worried, uncertain, wondering again about Morton Harper. What did the man have in mind? Who was he? Purcell said Harper had lent him money. Perhaps he had lent others in the wagon train money. It was not like a man to loan money and not follow it up to get back what was his. Behind all of this was a reason, and in the back of his mind Rock was afraid he knew that reason.

Sharon spoke suddenly. "What are you thinking of, Rock? You are always so silent. You seem so bitter sometimes, and I can never understand what you have in your mind."

"It isn't anything." He had no desire to mention Harper again. "I was just thinking about this country."

"You like it, don't you?"

"Like it?" He looked up suddenly, and his eyes changed. He smiled suddenly and with warmth. "Like it? I love it! This is a man's country! And that ahead? Wait until you see Bishop's Valley! Miles upon miles of tumbling streams, waving green grass dotted with cattle!

"You should see Bishop's Valley! You go down through a deep gorge along a roaring mountain stream, and you can look up at cliffs that rise for three thousand feet, and then suddenly the gorge widens and you look down a long valley that is six or seven miles wide and all of fifty miles long.

"On each side, high mountain ridges shut it in, and here and there deep gorges and ravines cut back into those ridges and there are green meadows and tumbling waterfalls. And all the hills around are timbered to their crests. It's a beautiful country!"

Sharon stared at him, enchanted. Rock had never talked like this before, and as she listened to him tell of the hills and the wild game, of deer, elk, bear, and mountain goats, of the catbirds calling in the willows and the hillsides white with groves of silver-columned birch, she suddenly forgot where she was and who was talking.

"You seem to love it so much!" she said. "Why did you ever leave?"

"It belongs to one man, to Hardy Bishop," Rock said. "He's carving a little empire there. He went there long before any other white man dreamed of anything but going on to California, before they thought of anything but getting rich from gold mines. They came through the country like a pack of vultures or wolves, taking everything, building nothing. They want only to get rich and get out.

"He was different. Once, when only a boy, he went into that

valley on a trapping venture, and he was never content until he came back. He drove a herd of cattle west when there were no cattle in this country, and he got them into that valley and turned them loose. He fought Indians and outlaws, he built a dam, built a home, built irrigation ditches where he wanted them, and planted trees.

"He made the valley, and you can't blame him if he wants to keep it his way now."

Long after Sharon lay in her blankets, she thought of that and of Rock Bannon. How tall he was! And how strange! He had risen suddenly and with scarcely a word had walked into the night, and then she heard him mount his horse and ride away. Yet even as she heard the dwindling hoof beats, she heard something else, the sound of other horses drawing near. Still wondering who the riders could be, she fell asleep.

Scarcely were they moving in the morning before a black mare wheeled alongside her wagon. Flushing suddenly, she saw Morton Harper, hat in hand, bowing to her.

"Good morning!" he said. "I hoped to catch up with you before this, but by tomorrow you'll be in green country again!"

"Yes, I know."

He looked at her quickly. "You know? Who told you?"

"Rock Bannon."

His face sharpened, and she could sense the irritation in the man. "Oh? Then he's still with you? I was hoping he had left you alone. I'm afraid he's not a good man."

"Why do you say that? He's been very helpful."

Harper shrugged. "I'd rather not say. You know of that killing in Laramie, and if that were the only one, it would not matter. There are others. He has killed five or six men. He's a troublemaker wherever he goes. I'm glad Purcell and your men understand that, for it will save a lot of trouble."

He smiled at her. "You look so lovely this morning that it is unbelievable that you have come so far across the prairies. It is a pity you have so far to go. I've been thinking some of settling in this country here." He waved ahead. "It is such a beautiful land, and there is nothing in California so desirable."

Rock Bannon had heard the horses the night before, and he had reined in long enough to see them come up to the fire. Harper he recognized at once. There were two men with him, one a lean, sharp-faced man with a long nose. The other man was short, chuckle-headed, and blunt featured. Bannon's lips tightened when he recognized Pete Zapata. The half-breed killer was notorious, a gunfighter and desperado of the worst stripe, but none of the wagon train would know that.

All that day he stayed away from the train, riding on ahead. He drank at the spring, killed an antelope and a couple of teal, and then rode back under a clump of poplars and waited for the wagon train to come up. They were already on Hardy Bishop's V Bar. Only a short distance behind the poplars, the long canyon known as Poplar Canyon ran down into Bishop's Valley.

He got up when he saw the first of the long caravan of wagons. Better than the others, he knew what this would mean and knew on how bad a trail they had started. He was standing there, close to the steel-dust stallion, when the wagons moved in.

The fresh water and green grass made everyone happy. Brown-legged children rushed downstream from where the drinking water was obtained, and there was laughter and merrymaking in the camp. Fires sprang up, and in a short time the camp was made and meals were being cooked.

Watchfully, Rock saw Morton Harper seated on a saddle at Cap Mulholland's fire. With them were the sharp-featured stranger, Satterfield, Lamport, and Pagones. They were deep in a conference. In a few minutes Tom Crockett walked over to join them.

Dud Kitchen was tuning his mandolin when he saw Bannon sitting under the willows.

"All alone?" Kitchen said with a grin and dropped on the grass beside Bannon. "Saw how you handled those guns in that Indian fight. Never saw the like. Make more tune with 'em than me with a mandolin!"

Rock chuckled. "But not so nice to hear." He nodded at the group of men around the fire. "Wonder what's up?"

Dud shrugged. "Harper's got some plan he's talkin' about. Sayin' they are foolish to go on when there's good country right here."

Rock Bannon sprang to his feet, his eyes afire with apprehension. "So that's it?" he said. "I might have known it!"

Kitchen was startled. "What's the matter? I think it would be a good idea, myself. This is beautiful country. I don't know that I've ever seen better. Harper says that down this draw behind us there's a long, beautiful valley, all open for settlement."

But Rock Bannon was no longer listening. Stepping across the branch of the creek, he started for the fire. Morton Harper was talking when Rock walked up.

"Why not?" Harper was saying. "You all want homes. Can you find a more beautiful country than this? That dry plain is behind you. Ahead lies the Salt Lake Desert, but in here, this is a little bit of paradise. Beyond this range of hills—you can reach it through Poplar Canyon—is the most beautiful valley you ever saw. It's just crying for people to come in and settle down! There's game in the hills and the best grazing land in the world, all for the taking!"

"What about Hardy Bishop?" Bannon demanded harshly.

Harper looked up, angered. "You, again? Every time these people try to do anything, you interfere! Is it your business where they stop? Is it your business if they remain here or go on to California? Are you trying to dictate to these people?"

Pike Purcell was on his feet, and Rock could see all the old dislike in the big Missourian's face. The other men looked at him with disapproval, too. Yet he went on recklessly, heedlessly.

"Hardy Bishop settled that valley. He's running two thousand head of cattle in there! You try to settle in that valley and you're asking for trouble! He won't stand for it."

"An' we won't stand for you buttin' in!" Purcell said suddenly. He dropped a hand to the big dragoon pistol in his holster. "I've had enough of your buttin' around, interferin' in our affairs. I'm tellin' you now, you shut up an' get out."

"Wait just a minute!" Bob Sprague stepped closer. "This man warned us about that Indian attack, or we'd all be dead, includin' you, Pike Purcell. He did more fightin' in that attack than any one of us, or two of us, for that matter. His advice has been good, and I think we should listen to him!"

Dud Kitchen nodded. "Speak up, Rock. I'll listen!"

"There's little to be said," Bannon told them quietly. "Only the land this man is suggesting you settle on was settled on over ten years ago by a man who fought Indians to get it. He fought Indians and outlaws to keep it. He won't see it taken from him now in his old age. He'll fight to keep it. I know Hardy Bishop. I know him well enough to be sure that if you move into that valley, many of the women in this wagon train will be widows before the year is out.

"What I don't know is Morton Harper's reason for urging you into this. I don't know why he urged you to take this trail, but I think he has a reason, and I think that reason lies in Bishop's Valley. You are coming west to win homes. You have no right to do it by taking what another man fought to win and to keep. There is plenty for all further west."

"That makes sense to me," Sprague said quietly. "I for one am moving west!"

"Well, I'm not!" Purcell said stubbornly. "I like this country, and me and the wife have seen enough dust and sun and Indians! We aim to stay!"

"That valley is fifty miles long, gentlemen," Harper said. "I think there is room enough for us all in Bishop's Valley."

"That seems right to me!" Cap said. He looked around at Tom Crockett, limping near the fire. "How about you, Tom?"

"I'm staying," Crockett said. "I like it here."

Satterfield nodded. "Reckon I'll find me a place to set up a blacksmith shop," he said. "But there's a sight of things we all need. There ain't no stores, no place to get some things we figured to get in California."

"That will be where I come in," the man with the sharp features smiled pleasantly. "I'm John Kies, and I have six wagonloads of goods coming over the trail to open a store in our new town!"

# III

Silently, Rock Bannon turned away. There was no further use in talking. He caught Sharon's eye, but she looked away, her gaze drawn to Mort Harper where he sat now, talking easily, smoothly, planning the new home, the new town.

Bannon walked back to his blankets and turned in, listening to the whispering of the poplar leaves and the soft murmur of the water in the branch. It was a long time before he fell asleep, long after the last talking had died away in the wagon train and when the fires had burned low.

When daylight came he bathed and saddled the stallion. Then, carefully, he checked his guns. At a sound, he glanced up to see Sharon Crockett dipping water from the stream.

"Good morning," he said. "Did you finally decide to stay?"

"Yes." She stepped toward him. "Rock, why are you always against everything we do? Why don't you stay, too? I'm sure Morton would be glad to have you. He's planned all this so well, and he says we'll need good men. Why don't you join us?"

"No, not this time. I stayed with the wagon train because I knew what you were going into. I wanted to help you—and I mean you. In what is to come, no one can help you. Besides, my heart wouldn't be in it."

"You're afraid of this crabby old man?" she asked scornfully. "Morton says as soon as Bishop sees we intend to stay he won't oppose us at all! He's just crabby and difficult because he's old, and he has more land than he needs. Are you afraid of him?"

Rock smiled. "You sure set a lot of store by this Harper fellow, don't you? Did he tell you that Bishop's riders were all crabby old men, too? Did Harper tell you why he carries Pete Zapata along with him?"

"Who is he?" Sharon looked up, her eyes curious, yet resentful.

"You've called me a killer," Bannon replied. "I have killed men. I may kill more, although I hope not, but Pete Zapata, that flat-faced man who rides with Harper, is a murderer. He's a killer of the most vicious type and the kind of man no decent man would have near him!"

Her eyes flared. "You don't think Morton Harper is decent? How dare you say such a thing behind his back?"

"I'll face him with it," Bannon said dryly. "I expect I'll face him with it more than once. But before you get in too deep, ask yourself again what he is getting out of all this. He goes in for talk of brotherly love, but he carries a gunman at his elbow!"

He turned and swung into the saddle as she picked up her bucket. He reined in the horse at a call. It was Bob Sprague.

"Hey, Rock! Want to come on west with us?"

He halted. "You're going on?"

"Uh-huh. Six wagons are going. We decided we liked the sound of what you said. We're pullin' on for California, and we'd sure admire to have you with us!"

Bannon hesitated. Sharon was walking away, her head held proudly. Did she seem to hesitate for his reply? He shrugged.

"No," he said. "I've got other plans."

Sharon Crockett, making frying-pan bread over the fire beside her wagon, stood up to watch Bob Sprague lead off six wagons, the owners of which had decided not to stay. All farewells had been said the night before, yet now that the time for leave-taking had come, she watched uneasily.

For years she had known Bob Sprague, ever since she was a tiny girl. He had been her father's friend, a steady, reliable man, and now he was going. With him went five other families, among them some of the steadiest, soberest men in the lot.

Were they wrong to take Morton Harper's advice? Her father, limping with the aid of a cane cut from the willows, walked back and stood beside her, his face somber. He was a tall man, almost as tall as Harper and Bannon, his hair silvery around the temples, his face gray with a slight stubble of beard. He was a fearless, independent man, given to going his own way and thinking his own thoughts.

Pagones walked over to them. "Did Bannon go along? I ain't seen him."

"I don't think he went," Crockett replied. "Sprague wanted him to go."

"No, he didn't go," said Satterfield, who had walked up to join them. Satterfield had been a frontier lawyer back in Illinois. "I saw him riding off down the canyon, maybe an hour ago."

"You think there will be trouble?" Pagones asked.

Satterfield shrugged. "Probably not. I know how some of these old frontiersmen are. They hate to see civilization catch up with them, but given time, they come around. Where's Harper?"

"He went off somewhere with that dark-lookin' feller who trails with him," Pagones said. "Say, I'm glad Dud Kitchen didn't go. I'd sure miss that music he makes. He was goin', then at the last minute changed his mind. He's goin' down with Harper and Cap to survey that townsite."

"Seem good to have a town again," Crockett said. "Where's it to be?"

"Down where Poplar Canyon runs into Bishop Valley. Wide, beautiful spot, they say, with plenty of water and grass. John Kies is puttin' in a store, I'm goin' to open an office, and Collins is already figurin' on a blacksmith shop."

"Father, did you ever hear of a man named Zapata?" Sharon asked thoughtfully. "Pete Zapata?"

Crockett looked at her curiously. "Why, no. Not that I recall. Why?"

"I was just wondering, that's all."

The next morning they hitched up the oxen and moved their ten wagons down Poplar Canyon to the townsite. The high, rocky walls of the canyon widened slowly, and the oxen walked on, knee deep in rich green grass. Along the stream were willow and poplar, and higher along the canyon sides she saw alder, birch, and mountain mahogany, with here and there a fine stand of lodgepole pine.

Tom Crockett was driving, so she ranged alongside, riding her sorrel mare.

As they rounded the last bend in the canyon, it spread wide before them, and she saw Morton Harper sitting his black mare some distance off. Putting the sorrel to a gallop, she rode down swiftly, hair blowing in the wind. Dud Kitchen was there with Zapata and Cap. They were driving stakes and lining up a street.

Before them the valley dropped into the great open space of Bishop's Valley, and she rode on. Suddenly, rounding a knoll, she stopped and caught her breath.

The long, magnificent sweep of the valley lay before her, green and splendid in the early-morning sun. Here and there over the grassland, cattle grazed, belly deep in the tall grass. It was overpowering; it was breathtaking. It was something beyond the grasp of the imagination. High on either side lifted the soaring walls of the canyon, mounting into high ridges, snowcapped peaks, and majestic walls of gray rock.

This was the cattle empire of Hardy Bishop. This was the place Rock Bannon had spoken of with such amazing eloquence.

*　　*　　*

She turned in her saddle at the sound of a horse's hoofs. Mort Harper rode up beside her, his face glowing.

"Look!" he cried. "Magnificent, isn't it? The most splendid view in the world. Surely, that's an empire worth taking!"

Sharon's head turned quickly, sharply. At something in Harper's eyes she caught her breath, and when she looked again at the valley, she was uneasy.

"What—what did you say?" she asked. "An empire worth taking?"

He glanced at her quickly and then laughed. "Don't pay any mind. I was thinking of Bishop, the man who claims all this. He took it. Took it from the Indians by main force." Then he added, "He's an old brute. He'd stop at nothing!"

"Do you think he will make trouble for us?" she inquired anxiously.

He shrugged. "Probably not. He might, but if he does, we can handle that part of it. Let's go back, shall we?"

She was silent during the return ride, and she kept turning over in her mind her memory of Bannon's question, "What's he going to get out of this?" Somehow, half hypnotized by Harper's eloquence, she had not really thought of that. That she thought of it now gave her a twinge of doubt. It seemed, somehow, disloyal.

For three days, life in the new town went on briskly. They named the town Poplar. Kies's Store was the first building up, and the shelves were heavy with needed goods. Kies was smiling and affable. "Don't worry about payment!" he assured them. "We're all in this together! Just get what you need, and I'll put it on the books. Then when you get money from furs or crops, you can pay me!"

It was easy. It was almost too easy. Tom Crockett built a house in a bend of the creek among the trees, and he bought dress goods for Sharon, trousers for himself, and bacon and flour. Then he bought some new tools.

Those first three days were hard, unrelenting labor, yet joyful labor, too. They were building homes, and there is always something warming and pleasant in that. At the end of those first three days, Kies's Store was up, and so were Collins's blacksmith shop, Satterfield's office, and Harper's Saloon and Theater. All of them pitched in and worked.

Then one day as she was leaving Kies's Store, she looked up to see three strange horsemen coming down the street. They were walking their horses, and they were looking around in ill-concealed amazement.

Mulholland had come out behind her, and at the sight of him, one of the horsemen, a big, stern-looking man with a drooping red mustache, reined his horse around.

"You!" he said. "What do you all think you're doin' here?"

"Buildin' us a town," Cap said aggressively. "Any objections?"

Red laughed sardonically. "Well, sir," he said, "I reckon *I* haven't, but I'm afraid the boss is sure goin' to raise hob!"

"Who's the boss?" Cap asked. "And what difference does it make? This is all free land, isn't it?"

"The boss is Hardy Bishop," Red drawled, glancing around. He looked approvingly at Sharon, and there seemed a glint of humor in his eyes. "And you say this is free land. It is and it ain't. You see, out here a man takes what he can hold. Hardy, he done come in here when all you folks was livin' fat and comfortable back in the States. He settled here, and he worked hard. He trapped and hunted and washed him some color, and then he went back to the States and bought cattle. Drivin' them cattle out here ten years ago was sure a chore, folks, but he done it. Now they've bred into some of the biggest herds in the country. I don't think Hardy's goin' to like you folks movin' in here like this."

"Is he so selfish?" Sharon demanded. "Why, there's land here enough for thousands of people!"

Red looked at her. "That's how you see it, ma'am. I reckon to your way of thinkin' back East, that might be true. Here, it ain't true. A man's needs run accordin' to the country he's in and the job he has to do. Hardy Bishop is runnin' cows. He expects to supply beef for thousands of people. To do that he needs a lot of land. You see, ma'am, if thousands of people can't raise their own beef, somebody's got to have land enough to raise beef for all those thousands of people. And Hardy, he come by it honest."

"By murdering Indians, I suppose!"

Red looked at her thoughtfully. "Ma'am, somebody's been tellin' you wrong. Plumb wrong. Hardy never murdered no Indians."

"What's going on here?" Morton Harper stepped into the street. To his right was Pete Zapata, to his left Pike Purcell. Lamport lounged in the door of the store.

"Why, nothin', mister," Red said thoughtfully. His gaze had sharpened, and Sharon saw his eyes go from Harper to Zapata. "We was just talkin' about land and the ownership of it. We're ridin' for Bishop, and—"

"And you can ride right out of here!" Harper snapped. "Now!"

Sharon was closer to the Bishop riders, and suddenly she heard the second man say softly:

"Watch it, Red! That's Zapata!"

Red seemed to stiffen in his saddle, and his hand, which had started to slip off the pommel of the saddle, with no aggressive intention, froze in position. Without a word, they turned their horses and rode away.

"That's the beginning," Harper stated positively. "I'm afraid they mean to drive us from our homes!"

"They didn't sound much like trouble," Cap ventured, hesitantly. "Talked mighty nice!"

"Don't be fooled by them!" Harper warned. "Bishop is an outlaw, or the next thing to it."

Tom Crockett was a man who loved the land. No sooner had he put a plow into the deep, rich soil of the canyon bottom than he felt he had indeed come home. The soil was deep and black, heavy with richness, land that had never known a plow. Working early and late, he had in the next day managed to plow several acres. Seed he bought from Kies, who seemed to have everything they needed.

There were several hours a day he gave to working on the buildings the others were throwing up, but logs were handy, and all but Zapata and Kies worked on the felling and notching of them. Kies stayed in his store, and Zapata lounged close by.

Morton Harper helped with the work, but Sharon noticed that he was never without a gun, and his rifle was always close by. At night in his saloon he played cards with Purcell and Lamport and anyone else who came around. Yet several times a day he managed to stop by, if only for a minute, to talk to her.

He stopped by one day when she was planting a vine near the door. He watched her for a few minutes, and then he stepped closer.

"Sharon," he said gently. "You shouldn't be doing this sort of thing. You're too beautiful. Why don't you let me take care of you?"

She looked at him, suddenly serious. "Is this a proposal?"

His eyes flashed, and then he smiled. "What else? I suppose I'm pretty clumsy at it."

"No," she returned thoughtfully, "you're not clumsy at it, but let's wait. Let's not talk about it until everyone has a home and is settled in a place of their own."

"All right." He agreed reluctantly. "But that won't be very long, you know."

It was not until they were eating supper that night that her thoughts suddenly offered her a question. What about Morton's home? He had not even started to build. He was sleeping in a room behind the saloon, such in name only as yet, for there was little liquor to be had.

The thought had not occurred to her before, but it puzzled and disturbed her. Tom Crockett was full of plans, talking of crops and the rich soil.

The next day Morton Harper was gone. Where he had gone to Sharon did not know, but suddenly in the middle of the morning she realized he was not among them. The black mare was gone, too.

Shortly after noon she saw him riding into town, and behind him came six wagons, loaded with boxes and barrels. They drew up before the store and the saloon.

He saw her watching and loped the mare over to her door.

"See?" he said, waving a hand. "The supplies! Everything we need for the coming year, but if we need more, I can send a rider back to the fort after more."

"Then you had them coming from the fort?" she asked. "You were farsighted."

He laughed, glancing at her quickly. "Well, I thought these things would sell in the mining camps out in California, but this is much, much better."

In spite of herself, Sharon was disturbed. All day as she went about her work, the thought kept recurring that those supplies offered a clue to something, yet she could find nothing on which to fasten her suspicions. Why should their arrival disturb her so much? Was it unusual that the man should start several wagonloads of supplies to California?

Pagones stopped by the spring to get a drink. He smiled at her, pushing back his hat from a sweating brow.

"Lots of work, ma'am. Your pa's sure getting in his plowing in a hurry. He'll have his seed in before the rest of us have started."

"Pag, how do the supplies reach the goldfields in California?" Sharon said suddenly.

He looked up over his second dipper of water. "Why, by sea, of course! Much cheaper that way. Why do you ask? Something botherin' you?"

"Not exactly. Only ever since those wagons came in this morning I've been wondering about them. Morton said he had started them for California, but thought they would sell better here. Why would he send them to California to sell when they can get supplies by sea?"

"Might mean a little ready money," Pagones suggested. He hung the dipper on a shrub. "Now that you mention it, it does seem kind of strange."

The expected trouble from Hardy Bishop did not materialize as soon as she expected. No other riders came near, although several times she noticed men, far out in the valley. All of Morton Harper's promises seemed to be coming true. He had said Bishop would not bother them.

Yet all was not going too smoothly. The last wagons had brought a load of liquor, and several of the men hung around the saloon most of the time. Purcell was there every evening, although by day he worked on his place. Pete Zapata was always there when not off on one of his lonely rides, and the teamsters who had brought the wagons to Kies's Store had remained, loitering about, doing nothing at all, but always armed. One of them had become the bartender.

During all this time, her work had kept Sharon close to the house and there had been no time for riding. Time and again she found herself going to the door and looking down toward the cluster of buildings that was fast becoming a thriving little village. And just as often she looked back up the trail they had followed when first coming into Poplar Canyon.

Not even to herself would she admit what she was looking for. She refused to admit that she longed to see the steel-dust stallion and its somber, lonely rider. She had overheard him say he would not leave, yet where was he?

The sound of a horse's hoofs in the trail outside brought her to the cabin door. It was Mary Pagones, daughter of George Pagones, who had long since proved himself one of the most stable men in the wagon train.

"Come on, Sharon—let's ride! I'm beginning to feel cramped with staying down here all the time."

Sharon needed no urging, and in a few minutes they were riding out of the settlement toward the upper reaches of the canyon.

"Have you seen that Pete Zapata staring at the women the way he does?" Mary asked. "He fairly gives me the creeps!"

"Somebody said he was a gunman," Sharon ventured.

"I wouldn't doubt it!" Mary was an attractive girl, always gay and full of laughter. The freckles over her nose were an added attraction rather than otherwise. "Dud doesn't like him at all. Says he can't see why Harper keeps him around."

As they rode out of Poplar Canyon, an idea suddenly occurred to Sharon, and without voicing it she turned her mare toward their old encampment, but as they burst through the last line of trees, disappointment flooded over her. There was no sign of Rock Bannon.

They had gone almost a mile further, when suddenly Mary reined in sharply.

"Why, look at that!" She pointed. "Wagon tracks coming out of that canyon! Who in the world would ever take a wagon in there?"

Sharon looked at them and then at the canyon. It was narrow mouthed, the only entrance into a wild, rugged region of crags and ravines, heavily forested and forbidding. Riding closer, she looked down. The wagon tracks were coming from the canyon, not going into it. She studied the mountains thoughtfully. Then, wheeling her horse, with Mary following, she rode out on their own trail. All the tracks she had observed were old.

She looked at Mary, and Mary returned the glance, a puzzled

frown gathering around her eyes. "What's the matter?" Mary asked. "Is something wrong?"

"I don't know," Sharon said. "There are no tracks here since we came over the trail, but there are tracks coming out of that canyon!"

Mary's eyes widened. "You mean those wagons of Harper's? Then they must have come over a different trail."

That wasn't what Sharon was thinking, but she just shook her head. "Don't say anything about it," she said.

They rode on. That wall of mountains would not offer a trail through, and if it did, where would it go? If it joined the Overland Trail to the north, it would still be almost twice as far as by the trail they had come, and through one of the most rugged sections she had ever seen. Suddenly, she knew. Those wagons had been here before. They had been back there, in some remote canyon, waiting.

Waiting for what? For a town to begin? But that was absurd. No one had known the town would begin until a few hours before. No one, unless it had been Morton Harper.

# IV

On, through hills of immeasurable beauty, the two girls rode. Great, rocky escarpments that towered to the skies and mighty crags, breasting their saw-toothed edges against the wind. Long, steep hillsides clad with alder and birch or rising to great, dark-feathered crests of lodgepole pine mingled here and there with an occasional fir.

Along the lower hillsides and along the mountain draws were quaking aspen, mountain mahogany, and hawthorn. They had come to the edge of a grove of poplar when they saw the horseman. They both saw him at once, and something in his surreptitious manner brought them to a halt. They both recognized him at the same instant.

"Sharon," Mary said, "it's that Zapata!"

"Ssh! He'll hear us!" Sharon held her breath. Suddenly, she was frightened at the idea of being found out here, even with Mary along, by Zapata. But Zapata seemed to have no eyes for them or even their direction. He was riding by very slowly, not over fifty yards away, carrying his rifle in his hands and watching something in the valley below that was beyond their vision.

Yet even as they watched he slid suddenly from the saddle and crouched upon some rocks on the rim. Then he lifted his rifle and fired!

"What's he shooting at?" Mary asked in a whisper.

"I don't know. A deer, probably. Let's get home!" Turning their horses, they rode back through the trees and hit the trail back to the settlement.

All the next day Sharon thought about that wagon trail out of the mountains. Several times she started to speak to her father, but he was preoccupied, lost in plans for his new home, and thinking of nothing but it. Later in the day she saw Dud Kitchen riding over. He reined in and slid from the saddle.

"Howdy, Sharon! Sure glad to see you all! We been talkin' some, Mary and I, about us gettin' up a sort of party. Seems like Satterfield plays a fiddle, and we thought we might have a dance, sort of. Liven things up a mite."

"That's a good idea, Dud," Sharon agreed. She looked up at him suddenly. "Dud, did Mary tell you anything about that wagon trail we saw?"

His blue eyes sharpened and he ran his fingers back through his corn-colored hair. "Yeah," he said, "she did."

"Dud, it looks to me like those wagons were out here before we were, just waiting. It begins to look like somebody planned to have us stop here."

"You mean Mort? But what would he do that for? What could he gain? And even if he did, you've got to admit it's a good place."

"Yes, it is, but just the same I don't like it."

Her father was walking toward them with George Pagones and Cap Mulholland.

"What's this you young folks figurin' to do?" Cap said, grinning. "Hear we're havin' us a party."

Her answer was drowned by a sudden rattle of horses' hoofs, and she saw three men swing down the canyon trail. When they saw the group before the house, they reined in. One of them was Red, the man who had called on them the first day. Another was—her breath caught—Rock Bannon!

"Howdy!" Red said. He looked down at the men and then recognized Cap. "Seen anything of a young feller, 'bout twenty or so, ridin' a bay pony?"

"Why, no," Cap said. "Can't say as I have. What's the trouble?"

"He's Wes Freeman, who rides for us. He was huntin' strays over this way yesterday and he never came back. We figured maybe he was hurt somehow."

"No, we haven't seen him," Crockett said.

Dud Kitchen was grinning at Rock. "Shucks, man! We figured you had left the country. What you doin'?"

Bannon grinned. "I'm ridin' for Hardy Bishop," he said. "Went over there right after I left you folks."

"What made you think your man might have come over here?"
Pagones asked. "Was he ridin' thisaway?"

"As a matter of fact," Red said, "he was ridin' back northeast of
here. Pretty rough country, except for one canyon that's got some
good grass in it."

The third man was short, thickset, and tough. "Hurry up, Red!"
he said. "Why beat around the brush. Tell 'em!"

"All right," Red said. "I'll just do that, Bat!" He looked down at
the little group before the house. "Fact of the matter is, Wes's horse
come in about sundown yesterday, come in with blood on the
saddle. We backtrailed the horse and we found Wes. We found him
in the open valley we spoke of. He was dead. He'd been shot
through the back and knocked off his horse. Then whoever shot him
had followed him up and killed him with a hunting knife."

Zapata! Sharon's eyes widened, and she looked around to see Dud
staring at her, gray faced. She had seen Zapata shoot!

In stunned silence the men stared up at the three riders. Rock
broke the silence.

"You can see what this means?" he said sternly. "Wes was a
mighty nice boy. I hadn't known him as long as these men, but he
seemed to be a right fine feller. Now he's been murdered—drygulched.
That's going to mean trouble."

"But why come to us?" Cap protested. "Sure, you don't believe
we—"

"We don't believe!" Bat broke in harshly. "We know! We trailed
three riders down out of those hills! Three from here! Wes was my
ridin' partner. He was a durned good boy. I'm goin' to see the man
who done that."

"Turn around."

The voice was cold and deadly. As one person, they turned. Pete
Zapata, his guns low slung on his hips, was staring at the three
riders. Flanking him were two men with shotguns, both of them
from the teamsters' crowd. The other two were Lamport and Purcell
of the wagon train.

Behind them, and a little to one side, was Morton Harper. He was
wearing two guns.

"Get out of here!" Harper snapped harshly. "Don't come around
here again, aimin' to make trouble. That's all you came for, and you
know it! You've been looking for an excuse to start something so you
could get us out of here, take our homes away from us. Now turn
your horses and get out!"

His eyes riveted on Rock Bannon. "As for you, Bannon," he said
sharply, "you're a traitor! You rode with us, and now you've gone
over to them. I think you're the cause of all this trouble. If a man of

yours is dead, I think it would be a good idea if these friends of yours backtrailed you. Now get moving, all of you!"

"This is a bad mistake, Harper," Rock said evenly. "I'm speaking of it before all these people." He nodded at the group in front of the house. "Bishop was inclined to let 'em stay, despite the fact that he was afraid they'd bring more after them. He listened to me and didn't run you off. Now you're asking for it."

"He listened to *you!*" Harper's voice was alive with contempt. "You? A trail runner?"

Red looked quickly at Rock and started to speak. Bannon silenced him with a gesture.

"We'll ride, Harper, but we want the man—or men—who killed Wes. And we want him delivered to us by sundown tomorrow! If not, we'll come and get him."

Turning abruptly, they started away. Wheeling, Zapata grabbed a shotgun from one of the teamsters. "I'll fix him, the bluffer!"

"Hold it!" Pagones had a six-shooter and was staring across it at Zapata. "We don't shoot men in the back."

For an instant, they glared at each other. Then Harper interposed. "Put it down, Pete. Let them go."

He looked around. "There'll be a meeting at the saloon tonight. All of you be there."

When they had all gone, Tom Crockett shook his head sadly. "More trouble, and all because of that Bannon. I almost wish we'd let him die on the trail."

"It wasn't Bannon, Father," Sharon said. "Those men were right, I think. Mary and I saw Zapata yesterday. Two of the horses they trailed back here were ours. The other one was his. We were not fifty yards away from him when he fired that shot. We didn't see what he shot at, but it must have been that man."

Crockett's face was gray. "Are you sure, Sharon? Are you positive?"

"Yes, I am."

"Then we must give him up," he said sadly. "If he killed, he should suffer for it. Especially, if he killed that way." He got up and reached for his hat. "I must go and tell Morton. He'll want to know."

She put a hand on his arm. "Father, you mustn't. Don't say anything to him until you've told the others. Pagones, I mean, and Cap. I'm afraid."

"Afraid of what? Morton Harper is a fine man. When he knows what happened, he'll want something done himself."

Putting on his hat he started across the road for the cluster of buildings. Only for an instant did she hesitate. Then she swung around and ran to her horse, standing saddled and bridled, as she had planned to ride over to Mary's. Dud Kitchen would be there, and Pagones.

They were sitting at the table when she burst into the room.

"Please come!" she said when she had explained. "I'm afraid!"

Without a word, they got up and buckled on their guns. It was only a few hundred yards to the saloon, and they arrived just a few moments after Tom Crockett had walked up to Harper.

"Morton, my daughter and Mary Pagones saw Zapata fire that shot yesterday," Crockett was saying. "I think we should surrender him to Bishop. We don't want to have any part in any killings."

Harper's face hardened and he started to speak. Zapata, overhearing his name, stepped to the door, his hand on a gun. Then Harper's face softened a little, and he shrugged.

"I'm afraid they were mistaken," he said carelessly. "You're being needlessly excited. Probably Pete was up that way, for he rides around a good deal, the same as the girls do. But shoot a man in the back? He wouldn't do it."

"Oh, but he did," Dud Kitchen interrupted. "What the girls say is true."

"You call me a liar?" Harper turned on him, his face suddenly flushed with anger.

"No," Kitchen replied stiffly, his face paling. "I ain't callin' no man a liar, 'specially no man who come over the trail with me, but I know what I seen with my own eyes.

"Mary, she done told me about that, and I'll admit I figured there was something wrong with what she said, so I went up and backtrailed 'em. I didn't have no idea about no killin' then, but I trailed the girls, and then I trailed Pete.

"Pete Zapata stalked that cowhand for two miles before he got the shot he wanted. I went over every inch of his trail. He was fixin' to kill him. Then I trailed him down to the body. I seen where he wiped his knife on the grass, and I seen some of them brown sort of cigarettes he smokes. Pete Zapata killed that man, sure as I'm alive!"

Zapata had walked, catfooted, to the edge of the wide plank porch in front of the saloon. He stood there now, staring at Dud.

"Trailed me, huh?" His hand swept down in a streaking movement before Dud could as much as move. His gun bellowed, and Dud Kitchen turned halfway around and dropped into the dust.

"Why, Mort!" Crockett's face was gray. "What does this mean? I—"

"You'd better all go back to your homes," Harper said sternly. "If Pete Zapata shot that man, and I don't admit for a minute that he did, he had a reason for it. As for this shooting here, Kitchen was wearing a gun, and he accused Zapata of murder."

Pagones's face was hard as stone. Two of the teamsters stood on the porch with shotguns. To have lifted a hand would have been to die.

"That settles it," Pagones said. "You can have your town! I'm leaving!"

"I reckon that goes for me, too," Crockett said sadly.

"I'm afraid you can't go," Harper said smoothly. There was a glint of triumph in his eyes. "My friend, John Kies, has lent you all money and supplies. Unless you can repay him what you owe, you'll have to stay until you have made a crop. California is a long ways away, and he couldn't be sure of collecting, there.

"Besides," he added, "Indians have rustled some of our stock. I have been meaning to tell you. Most of your oxen are gone." He shrugged. "But why worry? Stay here. This land is good, and these little difficulties will iron themselves out. There are always troubles when a new community begins. In a few years all this will be over and there will be children born here, a church built, and many homes."

Dud Kitchen was not dead. In the Pagones' house, Mary sat beside his bed. Satterfield had removed the bullet, and he sat at the kitchen table, drinking coffee.

"He's got him a chance," Satterfield said. "A good chance. I'm no doctor, just picked up a mite when I was in that Mexican War, but I think he'll come through."

Pagones, his heavy head thrust forward on his thick neck, stared into the fire, somber, brooding. He turned and looked at Satterfield and Crockett.

"Well," he said, "it looks bad. Looks like we're in a fight whether we want it or not. Hardy Bishop hasn't bothered us none, even after all of Mort Harper's preaching about him. Now Zapata has killed one of his men."

"That Red feller," Satterfield muttered, half to himself, "he don't look like no man to have trouble with. Nor Bat, neither!"

"Where does Rock stand?" Pagones demanded. "That's what I'm wonderin'."

"Said he was ridin' for Bishop," Satterfield replied. "That's plain enough."

"If we'd listened to him, this wouldn't have happened," Mary said.

There was no reply to that. The three men stood quiet, listening to Dud Kitchen's heavy breathing. The rap at the door startled them, and they looked up to see Rock Bannon standing there.

Sharon drew in her breath, and she watched him wide-eyed as he stepped into the room and closed the door after him. Hat in hand, his eyes strayed from them to the wounded man lying in the bed.

How tall he was! And his shoulders had seemed to fill the door when he entered. He wore buckskin trousers tucked into hand-tooled star boots and a checked shirt with a buckskin jacket, Mexican fashion, over it. On his hips were two big dragoon Colts in tied-down holsters.

"He hurt bad?" he asked softly.

"Yes, but Jim Satterfield says he's got a chance," Mary said.

Rock Bannon turned to look at them. "Well," he said, "you saw me ride in here today. You know I'm riding for Bishop. From what's happened, I reckon you know that war's been declared. You've got to make up your mind whose side you are on. I talked Hardy Bishop into lettin' you stay on against his better judgment. He was all for runnin' you off pronto, not because he had anything against you, but because he could see settlers gettin' a toehold in his domain.

"Now one of our boys has been killed. Even Bishop might have trouble holdin' the boys back after that. I've talked to 'em, and they want the guilty man. They don't care about nobody else. What happens now is up to you."

"Not necessarily," Pagones objected. "We'll call a vote on it."

"You know how that'll go," Bannon objected. "Ten of you came in here with Mort Harper. Then he brought in Kies and Zapata. Now he's got other men. Supposin' you three vote to turn over the guilty man. How many others will vote that way? Cap may think right, but Cap will vote pretty much as Harper says. So will Purcell and Lamport. Anyway you look at it, the vote is going to be to fight rather than turn Zapata over."

"No way to be sure of that," Satterfield objected. "Harper may decide to turn him over."

Bannon turned, his temper flaring. "Haven't you learned anything on this trip? Harper's using you. He brought you down here for his own reasons. He's out to steal Bishop's Valley from Hardy—that's what he wants. You're just a bunch of dupes!"

"You got any proof of that?" Crockett demanded.

"Only my eyes," Rock admitted, "but that's enough. He owns every one of you, lock, stock, and barrel. I heard about that matter of you being in debt to Kies. Don't you suppose he planned all that?"

The door opened and Mulholland came in; with him was Collins. Cap's face flushed when he saw Rock.

"You'd better light out. If Pete Zapata sees you, he'll kill you."

"That might not be so easy," Bannon said sharply. "All men don't die easy. Nor do they knuckle under to the first smooth talker who sells them a bill of goods."

Mulholland glared at him. "He promised us places, and we got 'em. Who's this Bishop to run us off? If it comes to war, then we'll fight."

"And die for Morton Harper? Do you think he'll let you keep what you have if he gets control of this valley? He'll run you out of here without a penny. You're his excuse, that's all. If the law ever comes into this, he can always say that Bishop used violence to stop free American citizens from settling on the land."

"That's just what he's doin'," Cap said. "If he wants war he can have it!"

"Then I'd better go," Rock said. "I came here hopin' to make some peace talk. It looks like Zapata declared war for you. Now you've got to fight Mort Harper's war for him."

"You were one of us once," Pagones said. "You helped us on the trail. Why can't you help us now?"

Rock Bannon looked up. His eyes hesitated on Sharon's face and then swept on. "Because you're on the wrong side," he said simply.

Sharon looked up and her eyes flashed.

"But you were one of us," she protested. "You should be with us now. Don't you understand loyalty?"

"I was never one of you after Mort Harper came," he said. Sharon flushed under his gaze. "Whatever I might have been, Harper took away from me. I ain't a smooth-talkin' man. Guess I never rightly learned to say all I feel, but sometimes them that says little feels a sight more."

He put one hand on the latch. "As for loyalty, my first loyalty's to Hardy Bishop," he said.

"But how could that be?" Sharon protested.

"He's my father," Rock said quietly, and then he stepped quickly and silently out the door.

"His father!" Pagones stared after him. "Well, I'll be danged!"

"That don't cut any ice with me," Mulholland said. "Nor his talk. I got the place I want, and I aim to keep it. Harper says there ain't any way they can drive us off. He says we've got guns enough to hold our own, and this canyon ain't so easy to attack. I'm glad it's comin' to a showdown. We might as well get it over."

"All I want is to get to work," Collins said stubbornly. "I got a sight of it ahead, so if that Bishop aims to drive me off, I wish he'd come and get it over with."

"All that talk about him usin' us," Satterfield said uneasily. "That didn't make sense!"

"Of course not!" Cap said hotly. "Bannon was against everything we tried to do, right from the start. He just never had no use for Mort Harper, that was all."

"Maybe there is something to what he says," Sharon interposed.

Cap glanced around irritably. "Beggin' your pardon, Sharon. This is man's talk."

"I'm not so sure," she flashed. "We women came across the plains with you! If we fight, my father may die. That makes it important to me, and if you think I'm going to stand by and let my home be turned into a shambles, you're wrong."

Her father started to speak, but she stepped forward. "Bannon said Harper was using you. Well, maybe he is and maybe he isn't, but there are a few things I'd like you to think about, because I've been thinking about them.

"Did Mort Harper look for this townsite? No, he rode right to it, and to me that means he had planned it before! What affair was it of his which trail we took? Yet he persuaded us, and we came down here. Who got us to stay? It was him! I'll admit, I wanted to stay, and most of us did, but I'm wondering if he didn't count on that. And what about those wagons of supplies that turned up just at the right time?"

"Why, they just follered him on from the fort," Mulholland protested.

"Did they?" Sharon asked. "Go up and look at the trail. Mary and I looked at it, and no wagons have come over it since we did. Anyway, would he let those wagons come across that Indian country without more protection than they had? Those wagons were already here, waiting for us. They were back up in a canyon northeast of the trail."

"I don't believe that!" Collins said.

"Go look for yourselves then," Sharon said.

"You sound like you were against us," Cap said. "Whose side are you on, anyway?"

"I'm on the side of the wagon train people, and you know it," she said. "But a lot of this doesn't look too good to me. The first day we were here I rode down in the valley with Mort, and he said something that had me wondering, something about taking it for himself."

"Don't make sense," Cap said stubbornly. "Anyway, womenfolks don't know about things like this."

Sharon was angry. In spite of herself, and knowing her anger only made Cap more stubborn, she said:

"You didn't think there were any Indians, either. You took Mort's word for that. If it hadn't been for Bannon, we'd all have been killed."

She turned quickly and went out of the cabin. Swinging into the saddle, she started across toward her own cabin. It was dark, and she could see the light in the saloon and the lights in Collins's blacksmith shop, where his wife and little Davy would be waiting for him to return.

Angry, she paid little attention where she was going until suddenly a horseman loomed in the dark near her. "Howdy!" he said, swinging alongside.

From his voice and bulk she knew him at once as Hy Miller, a big teamster who sometimes served as relief bartender. He had been drinking and his breath was thick.

She tried to push on, but he reached out and grabbed her wrist. "Don't be in no such hurry," he said, leering at her in the dimness. "I want to have a bit of palaver with you!"

"Well, I don't want to talk to you!" she said angrily. She tried to jerk her wrist away, but he only tightened his grip. Then he pulled her to him and slid his other arm around her waist. She struggled, and her mare sidestepped, pulling her from the saddle.

Miller dropped her and then slid from his own horse and grabbed her before she could escape. "I'll learn you a thing or two!" he said hoarsely. "It's about time you settlers were learnin' who's runnin' this shebang!"

What happened next, Sharon scarcely knew. She was suddenly wrenched from Miller's arms. She heard the crack of a blow, and Miller went down into the grass underfoot.

"Run for the house!" It was Bannon's voice. "Quick!"

Miller came up with an oath, and she saw him charge. Bannon smashed his left into the big teamster's mouth and staggered him, but the man leaped in, swinging with both hands. There was no chance for science or skill. In the dimness the two men fought like animals, tooth and nail, yet Bannon kept slamming his right to the bigger man's stomach. The teamster coughed and gasped, and then Rock swung a right to his chin that staggered him, and followed it up with a right and a left. Miller went down, and Bannon stooped and grasped his shirt collar in his left hand.

Holding the man at arm's length in a throttling grip, Bannon smashed him in the face again and again. Then he struck him in the body and hurled him to the ground.

Sharon, wide-eyed and panting, still stood there. "Get to your house," Bannon snapped. "Tell your father to go armed, always. This is only the beginning!"

As she fled, somebody behind her said, "Hey, what's goin' on here?"

Behind her, there was a pound of horse's hoofs, and she knew Rock was gone. Swiftly, when she reached the house, she stripped the saddle from the mare and turned her in the corral. Then she went into the house and lighted the lamp. A few minutes later, her father came in. She told him all that had happened.

He stood there, resting his fists on the table. Then he straightened.

"Honey," he said, "I'm afraid I did wrong to stop here. I wish now I'd gone on with Bob Sprague and the others. They'd be most to California by now. I'm afraid—I'm afraid!"

## V

Rock Bannon stopped that night in a line cabin six miles west of Poplar and across the valley. When morning came, he was just saddling up when Bat Chavez rode in. With him were Johnny Stark and Lew Murray. All three were armed.

Bat grinned at him. Then his eyes fell on the skinned knuckles, and he chuckled.

"Looks like you had some action."

"A little," Rock said and then explained briefly. "You watch yourselves," he said, "and stick together. That outfit's out for trouble."

"All I want's a shot at Zapata," Bat said harshly. "I'll kill him if I get it."

Rock mounted and rode north toward the ranch house. No act of his could avert trouble now. He had hoped to convince the settlers who came with the wagon train that they should break away from Mort Harper.

That would draw the lines plainly—the ranch against the land-grabbers. That Mulholland was an honest if stupid man, he knew. The others of the train, to a man, were honest, but some of them, such as Purcell and Lamport, were firm adherents of Harper's and believed in him. This belief they combined with a dislike of Rock Bannon.

It had been a hard task to persuade Hardy Bishop to let them stay. The old man was a fire-eater, and he knew what it would mean to let settlers get a toehold in his rich valley. Once in, they would encroach more and more on his best range until he was crowded back to nothing. Only his affection for Rock had convinced him, and the fact that he had gleaned from Rock's talk that among the settlers was a girl.

Rock Bannon knew what the old man was thinking. Lonely, hard-bitten, and tough, Bishop was as affectionate as many big bearlike men are. His heart was as big and warm as himself, and from the day he had taken Rock Bannon in when the boy had been orphaned at six, when Kaw Indians had killed his parents, Bishop had lived as much for Bannon as for his ranch. Now, more than anything, he wanted Rock settled, married, and living on the broad acres of Bishop's Valley.

It had been that as much as anything that had brought him around to Rock's way of thinking when Rock had planned to go east to Council Bluffs. Secretly, he had hoped the boy would come back with a wife; certainly, there were no women around Bishop's Valley but an occasional squaw. He had never seen this girl with the wagon train, but he had gleaned more than a little from Rock's casual comments, and what he heard pleased him.

Hardy Bishop was a big man, weighing nearly three hundred pounds now that he was heavy around the middle. Yet in the days of his raw youth he had tipped the beam at no less than two hundred and fifty pounds. On his hip even the big dragoon Colts looked insignificant, and he was scarcely less fast than Rock.

Seated deep in a cowhide-covered chair, he looked up when Rock came in, and grinned. He was just filling his pipe. There was a skinned place on Bannon's cheekbone, and his knuckles were raw.

"Trouble, you've had," Bishop said, his deep voice filling the room. "Been over to look at them settlers again? Think they killed Wes?"

"Not the settlers," Rock said. "One of the men with them."

He sat down on the butt of a log and quietly outlined the whole situation, explaining about Harper, Zapata, and the teamster.

"They had that stuff cached in the hills," Rock went on. "Red Lunney spotted it some time back. There were about a dozen men holed up back there with a lot of supplies, too many for themselves. He kept an eye on them, but they didn't wander around and made no trouble, so he left them alone.

"Evidently, Mort Harper had them planted there. The wagon train, as near as I can figure, he planned to use as a blind in case the government got into this. He could always say they were honest settlers looking for homes, and the government would be inclined to favor them. What he really wants is Bishop's Valley!"

"He'll have a time gettin' it!" Bishop said grimly. "I'll bank on that. I fought Indians all over these hills, but this here valley I bought fair and square from old War Cloud. We never had no Indian trouble until lately, when the wagon trains started comin' through. Those Mormons, they had the right idea. Treat Indians good, pay for what you get, and no shootin' Indians for the fun of it, like some folks do!

"Why, Rock! I trapped all over these here mountains. Lived with Indians, trapped with them, hunted with them, slept in their tepees. I never had trouble with them. I was through this country with Wilson Price Hunt's Astorians when I was no more'n sixteen, but a man growed. I was with John Day in this country after that, and he saw more of it than any other man.

"Took me two years to drive these cattle in here. First ever seen in this country! I drove them up from Santa Fe in six or seven of the roughest drives any man ever saw, with Indians doin' most of my drivin' for me. They said I was crazy then, but now my cattle run these hills and they eat this valley grass until their sides are fit to bust. One of these days you'll start drivin' these cattle east. Mark my words, there'll come a day they'll make you rich. And then some whippersnapper like this Harper—why!"

He rubbed his jaw irritably and then looked up at Rock. "You see that girl? That Crockett girl?"

"Uh-huh," Rock admitted. "I did."

"Why not stop this here cayusin' around and bring her home, son? Time you took a wife. Ain't no sense in a man runnin' loose too long. I did, and then hadn't my wife very long before she died. Fine girl, too."

"Hardy," Rock said suddenly, calling him by his first name as he had since Bishop first took him in hand as a child, "I don't want war with those people. They are askin' for it, and that Mulholland is simple enough to be led by the nose by Harper. Why don't you let me go get Zapata? I'll take him on myself. In fact," he added grimly, "I'd like to! Then we can take some of the boys, get Harper and his teamsters, and start them out of here."

"Separate the sheep from the goats, eh?" Bishop looked at him quizzically. "All right, son. I've gone along with you this long. You take the boys, you get that Harper out of there and start him back for Laramie.

"As for Zapata, do what you like. I've seen some men with guns, and you're the fastest thing I ever did see, and the best shot. But don't leave him alive. If I had my way, we'd string every one of 'em to a poplar tree, and right quick."

The old man grinned briefly at Bannon, leaned back, and lighted his pipe. So far as he was concerned, the subject was closed.

Bat Chavez was a man who made his own plans and went his own way. Loyal to the greatest degree, he obeyed Rock Bannon and Hardy Bishop without question. They were his bosses, and he liked and respected them both. However, he had another loyalty, and that was to the memory of Wes Freeman.

He and Wes had ridden together, hunted together, fought Indians together. Wes was younger, and Bat Chavez had always considered himself the other's sponsor, as well as his friend. Now Wes was dead, and to Bat Chavez that opened a feud that could only be settled by blood.

Johnny Stark and Lew Murray were like-minded. Both were young, hardy, and accustomed to live by the gun. They understood men like Zapata. Of the three, perhaps the only one who rated anything like an even break with Zapata was the half-Mexican, half-Irish Chavez. However, no one of them would have hesitated to draw on sight.

They weren't looking for trouble, but they were ready. In that frame of mind they started down the valley to move some of the cattle away from the mouth of Poplar Canyon. No one of them knew what he was riding into, and had they known, no one of them would have turned back. . . .

Mort Harper, seated in his own living quarters in the back of the saloon, was disturbed. Things had not gone as he had planned. Secure in his familiarity with men of Hardy Bishop's type, he had been positive that the arrival of the wagon train and the beginning of their settlement would precipitate trouble. He had counted on a sudden attack by Bishop and perhaps the killing of one or more of the settlers. Nothing more, he knew, would have been required to unite them against the common enemy. Peace loving they might be, but they were men of courage and men who believed in independence and equal rights for all. Typically American, they wouldn't take any pushing around.

On his knowledge of their character and that of Bishop he had built his plans. Over a year before he had seen Bishop's Valley, and the sight had aroused a lust for possession that he had never known could live within him. Since that day he had lived for but one thing: to possess Bishop's Valley, regardless of cost.

It was beyond the reach of law. Few people in the country had any idea the valley existed or that it had been settled. His first thought was to ride in with a strong band of outlaws recruited from the offscourings of the border towns and take the place by main force, but times, he knew, were changing.

Morton Harper was shrewd enough to understand that the fight might arouse government inquiry. Fremont and Carson knew this country, and it was possible the Army might soon move into it. It would behoove him to have justice on his side.

The wagon trains offered that chance. From the first he had seen what a good chance it was. At the fort he watched them go through, and he saw the weariness of the women and children, the haggard lines of the men's faces. The novelty of the trip was over, and miles upon miles remained before they could reach Oregon. Now, if he could but get some of them into the valley country, he believed he could persuade them, by some method, to stay on. With that end in view, he watched until he saw the wagon train he wanted.

Those who were led by able and positive men he avoided. He talked to a number, but when he encountered Cap Mulholland, he was quick to perceive his opportunity.

In his visit to the camp he noted that Tom Crockett was a mild, tolerant man, friendly, and interested mainly in finding a new home and getting a plow into the ground. Pagones was a strong, able man, but not outspoken, nor likely to push himself into a position of leadership.

Pike Purcell and Lamport were honest, able men, but ignorant and alike in their dislike of Rock Bannon. Lamport, who was unmarried and thoroughly undesirable, had fancied himself for an inside track with Sharon Crockett until Bannon joined the train.

As Rock Bannon was constantly with her, first as a wounded man needing care and later as a rider, Lamport grew jealous. Purcell, married to a nagging wife, had looked after Sharon with desire. His own dislike of Bannon stemmed from the same source, but grew even more bitter because Pike sensed Bannon was the better man. Pike hated him for it.

Mort Harper was quick to curry the favor of these two. He talked with them, flattered them in subtle fashion, and bought them drinks. He learned that Purcell was desperately hard up and lent him some money. He gave Lamport a gun he had admired.

The only flaw in the picture had been Rock Bannon, and in Rock, Harper was quick to recognize a formidable and dangerous antagonist. He also realized he had an excellent weapon in the veiled enmity of Purcell and Lamport.

His plans had gone ahead very well until an attack by Bishop failed to materialize. Despite himself, he was disturbed. Would the old man really let them settle there? He caused a few cattle to be killed for meat and left evidence about. That Rock Bannon had found the remains of the slaughtered cattle and buried them, he could not know. The expected attack failed to come and he sensed a falling away from him on the part of the settlers.

The only way he could hope to get the valley was by precipitating open warfare, killing all of the Bishop forces, and taking possession. Then in due time he could eliminate the settlers themselves and reign supreme, possessor of one of the largest cattle empires in the country.

Pete Zapata was under no orders to kill, but the fact that he had killed Wes Freeman fell in line with Harper's plans. Yet he could sense the disaffection among the settlers. Crockett and Pagones could be a strong force against him if they became stubborn. Something was needed to align them firmly on his side.

That chance came, as he had hoped it would come. With Pete Zapata, Hy Miller, Pike Purcell, Lamport, and Collins, he was riding down into the valley when they saw Bat Chavez and the two Bishop riders approaching. Had Harper continued with his party along the trail on which they had started, the paths of the two groups would not have intersected, but Harper reined in and waited.

Chavez wasn't the man to ride around trouble. In Lew Murray and Johnny Stark he had two companions who had never ridden around anything that even resembled trouble. With guns loosened in holsters they rode on.

"Howdy!" Bat Chavez said. His eyes swung and fastened on Pete Zapata. "Where you ridin'?"

"Who's askin'?" Purcell demanded truculently. "We go where we want."

"Not on this range, you don't! You stick to your valley. This here's Bishop range."

"He own everything?" Miller demanded. "We ride where we please!"

"Looks like you been ridin' where somebody else pleased," Johnny Stark said, grinning. "In fact, that face looks like somebody rid all over you with spikes in his boots."

Miller's face flamed. "There was three of 'em!" he snapped. "You couldn't do it. I think it's time we taught you Bishop riders a lesson, anyways."

"You mean," Chavez demanded insolently, "like that murderin' Zapata killed Wes Freeman—in the back?"

Zapata's hand flashed for his gun, and Chavez was scarcely slower. Only the jerk of Zapata's horse's head saved him, as the horse took the bullet right through the head. It leaped straight up into the air, jerking Zapata's gun and spoiling his aim.

There was a sudden flurry of gunshots, and Mort Harper was quick to sense his chance. He drew his six-shooter and calmly shot Collins through the back.

The attack broke as quickly as it had begun. Zapata's horse had leaped and then hit the ground, stone dead. Thrown from the horse, Zapata lost his gun and sprawled in the grass, showing no desire to get up and join the fight or even hunt for his gun.

Outnumbered, and with Murray shot through the leg, the Bishop riders drew off. Purcell had been burned along the cheek, and Miller's horse was killed, so the battle ended after only a few seconds with two horses and one man dead. In the excitement, only Mort Harper had seen the flare of pained astonishment and accusation in Collins's eyes.

The blacksmith's mouth refused to shape words, and he died there in the grass. Harper looked down at him, a faint smile on his face. Collins had been a popular man, quiet and well liked. This would do what all Harper's other plans had failed to do.

"Collins got it?" Pike stood over him, his hard face saddened. "He was a good man." Collins was the only man in the wagon train Pike Purcell had known before the trip began. They had come through the war together.

"Might as well bury him, I guess," Mort said.

Pike looked up. "No, we'll tote him back home. His widow will be wantin' to see him. Reckon it'll go hard with her."

Mort Harper's lips thinned, but there was nothing more he could say without arousing suspicion. Silently, the little cavalcade started back. Collins's body was tied to Pike's horse, and Pike walked alongside, trailed by Zapata and Miller.

For two days ominous quiet hung over the town of Poplar. Collins had been buried, and the faces of the settlers as they gathered about to see his body lowered into the grave proved to Harper how right he had been. No longer was there any doubt or hesitation. Now they were in the fight. He had walked back from that grave filled with triumph. Only a few days longer, and then he would begin the war in earnest.

Tom Crockett was a quiet man, but his face was stern and hard as he walked back home beside Sharon.

"Well, we tried to avoid it, but now it's war," he said. "I think the sooner we have some action the better."

Sharon said nothing, but her heart was heavy within her. She no longer thought of Mort Harper. His glamour had faded, and always now, there was but one man in her thoughts, the tall, shy, hesitant Rock Bannon.

She always marveled that a man so hard, so sure of himself when with men, horses, or guns, could be so quiet and diffident with women. As a matter of fact, Rock Bannon had never seen any woman but an Indian squaw until he was eighteen years old, in Santa Fe.

Rock Bannon had never talked to a woman until he was twenty. In his life until now, and he was twenty-seven, he had probably talked to no more than six or seven women or girls.

With deepening sadness and pain, she realized that the killing of Collins had done all they had hoped to avoid. There would be war now, and knowing her father as she did, she knew the unrelenting stubbornness in him once he was resolved upon a course.

She had seen him like this before. He always sought to avoid trouble, always saw the best in people, yet when the battle line was laid down, no man would stay there longer than Tom Crockett.

Only one man was silent on the walk back from the grave. Dud Kitchen, weak and pale from his own narrow escape, was out for the first time. He was very tired, and he was glad when he was back in the Pagones' house and could lie down and rest. He was up too soon; he knew that, but Collins had been his friend. Now, lying alone in the gathering darkness and hearing the low mutter of men's voices in the other room, he was sorry he had gone.

He had gone over to the Collins house to see his old friend once before he was buried, and he was there when the widow and Satterfield had dressed him in his Sunday-go-to-meeting clothes. He saw something then that filled the whole inside of him with horror.

He saw not only that Collins had been shot in the back, but something more than that, and it was that thing that disturbed him.

Dud Kitchen was a friendly, cheerful young man who liked nothing better than to sing and play the mandolin. Yet in his life from Missouri to Texas, he had had more than a little experience with guns. Once, too, he had gone down the river to New Orleans, and he had learned things on that trip.

Among other things, he knew that the dragoon Colt had the impact of an ax and would blow a hole in a man big enough to run a buffalo through, or so it was phrased on the frontier. The hole in Collins had been small at the point of entry, but it had been wide and ugly at the point of exit.

Opening the door between the living room and the kitchen of the Pagones' house, Pike walked in to look down at Dud. "Better get yourself well, Dud," Pike said. "We'll need all hands for this fuss."

"Was it bad, Pike?" Kitchen asked. His voice was faint, and in the dim light Pike could not see what lay in the younger man's eyes.

"No, I figger it wasn't so bad," Pike said. "Only a few shots fired. It was over so quick I scarce got my gun out. That Bat Chavez, him and Zapata were fastest, but Pete's horse swung around and spoiled his aim for him. Guess it saved his life, though, 'cause Bat's bullet hit the horse right in the head. Between the eyes.

"The horse rared up and throwed Pete, and I jumped my horse away to keep from gettin' in a tangle. Lamport, he scored a shot on one of them other fellers. We seen him jerk and seen the blood on him as they were ridin' off."

Dud Kitchen waited for a long moment, and then he said carefully: "Who killed Collins?"

Purcell seemed to scowl. "Don't rightly know. There was a sight of shootin' goin' on. Might have been any one of them three. Don't you worry about that. We'll get all three of them, so we won't miss gettin' the right one."

"Have they got good guns?" Dud asked. "I'll bet they have!"

"Same as us. Dragoon Colts. One of 'em had an old Walker though. Big gun, too. Shoots like a rifle."

After Pike Purcell was gone Dud Kitchen lay alone in the dark room, thinking. His thoughts frightened him, and yet, he was himself down from a shot by Zapata, who was on their own side. Collins had been shot in the back.

Whatever he had been shot by, Dud Kitchen was willing to take an oath it had not been by either a Walker or a Dragoon Colt. The hole was much too small, though the chest of the man had been frightfully torn. Sometimes men cut their bullets off flat across the nose to make them kill better. Dud had seen that done. It usually tore a man up pretty bad.

## VI

Johnny Stark brought the news of the fight to Rock Bannon. He was with Bishop at the time, and the old man's face hardened.

"Well, there it is, Rock! We can't give them any more time now. They've had their chance, and from now on she'll be open warfare!"

Bishop looked up at Stark. "Take six men back with you. Have Monty go with the buckboard and bring Lew here to the ranch house where he can have proper care. You tell Red I want to see him, but he'll be in charge when he goes back."

Rock got up and paced the floor. He ran his fingers through his shock of black, curly hair. His face was stern and hard. He knew what this meant. One man had gone down, Johnny said. From his description of the man it would be Collins, one of the good men. That would serve to unite the settlers in a compact lot. Despite all his desires to avoid trouble, they were in for it now, and it would be a case of dog eat dog. What would Sharon think of all this?

Hastily, he computed the numbers at the townsite. Their numbers were still slightly inferior to those on the Bishop ranch, but because of expected Indian trouble and the stock, many of the Bishop hands must remain on the far ranges.

"I'm going out," he said at last. "I'm going down to Poplar. Also, I'm going to have a look in that canyon where Harper's stuff was cached."

"You watch yourself, boy!" Bishop said. He heaved himself up in his chair. "You take care! I'm figurin' on you havin' this ranch, and I ain't wantin' to will it to no corpse."

Rock hurried down to the corral and saw Johnny Stark leading out the steel dust, all saddled and ready.

"I figured you'd be ridin', Rock," he said grimly. He handed the reins to him and started to turn away, but then he stepped back.

"Rock," he said, "somethin' I been goin' to tell somebody. I forgot to mention it back there. Rock, I don't think any of us killed Collins!"

Bannon wheeled and grabbed the cowhand by the arm. His eyes were like steel.

"What do you mean? Give it to me, quick!"

"Hey!" Johnny said. "Ease up on that arm!" He grinned. "You got a grip like a bear trap." He rubbed his arm. "Why, I been thinkin' about that ever since. Bat, he was thinkin' only of Zapata. I shot at that Miller, the guy you whupped. I got his horse. Lew, he burned that long, lean mountain man along the cheek, tryin' for a head shot. Actually, this here Collins hombre was off to our left. None of us shot that way."

"You're sure about that?" Bannon demanded.

His mind was working swiftly. If one thing would arouse anger against Bishop among the settlers it would be the killing of one of their own number, and particularly one so well liked as Collins had been.

Bannon stared at the rider. "Did you see anybody near him? Who was over at that side?"

"This here Collins hombre who got shot, he was in the front rank," Johnny said. "Then there was a heavyset, sandy sort of guy with a beard and a tall hombre with a white hat with a dark coat."

The bearded man would be Lamport. The man in the white hat was Mort Harper.

Rock Bannon swung a leg over the saddle. "Johnny, you tell Red to sit tight," he said. "I'm riding to Poplar."

"Want me along?" Stark asked eagerly. "You better take some help. Those hombres are killin' now. They are in a sweat, all of them."

Rock shook his head. "No, I'll go it alone," he said. "Tell Red to wait at the cabin."

Rock wheeled the steel dust and cut across the valley. There was still a chance to avoid a battle if he could get to Poplar in time, yet he had a feeling that Harper would not wait. Hostilities had begun, and that was what he had been playing for all the time. Now he had his excuse to wipe out the Bishop forces, and he would be quick to take advantage of it.

Before he was halfway down the valley, he reined in on the slope of a low hill. Miles to the south he could see a group of horsemen cutting across toward the line cabin. Bat Chavez was there alone with the wounded Murray.

Red would be starting soon, but would get there too late to help Bat or Murray. Within a matter of a half hour they would be attacking. From where he was it would take him all of that time and probably more to reach them. There was no time to go back. Wheeling the steel dust he started down the valley, angling away from the group of riders.

In the distance around the peaks towering against the sky, dark clouds were banking. A jagged streak of lightning ripped the horizon to shreds of flame and then vanished, and there was a distant roll of thunder, muttering among the dark and distant ravines like the echoes of distant battle.

The gray horse ran through the tall grass, sweeping around groves of aspen and alder, keeping to the low ground. He splashed through a swale, crested a long low hill that cut athwart the valley, and turned at right angles down the draw toward the cover of the far-off trees. The cool wind whipped against his face, and he felt a breath of moist wind as it shifted, feeling for the course of the storm.

The big horse was running smoothly, liking the feel of running as he always did, letting his powerful muscles out and stretching them. Leaning forward to break the wind and let the weight of his body help the running horse Rock Bannon talked to him, speaking softly to the stallion. He knew it loved his voice, for between horse and man there was that companionship and understanding that come only when they have known many trails together, shared the water of the same creeks, and run over long swells of prairie as they were running now.

Then he heard the distant sound of a rifle, followed by a roll of shots.

"Bat, I hope to heaven you're under cover!" he muttered. "I hope they didn't surprise you!"

He eased the horse's running now because he might rush upon some of them sooner than he expected. He slid his rifle from the scabbard and raced into the trees. The sound of firing was nearer now. He slowed the horse to a walk, letting him take a blow, his eyes searching the brush. There was still some distance to go, but there was firing, and that meant that Bat was under cover. They had not caught him flat-footed at least.

He swung the horse up into the rocks and slid from the saddle, easing forward to the rim of the shelf overhanging the line cabin. Lying face down among the rocks, he could see puffs of smoke from the brush around the cabin. Waiting until he saw a gleam of light on a rifle, he fired.

Almost instantly, a man some distance away leaped up and started to run for a boulder. Swinging the rifle he snapped a shot at him, and the man went to his knees and then started to crawl for shelter.

A rifle bellowed down below, and a shot glanced off a rock, kicking splinters into Bannon's face. He eased back and worked down the slope a bit, studying the situation below. One man was wounded, at least.

Suddenly, a horseman leaped a horse from behind some trees, and dragging a flaming mass of brush, raced toward the cabin. It was a foolhardy thing to do, but instantly, Bannon saw his purpose. The rifle fire had attracted Bat Chavez to the other side of the cabin. Rock lifted his own rifle and steadied it. A flashing instant of aim, and then he fired.

*     *     *

The horseman threw up his arms and toppled back off the horse, right into the mass of flaming brush. He screamed once, horribly, and then rolled clear, fighting the fire in his garments and dragging himself in the dust. Another man rushed from the brush to aid him, and Rock held his fire.

Suddenly, there was a heavy roll of thunder. Looking around, he saw the clouds had come nearer, and now there was a sprinkle of rain. At the same instant he heard the pounding of horses' hoofs. Snapping a quick shot at the brush, he heard a startled yell. Then the attackers broke from the brush and, scrambling to their saddles, charged away across the valley. At that moment, the rain broke with a thundering roar, a veritable cloudburst.

Rushing to the steel dust, he swung into the saddle. He put the animal around to a steep slide of shale and rode down to the barn near the corral. Johnny rushed up to him.

"You all right?"

"Yeah. How's Bat?"

"Don't know. Red went in. You go ahead. I'll fix your horse up."

Rock sprinted for the house and got in, slamming the door after him. Bat looked around, grinning widely.

"Man, was I glad to hear that rifle of yours," he said. "They had me surrounded. Lew wanted to get into it, but I was afraid his wound would open and start bleedin' again. Well, we drove 'em off."

"You get anybody?"

"Scratched a couple. Maybe got one. You got one that first shot. I seen him fall. That'll be one down and two bad hurt, maybe four. Looks like we come out of that on top."

"I was headed for Poplar and saw them comin'. I was afraid you'd be outside and they'd split up on you."

Chavez spat. "They mighty near did. I'd just been to the spring for water."

Rock stared into the fire. This would mean nothing one way or another. They had been turned back from the first attack, but they would not be convinced. He had killed a man. Who was it? That would matter a great deal, he knew. Certainly, if it was another of the settlers he would have small chance of selling them on quitting.

Yet he was just as resolved now as before the attack. This thing must be stopped. It was never too late to try. The rain was roaring upon the roof. They would never expect him in a flood like that. They would be inside and expecting everyone else to be there, too. If he circled around and came down the canyon, it would be the best chance. If they were keeping watch at all it would be from this direction. He would start in a few minutes. They were making coffee now. . . .

Sharon was outside when she saw the rain coming, and she waited for it, liking the cool air. Over the distant mountains across the valley, there were vivid streaks of lightning. It was already storming there, a frightful storm by all appearances.

She was alone and glad of it. Mary had wanted her to come to the Collins house, where several of the women had gathered, but she knew she could not stand to be cooped up now. She was restless, worried. Her father was out there, and for all his courage and willingness to go, Tom Crockett was no fighting man. He was not like Bannon. Strangely now, she was but little worried about him. He was hard, seemingly impervious to harm.

Even now he might be over there across the valley. He might be killing her father, or her father might be shooting him. Twelve men had ridden away. Eight of them were settlers. Collins was dead and Dud Kitchen still too weak to ride, but the others had gone to a man. Mulholland, Satterfield, Pagones, Lamport, Purcell, Olsen, and Greene. And, of course, her father.

Then the rain came, a scattering of big drops and then the rolling wall of it. She turned and went inside. There were a few places where the roof was not too tight. She put pans under them and lighted a light, which she put on the table near the window. Her father's leg was still not overly strong, and it worried her to think he was out there in all this.

She caught a glimpse of herself in the mirror, a tall, lovely girl with a great mass of red gold hair done in two thick braids about her head, her face too pale, her eyes overly large.

She heard them coming before she saw them, and saw a horseman break away from the others and cross the grass, now worn thin from much travel. When the horse was stabled he came in, stamping his feet and slipping out of his slicker. His gray hat was black with rain, and she took it close to the fire. The coffee was ready, and she poured a cup and then went for a bowl to get some thick soup for him.

He sat down at the table, sat down suddenly, as if his legs had been cut off, and she noticed with a sudden qualm that he looked old, tired. His eyes lifted to hers and he smiled wanly.

"Guess I'm no fighting man, Sharon," he said. "I just wasn't cut out for it. When that man fell into the flames today, I nearly wilted."

"Who was it?" she asked quickly. "One of our men?"

"No, it was a teamster. One of the bunch that hangs around the saloon. His name was Osburn. We rushed the house, and one of the men inside opened fire. Wounded one of the men, first shot. We had the house surrounded though, and would have had them in a few minutes. Then someone opened up on us from the cliff.

"It was Bannon, I'm sure of that. He killed Hy Miller. Got him with his first shot, although how he saw him I can't imagine. Then he wounded Satterfield. Shot him through the leg, about like I was. This Osburn got on a horse, and—" His voice rambled on, and all she could think about was that her father was home, that her father was safe.

After it all, when his voice had died away and he was eating the hot soup, she said, "And Bannon? Was he hurt?"

"No, he wasn't hurt. He never seems to get hurt. He's a hard man, Sharon."

"But a good man, Father!" she said suddenly. "He's a good man. Oh, I wish things were different!"

"Don't think it, Sharon," her father said, shaking his head. "He's not for you. He's a wild, ruthless man, a man who lives by the gun. Collins is dead, and by one of this man's friends, and they'll never let up now, nor will we. It's a war to the end."

"But why, Father? Why?" Sharon's voice broke. "Oh, when I think that we might have gone by the other trail! We might have been in Oregon now. Sometimes I believe that everything Bannon ever said about Mort Harper was true. All we've done is to come on here into this trap, and now our oxen are gone, all but the two you use to plow, and we're in debt."

"I know." Crockett stirred restlessly. "But it might have been as bad wherever we went. You must understand that. We may be mistaken in Mort. He's done what he could, and he's standing by us in this fight."

The fire flickered and hissed with the falling drops of rain in the chimney, and Sharon crossed and knelt beside the fire, liking the warm feel of it on her knees. She sat there, staring into the flames, hearing the unrelenting thunder of the rain, and wondering where Rock Bannon was.

Where would it all end? That boy, Wes Freeman, slain in the hills. Then Collins and now Miller. Dud Kitchen recovering from a wound. Jim Satterfield down, and the whole affair only beginning and no end in sight. The door opened suddenly and without warning, and she whirled, coming to her feet with her eyes wide.

Disappointment swept over her, and then fear. Pete Zapata was closing the door after him. He was smiling at her, his queer, flat face wet with rain, his narrow rattler's eyes searching the corners of the room.

"Not here?" he whispered hoarsely. "Pretty soon, maybe."

"Who—who do you mean?" she gasped.

Her father was sitting up very straight, his eyes on the man. Zapata glanced at him with thinly veiled contempt and then shrugged.

"Who? That Rock Bannon. A few minutes ago he came down the

canyon on his horse, now he is here somewhere. Who knows? But soon he will come here, and when—" He smiled, showing his yellow teeth between thick lips. His eyes shifted from her to her father. "If one speaks to warn him, I'll kill the other one, you see?"

Fear left her lips stiff, her eyes wide. Slowly, she turned back to the fire. Bannon would come here. Zapata was right. She knew he would come here. If Rock had come again to Poplar, he would not leave without seeing her. He might come at any minute. She must think, she must somehow contrive to warn him—somehow!

The steel dust liked the dim, shallow cave in which Rock stopped him, but he didn't like being left alone. He whimpered a little and made believe to snort with fear as Bannon started to move away, but when Rock spoke, the stallion quieted, resigned to what was to come.

Rock Bannon moved out swiftly, keeping under the trees but working his way closer and closer to the house of Pagones. He didn't know what he was getting into, but Pagones was the most reliable of them all, and the strongest one. If resistance to Harper was to come, it must come from him. Crockett lacked the force of character, even though he might have the will. Besides, Pagones knew that one of Harper's men had shot down Dud Kitchen.

Pagones hadn't chosen his potential son-in-law. Mary had done that for herself, but Pagones couldn't have found anyone he liked better. Dud was energetic, tireless, capable, and full of good humor. George Pagones, in his heart, had never felt sure of Mort Harper. He had listened with one part of his mind to Bannon's protests, even while the smooth words of Harper beguiled him.

Pagones had returned wet and tired. Like Crockett, he had no love of killing. He had seen Osburn tumble into the flames, and he had seen Miller killed. Knowing the trouble Miller had caused and how he had attacked Sharon while drunk, Pagones was not sorry to see him die. If it had to be someone, it might as well have been Miller. Yet seeing any man die is a shock, and he had been close to the man.

Many men are aggressive and willing enough to fight, but when they see death strike suddenly and horribly their courage oozes away. Pagones had the courage to defend himself, but his heart was not in this fight, and the action of the day had served to make him very thoughtful.

Something was worrying Dud Kitchen. He had been noticing that for several days, yet there had been no chance to talk to him when the womenfolk were not around. He felt the need of talking to him now and got up and went into the room. He was there, beside the bed, when a breath of cold air struck him and he heard a startled gasp from his wife.

Gun in hand he stepped back to the door. Rock Bannon was closing it after him. He turned now and looked at the gun in Pagones's hand. Bannon smiled grimly.

"Well, you've got the drop on me, Pag. What happens now?"

"What do you want here?" Pagones demanded sternly. "Don't you know if you keep coming back, they'll kill you?"

"Just so it isn't you, Pag," Bannon said. "I always reckoned you a friend."

Pagones holstered his gun. "Come in," he said. "I take it you've come to talk."

Mary and his wife stood facing him, their eyes shining with apprehension. There was a scuffling of feet from the other room, and Dud Kitchen was in the door.

"Howdy," he said. "They'll kill you, Rock. I heard Zapata say he was after you. He said he was going to get you next."

"All right." Rock dropped into a chair, his right-hand holster in his lap, the ivory gun butt near his right hand. His dark blue shirt was open at the neck, his leather jacket unbuttoned. The candle and firelight flickered on the bright butts of the cartridges in his twin belts.

Dud's face was very pale, but somehow Rock sensed that Dud was glad to see him, and it made him feel better and made the talk come easier. Pagones's cheekbones glistened in the firelight, and his eyes were steady on Bannon's face as he waited for him to begin. It was very still in the room. A drop of water fell into the fire and hissed itself into extinction.

Mary Pagones stooped, her freckles dark against the pallor of her face, and dropped a handful of small sticks on the fire.

"Pag," Bannon began slowly, "I've never wanted this fight. I don't think you have. I don't think Crockett did either, or Dud here. There's no use me tryin' to talk to Tom. He's a good man and he knows what he wants, but he hasn't force enough to make it stick. He couldn't stand against Harper. There's only one man here can do that, Pagones, and that's you."

"Harper's my friend," Pagones said evenly. "He led us here. This is his fight and ours."

"You don't believe that," Rock said. "Not down inside, you don't. Collins's death brought you into it. That made it your fight and Crockett's fight. The truth is, all you men want is homes. That's what your wife wants, and Mary. That's what Sharon wants, too. That's what Cap wants, and the rest of them.

"What Mort Harper wants is land and power. He intends to have them, no matter who dies or when. I've been here before to try to stop this trouble. I'm here again now.

"One of our men died first, and he was a good boy. He was murdered, Pagones, murdered like no man in the wagon train would kill any man. Purcell didn't like me. Neither did Lamport. Cap was your leader, but he listened too quick to that glib tongue of Harper's."

"We all did," Dud said. "I listened, too. I listened for a while, anyway." Mary moved up behind his chair and put her hand on his shoulder. He looked up quickly, and she smiled.

"Get to the point!" Pagones said. All that Bannon said was true. He knew it as well as Rock. He had listened to Harper, but secretly he had always been afraid that Bannon was right. He had been afraid of this trail. They had no oxen now, and they had no money. They were here, and they could not escape.

Rock leaned a hand on his knee. "Pagones, my boys say they didn't kill Collins!"

## VII

Dud Kitchen drew in his breath, and Mary looked at him in sudden apprehension.

"What's that you say?" Pagones demanded.

"I repeat. I talked to my boys, and they say they didn't kill Collins. Bat Chavez couldn't see anything but Zapata, Stark and Murray weren't even facing toward Collins then. They say they didn't kill him."

"There was a lot of shooting," Pagones said. "Anything might of happened."

"That's right," Bannon agreed. "But my boys don't think they shot Collins, and that leaves a big question."

"It don't leave no question for me!" Dud flared suddenly. "I saw that wound of Collins's! And he was shot in the back!"

Pagones's face hardened. He stared down at the floor, his jaw muscles working. Was nothing ever simple anymore? Was there nothing on which a man could depend? How had he got into this mess, anyway? What should he do?

"Who do you think?" he asked. "You mean Zapata?"

Their eyes were all on Rock Bannon, waiting, tense. "No," he said. "I mean Mort Harper!"

"But, man, that's crazy!" Pagones leaped to his feet. "What would be the object? Is there any reason why he would kill a man on his own side?"

"You know the answer to that as well as I," Bannon said. He got up, too. "He wanted you in this fight, and that was the only way he could get you. Purcell and Lamport were fire-eaters. They were in, but they weren't enough. He wanted the rest of you, the good, sober, industrious citizens, the men whose reputations at home were good, the men who would look honest to the military if they ever came west."

"I saw that wound," Kitchen repeated. "Collins was killed with a small gun, a small gun with flat-nose or split-ended bullets."

"Who has such a gun?" Pagones said. "You all know that Harper carries a Dragoon, like the rest of us."

"In sight, he does," Bannon agreed. "Mort Harper may pack another one."

He stopped, feet wide apart. "I've got to get out of here, Pag. I've got to get going and fast. There's not much chance of anybody being out tonight, but I can't gamble on that. I've got to get away from here, and this is the last time I'll come. I've tried to tell you about Mort Harper for a long time. You've got your last chance to break away, because I'm telling you flat: if you don't break away there won't be a building standing on this ground within forty-eight hours."

Pagones's head jerked up. "Is that an ultimatum?"

"You bet it is!" Bannon snapped. "If I'd let Bishop have his head, you'd have all been out of here long ago. Wes would be alive now, and Collins, and Murray wouldn't be packin' that slug in his leg, and Dud would be on his feet. If I'd not kept Bishop off you, he would have faced you with forty armed men and ordered you off before you had a stake down or a foundation laid.

"Those boys of ours are spoilin' for a fight. They hate Harper's innards, and they want Zapata. He's a murderin' outlaw, and they all know it."

"I don't know that I can do anything," Pagones protested. "We have to think of Zapata as it is. Harper's the only thing that keeps him and those teamsters off our places and away from our women, anyway!"

Rock Bannon started for the door. With his hand on the latch, he turned, sliding into his slicker.

"You step aside and there won't be any Zapata or his friends!" he declared. "We'll wipe them out so fast they'll only be a memory. We just don't want to kill good people. You can keep your places. We let you come in, and we'll let you stay."

He turned and slipped out the door into the rain. For an instant, he hesitated, letting his eyes grow accustomed to the dark. Rain fell in slanting sheets, striking his face like hailstones and rattling against his oilskin slicker like on a tin roof. Water stood in puddles on the ground, and when he stepped down a large drop fell from a tree down the back of his neck.

He hesitated, close against the wet tree trunk, and stared into the night. There was a glow of light from the window of the Crockett

place. Somebody was still up. He hesitated, knowing it was dangerous to remain longer, yet longing for a sight of Sharon, for the
chance to take her in his arms.

He never had. He had never kissed her, never held her hand. It
was all a matter of their eyes, and yet he felt she understood and,
perhaps, a little responded to his feeling.

There were lights from the saloon. They would all be down there
now, playing cards, drinking. It was a pity he had none of the boys
here. They could go in and wipe them out in one final, desperate
battle. Lightning flashed and revealed the stark wet outlines of the
buildings, the green of the grass, worn down now, between him and
the Crockett cabin.

He stepped out from the tree and started across the open, hearing
the far-off thunder muttering among the peaks of the mountains
beyond the valley, muttering among the cliffs and boulders like a
disgruntled man in his sleep.

He did not fasten his slicker, but held it together with his left
hand and kept his right in his pocket, slopping across the wet ground
with the rain battering the brim of his hat, beating with angry,
skeleton fingers against the slicker.

Under the trees, he hesitated, watching the house. There was no
horse around. Suddenly, a column of sparks went up from the
chimney, as if someone had thrown some sticks on the fire. He
started to move, and another cluster of sparks went up. He hesitated. A signal? But who would know he was near?

A third time. Three times was a warning, three smokes, three rifle
shots—what could it be? Who could know he was here? It was
nonsense, of course, but the sparks made him feel uneasy.

Then again, three times, once very weakly, sparks mounted from
the chimney. Somebody was playing with the fire, tapping with a
stick on the burning wood or stirring the fire.

No matter. He was going in. He felt cold, and the warmth of the
room would be good again before he began his long ride to the line
cabin. A long ride, because it would be foolhardy to go down the
canyon toward the valley.

He stepped out from under the tree and walked up to the house.
His boots made sucking noises in the mud before the door. Lightning flashed and water glistened on the smooth boards of the door.
He should knock, but he stepped up and, keeping to the left of the
door, reached across with his left hand and drew the door wide.

A gun blasted, and he saw the sudden dart of fire from the
darkness by the fireplace. The bullet smashed into the door, and
then he went in with a rush.

He caught a glimpse of Sharon, her eyes wide with fright, scrambling away from the fire. Zapata lunged from the shadows, his face

set in a snarl of bared teeth and gleaming eyes. His gun blasted again, and a bullet snatched at Rock's jacket. Bannon thumbed his gun.

Zapata staggered, as though struck by a blow in the stomach. As Rock started for him, he leaped for an inner door. Rock lunged after him, firing again. There was a crash as Zapata went through a sack-covered window.

Wheeling, Rock leaped for the door and went out. Zapata's gun barked, and something laid a white hot iron across his leg. Rock brought his gun up, turned his right side to the crouching man, and fired again, fired as though on a target range.

Zapata coughed, and his pistol dropped into the mud. He clawed with agonized fingers at his other gun, and Rock Bannon could see the front of his shirt darkening with the pounding rain and with blood. Then Bannon fired again, and Zapata went down, clawing at the mud.

A door slammed, and there was a yell. Rock wheeled and saw Sharon in the doorway. "I can't stop," he said. "Talk to Pagones." And even as he spoke, he was running across the worn grass toward the trees.

A rifle barked and then another; then there were intermittent shots. Crying with fear for him, Sharon Crockett stood in the door, staring into the darkness. Lightning flared, and through the slanting rain she caught a brief glimpse of him. A rifle flared, and then he was gone into the trees. A moment later, they heard the pounding of hoofs.

"They'll never catch him on that horse," Tom Crockett said. "He got away!"

Sharon turned, and her father was smiling. "Yes, Daughter, I'm glad he got away. I'm glad he killed that murderer."

"Oh, Father!" Then his arms were around her, and as running feet slapped in the mud outside, he pushed the door shut. "He'll get away," she cried. "He must get away."

The door slammed open, and Mort Harper shoved into the room. Behind him were four men, their faces hard, their guns ready.

"What was he doing here?" Harper demanded. "That man's a killer! He's our enemy. Why should he come here?"

"I don't know why he came!" Crockett said coldly. "He never had a chance to say. Zapata had been waiting for him all evening. He seemed to believe he would be here. When Bannon came in, he fired and missed. He won't miss again."

Harper stared at him, his face livid and angry under the glistening dampness of the rain.

"You seem glad!" he cried.

"I am!" Crockett said. "Yes, I'm glad! That Zapata was a killer, and he deserved killing."

"And I'm glad," Sharon said, her chin lifted. "I'm glad Bannon killed him, glad that Bannon got away."

There was an angry mutter from the men behind Harper, but Mort put up a restraining hand. "So? This sounds like rebellion. Well, we'll have none of that in this camp. I've been patient with you people, and especially patient with you, Sharon, but my patience is wearing thin."

"Who cares about your patience?" Anger rose in Sharon's eyes. "Your soft talk and lies won't convince us any longer. We want our oxen back tomorrow! We've had enough of this. We'll get out of here tomorrow if we have to walk."

"No, you won't," Harper said. "Come on, boys. We'll go now."

"Let's teach 'em a lesson, Boss," one man said angrily. "To blazes with this palaver!"

"Not now," Harper said. His nostrils were flared with anger, and his face was hard. "Later!"

When the door closed after them, Tom Crockett's face was white. "Well, Sharon," he said quietly, "for better or worse, there it is. Tomorrow we may have to fight. Your mother helped me fight Indians once, long ago. Could you?"

Sharon turned, and suddenly she smiled. "Do you need to ask?"

"No." He smiled back, and she could see a new light in his eyes, almost as if the killing of Zapata and the statement to Harper had made him younger, stronger. "No, I don't," he repeated. "You'd better get some sleep. I'm going to clean my rifle."

Rock Bannon's steel dust took the trail up the canyon at a rapid clip. They might follow him, Bannon knew, and he needed all the lead he could get. Some of those men had been in these hills for quite some time, yet if he could get away into the wilderness around Day's River, they would never find him.

Shooting it out with six or seven desperate killers was no part of his plan, and he knew the teamsters who had come to Poplar were just that, a band of renegades recruited from the scourings of the wagon trains passing through the fort. After the immediate dash, however, he slowed down to give the steel dust better footing.

He turned northeast when he came out of Poplar Canyon and rode down into a deep draw that ended in a meadow. The bottom of the draw was roaring with water that had run off the mountains, but as yet it was no more than a foot deep. Far below, he could hear the thunder of Day's River, roaring at full flood now.

The canyon through the narrows would be a ghastly sight with its weight of thundering white water. Always a turmoil, now it would be doubled and tripled by the cloudburst. Rain slanted down, pouring unceasingly on the hills.

The trail by which he had come would be useless on his return. By now the water would be too deep in the narrow canyon up which he had ridden. He must find a new trail, a way to cut back from the primitive wilderness into which he was riding and down through the valley where Freeman had been killed, and then through the mountains.

Briefly, he halted the big stallion in the lee of a jutting shoulder of granite where wind and rain were cast off into the flat of the valley. Knowing his horse would need every ounce of its strength, he swung down. His shoulder against the rock, he studied the situation in his mind's eye.

His first desperate flight had taken him northeast into the wild country. Had he headed south he must soon have come out on the plains beyond the entrance to Bishop's Valley, where he would have nothing but the speed of his own horse to assist his escape.

He was needed here, now. Any flight was temporary, so in turning north he had kept himself within striking distance of the enemy. His problem now was to find a way through the rugged mountain barrier, towering thousands of feet above him, into Bishop's Valley, and across the valley to home.

No man knew these mountains well, but Hardy Bishop best of all. Next to him, Rock himself knew them best, but with all his knowledge they presented a weird tangle of ridges, canyons, jagged crests, peaks, and chasms. At the upper end of the valley, the stream roared down a gorge often three thousand feet deep and with only the thinnest of trails along the cliffs of the narrows.

The isolated valley might have been walled for the express purpose of keeping him out, for as he ran over the possible routes into the valley, one by one he had to reject them. Bailey's Creek would be a thundering torrent now, water roaring eight to ten feet deep in the narrow canyon. Trapper's Gulch would be no better, and the only other two routes would be equally impassable.

Rock stared at the dark bulk of the mountain through the slanting rain. He stared at it, but could see nothing but Stygian darkness. Every branch, every rivulet, and every stream would be a roaring cataract now. If there was a route into the valley now it must be over the ridge. The very thought made him swallow and turn chill. He knew what those ridges and peaks were in quiet hours. They could be traveled, and he had traveled them, but only when he could see and feel his way along. Now, with lightning crashing, with thunder butting against the cliffs, and with clouds gathered around them, it would be an awful inferno of lightning and granite, a place for no living thing.

Yet, the thought in the back of his mind kept returning. Hardy Bishop was alone, or practically so. He had sent Red to the line cabin nearest Harper with most of the fighting men. Others were in a cabin near the narrows, miles away. Only two men would be at home aside from the cook.

Rock Bannon did not make the mistake of underestimating his enemy. Mort Harper had planned this foray with care. He would not have begun without a careful study of the forces to be arrayed against him. He would know how many men were at the line cabin, and the result of his figuring must certainly be to convince him that the ranch house was unprotected, and Hardy Bishop, the heart, soul, and brain of the Bishop empire, was there.

There was a route over the mountain. Once, by day, Bannon had traveled it. He must skirt a canyon hundreds of feet deep along a path that clung like an eyebrow to the sheer face of the cliff. He must ride across the long swelling slope of the mountain among trees and boulders, and then between two peaks, and angle through the forest down the opposite side.

At best, it was a twelve-mile ride, and might stretch that a bit. Even by day it was dangerous and slow going. And he needed only his own eyes to convince him that lightning was making a playground of the hillside now.

"All right, boy," he said gently to the horse. "You aren't going to like this, but neither am I." He swung into the saddle and moved out into the wind.

As he breasted the shoulder of granite, the wind struck him like a solid wall, and the rain lashed at his garments, plucking at the fastenings of his oilskin. He turned the horse down the canyon that would take them to the cliff face across which he must ride. He preferred not to think of that.

As he drew near, the canyon walls began to close in upon him, until it became a giant chute down which the water thundered in a mighty Niagara of sound. Great masses of water churned in an enormous maelstrom below and the steel dust snorted and shied from its roaring.

Rock spoke to the horse and touched it on the shoulder. Reassured, it felt gingerly for the path and moved out. A spout of water gushing from some crack in the rock struck him like a blow, drenching him anew and making the stallion jump. He steadied the horse with a tight rein and then relaxed and let the horse have his head. He could see absolutely nothing ahead of him.

Thunder and the rolling of gigantic boulders reverberated down the rock-walled canyon, and occasional lightning-lit flares showed him glimpses of a weird nightmare of glistening rock and tumbling white water that caught the flame and hurled it in millions of tiny shafts on down the canyon.

The steel dust walked steadily, facing the wind but with bowed head, hesitating only occasionally to feel its way around some great rock or sudden, unexpected heap of debris.

The hoarse wind howled down the channel of rock, turning its shouting to a weird scream on corners where the pines feathered down into the passage of the wind. Battered by rain and wind, Rock Bannon bent his head and rode on, beaten, soaked, bedraggled, with no eyes to see, only trusting to the surefooted mountain horse and its blind instinct.

Once when the lightning lifted the whole scene into stark relief, he glimpsed a sight that would not leave him if he lived to be a hundred. For one brief, all-encompassing moment he saw the canyon as he never wanted to see it again.

The stallion had reached a bend and for a moment, hesitated to relax its straining, careful muscles. In that instant, the lightning flared.

Before them, the canyon dropped steeply away, like the walls of a gigantic stairway, black, glistening walls slanted by the steel of driving rain, cut by volleys of hail, and accompanied by the roar of the cataract below.

Two hundred feet down the white water roared, and banked in a cul-de-sac in the rock was a piled-up mass of foam, fifteen or twenty feet high, bulging and glistening. At each instant, wind or water ripped some of it away and shot it, churning, down the fury of raging water below. Thunder roared a salvo, and the echoes responded, and a wild cliff-clinging cedar threshed madly in the wind, as if to tear free its roots and blow away to some place of relief from the storm.

Lightning crackled, and thunder drummed against the cliffs, and the scene blacked out suddenly into abysmal darkness. The steel dust moved on, rounding the point of the rock and starting to climb. Then, as if by a miracle, they were out of the canyon, but turning up a narrow crevice in the rock with water rushing, inches deep, beneath the stallion's feet. A misstep here and they would tumble down the crevice and pitch off into the awful blackness above the water. But the stallion was surefooted, and suddenly they came out on the swell of the mountain slope.

The lightning below was nothing to this. Here darkness was a series of fleeting intervals shot through with thunderbolts, and each jagged streak lighted the night like a blaze from Hades. Gaunt shoulders of the mountain butted against the bulging weight of cloud, and the skeleton fingers of long-dead pines felt stiffly of the wind.

Stunned by the storm, the stallion plodded on, and Rock swayed in the saddle, buffeted and hammered, as they walked across that bare, dead slope among the boulders, pushing relentlessly, tirelessly against the massive wall of the wind. A flash of lightning, and a tree ahead detonated like a shell, and bits of it flew off into space with the wild complaining of a ricocheted bullet. The stub of the tree smoked, sputtered with flame, and went out, leaving a vague smell of charred wood and brimstone.

A long time later, dawn felt its way over the mountains beyond and behind him, and the darkness turned gray, and then rose and flame climbed the peaks. Rock rode on, sullen, beaten, overburdened with weariness. The high cliffs behind him turned their rust-colored heights to jagged bursts of frozen flame, but he did not notice. Weary, the stallion plodded down the last mile of slope and into the rain-flattened grass of the plain.

The valley was empty. Rock lifted his red-rimmed eyes and stared south. He saw no horsemen, no movement. He had beaten them. He would be home before they came. And once he was home he could stand beside the big old man who called him son, and they would face the world together, if need be.

Let Harper come. He would learn what fighting meant. These men were not of the same flesh or the same blood, but the response within them was the same, and the fire that shaped the steel of their natures was the same. They were men bred to the Colt. Bred to the law of strength. Men who knew justice, but could fight to defend what was theirs and what they believed.

He was not thinking that. He was thinking nothing. He was only moving. The steel dust plodded on into the ranch yard, and he fell rather than stepped from the saddle. Springer rushed out to get his horse.

"My stars, man! How'd you get here?"

"Over the mountain," Bannon said, and walked toward the house.

Awed, Springer turned and looked toward the towering, six-thousand-foot ridge. "Over the mountain," he said. "Over the mountain!" He stripped the saddle from the big horse and turned it into the corral, and then almost ran to the bunkhouse to tell Turner. "Over the mountain!"

Hardy Bishop looked up from his great chair, and his eyes sharpened. Rock raised a hand and then walked on through the room, stripping his sodden clothing as he went. When he reached the bed he pulled off one boot and then rolled over and stretched out, his left spur digging into the blanket.

*     *     *

Bishop followed him to the room and stared down at him grimly; then he walked back and dropped into the chair. Well, he reflected, for that he could be thankful. He had a man for a son.

It was a long time ago that he first came into this valley with old John Day. They had come down through the narrows and looked out over the wide, beautiful length of it, and he had seen what he knew he was looking for. He had seen Paradise.

There were men in the West then, men who roamed the streams for beaver or the plains for buffalo. They lived and traded and fought with the Indians, learning their ways and going them one better. They pushed on into new country, country no white man had seen.

There were men like John Coulter, who first looked into the Yellowstone region; old Jim Bridger, who knew the West as few men. There were John Day, Smith, Hoback, Wilson Price Hunt, Kit Carson, and Robert Stuart. Most of them came for fur or game, and later they came for gold, but there were a few even then who looked for homes, and of the first was Hardy Bishop.

He had settled here, buying the land from the Indians and trading with them long before any other white man dwelled in the region. Once a whole year had passed when he saw not even a trapper.

The Kaws were usually his friends, but the Crows were not, and occasionally raiding parties of Blackfeet came down from the north. When they were friendly, he talked or traded, and when they wanted to fight, he fought. After a while, even the Crows left him alone, learning friendship was more profitable than death, and many had died.

Bad days were coming. From the seat in the great hidebound chair, Hardy Bishop could see that. The trouble with Indians would be nothing to the trouble with white men, and he was glad that Rock was a man who put peace first, but who handled a gun fast.

He raised his great head, his eyes twinkling. They were keen eyes that could see far and well. Even the Indians respected them. He could, they said, trail a snake across a flat rock, or a duck downstream through rough water. What he saw now was a horseman, riding toward the ranch. One lone horseman, and there was something odd in the way he rode.

It was not a man. It was a woman. A white woman. Hardy Bishop heaved himself ponderously from the chair. It had been almost ten years since he had seen a white woman! He walked slowly to the door, hitching his guns around just in case.

The sun caught her hair and turned it to living flame. His dark eyes kindled. She rode up to the steps, and he saw Springer and Turner in the bunkhouse door, gaping. She swung down from her black mare and walked over to him. She was wearing trousers and a man's shirt. Her throat was bare in the open neck. He smiled. Here was a woman!

## VIII

Sharon looked up at Bishop, astonished. Somehow, she had always known he would be big, but not such a monster of a man. Six feet four he stood, in his socks, and weighing three hundred pounds. His head was covered with a shock of iron-gray hair, in tight curls. His eyes twinkled, and massive forearms and hands jutted from his sleeves.

"Come in! Come in!" he boomed. "You'll be Sharon Crockett, then. I've heard of you. Heard a sight of you!"

He looked around as she hesitated on the steps. "What's the matter? Not afraid of an old man, are you? Come in."

"It isn't that. Only we've come here like this—and it was your land, and—"

"Don't explain." He shook his head. "Come in and sit down. You're the first white woman who ever walked into this house. First one ever saw it, I reckon. Rock, he's asleep. Dead to the world."

"He's safe then?" she asked. "I was afraid. I saw them go after him."

"There was trouble?" he looked at her keenly. "What happened?"

She told him about the killing of Pete Zapata and what happened afterward. "That's why I'm here," she said. "In a way, I'm asking for peace. We didn't know. We were foolish not to have listened to Rock in the beginning, when he told us about Mort. My father and the settlers want peace. I don't know about Pike Purcell and Lamport, but I can speak for the rest of us."

Bishop nodded his head. "Rock told me what he was goin' for. So he killed Zapata? That'll please the boys." He turned his head. "Dave!" he bellowed.

A face covered with a shock of mussed hair and beard shoved into the door. "Bring us some coffee! And some of that cake! We've got a lady here, by—" He flushed. "Excuse me, ma'am. Reckon my manners need a goin' over. We cuss a sight around here. A sight too much, I reckon.

" 'Course, I ain't never figured on gettin' into heaven, anyways. I been pretty much of a sinner and not much of a repenter. Reckon they'd have to widen the gate some, anyway. I'd be a sight of weight to get into heaven. Most likely, they'd have to put some cribbin' under the cloud I set on, too."

He chuckled, looking at her. "So you're the girl what's goin' to marry Rock?"

She jumped and flushed. "Why! Why, I—"

"Don't let it get you down, ma'am! Reckon I'm a blunt old codger. It's true enough, the boy ain't said a word to me about it, but I can see what's in his eyes. I ain't raised the lad for nothin'. When he took off on this rampage, I was hopin' he'd find himself a gal.

"You like him, ma'am?" He looked at her sharply, his eyes filled with humor. "You goin' to marry him?"

"Why, I don't know," she protested. "I don't know that he wants me."

"Now listen here! Don't you go givin' me any of that demure, folded-hands palaver. That may go for those young bucks, but not for me. You know as well as I do if a woman sets her cap for a man he ain't got a chance. Only if he runs. That's all! Either give up and marry the gal or get clean out of the country and don't leave no address behind. Nor no trail sign, neither!

"You might fool some young sprout with that 'he hasn't asked me' business, but not me. I seen many a young buck Indian give twenty head of ponies for some squaw when he could have had better ones for ten. Just because she wanted him like and caused him to figure the price was cheap.

"No, sir! I'd rather try to get away from a bear trap on each foot and each hand than a woman with her head set on marriage."

Flushed with embarrassment, she ignored what he had said.

"Then—then, you'll let us have peace, sir? You won't be fighting us if we draw off from Harper?"

"Of course not, ma'am! I reckon it'd be a right nice thing to have a few folks around once in a while!" His eyes flashed. "But no more, you understand. Only this bunch of yours. No more!"

"And we can have our land, then?" she persisted.

"Sure, you can have it. You can have what them other fellers got, too, when they get out. Sure, you can have it. I can't set my hand to paper on it, though, because I never did learn to write. That's true, ma'am! Never learned to write, nor to read. But I can put my name on the side of a house with a six-shooter. I can do that. But them pens! They always figured to be a sight too small for my hands. No, I can't read printin', but I can read sign. I trailed a Blackfoot what stole a horse from me clean to Montana one time. Trailed him six hundred miles, believe me or not. Yes, ma'am, I come back with the horse and his scalp. Took it right in his own village."

A startled yell rang out, and Springer burst through the door.

"Boss! Boss! Here they come! Oh, quick, man! Here they—"

His voice died in the report of a gun, and Hardy Bishop lunged from his chair to see men charging the porch.

Turner had started from the bunkhouse, but the rush of the horses rode him down. They heard his wild, agonized screams as he went down under the pounding hoofs. Sharon never saw the old man reach for his guns, but suddenly they were spouting flame. She saw a man stagger back from the door clutching at his breast, blood pouring over his hand.

Then a wild figure wearing one boot appeared from the other room, swinging gun belts about his hips. Then Rock Bannon, too, was firing.

A sound came at a rear window, and he turned and fired from the hip. A dark form looming there vanished. The attack broke, and Rock Bannon rushed to the rifle rack and jerked down two Henry rifles. Then he ran back, thrusting one at Bishop.

The old man dropped to his knees beside a window. "Come up on us fast!" he said. "I was talkin' to this gal."

Rock's eyes swung to her, and then amazement faded to sudden grimness. With horror, she saw suspicion mount in his eyes.

A wild chorus of yells sounded from outside, and then a volley of shots smashed through the windows. The lamp scattered in a thousand pieces, and from the kitchen they heard a cursing and then the crash of a buffalo gun.

"How many did you see?" Rock demanded.

"Most like a dozen," Bishop said. "We got two or three that first rush!"

"A dozen?" He wheeled to the girl. "Did the settlers come? Did they? Are they fighting us now?"

"Can't be that," Bishop said, staring out at the ranch yard, his eyes probing the corral. "No chance of that. This girl come with peace talk."

"And while she was talking, they rode in on us!" Rock raged.

Sharon came up, her eyes wide. "Oh, you can't believe that! You can't! I—"

The thud of bullets into the logs of the house drowned her voice, along with the crashing of guns. Rock Bannon was slipping from window to window, moving on his feet like an Indian. He had yanked off his other boot now. A shot smashed the water olla that hung near the door. Bannon fired, and a man toppled from behind the corner of the corral and sprawled on the hard-packed ground near the body of Turner.

"They're goin' to rush us," Bannon said suddenly. He began loading his Colts. "Get set, Hardy. They are goin' to rush."

"Let 'em come! The sneak-thievin', pelt-robbin', trap-lootin' scum! Let 'em come! More'll come than'll go back!"

As the outlaws rushed suddenly, charging in a scattered line, the old man burst through the door, his Colt smoking.

A man screamed and grabbed his middle and took three staggering steps and then sprawled his full length on the ground. Another man went down, and then a gun bellowed and the old man winced, took another step, and then toppled back into the room.

Sharon stared at him in horror and then ran to him. He looked shocked.

"Hit me! They hit me! Give me my gun, ma'am. I'll kill the scum like the trap-robbin' wolverines they are!"

"Ssh, be still," she whispered. She began tearing the shirt away from the massive chest to search for the wound.

Steadily, using now one gun and then the other, Rock Bannon fired. He could sense uncertainty among the attackers. They had shot the old man, but four of their own number were down, and probably others were wounded. They were beginning to lose all desire for battle.

Watching closely, Rock saw a flicker of movement behind a corral trough. He watched, lifted his rifle, and took careful aim, and when the movement came again, he fired, just under the trough.

A yell rang out, and he saw a man lift up to his full height and then topple over.

"All right!" Bannon shouted. "Come on and get me! You wanted me! But you'd better come before the boys get in from north camp, or they'll spoil my fun."

They wouldn't believe him, but it might make them doubtful. He heard voices raised in argument. Then there was silence. He reloaded all the guns, his own, Bishop's Henry, and the old man's six-guns. It was midafternoon, and the sun was hot. If they waited until night, he was going to have a bad time of it.

There was a chance, however, that they would believe his story or fear that someone from the line cabin might ride far enough this way to hear the shots. If both groups came, they would be caught between two fires and wiped out.

An hour passed, and there was no sound.

"Rock!" Sharon was standing behind him. "We'd better get him on a bed."

He avoided her eyes, but got up and put his rifle down. It was a struggle, but they lifted Bishop off the floor and put him on his homemade four-poster. While Sharon bent over him, bathing the wound and treating it as best she could, Rock walked back to the windows.

Like a caged panther, he prowled from window to window. Outside, all was still. Only the bodies of the dead lay on the hard-packed ground of the ranch yard. A dust devil started somewhere on the plain and twisted in the grass of the meadow and then skipped across the ranch yard, stirring around the body of Turner and blowing in his hair.

Turner was dead. The old man had been with them almost as long as Rock himself. He had been like one of the family. And Bob Springer was gone, blasted from life suddenly, all the young man's enthusiastic plans for a ranch of his own. Well, they would pay. They would pay to the last man.

The steel dust had come back from the end of the corral near the creek. He seemed curious and approached the body lying near the trough with delicate feet, ready to shy. He snuffed at the body, caught the scent of blood, and jerked away, eyes distended and nostrils wide.

There was no one in sight. Apparently, the attackers had drawn off. They had anticipated no such defense as this. They had had no idea that Rock Bannon was home, nor had they realized what a fighter the old man could be. They had to learn what the Crows had learned long since.

Rock waited another hour, continuing his slow prowl. Within the house he was comparatively safe, and he knew that to go out before he was sure was to tempt fate. From time to time he went into the bedroom where Bishop lay on the four-poster. He was unconscious or asleep, Sharon sitting beside him.

He avoided her eyes, yet the thought kept returning, filling him with bitterness, that she had ridden here with peace talk and that under cover of her talk Harper's men had made their approach. Knowing Bishop, he knew that unless his attention had been diverted, no rider or group of riders could have reached the ranch without being seen.

Had she planned with Mort Harper to do this thing? Everything he knew about the girl compelled him to believe she would do nothing of the kind, yet the thought persisted; it was almost too much of a coincidence.

After all, what reason had he to believe otherwise? Hadn't she admired Harper? Hadn't Pete Zapata been waiting in her cabin for him? Perhaps she had tried to warn him by throwing sticks on the fire, or it could have been an accident. The fact remained that while visiting her he had almost been killed in a trap laid by Zapata, and while she had been making peace talk with Bishop, the raiding party had struck. It was not her fault they were not dead, both of them.

He knew she came to the door from time to time, and once she started to speak, but then turned away as he avoided her eyes.

Rock was crouching by a window when the sound of horse's hoofs brought him to his feet. It was Bat Chavez astride a slim, fast buckskin. The horse shied violently at Turner's body, and Bat had a hard time getting him to the door.

Bannon rushed out. "Everything all right at the line cabin?"

"Shucks, man!" Bat exploded. "That's what I was goin' to ask you. What happened here?"

"They hit us. Dave opened up from the kitchen, Hardy and I shot it out up here. Bishop's down, hit pretty bad. They got Springer and Turner, as you can see."

"Saw them cuttin' across the valley for Poplar a few minutes ago. The boys are gettin' restless, Rock. They want to ride over and wind this up."

"No more than I do," Bannon said shortly. "Yes, we're goin'. We'll ride over and wipe that place out."

"Oh, no! You mustn't." Sharon had come into the door behind Rock. "Please, Rock! You mustn't. The settlers don't want to fight anymore. It's just Harper's crowd."

"Maybe that's true," Bannon said, "but I've seen no sign of them quittin' yet. There were at least twelve men in this bunch. Did Harper have twelve men of his own? Not that I saw, he didn't. And Zapata's dead. So's Miller. Where would he get twelve men?"

He turned back to Chavez. "Get some food into you, Bat, and then ride back. I'll be down before long, and when I am, we'll cross that valley. If the settlers get in the way, they'll get what the rest of them got—what they gave Turner and Springer here! We've dallied long enough."

Rock Bannon turned and walked back into the house. Sharon stared at him, her face white.

"Then you won't believe me?" she protested. "You'll go over there and kill innocent people?"

"Who killed Springer and Turner?" Rock demanded harshly. "In what way had they offended? I don't know that your settlers are innocent. I tried to tell them what they were going into, and they wouldn't believe me. Well, they came, and if they get their tails in a crack they've only themselves to blame.

"I argued with them. I argued with Bishop to give them a break, and now this happens. There were twelve men in that attack on us. At least twelve! Well, some of them died out here, but you and I both know that Harper didn't have twelve men. Perhaps eight, at best. They came in here and killed two of our boys and wounded Bishop. That old man in there has been a father to me. He's been more than most fathers. He's been a guide and a teacher, and all I know I learned from him. He may die, and if he does the fault was mine for ever letting this bunch of squatters in here."

The girl clasped her hands in distress. "Please, Rock!" she protested. "You can't do this. Most of your men don't know one from the other. The settlers would be killed whether they fought or not. Their homes will be burned."

"If they don't fight they won't be hurt," he insisted stubbornly. "Next time that Harper attacks, he might get us all. Anyway, it looks to me like they were plenty willing to ride in on Harper's coattails and get all they could while the getting was easy."

"That's not true," she protested hotly. "They wanted to do the right thing. They thought they were doing the right thing. They believed Harper was honest."

Rock slid into his buckskin coat and picked up his hat. His face was grim and hard. He could not look at Sharon. He knew if their eyes ever met it would tear the heart out of him. Yet he also knew he had waited too long now, that if he had resorted to guns long ago, so many things might not have happened. Springer might be living, and Turner, and Collins, the settler.

He started for the door, picking up his rifle from where he had left it. "Rock," Sharon said, "if you go back, I will too. The first one of your men who puts a hand on a settler's home, I'll kill with my own rifle."

For the first time he looked at her, and her eyes were flashing with pain and anger. "Go, then!" he said brutally. "But if you're half as smart as I think you are, you'll take your friends and head for the hills. Go! I'll give you a start. Warn Harper, too, if you want. Let him know we're coming. But if you want to save that precious pack of settlers, get them out of Poplar. Take to the hills until this is over—but be out of town before my boys ride in!"

He walked to the door and went out. She saw him stop by the corral and pick up a rope and then go to the corral for the steel dust. Running from the house, she threw herself into the saddle of her own black mare, which had been tied at the corner of the house. Spurring her to top speed, she sprang out on the long ride across the valley.

Rock Bannon did not look up or turn his head, but in his heart and mind the hard hoofs pounded like the pulse in his veins, pounded harder and harder, and then vanished with the dying sound of the running horse.

He saddled the steel dust, and as Bat Chavez walked from the house, Rock swung into the saddle. "Dave!" he yelled at the cook. "You watch over Hardy. We won't be long gone."

Abruptly, he swung the stallion south. Chavez rode beside him, glancing from time to time at Rock. Finally, he burst out. "Bannon, I think that gal's on the level. I sure do!"

"Yes?" Rock did not turn his head. "You let me worry about that!"

## IX

Pike Purcell was a grim and lonely man. He had been loitering all day around the saloon. Only that morning before riding away to the attack on the Bishop ranch house, in which he and Lamport had taken part, Dud Kitchen had told him about the bullet that killed Collins.

Pike was disturbed. His heart had not been in the fight at the ranch, and he had fired few shots. In fact, he and Lamport had been among the first to turn away from the fight. Purcell was thoroughly disillusioned with Mort Harper. The attack on the ranch had been poorly conceived and carried out even more poorly. Purcell didn't fancy himself as a leader, but he knew he could have done better.

Men had died back there—too many of them. Pike Purcell had a one-track mind, and that one track was busy with cogitation over the story told him by Dud. He could verify the truth of the supposition. Mort Harper had been behind Collins. It worried him, and his loyalty, already shaken by inadequate leadership, found itself on uncertain ground.

On the ride back there had been little talk. The party was sullen and angry. Their attack had failed under the straight shooting of Bishop and Bannon. They were leaving six men behind, six men who were stone dead. Maybe they had killed two, but that didn't compensate for six. Bishop was down, but how badly none of them knew.

Cap Mulholland had ridden in the attack as well. Never strongly inclined toward fighting, he had had no heart in this fight. He had even less now. Suddenly, he was realizing with bitterness that he didn't care if he never saw Mort Harper again.

"They'll be comin' for us now," Cap said.

"Shut up!" Lamport snapped. He was angry and filled with bitterness. He was the only one of the settlers who had thrown in completely with Harper's crowd, and the foolishness of it was now apparent. Defeat and their own doubts were carrying on the rapid disintegration of the Harper forces. "You see what I saw?" he demanded. "That Crockett girl was there. She was the one dragged Bishop's body back. I seen her!"

Harper's head jerked up. "You lie!" he snapped viciously.

Lamport looked across at Harper. "Mort," he said evenly, "don't you tell me I lie."

Harper shrugged. "All right, maybe she was there, but I've got to see it to believe it. How could she have beaten us to it?"

"How did Bannon beat us back?" Lamport demanded furiously. "He was supposed to be lost in the hills."

"He must have come back over the mountain," Gettes put in. He was one of the original Harper crowd. "He must have found a way through."

"Bosh!" Harper spat. "Nothing human could have crossed that mountain last night. A man would be insane to try it."

"Well," Pike said grimly, "Bannon got there. I know good and well he never rode none of those canyons last night, so he must've come over the mountain. If any man could, he could."

Harper's eyes were hard. "You seem to think a lot of him," he sneered.

"I hate him," Pike snapped harshly. "I hate every step he takes, but he's all man!"

Mort Harper's face was cruel as he stared at Pike. Purcell had ridden on, unnoticing.

Pike did not return to his cabin after they reached Poplar. Pike Purcell was as just as he was ignorant and opinionated. His one quality was loyalty, that and more than his share of courage. Dud Kitchen's story kept cropping up. Did Harper own a small gun?

Suddenly, he remembered. Shortly after they arrived at Poplar he had seen such a gun. It was a .34 Patterson, and Mort Harper had left it lying on his bed.

Harper was gone somewhere. The saloon was empty. Purcell stepped in, glanced around, and then walked back to Harper's quarters. The room was neat, and things were carefully arranged. He crossed to a rough wooden box on the far side of the room and lifted the lid. There were several boxes of .44s, and a smaller box. Opening it, he saw a series of neat rows of .34 caliber cartridges, and across the lead nose of each shell was a deep notch!

He picked up one of the shells and stepped back. His face was gray as he turned toward the door. He was just stepping through when Mort Harper came into the saloon.

Quick suspicion came into Mort's eyes. "What are you doin' in there?" he demanded.

"Huntin' for polecat tracks," Purcell said viciously. "I found 'em!" He tossed the shell on the table. It was the wrong move, for it left his right hand outstretched and far from his gun.

At such a time things happen instantaneously. Mort Harper's hand flashed for his gun, and Purcell was late, far too late. He had his hand on the butt when the bullet struck him. He staggered back, hate blazing in his eyes, and sat down hard. He tugged at his gun, and Harper shot him again.

Staring down at the body of the tall, old mountaineer, Mort Harper saw the end of everything. So this was how things finished? An end to dreams, an end to ambition. He would never own Bishop's Valley now. He would never own the greatest cattle empire in the West, a place where he would be a king on his own range, with nothing to control his actions but his own will.

He had despised Purcell for his foolishness in following him. He had led the settlers like sheep, but now they would survive and he would die. In a matter of hours, perhaps even minutes, Bannon would be coming, and then nothing would be left here but a ruin.

At that moment he heard a pounding of horse's hoofs and looked up to see Sharon go flying past on her black mare.

There was something left. There was Sharon. Rock Bannon wanted her. Sudden resolution flooded him. She was one thing Bannon wouldn't get! Mort Harper ran to his quarters, threw a few things together, and then walked out. Hastily, under cover of the pole barn, he saddled a fresh horse, loaded his gear aboard, swung into the saddle, and started up the canyon toward the Crockett home.

Cap Mulholland watched him go, unaware of what was happening. Dud Kitchen had heard the shots and had returned for his own guns. He watched Harper stop at the Crockett place, unaware of the stuffed saddlebags. When he saw the man swing down, he was not surprised.

Sharon had caught Jim Satterfield in the open and told him they should flee the village at once. At this moment Satterfield was headed for the Pagones' house as fast as he could move. Sharon ran into her house, looking for her father, but as usual, he was in the fields. There was not a moment to lose. She ran out and was about to swing into the saddle when Mort Harper dismounted at the front steps. He heard her speak to the horse and stepped around the house.

"Sharon!" he said. "You're just in time."

She halted. "What do you mean?" she demanded coolly.

He rushed to her excitedly. "We're leaving! We must get away now. Just you and me! The Bishop crowd will be coming soon, and they'll leave nothing here. We still have time to get away."

"I'm going to get my father now," she said. "Then we'll go to the hills."

"There's no time for that—he'll get along. You come with me!" Harper was excited, and he did not see the danger lights in Sharon's eyes.

"Go where?" she inquired.

Mort Harper stared at her impatiently. "Away! Anywhere for the time being. Later we can go on to California together, and—"

"Aren't you taking too much for granted?" She reached for the black mare's bridle. "I'm not going with you, Mort. I'm not going anywhere with you."

It was a real shock. He stared at her, unbelieving and impatient.

"Don't be foolish!" he snapped. "There's nothing here for you. You were practically promised to me. If it's marriage you want, don't worry about that. We can go on to California and be married there."

"It is marriage I want, Mort, but not to you. Never to you. For a little while I was as bad as the others, and I believed in you. Then I saw the kind of men you had around you, how you'd deliberately led us here to use us for your own ends. No, Mort. I'm not marrying you and I'm not going away with you." She made no attempt to veil the contempt in her voice. "If you're afraid, you'd better get started. I'm going for my father."

Suddenly, he was calm, dangerously calm. "So? It's that Rock Bannon, is it? I never thought you'd take that ignorant cowhand seriously. Or," he sneered, "is it your way of getting Bishop's Valley?"

"Get out!" she said. "Get out now! Dad and Pagones will be here in a moment, and when I tell them what you've said, they'll kill you."

"Kill me? Those two?" He laughed. Then his face stiffened. "All right, I'll get out, but you're coming with me!"

He moved so swiftly she had no chance to defend herself. He stepped toward her suddenly and she saw his fist start. The shock of the blow was scarcely greater than the shock of the fact that he had struck her. Dimly, she realized he had thrown her into the saddle and was lashing her there. She thought she struggled, but she lived those moments only in a half world of consciousness, a half world soon pounded into oblivion by the drum of racing horses. . . .

It was Satterfield who finally got Crockett from the fields. The Bishop riders were already in sight when Tom raced into his house, caught up his rifle, and called for Sharon. She was gone, and he noted that her black mare was gone. She was away, that was the main thing. With Jim, he ran out into the field, where he was joined by Pagones, his wife and daughter, and Dud Kitchen.

The others were coming. It was a flight, and there was no time to prepare or take anything but what lay at hand. Cap Mulholland, his face sullen, went with them, his wife beside him. The Olsens and Greene joined them, and in a compact group they turned away toward the timber along the hillside.

Lamport did not go. He had no idea that Mort Harper was gone. John Kies was in his store, awaiting the uncertain turn of events. Kies had worked with Mort before, and he trusted the younger man's skill and judgment.

It was over. It was finished. Lamport stared cynically at the long buildings of the town. Probably it was just as well, for he would do better in the goldfields. Steady day-to-day work had never appealed to him. Pike Purcell had been an honest but misguided man. Lamport was neither. From the first he had sensed the crooked grain in the timber of Mort Harper, but he didn't care.

Lamport felt that he was self-sufficient. He would stay in as long as the profits looked good, and he would get out when the luck turned against them. He had seen the brilliant conception of theft that had flowered in the brain of Mort Harper. He saw what owning that valley could mean.

It was over now. He had lived and worked with Purcell, but he had no regret for the man. Long ago he had sensed that Harper would kill him someday. Of all the settlers, Lamport was the only one who had read Harper aright, perhaps because they were of the same feeling.

Yet there was a difference. Lamport's hate was a tangible, deadly thing. Harper could hate and he could fight, but Harper was completely involved with himself. He could plot, wait, and strike like a rattler. Lamport had courage with his hate, and that was why he was not running now. He was waiting, waiting in the full knowledge of what he faced.

His hate for Rock Bannon had begun when Bannon rode so much with Sharon. It had persisted, developing from something much deeper than any rivalry over a woman. It developed from the rivalry of two strong men, of two fighting men, each of whom recognizes in the other a worthy and dangerous foe.

Lamport had always understood Harper. Of all those that had surrounded him, Lamport was the only one Mort Harper had feared. Pete Zapata he had always believed he could kill. Lamport was the one man with whom he avoided trouble. He even avoided conversation with him when possible. He knew Lamport was dangerous, and he knew he would face him down if it came to that.

He was a big man, as tall as Rock Bannon, and twenty pounds heavier. When he walked, his head thrust forward somewhat and he stared at the world from pale blue eyes beneath projecting shelves of beetling brows. In his great shoulders there was a massive, slumbering power. Lamport's strength had long since made him contemptuous of other men, and his natural skill with a gun had added to that contempt. He was a man as brutal as his heavy jaw, as fierce as the light in his pale eyes.

Surly and sullen, he made friends with no one. In the biting envy and cantankerousness of Pike Purcell he had found companionship if no more. Lamport was not a loyal man. Purcell's death meant nothing to him. He waited for Rock Bannon now, filled with hatred for the victor in the fight, the man who would win.

Thinking back now, Lamport could see that Rock had always held the winning hand. He had known about Bishop, was akin to him, had known what awaited here. Also, from the start his assay of Harper's character had been correct.

From the beginning, Lamport had accepted the partnership with Purcell, rode with the wagon train because it was a way west, and threw in with Harper for profit. In it all, he respected but one man, the man he was now waiting to kill.

When he heard the horses coming, he poured another drink in the deserted bar. Somewhere around, there were three or four more men. The rest had vanished like snow in a desert sun. Hitching his guns into place, he walked to the door and out on the plank porch.

John Kies's white face stared at him from an open window of the store.

"Where's Mort?" Kies said. "That's them coming now."

Lamport chuckled and spat into the dust. He scratched the stubble on his heavy jaw and grinned sardonically at Kies.

"He's around, I reckon, or maybe he blowed out. The rest of 'em have."

Stark fear came into the storekeeper's face. "No! No, they can't have!" he protested. "They'll have an ambush! They'll— "

"You're crazy!" Lamport sneered. "This show is busted. You should know that. That's Bannon comin' now, and when that crowd of his gets through, there won't be one stick on another in this town."

"But the settlers!" Kies wailed. "They'll stop him."

Lamport grinned at him. "The settlers have took to the hills. They are gone! Me, I'm waitin' to kill Rock Bannon. Then if I can fight off his boys, I'm goin'."

They came up the street, walking their horses. Rock was in the lead, his rifle across his saddle bows. To his right was Bat Chavez, battle hungry as always. To his left was Red, riding loosely on a paint pony. Behind them, in a mounted skirmishing line, came a dozen hard-bitten Indian-fighting plainsmen, riders for the first big cow spread north of Texas.

A rifle shot rang out suddenly from a cabin in the back of the store, then another. A horse staggered and went down, and Bat Chavez wheeled his horse and with four riders, raced toward the cabin. The man who waited there lost his head suddenly and bolted.

A lean blond rider in a Mexican jacket swept down on him, rope twirling. It shot out, and the horse went racing by, and the burly teamster's body was a bounding thing, leaping and tumbling through the cactus after the racing horse. Chavez swung at once, and turned back toward the saloon. The riders fanned out and started going through the town. Where they went, there were gunshots, then smoke.

Rock Bannon saw Lamport standing on the porch. "Don't shoot!"

he commanded. He walked the steel dust within twenty feet. Lamport stood on the edge of the porch, wearing two guns, his dark, dirty red wool shirt open at the neck to display a massive, hairy chest.

"Howdy, Rock!" Lamport said. He spat into the dust. "Come to take your lickin'?"

"To give you yours," Rock said coolly. "How do you want it?"

"Why, I reckon we're both gun handy, Rock," Lamport said, "so I expect it'll be guns. I'd have preferred hand muckin' you, but that would scarcely give you an even break."

"You reckon not?" Rock slid from the stallion. "Well, Lamport, I always figure to give a man what he wants. If you think you can take me with your hands, shed those guns and get started. You've bought yourself a fight."

Incredulous, Lamport stared at him. "You mean it?" he said, his eyes brightening.

"Stack your duds and grease your skids, coyote!" Rock said. "It's knuckle and skull now, and free fighting if you like it!"

"Free, he says!" A light of unholy joy gleamed in Lamport's eyes. "Free it is!"

"Watch yourself, Boss!" Red said, low voiced. "That hombre looks like blazin' brimstone on wheels!"

"Then we'll take off his wheels and kick the brimstone out!" Rock said. He hung his guns over the saddle horn as Bat Chavez rode around the corner.

Lamport faced him in the dust before the saloon, a huge grizzly of a man with big iron-knuckled hands and a skin that looked like a stretched rawhide.

"Come and get it!" he sneered, and rushed.

As he rushed, he swung a powerful right. Rock Bannon met him halfway and lashed out with his own right. His punch was faster, and it caught the big man flush, but Lamport took it on the mouth, spat blood, and rushed in, swinging with both fists. Suddenly he caught Bannon and hurled him into the dust with such force that a cloud of dust arose. Rock rolled over like a cat, gasping for breath, and just rolled from under Lamport's driving boots as the big man tried to leap on him to stamp his life out.

Rock scrambled to his feet and lunged as he picked his hands out of the dust, butting Lamport in the chest. The big renegade jerked up a stiff thumb, trying for Rock's eye, but Bannon rolled his head away and swung a left to the wind and then a driving right that ripped Lamport's ear, starting a shower of blood.

Lamport now charged again and caught Bannon with two long swings on the head. His skull roaring with pain and dizziness, Rock braced himself and started to swing in a blind fury, both hands going with every ounce of power he could muster.

Lamport met him, and spraddle-legged, the two started to slug. Lamport was the bigger, and his punches packed terrific power, but were a trifle slower. It was nip and tuck, dog eat dog, and the two battled until the breath gasped in their lungs and whistled through their teeth. Lamport ducked his battered face and started to walk in, stemming the tide of Bannon's blows by sheer physical power.

Rock shifted his attack with lightning speed. He missed a right, and following it in with the weight of his body, he slid his arm around Lamport's thick neck. Grabbing the wrist with his left hand, he jerked up his feet and sat down hard, trying to break Lamport's neck.

But the big renegade knew all the tricks, and as Rock's feet flew up, Lamport hurled his weight forward and to the left, falling with his body half across Bannon. It broke the hold, and they rolled free. Rock came to his feet, and Lamport, catlike in his speed, lashed out with a wicked kick for his head.

Rock rolled away from it and hurled himself at Lamport's one standing leg in a flying tackle. The big man went down, and as they scrambled up, Rock hit him with a left and right, splitting his right cheek in a bone-deep gash and pulping his lips.

Lamport was bloody and battered now, yet he kept coming, his breath wheezing. Rock Bannon stabbed a left into his face, set himself, and whipped a right uppercut to the body. Lamport gasped. Bannon circled and then smashed him in the body with another right and then another and another. Lamport's jaw was hanging open now, his face battered and bleeding from a dozen cuts and abrasions. Rock walked in, measured him, and then crossed a right to his chin. He followed it up with two thudding, bone-crushing blows. Lamport reeled, tried to steady himself, and then measured his length in the dust.

Rock Bannon weaved on his feet and then walked to the watering trough and ducked his head into it. He came up spluttering and then splashed water over his face and body, stripping away the remnants of his torn shirt.

"We got 'em all, Boss," Red said. "You want we should go after the settlers?"

"No, and leave their homes alone. Where's Kies?"

"The storekeeper? Inside, I guess."

Rock strapped on his guns and strode up the steps of the store with Red and Chavez at his heels. Kies was waiting behind the counter, his face white.

"Kies," Rock said. "Have you got the bills for the goods you sold the settlers?"

"The bills?" Kies's frightened eyes showed doubt and then dismay.
"Why, yes."

"Get 'em out."

Fumblingly, Kies dug out the bills. Quickly, Bannon scanned
through them. Then he took a match and set fire to the stack as they
lay on the counter.

Kies sprang for them. "What are you doing?" he screamed.

"You're payin' the price of hookin' up with a crooked bunch,"
Bannon said grimly, as Chavez held the angry storekeeper. "You got
a horse?"

"Yes, I have a—horse, but I—"

"Red," Bannon turned. "Give this man some shells, a rifle, a
canteen, and two days' grub, skimpy rations. Then put him on a
horse and start him on his way. If he tries to load that rifle or if he
doesn't ride right out of the country, hang him."

"But the Indians!" Kies protested. "And my store!"

"You haven't got a store," Bannon told him harshly. "You'll have
to look out for the Indians yourself."

"Boss," Chavez touched him on the shoulder. "Hombre here
wants to talk."

Rock Bannon wheeled. Tom Crockett, Pagones, and Dud Kitchen
were standing there.

"Bannon," Crockett said, "Harper took my girl. Kitchen saw him
tying her to a horse."

Rock's face went white and then stiffened. "I reckon he was the
one she wanted," he said. "She had Zapata waitin' for me, and she
led that raid to the ranch."

"No, she didn't do that, Rock," Pagones said. "The raid wasn't
even organized when she left. As for Zapata—"

"He forced himself on us," Crockett protested. "And she was tied
to the saddle. She didn't want to go with Harper. She was in love
with you."

"That's right, Rock," Pagones assured him. "Mary's known that for
weeks."

"All right," Rock said. He jerked a shirt from a stack on the
counter and began getting into it. "I'll find 'em."

"Who goes along with you?" Bat asked eagerly.

"Nobody," Bannon said. "This is my job."

# X

The steel-dust stallion liked the feel of the trail. He always knew
when he was going someplace that was beyond the place where
distance lost itself against the horizon. He knew it now, knew in

the sound of Rock Bannon's voice and the easy way he sat in the saddle.

Rock rode through the poplars where the wagon train had spent its last night on the trail, and as he passed, he glanced down at the ruts, already grown with grass. It seemed such a long time ago, yet it was scarcely more than days since the wagons had waited here. He had observed them from the mountains, looking back for the last time as he rode away from the train.

He turned the stallion up the long, grassy canyon where Freeman had been killed. The trail Mort Harper had left was plain enough. So far, he had been running; later, he would try to cover it. Yet Bannon was already looking ahead, planning, trying to foresee what plan, if any, could be in the man's mind.

The Day's River region was one of the most rugged in all America. No man knew it well; few knew it even passingly well. Unless a man chose carefully of the trails that offered, he would run into a blind canyon or end in a jump off or at some blind tangle of boulders.

There were trails through. The Indians had used them. Other Indians, ages before, had left picture writing on the canyon walls, some of them in places almost impossible to reach. No man knew the history of this region.

There were places here with a history stranger than any written—an old weapon washed from the sands of a creek, a strange date on a canyon wall. There was one place miles from here where the date 1642 was carved on a canyon wall among other dates and names, and no man has yet accounted for that date or said who put it there or how he came to be in the country.

From Grass Canyon the trail of the two horses led into a narrow draw with very steep sides overgrown with birch, balsam, and cottonwood. His rifle ready, although anticipating no trouble at this stage, Rock pushed on.

The draw now opened on a vast region of jagged mountain ridges, gorges, cliffs, and mesas. The stallion followed the trail along the edge of a meadow watered by a brawling mountain stream. Some teal flew from the pool of water backed up by a beaver dam, and Rock heard the sharp, warning slap of the beaver's tail on the water.

The trail dipped now down a narrow passage between great rock formations that towered heavenward. On one side was an enormous mass of rock like veined marble, and on the other a rock of brightest orange fading to rust red, shot through with streaks of purple.

Boulders scattered the space between the walls, and at times passage became difficult. At one place great slabs of granite had sloughed off from high above and come crashing down upon the rocks below. Far ahead he could see the trail leaving the lowlands and climbing, threadlike, across the precipitous wall of the mountain.

Studying the trail and the speed of the horses he was following, Rock could see that Mort was trying for distance, and fast. Rock knew, too, that unless Harper was far ahead, he would, if watching his back trail, soon know he was followed. From the incredible heights ahead, the whole series of canyons and gorges would be plainly visible except when shoulders of rock or boulders intervened.

The trail up the face of the cliff had been hewn by nature from the solid rock itself, cutting across the face of an almost vertical cliff and only emerging at times in bare rock ledges or dipping around some corner of rock into a cool, shadowed gorge.

"He's headin' for Big Track," Rock told himself suddenly. "He sure is. He's headin' for Big Track Hollow."

He knew the place, and certainly, if Harper was following a known or planned route, he could choose no better. Big Track Hollow was a basin over six thousand feet above sea level where there was a wealth of grass, plenty of water, and sheltering woods.

It would be the best place in this region to hole up for any length of time. Long ago, somebody had built a cabin there, and there were caves in the basin walls. It took its name from gigantic dinosaur tracks that appeared in the rock all along one side.

For Harper the place had the distinct advantage of offering four separate avenues of escape. Each one would take him over a trail widely divergent from the others, so once a follower was committed to one trail he would have to retrace his steps and start over again to find his quarry. The time consumed would leave him so far behind that it would be impossible to catch up.

Rock Bannon stared thoughtfully at the tracks. It would soon be night, and the two must stop. Yet they had sufficient lead on him to make it difficult to overtake them soon, and at night he could easily get off the trail and lose himself in the spiderweb of canyons.

Reluctantly, he realized he must camp soon. The landscape everywhere now was rock, red rock cliffs towering against the sky, cathedral-shaped buttes and lofty pinnacles. He rode down the steep trail, dipping into shadowy depths and riding along a canyon that echoed with the stallion's steps. It was like riding down a long hallway carved from solid rock, lonely and empty.

There was no sound but the walking of the horse and the creak of the saddle leather. Dwarfed by the lofty walls, he moved as a ghost in a vast, unreal world. Yet he rode warily, for at any point Harper might elect to stop and waylay him.

Now the trail down the long avenue between the walls began to rise, and suddenly he emerged upon a plateau that seemed to hang upon the rim of the world.

Far away and below him stretched miles upon miles of the same broken country, but there were trees and grass in the valleys below, and he turned the horse at right angles and then reined in. Here for a space was gravel and rock. He studied the ground carefully and then moved on.

The trail was difficult now, and in the fading light he was compelled to slip from the saddle, rifle in hand, and walk along over the ground. They wound around and around, steadily dropping. Then ahead of him he saw a pool and beside it a place where someone had lain to drink.

Sliding to the ground, he stripped the saddle from the stallion and tethered him on a grassy plot. Then he gathered dry sticks for a fire, which he made, keeping it very small and in the shadow of some boulders. When the fire was going he made coffee and then slipped back from the fire and carefully scouted the surrounding darkness.

Every step of the way was a danger. Mort Harper was on the run now, and he would fight like a cornered rat, where and when and how he could find the means.

Before daylight, Rock rolled out, packed his gear, and saddled the stallion. Yet when it was light enough to see, there was no trail. The water of the stream offered the best possibility, so he rode into it himself, scanning the narrow banks with attention.

Finally, after being considerably slowed down by the painstaking search, he found where they had left the stream. A short distance further, after seeing no marks, he found a bruised clump of grass where a horse had stepped and slipped.

He had gone no more than four miles when he found where they had camped. There had been two beds, one back in a corner of rocks away from the other, and cut off from the trail by it. Mort Harper was taking no chances. Yet when Rock looked around, he glimpsed something under a bush in the damp earth.

Kneeling, he put his head under the bush. Scratched in the earth with a stick were the words BE CAREFUL and then BIG TRACK.

He had been right then. Harper was headed for Big Track. If that was so, they were a good day's ride from there. Bannon thought that over while climbing the next ridge. Then he made a sudden decision. From the ridge, he examined the terrain before him and then wheeled his horse. As he did so a shot rang out. Leaping from the horse to a cleft in the rock, he lifted his rifle and waited.

The country on the other side of the ridge was fairly open, but with clumps of brush and boulders. To ride down there after a rifleman, and Harper was an excellent shot, would be suicide. Only his wheeling of the stallion had saved his life at that moment.

Sliding back from the cleft, he retreated down the hillside to the steel dust. He swung into the saddle, and keeping the ridge between him and the unseen marksman, he started riding east. He had made his decision, and he was going to gamble on it.

If he continued to follow, as he was following now, he would fall further and further behind, compelled to caution by Harper's rifle and the difficulty of following the trail. If Harper reached Big Track Hollow first, it would be simple for him to take a trail out of there, and then it would be up to Bannon to find which trail.

Rock Bannon had never heard of a cutoff to Big Track, but he knew where he was and he knew where Big Track was. Ahead of him a draw opened and he raced the steel dust into it and started along it, slowing the horse to a canter. Ahead of him and on the skyline, a sharp pinnacle pointed at the sky. That was his landmark.

The country grew rougher, but he shifted from draw to draw, cut across a flat, barren plateau of scattered rocks and rabbit grass, and traversed a lava flow, black and ugly, to skirt a towering rust-red cliff. A notch in the cliff ahead seemed to indicate a point of entry, so he guided the stallion among the boulders. A lizard darted from under the stallion's hoofs, and overhead a buzzard wheeled in wide, lonely circles.

The sun was blazing hot now, and the rocks caught and multiplied the heat. He skirted the gray, dirty mud shore of a small alkaline lake and rode into a narrow cleft in the mountain.

At one point it was so narrow that for thirty yards he had to pull one foot from the stirrup and drag the stirrup up into the saddle. Then the cleft opened into a spacious green valley, its sides lined with a thick growth of quaking aspen. There was water here, and he stopped to give the stallion a brief rest and to drink.

They had been moving at a rapid clip for the distance and the heat. Yet the horse looked good. Again he checked his guns. It was nip and tuck now. If he were to make Big Track before they reached it, or by the same time, he must hurry. If he failed, then there was not one chance in a dozen that he would ever see Sharon again.

Now, every movement, every thought, and every inflection of her voice returned to him, filling him with desperation. She was his. He knew it in every fiber of his being. She was his and had always been his, not only, he understood now, in his own heart, but in hers. He had always known what Mort Harper was. He should never have doubted the girl. It was amazing to him now that he had doubted her even for an instant.

So on he went, though the sun blazed down on the flaming rocks in a torment and the earth turned to hot brass beneath the stallion's feet. The mountains grew rougher. There was more and more lava, and then when it seemed it could get no worse, he rode out upon a glaring white alkali desert that lasted for eight miles at midday, stifling dust and blazing sun.

Rock Bannon seemed to have been going for hours now, yet it was only because of his early start. It was past one in the afternoon, and he had been riding, with but one break, since four in the morning.

On the far side of the desert, there was a spring of water that tasted like rotten eggs—mineral water. He drank a little, rubbed the horse down with a handful of rabbit grass, and let him graze briefly. Then he mounted again, and went on, climbing into the hills.

Big Track was nearer. Somewhere not far from the great sky-stabbing pinnacle he had seen. Sweat streamed down his face and down his body under the new shirt. He squinted his eyes against the sun and the smart of the sweat. He had to skirt a towering peak to get to the vicinity of Big Track.

He was riding now with all thought lost, only his goal in mind, and a burning, driving lust to come face to face with Mort Harper. Somewhere ahead he would be waiting; somewhere ahead they would meet.

The sun brought something like delirium, and he thought again of the long days of riding over the plains, of Sharon's low voice and her cool hands as he wrestled with pain and fever, recovering from the wounds of a lone battle against Indians. He seemed to feel again the rocking roll of the wagon over the rutted, dusty trail, tramped by the thousands heading for the new lands in the West.

Why had he waited so long to speak? Why hadn't he been able to find words to tell the girl he loved her? Words had always left him powerless; to act was easy, but somehow to shape into words the things he felt was beyond him, and women put so much emphasis on words, on the saying of things, and the way they were said.

He swung down from the saddle after a long time and walked on, knowing even the great stallion's strength was not without limit. The wild, strange country through which he was going now was covered with blasted boulders, the rough, slaglike lava, and scattered pines, dwarfish and wind bedraggled, whipped into agonized shapes by the awful contortions of the wind.

Then he saw the stark pinnacle almost ahead, and he saw, beyond it, the green of Big Track. He climbed back into the saddle again, and mopped the sweat from his face. The big horse walked wearily now, but the goal was reached. Rock Bannon loosened the guns in their holsters, and grim faced, he turned down a natural trail that no man had ridden before him, and into the green lush splendor of Big Track Hollow.

The smell of the grass was rich and almost unbelievable, and he heard a bird singing and the sudden whir of wings as some game bird took off in sudden flight. Water sounded, and the gray stallion quickened his pace. He skirted a wide-boled aspen and rode through a grass scattered with purple and pink asters, white sego lilies, and red baneberry. Then he saw the water and rode rapidly toward it.

He dropped from the saddle, taking a quick look around. No human sound disturbed the calm, utter serenity of Big Track. He dropped to his chest on the ground and drank, and beside him, the steel dust drank and drank deep.

Suddenly, the stallion's head came up sharply. Warned, Rock felt his every muscle tense. Then he forced himself to relax. The horse was looking at something, and the calling of birds was stilled. He got slowly to his feet, striving to avoid any sudden movement, knowing in every muscle and fiber of his being that he was being watched. He turned slowly, striving for a casual, careless manner.

Mort Harper was standing a short distance away, a pistol in his hand. He was thinner, wolfish now, his face darkened by sun and wind, his eyes hard and cruel. Backed in a corner, all the latent evil of the man had come to the fore. Quick fear touched Rock.

"Howdy," he said calmly. "I see you're not takin' any chances, Mort. Got that gun right where it'll do the most good."

Harper smiled, and with his teeth bared he looked even more vulpine, even more cruel. "We both know what it means to get the drop," Harper said. "We both know it means you're a dead man."

"I ain't so sure," Bannon said, shrugging. "I've heard of men who beat it. Maybe I'm one of the lucky ones."

"You don't beat this one," Mort said grimly. "I've come to kill you, man." Suddenly his eyes darkened with fury. "I'd like to know how in blazes you got here!" he snapped.

"Figured you'd head for this place if you knew the country at all," Bannon replied with a shrug. "So I cut across country."

"There's no other trail," Harper said. "It can't be done."

Rock Bannon stared at him coldly. "Where I want to go, there's always a trail," Bannon said. "I make my trails, Mort Harper, I don't try to follow and steal the work of other men."

Harper laughed. "That doesn't bother me, Rock. I've still got the edge. Maybe I lost on that steal, but I've got your woman. I've got her and I'll keep her! Oh, she's yours, all right—I know that now. She's yours, and a hellcat with it, but it'll be fun breaking her, and before I take her out of these hills she'll be broken or dead.

"I've got her, and she's fixed so if anything happens to me, you'll never find her and she'll die there alone. It'll serve both of you right. Only I'm not going to die—you are."

"All rat," Rock said coldly. "A rat, all the way through. I don't imagine you ever had a square, decent thought in your life. Always out to get something cheap, to beat somebody, to steal somebody else's work and fancying yourself a smart boy because of it."

Rock Bannon smiled suddenly. "All right, you're going to kill me. Mind if I smoke first?"

"Sure!" Mort sneered. "You can smoke, but keep your hands high, or you'll die quick. Go ahead, have your smoke. I like standing here watching you. I like remembering that you're Rock Bannon and I'm Mort Harper and this is the last hand of the game and I'm holding all winning cards. I've got the girl and I've got the drop."

Carefully, Rock dug papers and tobacco from his breast pocket. Keeping his hands high and away from his guns, he rolled a cigarette.

"Like thinking about it, don't you, Harper? Killing me quick would have spoiled that. If you'd shot me while I was on the ground, it wouldn't have been good. I'd never have known what hit me. Now I do know. Tastes good, doesn't it, Mort?"

He dug for his matches and got them out. He struck one, and it flared up with a big burst. Rock smiled, and holding the match in his fingers, the cigarette between his lips, he grinned at Mort.

"Yes," he said, "it tastes good, doesn't it? And you've got the girl somewhere? Got her hid where I can't find her? Why, Mort, I'll have no trouble. I can read your mind. I can trail you anywhere. I could trail a buzzard flying over a snowfield, Mort, so trailing you would be—"

The match burned down to his fingers and he gestured with it; then as the flame touched his fingers he let out a startled yelp and dropped the match, jerking his hand from the pain—the hand swept down and up, blasting fire!

Mort Harper, distracted by the gesture and the sudden yelp of pain, was just too late. The two guns boomed together, but Mort twisted with sudden shock, and he took a full step back, his face stricken.

Rock Bannon stepped carefully to one side for a better frontal target, and they both fired again. He felt something slug him, and a leg buckled, but he fired again and then again. He shifted guns and fired a fifth shot. Harper was on his knees, his face white and twisted. Rock walked up to him and kicked the smoking gun from his hand.

"Where is she?" he demanded. "Tell me!"

Mort's hate-filled face twisted. "Go to the devil!" he gasped hoarsely. "You go—plumb to the devil!"

He coughed, spitting blood. "Go to the devil!" he said again. Suddenly his mouth opened wide and he seemed to gasp wildly for breath that he couldn't get. Then he fell forward on his face, his fingers digging into the grass, as blood stained the mossy earth beneath him.

Rock walked back to the horse, and stood there, gripping the saddle horn. He felt weak and sick, yet he didn't believe he had been hit hard. There was a dampness on his side, but when he pulled off the new shirt, he saw that only the skin was cut in a shallow groove along his side above the hipbone.

Digging stuff from his saddlebags, he patched the wound as best he could. It was only then he thought of his leg.

There was nothing wrong with it, and then he saw the wrenched spur. The bullet had struck his spur, twisting and jerking his leg but doing no harm.

Carefully, he reloaded his guns. Then he called loudly. There was no response. He called again, and there was no answering sound. Slowly, Rock began to circle, studying the ground. Harper had moved carefully through the grass and had left little trail. Rock returned for his horse, and mounting, he began to ride in slow circles.

Somewhere, Mort would have his horses, and the girl would not be far from them. From time to time he called. Two slow hours passed. At times, he swung down and walked, leading the stallion. He worked his way through every grove, examined every boulder patch and clump of brush.

Bees hummed in the still, warm air. He walked on, his side smarting viciously, his feet heavy with walking in the high-heeled boots. Suddenly, sharply, the stallion's head came up and he whinnied. Almost instantly, there was an answering call. Then Rock Bannon saw a horse, and swinging into the saddle he loped across a narrow glade toward the boulders.

The horse was there, and almost at once he saw Sharon. She was tied to the top of a boulder, out of sight from below except for a toe of her boot. He scrambled up and released her and then unfastened the handkerchief with which she had been gagged.

"Oh, Rock!" Her arms went about him, and for a long moment they sat there, and he held her close.

After a long time she looked up. "When I heard your horse, I tried so hard to cry out that I almost strangled. Then when my mare whinnied, I knew you'd find us."

She came to with a start as he helped her down. "Rock! Where's Mort? He meant to kill you."

"He was born to fail," Rock said simply. "He was just a man who had big plans, but couldn't win out with anything. At the wrong time he was too filled with hate to even accomplish a satisfactory killin'."

Briefly, as she bathed her face and hands, he told her of what had happened at Poplar. "Your folks will all be back in their homes by now," he said. "You know, in some ways, Lamport was one of the best of the lot. He was a fighter—a regular bull. I hit him once with everything I had, every bit of strength an' power and drive in me, and he only grunted."

They sat there in the grass, liking the shade of the white-trunked aspens.

"Dud and Mary are getting married, Rock," Sharon said suddenly.

He reddened slowly under his tan and tugged at a handful of grass. "Reckon," he said slowly, "that'll be two of us!"

Sharon laughed gaily and turned. "Why, Rock! Are you asking me to marry you?"

"Nope," he said, grinning broadly. "I'm tellin' you! This here's one marriage that's goin' to start off right."

The steel dust stamped his hoofs restlessly. Things were being altogether too quiet. He wasn't used to it.

# AUTHOR'S NOTE
# A Man Called Trent

*Society has never been comfortable with killers. In times of warfare and troubles they have been tolerated, but have always been discomforting to have around. A marshal or sheriff with such a reputation might be tolerated as long as he was necessary, but as soon as the need passed, most citizens wanted to be rid of him.*

*Contrary to western motion pictures, nobody went around cultivating a reputation as a gunfighter unless he was a psychopath. A gunfighter was simply a man who was good with a gun. His coordination, his coolness in a tight situation, and his steadiness of nerve and hand also might have been better than others'. At a time when gunfighting was the accepted way of settling disputes, a man with a steady hand and eye came up a winner. By the time he had won two or three times, he had a reputation. Some admired him for his ability, but far more were uneasy in his presence.*

*A man such as Lance Kilkenny would not want such a reputation, and, as in this story, might flee from it. But a reputation is hard to escape in a country of a small but constantly shifting population. Moreover, the motivations and skills that won the reputation in the first place would always be with him.*

*There are always those who will ride roughshod over the rights of others if they can make a dollar by doing so, and each one believes he is manifest destiny. But there are always those who will resist. And there are always those who believe that because they have wealth or power, they are different from those without it.*

*Such people as Jared Tetlow in this story were all too familiar. In Wyoming a number of large ranchers or their superintendents, aided by men who were politically powerful, actually recruited fifty-odd gunfighters to come secretly into Wyoming and kill more than eighty men. The men to be killed were called "rustlers," but as a matter of fact most of them were simply nesters, people who had moved to government land, built cabins, and laid claim to land and waterholes* the big cattlemen wanted. So these gunmen were imported for the purpose of committing murder, nothing more nor less.

Sheepmen were often killed by cattlemen because of the mistaken impression that cattle would not feed where sheep were. That this was utter nonsense made no difference. The killings were carried out by self-righteous cattlemen accustomed to the use of power.

These wars were not "made up" by writers. They actually happened and were not infrequent. From the standpoint of ecology, the big cattlemen were closer to being right than the nesters, but that had nothing to do with justice or common decency.

# A MAN CALLED TRENT

## Chapter I
## *The Challenge*

Smoke lifted wistfully from the charred timbers of the house, and smoke lifted from the shed that had been Moffitt's barn. The corral bars were down and the saddle stock run off, and where Dick Moffitt's homestead had been in the morning, there was now only desolation, emptiness, and death.

Dick Moffitt himself lay sprawled on the ground. The dust was scratched deeply where his fingers had dug in the agony of death. Even from where he sat on the long-legged buckskin, the man known as Trent could see he had been shot six times. Three of those bullets had gone in from the front. The other three had been fired directly into his back by a man who stood over him. And Dick Moffitt wore no gun.

The little green valley was still in the late afternoon sun. It was warm, and there was still a faint heat emanating from the charred timber of the house.

The man who called himself Trent rode his horse around the house. Four or five men had come here. One of them riding a horse with a split right rear hoof. They had shot Moffitt down and then burned his layout.

What about the kids? What about Sally Crane, who was sixteen? And young Jack Moffitt, who was fourteen? Whatever had happened, there was no evidence of them here. He hesitated, looking down the trail. Had they been taken away by the killers? Sally, perhaps, but not Jack. If the killers had found the two, Jack would have been dead.

Thoughtfully, Trent turned away. The buckskin knew the way was toward home, and he quickened his pace. There were five miles to go, five miles of mountains and heavy woods, and no clear trails.

This could be it. Always, he had been sure it would come. Even when happiest, the knowledge that sooner or later he must sling his gun belts on his hips had been ever present in the back of his mind. Sooner or later there would be trouble, and he had seen it coming here along the rimrock.

Slightly more than a year ago he had built his cabin and squatted in the lush green valley among the peaks. No cattle ranged this high. No wandering punchers drifted up here. Only the other nesters had found homes, the Hatfields, O'Hara, Smithers, Moffitt, and the rest.

Below, in the vicinity of Cedar Bluff, there was one ranch—one and only one. On the ranch and in the town, one man ruled supreme. He rode with majesty, and when he walked, he strode with the step of kings.. He never went unattended. He allowed no man to address him unless he spoke first, he issued orders and bestowed favor like an eastern potentate, and if there were some who disputed his authority, he put them down, crushed them.

King Bill Hale had come west as a boy, and he had had money even then. In Texas he had driven cattle over the trails and had learned to fight and sling a gun, and to drive a bargain that was tight and cruel. Then he had come west, moved into the town of Cedar Bluff, built the Castle, and drove out the cattle rustlers who had used the valley as a hideout. The one other honest rancher in the valley he bought out, and when that man had refused to sell, Hale had told him to sell, or else. And he had cut the offered price in half. The man sold.

Cedar Bluff and Cedar Valley lived under the eye of King Bill. A strong man and an able one, Hale had slowly become power mad. The valley was cut off from both New Mexico and Arizona. In his own world he could not be touched. His will was law.

He owned the Mecca, a saloon and gambling house. He owned the stage station, the stage line itself, and the freight company that hauled supplies in and produce out. He owned the Cedar Hotel, the town's one decent rooming house. He owned sixty thousand acres of good grazing land and controlled a hundred thousand more. His cattle were numbered in the tens of thousands, and two men rode beside him when he went among his other men. One was rough, hard-scaled Pete Shaw, and the other was his younger son, Cub Hale.

Behind him trailed the gold-dust twins, Dunn and Ravitz, both gunmen.

The man who called himself Trent rarely visited Cedar Bluff. Sooner or later, he knew, there would be someone from the outside, someone who knew him, someone who would recognize him for what and who he was, and then the word would go out.

"That's Kilkenny!"

Men would turn to look, for the story of the strange, drifting gunman was known to all in the West, even though there were few men anywhere who knew him by sight, few who could describe him or knew the way he lived.

Mysterious, solitary, and shadowy, the gunman called Kilkenny had been everywhere. He drifted in and out of towns and cow camps, and sometimes there would be a brief and bloody gun battle, and then Kilkenny would be gone again, and only the body of the man who had dared to try Kilkenny remained.

So Kilkenny had taken the name of Trent, and in the high peaks he had found the lush green valley where he built his cabin and ran a few head of cows and broke wild horses. It was a lonely life, but when he was there he hung his guns on a peg and carried only his rifle, and that for game or for wolves.

Rarely, not over a dozen times in the year, he went down to Cedar Bluff for supplies, packed them back, and stayed in the hills until he was running short again. He stayed away from the Mecca, and most of all, he avoided the Crystal Palace, the new and splendid dance hall and gambling house owned by the woman, Nita Riordan.

The cabin in the pines was touched with the red glow of a sun setting beyond the notch, and he swung down from the buckskin and slapped the horse cheerfully on the shoulder.

"Home again, Buck! It's a good feeling, isn't it?"

He stripped the saddle and bridle from the horse and carried them into the log barn; then he turned the buckskin into the corral and forked over a lot of fresh green grass.

It was a lonely life, yet he was content. Only at times did he find himself looking long at the stars and thinking about the girl in Cedar Bluff. Did she know he was here? Remembering Nita from the Live Oak country, he decided she did. Nita Riordan knew all that was going on; she always had.

He went about the business of preparing a meal, and thought of Parson Hatfield and his tall sons. What would the mountaineer do now? Yet, need he ask that question? Could he suspect, even for a moment, that the Hatfields would do anything but fight?

They were the type. They were men who had always built with their hands and who were beholden to no man. They were not gunfighters, but they were lean, hard-faced men, tall and stooped a little, who carried their rifles as if they were part of them. And big Dan O'Hara, the talkative, friendly Irishman who always acted as though campaigning for public office—could he believe that Dan would do other than fight?

                      *       *       *

War was coming to the high peaks, and Trent's face grew somber as he thought of it. War meant that he would once more be shooting, killing. He could, of course, mount in the morning and ride away. He could give up this place in the highlands and go once more, but even as the thought came to him, he did not recognize it as even a remote possibility. Like O'Hara and the Hatfields, he would fight.

There were other things to consider. The last time he had been to Cedar Bluff, there had been a letter from Lee Hall, the ranger.

> We're getting along all right here, but I thought you would like to know: Cain Brockman is out. He swears he will hunt you down and kill you for killing his brother and whipping him with your fists. And he'll try, so be careful.

He dropped four slices of bacon into the frying pan, humming softly to himself. Then he put on some coffee water and sat watching the bacon. When it was ready, he took it out of the pan and put it on a tin plate. He was reaching for the coffee when he heard a muffled movement.

Instantly, he froze in position. His eyes fastened on the blanket that separated his bedroom from the living room of the two-room cottage. His guns were hanging from a peg near the cupboard. He would have to cross the room to them. His rifle was nearer.

Rising, he went about the business of fixing the coffee, and when close to the rifle, he dropped his hand to it. Then, swinging it hip high, he crossed the room with a bound and jerked back the blanket.

Two youngsters sat on the edge of his homemade bed, a slender, wide-eyed girl of sixteen and a boy with a face thickly sprinkled with freckles. They sat tight together, frightened and pale.

Slowly, he let the gun butt down to the floor. "Well, I'll be—! Say, how did you youngsters get here?"

The girl swallowed and stood up, trying to curtsey. Her hair, which was very lovely, hung in two thick blond braids. Her dress was cheap and cotton, and now after rough treatment, was torn and dirty. "We're—I mean, I'm Sally Crane, and this is Jackie Moffitt."

"They burned us out!" Jackie cried out, his face twisted and pale. "Them Haleses done it! An' they kilt Pappy!"

"I know." Trent looked at them gravely. "I came by that way. Come on out here an' we'll eat. Then you can tell me about it."

"They come in about sunup this mornin'," Jack said. "They told Pap he had two hours to get loaded an' movin'. Pap, he allowed he wasn't movin'. This was government land an' he was settled legal, an' he was standin' on his rights."

"What happened?" Trent asked. He sliced more bacon and dropped it in the pan.

"The young'un, he shot Pap. Shot him three times afore he could move. Then after he fell, he emptied his gun into him."

Something sank within Trent, for he could sense the fight that was coming. The "young'un" would probably be Cub Hale. He remembered that slim, erect, pantherlike young man in white buckskins and riding his white horse, that young, handsome man who loved to kill. Here it was, and there was no way a man could duck it. But no. It wasn't his fight. Not yet, it wasn't.

"How'd you kids happen to come here?" he asked kindly.

"We had to get away. Sally was gettin' wood for the house, an' when I met her we started back. Then we heard the shootin', an' when I looked through the brush, I seen the young'un finishin' Pap. I wanted to fight, but I ain't got no gun."

"Did they look for you?" Trent asked.

"Uh-huh. We heard one of 'em say he wanted Sally!" Jackie glanced at the girl, whose face was white, her eyes wide. "They allowed there wasn't no use killin' her—yet!"

"You had horses?" Trent asked.

"Uh-huh. We done left them in the brush. We wasn't sure but what they'd come here, too. But we come here because, Pap, he done said if anythin' ever happened to him, we was to come here first. He said you was a good man, an' he figgered you was some shakes with a gun."

"All right." Trent dished them out some food. "You kids can stay here tonight. I got blankets enough. Then in the mornin' I'll take you down to Parson's."

"Let me fix that," Sally pleaded, reaching for the skillet. "I can cook."

"She sure can," Jackie declared admiringly. "She cooked for us all the time."

A horse's hoof clicked on a stone, and Trent doused the light instantly. "Get down," he whispered hoarsely. "On the floor. Let's see who this is."

He could hear the horses coming closer, two of them from the sound. Then a voice rang out sharply.

"Halloo, the house! Step out here!"

From inside the door, Trent replied shortly. "Who is it? What d'you want?"

"It don't make a damn who it is! Trent, we're givin' you till noon tomorrow to hit the trail! You're campin' on Hale range! We're movin' everybody off!"

Trent laughed harshly. "That's right amusin', friend!" he said dryly. "You go back an' tell King Bill Hale that I'm stayin' right where I am. This is government land, filed on all fittin' an' proper."

He glimpsed the light on a gun barrel and spoke sharply. "Don't try it, Dunn. I know you're there by your voice. If you've got a lick of sense you know you're outlined against the sky. A blind man could get you both at this range."

Dunn cursed bitterly. Then he shouted, "You won't get away with this, Trent!"

"Go back an' tell Hale I like it here, an' I'm plannin' to stay!"

When they had gone Trent turned to the youngsters. "We'll have a little time now. Sally, you take the bed in the other room, Jackie an' me, we'll bunk out here."

"But—?" Sally protested.

"Go ahead. You'll need all the sleep you can get. I think the trouble has just started. But don't be afraid. Everything is goin' to be all right."

"I'm not afraid." Sally Crane looked at him with large, serious eyes. "You'll take care of us, I know."

He stood there a long minute staring after her. It was a strange feeling to be trusted, and trusted so implicitly. The childish sincerity of the girl moved him as nothing had ever moved him before. He recognized the feeling for what it was, the need within himself to protect and care for something beyond himself. It was that, in part, that during these past years had led him to fight so many fights that were not his. And yet, was not the cause of human liberty and freedom always every man's trust?

Jackie was going about the business of making a bed on the floor as though he had spent his life at it. He seemed pleased with this opportunity to show some skill, some ability to do things.

Trent reached up and took down his guns and checked them as he had every night of the entire year in which they had hung from the peg. For a minute after he completed the check, he held them. He liked the feel of them, even when he hated what they meant. Slowly, he replaced them on the peg.

# Chapter II
## *The Right to Bear Arms*

The early-morning sun was just turning the dew-drenched grass into settings for diamonds when Trent was out of his pallet and roping some horses. Yet, early as it was, when he returned to the cabin the fire was going and Sally was preparing breakfast. She smiled at him, but her eyes were red and he could see she had been crying.

Jackie, beginning to realize now the full meaning of the tragedy, was showing his grief through his anger, but was very quiet. Trent was less worried about Jackie than about Sally.

Only six years before, according to what Dick Moffitt had told him, Sally Crane had been found hiding in the bushes. Her father's wagons had been burned and her parents murdered by renegades posing as Indians. Since then, Dick had cared for her. Dick's wife had died scarcely a year before, and the girl had tried to take over the household duties, yet even to a western girl, hardened to a rough life, two such tragedies, each driving her from a home, might be enough to upset her life.

When breakfast was over he took them out to the saddled horses. Then he walked back to the cabin alone, and when he returned he carried an old Sharps rifle. He looked at it a moment, and then he glanced up at Jackie. The boy's eyes were widening, unbelieving, yet bright with hope.

"Jackie," Trent said quietly, "when I was fourteen I was a man. Had to be. Well, it looks like your pappy dyin' has made you a man, too. I'm goin' to give you this Sharps. She's an old gun, but she can shoot. But Jackie, I'm not givin' this gun to a boy. I'm givin' it to a man. I'm givin' it to Jackie Moffitt, an' he's already showed himself pretty much of a man.

"A man, Jackie, he don't ever use a gun unless he has to. He don't go around shootin' heedless like. He shoots only when he has to, an' then he don't miss. This gun's a present, Jackie, an' there's no strings attached, but it carries a responsibility, an' that is never to use it against a man unless it's in defense of your life or the lives or homes of those you love.

"You're to keep it loaded always. A gun ain't no good to a man unless it's loaded, an' if it's seen settin' around people won't be handlin' it careless. They'll say 'that's Jackie Moffitt's gun, an' it's always loaded.' It's always guns people think are empty that kill people by accident."

"Gosh!" Jackie stared in admiration at the battered old Sharps. "That's a weapon, man!" Then he looked up at Trent, and his eyes were filled with tears of sincerity. "Mister Trent, I sure do promise! I'll never use no gun unless I have to!"

Trent swung into the saddle and watched the others mount. He carried his own Winchester, one of the new '73 models that were replacing the old Sharps on the frontier.

He was under no illusions. If King Bill Hale had decided to put an end to the nesters among the high peaks, he would probably succeed. But Hale was so impressed with his own power that he was not reckoning with the Hatfields, O'Hara, or himself.

"Y'know, Jackie," Trent said thoughtfully, "there's a clause in the

Constitution that says the right of an American to keep and bear arms shall not be abridged. They put that in there so a man would always have a gun to defend his home or his liberty.

"Right now there's a man in this valley who is tryin' to take the liberty an' freedom of some men away from 'em. When a man starts that, and when there isn't any law to help, you got to fight. I've killed men, Jackie, an' it ain't a good thing, no way. But I never killed a man unless he deserved killin' an' unless he forced me to a corner where it was me or him.

"This here country is big enough for all, but some men get greedy for money or power, an' when they do the little men have to fight to keep what they got. Your pappy died in a war for freedom just as much as if he was killed on a battlefield somewheres.

"Whenever a brave man dies for what he believes, he wins more'n he loses. Maybe not for him, but for men like him that want to live honest an' true."

The trail narrowed and grew rougher, and Trent felt a quick excitement within him, as he always did when he rode up to this windy plateau. They went up through the tall pines toward the knifelike ridges that crested the divide, and when they finally reached the plateau he reined in, as he always did when he reached that spot.

Off over the vast distance that was Cedar Valley lay the blue haze that deepened to purple against the far-distant mountains. Here the air was fresh and clear, crisp with the crispness of the high peaks and the sense of limitless distance.

Skirting the rim, Trent led on and finally came to the second place he loved, a place he not only loved but which was a challenge to all that was in him. For here the divide, with its skyscraping ridges, was truly a divide. It drew a ragged, mountainous line between the lush beauty of Cedar Valley and the awful waste of the scarred and tortured Smoky Desert.

Always, there seemed a haze of dust or smoke hanging in the sky over Smoky Desert, and what lay below it, no man could say, for no known trail led down the steel canyon to the waste below. An Indian had once told him his fathers knew of a trail to the bottom, but no living man knew it, and no man seemed to care, nobody but Trent, drawn by his own loneliness to the vaster loneliness below.

Far away were ragged red mountains, red, black, and broken like the jagged stumps of broken teeth gnawing at the sky. It was, he believed, the far edge of what was actually an enormous crater, greater than any other of its kind on earth.

"Someday," he told his companions, "I'm goin' down there. It looks like the mouth of hell itself, but I'm goin' down."

Parson Hatfield and his four tall sons were all in sight when the three rode up to the cabin. All were carrying their long Kentucky rifles.

"Alight, Trent," Parson drawled, widening his gash of a mouth into a smile. "We was expectin' most anybody else. Been some ructions down to the valley."

"Yeah." Trent swung down. "They killed Dick Moffitt. These are his kids, Parson. I figgered maybe you could make a place for 'em."

"You thought right, son. The good Lord takes care of his own, but we have to help. There's always room for another beneath the roof of a Hatfield."

Quincy Hatfield, oldest of the lean, rawboned Kentucky boys, joined them. "Howdy," he said. "Did Pap tell you all about Leathers?"

"Leathers?" Trent frowned in quick apprehension. "What about him?"

"He ain't a-goin' to sell anything to us no more." The tall young man spat and shifted his rifle to the hollow of his arm. "That makes the closest store over at Blazer, an' that's three days across the mountains."

Trent shrugged, frowning. "Aims to freeze us out or kill us off." He glanced at Parson speculatively. "What are you plannin'?"

Hatfield shook his head. "Nothin' so far. We sort of figgered we might get together with the rest of the nesters an' try to figger out somethin'. I had Jake ride down to get O'Hara, Smithers, an' young Bartram. We got to have us a confab."

Parson Hatfield rubbed his long, grizzled jaw and stared at Trent. His gray eyes were inquisitive, sly. "Y'know, Trent, I always had me an idea you was some shakes of a battler yourself. Maybe if you'd wear some guns you'd make some of them gunslick hombres of Hale's back down cold."

Trent smiled. "Why, Parson, I reckon you guess wrong. Me, I'm a peace-lovin' hombre. I like the hills, an' all I ask is to be let alone."

"An' if they don't let alone?" Parson stared at him shrewdly, chewing his tobacco slowly and watching Trent with his keen gray eyes.

"If they don't let me alone? An' if they start killin' my friends?" Trent turned to look at Hatfield. "Why, Parson, I reckon I'd take my guns down from that peg. I reckon I'd fight."

Hatfield nodded. "That's all I wanted to know, Trent. I ain't spent my life a-feudin' without knowin' a fightin' man when I see one. O'Hara an' young Bartram will fight. Smithers, too, but he don't stack up like no fightin' man. My young'uns, they cut their teeth on a rifle stock, so I reckon when the fightin' begins I'll be bloodin' the two young'uns like I did the two older back in Kentucky."

Trent kicked his toe into the dust. "Don't you reckon we better get the womenfolks off to Blazer? There ain't many of us, Parson, an' Hale must have fifty riders. We better get them out while the gettin' is good."

"Hale's got more'n fifty riders, but the women'll stay, Trent. Ma, she ain't for goin'. You ain't got no woman of your own, Trent, so I don't reckon you know how unpossible ornery they can be, but Ma, she'd be fit to be tied if it was said she was goin' to go to Blazer while we had us a scrap.

"Ma loaded rifles for me in Kentucky when she was a gal, an' she loaded 'em for me crossin' the plains, an' she done her share of shootin'.

"Trent, I'd rather face all them Haleses than Ma if we tried to send her away. She always says her place is with her menfolks, an' there she'll stay. I reckon Quince's wife feels the same, an' so does Jesse's woman."

Trent nodded. "Parson, we got us an argument when the rest of them get here. They've got to leave their places an' come up here. Together, we could make a pretty stiff fight of it. Scattered, they'd cut us down one by one."

He swung into the saddle. "I'm goin' down to Cedar. I'm goin' to see Leathers."

Without waiting for a reply, Trent swung the buckskin away and loped down the trail. He knew very well he was taking a chance. The killing had started. Dick Moffitt was down. They had burned his place, and within no time at all, the Hale riders would be carrying fire and blood through the high hills, wiping out the nesters. If he could but see King Bill, there might be a chance.

Watching him go, Parson Hatfield shook his head doubtfully and then turned to his eldest. "Quince, you rope yourself a horse, boy, an' you an' Jesse follow him into Cedar. He may get hisself into trouble."

A few minutes later the two tall, loose-limbed mountain men started down the trail on their flea-bitten mustangs. They were solemn, dry young men who chewed tobacco and talked slowly, but they had grown up in the hard school of the Kentucky mountains, and they had come west across the plains.

# Chapter III
## *A Tough Job Ahead*

Unknowing, Trent rode rapidly. He knew what he had to do, yet even as he rode, his thoughts were on the Hatfields. He liked them. Hardworking, honest, opinionated, they were fierce to resent any intrusion on their personal liberty, their women's honor, or their pride.

They were the kind of men to ride the river with. It was such men who had been the backbone of America, the fence-corner soldier, the man who carried his rifle in the hollow of his arm, but the kind of men who knew that fighting was not a complicated business but simply a matter of killing and keeping from being killed.

They were men of the blood of Dan Boone, Kit Carson, Jim Bridger, the Green Mountain Boys, Dan Freeman, and those who whipped the cream of the British regulars at Concord, Bunker Hill, and New Orleans.

They knew nothing of Prussian methods of close-order drill. They did nothing by the numbers. Many of them had flat feet and many had few teeth. But they fought from cover and they made every shot count—and they lived while the enemy died.

The Hale Ranch was a tremendous power, and they had many riders, and they were men hired for their ability with guns as well as with ropes and cattle. King Bill Hale, wise as he was, was grown confident, and he did not know the caliber of such men as the Hatfields. The numbers Hale had might lead to victory, but not until many men had died.

O'Hara? The big Irishman was blunt and hard. He was not the shrewd fighter the Hatfields were, but he was courageous, and he knew not the meaning of retreat.

Himself? Trent's eyes narrowed. He had no illusions about himself. As much as he avoided trouble, he knew that within him there was something that held a fierce resentment for abuse of power, for tyranny. There was something in him that loved battle, too. He could not dodge the fact. He would avoid trouble, but when it came he would go into it with a fierce love of battle for battle's sake.

Someday, he knew, he would ride back to the cattle in the high meadows, back to the cabin in the pines, and he would take down his guns and buckle them on, and then Kilkenny would ride again.

The trail skirted deep canyons and led down toward the flat bottomland of the valley. King Bill, he knew, was learning what he should have known long ago, that the flatlands, while rich, became hot and dry in the summer weather, while the high meadows remained green and lush, and there cattle could graze and grow fat. And King Bill was moving to take back what he had missed so long ago.

Had the man been less blinded by his own power and strength, he would have hesitated over the Hatfields. One and all, they were fighting men.

Riding into Cedar Bluff would be dangerous now. Changes were coming to the West, and Trent had hoped to leave his reputation in

Texas. He could see the old days of violence were nearing an end. Billy the Kid had been killed by Pat Garrett. King Fisher and Ben Thompson were heard of much less; one and all, the gunmen were beginning to taper off. Names that had once been mighty in the West were already drifting into legend.

As for himself, few men could describe him. He had come and gone like a shadow, and where he was now, no man could say, and only one woman.

King Bill even owned the law in Cedar. He had called an election to choose a sheriff and a judge. Yet there had been no fairness in that election. It was true that no unfair practices had been tolerated, but the few nesters and small ranchers had no chance against the fifty-odd riders from the Hale Ranch and the townspeople who needed the Hale business or who worked for him.

Trent had voted himself. He had voted for O'Hara. There had been scarcely a dozen votes for O'Hara. One of those votes had been that of Jim Hale, King Bill's oldest son. Another, he knew, had been the one person in Cedar whom he had studiously avoided, the half-Spanish, half-Irish girl, Nita Riordan.

Trent had avoided Nita Riordan because the beautiful girl from the Texas Mexican border was the one person who knew him for what he was—who knew him as Kilkenny, the gunfighter.

Whenever Trent thought of the trouble in Cedar he thought less of King Bill but more of Cub Hale. The older man was huge and powerful physically, but he was not a killer. It was true that he was responsible for deaths, but they were of men whom he believed to be his enemies or to be trespassing on his land. But Cub Hale was a killer.

Two days after Trent had first come to Cedar Bluff he had seen Cub Hale kill a man. It was a drunken miner, a burly, quarrelsome fellow who could have done with a pistol barrel alongside the head, but needed nothing more. Yet Cub Hale had shot him down, ruthlessly, heedlessly.

Then there had been the case of Jack Lindsay, a known gunman, and Cub had killed him in a fair, standup fight, with an even break all around. Lindsay's gun had barely cleared its holster when the first of three shots hit him. Trent had walked over to the man's body to see for himself. You could have put a playing card over those three holes. That was shooting.

There had been other stories of which Trent had only heard. Cub had caught two rustlers, red-handed, and killed them both. He had killed a Mexican sheepherder in Magdalena. He had killed a gunfighter in Fort Sumner, and gut shot another one near Socorro, leaving him to die slowly on the desert.

And besides Cub, there were Dunn and Ravitz. Both were graduates of the Lincoln County War. Both had been in Trail City and had left California just ahead of a posse. Both were familiar names among the dark brotherhood who lived by the gun. They were strictly cash-and-carry warriors, men whose guns were for hire.

"Buck," Trent told his horse thoughtfully, "if war starts in the Cedar hills, there'll be a power of killin'. I got to see King Bill. I got to talk reason into him."

Cedar Bluff could have been any cow town. Two things set it off from the others. One was the stone stage station, which also contained the main office of the Hale Ranch; the other was the huge and sprawling Crystal Palace, belonging to Nita Riordan.

Trent loped the yellow horse down the dusty street and swung down in front of Leathers's General Store. He walked into the cool interior. The place smelled of leather and drygoods. At the rear, where they dispensed food and other supplies, he halted.

Bert Leathers looked up from his customer as Trent walked in, and Trent saw his face change. Leathers wet his lips and kept his eyes away from Trent. At the same time, Trent heard a slight movement, and glancing casually around, he saw a heavyset cowhand wearing a tied-down gun lounging against a rack of saddles. The fellow took his cigarette from his lips and stared at Trent from shrewd, calculating eyes.

"Need a few things, Leathers," Trent said casually. "Got a list here."

The man Leathers was serving stepped aside. He was a townsman, and he looked worried.

"Sorry, Trent," Leathers said abruptly, "I can't help you. All you nesters have been ordered off the Hale range. I can't sell you anything."

"Lickin' Hale's boots, are you?" Trent asked quietly. "I heard you were, Leathers, but doubted it. I figgered a man with nerve enough to come west an' set up for himself would be his own man."

"I am my own man!" Leathers snapped, his pride stung. "I just don't want your business!"

"I'll remember that, Leathers," Trent said quietly. "When all this is over, I'll remember that. You're forgettin' something. This is America, an' here the people always win. Maybe not at first, but they always win in the end. When this is over, if the people win, you'd better leave—understand?"

Leathers looked up, his face white and yet angry. He looked uncertain.

"You all better grab yourself some air," a cool voice suggested.

Trent turned, and he saw the gunhand standing with his thumbs in his belt, grinning at him. "Better slide, Trent. What the man says is true. King Bill's takin' over. I'm here to see Leathers doesn't have no trouble with nesters."

"All right," Trent said quietly, "I'm a quiet man myself. I expect that rightly I should take the gun away from you an' shove it down your throat. But Leathers is probably gunshy, an' there might be some shootin', so I'll take a walk."

"My name's Dan Cooper," the gunhand suggested mildly. "Any time you really get on the prod about shovin' this gun down my throat, look me up."

Trent smiled. "I'll do that, Cooper, an' if you stay with King Bill I'm afraid you're going to have a heavy diet of lead. He's cuttin' a wide swath."

"Uh-huh." Cooper was cheerful and tough. "But he's got a blade that cuts 'em off short."

"Ever see the Hatfields shoot?" Trent suggested. "Take a tip, old son, an' when those long Kentucky rifles open up, you be somewhere else."

Dan Cooper nodded sagely. "You got somethin' there, pardner. You really have. That Parson's got him a cold eye."

Trent turned and started for the street, but Cooper's voice halted him. The gunhand had followed him to the door.

"Say," Cooper's voice was curious. "Was you ever in Dodge?"

Trent smiled. "Maybe. Maybe I was. You think that one over, Cooper."

He looked at the gunhand thoughtfully. "I like you," he said bluntly, "so I'm givin' you a tip. Get on your horse an' ride. King Bill's got the men, but he ain't goin' to win. Ride, because I always hate to kill a good man."

Trent turned and walked down the street. Behind him, he could feel Dan Cooper's eyes on his back.

The gunman was scowling. "Now who the hell?" he muttered. "That hombre's salty, plumb salty."

Three more attempts to buy supplies proved to Trent he was frozen out in Cedar Bluff. Worried now, he started back to his horse. The nesters could not buy in Cedar Bluff, and that meant their only supplies must come by the long wagon trip across country from Blazer. Trent felt grave doubts that Hale would let the wagons proceed unmolested, and their little party was so small they could not spare men to guard the wagons on the three-day trek over desert and mountains.

"Trent!" He turned slowly and found himself facing Price Dixon, a dealer from the Crystal Palace. "Nita wants to see you. Asked me to find you and ask if you'd come to see her."

For a long moment, Trent hesitated. Then he shrugged. "All

right," he said, "but it won't do any good to have her seen with me. We nesters aren't looked upon with much favor these days."

Dixon nodded, sober faced. "Looks like a shootout. I'm afraid you boys are on the short end of it."

"Maybe."

Dixon glanced at him out of the corner of his eyes. "Don't you wear a gun? They'll kill you someday."

"Without a gun you don't have many fights."

"It wouldn't stop Cub Hale. When he decides to shoot, he does. He won't care whether you are packin' a gun or not."

"No. It wouldn't matter to him."

Price Dixon studied him thoughtfully. "Who are you, Trent?" he asked softly.

"I'm Trent, a nester. Who else?"

"That's what I'm wondering. I'm dry behind the ears. I've been dealing cards in the West ever since the War Between the States. I've seen men who packed guns, and I know the breed. You're not Wes Hardin, and you're not Hickok, and you're not one of the Earps. You never drink much, so you can't be Thompson. Whoever you are, you've packed a gun."

"Don't lose any sleep over it."

Dixon shrugged. "I won't. I'm not taking sides in this fight or any other. If I guess, I won't say. You're a friend of Nita's, and that's enough for me. Besides, Jaime Brigo likes you." He glanced at Trent. "What do you think of him?"

"Brigo?" Trent said thoughtfully. "Brigo is part Yaqui, part devil, and all loyal, but I'd sooner tackle three King Bill Hales than him. He's poison."

Dixon nodded. "I think you're right. He sits there by her door night after night, apparently asleep, yet he knows more about what goes on in this town than any five other men."

"Dixon, you should talk Nita into selling out. Good chance of getting the place burned out or shot up if she stays. It's going to be a long fight."

"Hale doesn't think so."

"Parson Hatfield does."

"I've seen Hatfield. He looks like something I'd leave alone." Dixon paused. "I was in Kentucky once, a long time ago. The Hatfields have had three feuds. Somehow, there's always Hatfields left."

"Well, Price," Trent threw his cigarette into the dust, "I've seen a few fighting men, too, and I'm glad the Hatfields are on my side, an' particularly the Parson."

## Chapter IV
### *One Girl in a Million*

The Crystal Palace was one of those places that made the western
frontier what it was. Wherever there was money to spend, gambling
joints could be found, and some became ornate palaces of drinking
and gambling like the Palace. They had them in Abilene and Dodge,
but not so much as farther west.

Cedar Bluff had the highly paid riders of the Hale Ranch. They
also drew miners from Rock Creek. The Palace was all gilt and glass,
and there were plenty of games going, including roulette, faro, and
dice. Around the room at scattered tables were at least a dozen
poker games.

Nita Riordan, Trent decided, was doing all right. This place was
making money and lots of it. Trent knew a lot about gambling
houses, enough to know what a rake-off these games would be
turning in to the house. There was no necessity for crooked games.
The percentage was entirely adequate.

They crossed the room, and Trent saw Jaime Brigo sitting on a
chair against the wall as he always sat. The sombrero on the floor was
gray and new. He wore dark tailored trousers and a short velvet
jacket, also black. The shirt under it was silk and blue. He wore, as
always, two guns.

He looked up as Trent approached, and his lips parted over even
white teeth. "*Buenos días, Señor!*" he said.

Price stopped and nodded his head toward the door. "She's in
there."

Trent faced the door, drew a deep breath, and stepped inside. His
heart was pounding, and his mouth was dry. No woman ever stirred
him so deeply or made him realize so much what he was missing in
his lonely life.

It was a quiet room, utterly different from the garish display of the
gambling hall behind him. It was a room to live in, the room of one
who loved comfort and peace. On a ledge by the window were
several potted plants; on the table lay an open book. These things he
absorbed rather than observed, for all his attention was centered
upon Nita Riordan.

She stood across the table, taller than most women, with a slender
yet voluptuous body that made a pulse pound in his throat. She was
dressed for evening, an evening walking among the tables of the
gambling room, and she was wearing a black and spangled gown,
utterly different from the room in which she stood.

Her eyes were wide now, her full lips parted a little, and as he stopped across the table he could see the lift of her bosom as she took a deep breath.

"Nita!" he said softly. "You've not changed. You're the same."

"I'm older, Lance," she said softly, "more than a year older."

"Has it been only a year? It seems so much longer." He looked at her thoughtfully. "And you are lovely, as always. I think you could never be anything but lovely and desirable."

"And yet," she reminded him, "when you could have had me, you rode away. Lance, do you live all alone in that cabin of yours? Without anyone?"

He nodded. "Except for memories. Except for the thinking I do. And the thinking only makes it worse, for whenever I think of you, and all that could be, I remember the Brockmans, Bert Polti, and all those others back down the trail. Then I start wondering how long it will be before I fall in the dust myself."

"That's why I sent for you," Nita told him. Her eyes were serious and worried. She came around the table and took his hands. "Lance, you've got to go. Leave here, now! I can hold your place for you, if that's what you want. If that doesn't matter, say so and I'll go with you. I'll go with you anywhere, but we must leave here."

"Why?" It was like him to be direct. She looked up into his dark, unsmiling face. "Why, Nita? Why do you want me to go?"

"Because they are going to kill you!" she exclaimed. She caught his arm. "Lance, they are cruel, ruthless, vicious. It isn't King Bill. He's their leader, but what he does he believes to be right. It's Cub.

"He loves to kill. I've seen him. Last week he killed a boy in the street in front of my place. He shot him down and then emptied his gun into him with slow, methodical shots. He's a fiend!"

Lance shook his head. "I'll say, no matter."

"But listen, Lance!" she protested. "I've heard them talking here. They are sure you'll fight. I don't know why they think so, but they do. They've decided you must die, and soon. They won't give you a chance. I know that."

"I can't, Nita. These people in the high meadows are my friends. They depend upon me to stand by them. I won't be the first to break and run, or the last. I'm staying. I'm going to fight it out here, Nita, and we'll see who is to win, the people or a man of power and greed."

"I was afraid you'd say that." Nita looked at him seriously. "Hale is out to win, Lance. He's got men. They don't know you're Lance Kilkenny. I've heard them talking, and they do suspect that you're something more than a nester named Trent. But Hale is sure he is right, and he'll fight to the end."

Trent nodded. "I know. When a man thinks he is right, he will fight all the harder. Has anybody tried to talk to him?"

"You can't. You can't even address him. He lives in a world of his own. In his way, I think he is a little insane, Lance, but he does have ability, and he has strength. He's a fighter, too."

Trent studied her thoughtfully. "You seem to know him. Has he made you any trouble?"

"Why do you ask that?" Nita asked quickly.

"I want to know."

"He wants to marry me, Lance."

Trent tightened and then stared at her. "I see," he said slowly. "And you?"

"I don't know." She hesitated, looking away. "Lance, can't you see? I'm lonely. Dreadfully, frighteningly lonely. I have no life here, just a business. I know no women but those of the dance hall. I see no one who feels as I do, thinks as I do.

"King Bill is strong. He knows how to appeal to a woman. He has a lot to offer. He has a son as old as I, but he's only forty, and he's a powerful man, Lance. A man a woman could be proud of. I don't like what he's doing, but he does think he's right.

"No," she said finally, "I won't marry him. I'll admit, I've been tempted. He's a little insane, I think. Drunk with power. He got too much and got it too easily, and he believes he is better than other men because he has succeeded. But whatever you do, Lance, don't underrate him. He's a fighter."

"You mean he'll have his men fight?" Trent asked.

"No. I mean *he* is a fighter. By any method. With his fists, if he has to. He told me once in such a flat, ordinary voice that it startled me that he could whip any man he ever saw with his hands."

"I see."

"Shaw, his foreman, tells a story about King Bill beating a man to death in El Paso. He killed another one with his fists on the ranch."

"I've got to see him today. I've got to convince him that we must be left alone."

"He won't talk to you, Lance." Nita looked at him with grave, troubled eyes. "I know him. He'll just turn you over to his cow-hands, and they'll beat you up or kill you."

"He'll talk to me."

"Don't go down there, Lance. Please don't."

"Has he ever made any trouble for you?"

"No." She shook her head. "So far, he has listened to me and has talked very quietly and very well. No one has made any trouble yet, but largely because they know he is interested in me. Some men tried to hold me up one night, but Jaime took care of that. He killed them both, and that started some talk. But if King Bill decides he wants this place—or me—he'll stop at nothing."

"Well,"—he turned—"I've got to see him, Nita. I've got to make one attempt to stop this before anyone else is killed."

"And if you fail—?"

He hesitated, and his shoulders drooped. Then he looked up, and he smiled slowly. "If I fail, Nita, I'll buckle on my guns, and they won't have to wait for war. I'll bring it to Cedar myself!"

He stopped in the outer room and watched Price Dixon dealing cards, but his mind wasn't on the game. He was thinking of King Bill.

Hale was a man who fought to win. In this little corner of the West, there was no law but that of the gun. Actually, there were but two trails in and out of Cedar Valley. What news left the valley would depend on Hale. The echoes of the war to come need never be heard beyond these hills.

Only one trail led into Cedar Bluff, and one led out. Most of the traffic went in and out on the same route. The other trail, the little-used route to Blazer, was rough and bad. Yet in Blazer, too, Hale owned the livery stable, and he had his spies there as all around.

Hale himself lived in the Castle, two miles from Cedar. He rode into town once each day and stopped in at the Mecca for a drink and again at the Crystal Palace. Then he rode out of town. He went nowhere without his gunmen around him. Thinking of that, Trent decided on the Mecca. There would be trouble unless everything happened just right. He didn't want the trouble close to Nita.

He knew what Nita meant when she said she was lonely. There had never been a time when he hadn't been lonely. He had been born on the frontier in Dakota, but his father had been killed in a gun battle, and he had gone to live with an uncle in New York, and later in Virginia.

Trent walked out on the street. It was late now, and the sun was already gone. It would soon be dark. He walked down to the buckskin and led him to a watering trough. Then he gave him a bundle of hay and left him tied at the hitching rail.

There were few people around. Dan Cooper had left the store and was sitting on the steps in front now. He watched Trent thoughtfully. Finally, he got up and walked slowly down the walk. He stopped near the buckskin.

"If I was you, Trent," he said slowly, "I'd get on that horse an' hit the trail. You ain't among friends."

"Thanks." Trent looked up at Cooper. "I think that's friendly,

Cooper. But I've got business. I don't want a war in Cedar Bluff, Cooper. I want to make one more stab at stopping it."

"An' if you don't?" Cooper studied him quizzically.

"If I don't?" Trent stepped up on the boardwalk. "Well, I'll tell you like I've told others. If I don't, I'm going to buckle on my guns and come to town."

Dan Cooper began to roll a cigarette. "You sound all-fired sure of yourself. Who are you?"

"Like I said, old son, I'm a nester, name of Trent."

He turned and strolled down the walk toward the Mecca, and even as he walked, he saw a small cavalcade of horsemen come up the road from the Castle. Four men, and the big man on the bay would be King Bill Hale.

Hale got down, and strode through the doors. Cub followed. Ravitz tied King Bill's horse, and Dunn stood for a moment, staring at Trent, whom he could not quite make out in the gathering gloom. Then he and Ravitz walked inside.

# Chapter V
## *May the Best Man Win*

Walking up, Trent pushed open the swinging doors. He stopped for an instant inside the door. The place was jammed with Hale cowhands. At the bar, King Bill was standing, his back to the room.

He was big—no taller than Trent, and perhaps an inch shorter than Trent's six-one, but much heavier. He was broad and powerful, with thick shoulders and a massive chest. His head was a block set upon the thick column of a muscular neck. The man's jaw was broad, his face brown and hard. He was a bull. Looking at him, Trent could guess that the stories of his killing men with his fists were only the truth.

Beside him, in white buckskin, was the slender, catlike Cub Hale. And on either side of the two stood the gunmen Dunn and Ravitz.

Trent walked slowly to the bar and ordered a drink. Dunn, hearing his voice, turned his head slowly. As his eyes met Trent's, the glass slipped from his fingers and crashed on the bar, scattering rye whiskey.

"Seem nervous, Dunn," Trent said quietly. "Let me buy you a drink."

"I'll be hanged if I will!" Dunn shouted. "What do you want here?"

Trent smiled. All the room was listening, and he knew that many of the townspeople, some of whom might still be on the fence, were present.

"Why, I just thought I'd ride down an' have a talk with King Bill," he said quietly. "It seems there's a lot of war talk, an' somebody killed a harmless nester the other day. It seemed like a man like King Bill Hale wouldn't want such things goin' on."

"Get out!" Dunn's hand hovered above a gun. "Get out or be carried out!"

"No use you makin' motions toward that gun," Trent said quietly. "I'm not heeled. Look for yourself. I'm makin' peace talk, an' I'm talkin' to King Bill."

"I said—get out!" Dunn shouted.

Trent stood with his hands on his hips, smiling. Suddenly, Dunn's hand streaked for his gun, and instantly, Trent moved.

One hand dropped to Dunn's gun wrist, while his right whipped up in a short, wicked arc and exploded on Dunn's chin. The gunman sagged, and Trent released his gunhand and shoved him from him so hard he fell headlong into a table. The table crashed over, and among the scattered cards and chips, Bing Dunn lay, out cold.

In the silence that followed, Trent stepped quickly up to King Bill.

"Hale," he said abruptly, "some of your men killed Dick Moffitt, shot him down in cold blood and then burned him out. Those same men warned me to move out. I thought I'd come to you. I've heard you're a fair man."

King Bill did not move. He held his glass in his fingers and stared thoughtfully into the mirror back of the bar, giving no indication that he heard. Cub Hale moved out from the bar, his head thrust forward, his eyes eager.

"Hale," Trent said sharply, "this is between you an' me. Call off your dogs! I'm talkin' to you, not anybody else. We want peace, but if we have to fight to keep our land, we'll fight! If we fight, we'll win. You're buckin' the United States government now."

Cub had stepped out, and now his lips curled back in a wolfish snarl as his hand hovered over his gun.

"What's the matter, Hale?" Trent persisted. "Making a hired killer of your son because you're afraid to talk?"

Hale turned deliberately. "Cub, get back. I'll handle this!"

Cub hesitated, his eyes alive with eagerness and disappointment.

"I said," Hale repeated, "to get back."

He turned. "As for you, you squatted on my land. Now you're gettin' off, all of you. If you don't get off, some of you may die. That's final!"

"No!" Trent's voice rang out sharply. "It's not final, Hale! We took those claims legal. You never made any claim to them until now. You got more land now than you can handle, and we're stayin'. I filed my claim with the United States, so did the others. If we don't get justice, we'll get a United States marshal in here to see why."

"Justice!" Hale sneered. "You blasted nesters'll get all the justice you get from me. I'm givin' you time to leave—now get!"

Trent stood his ground. He could see the fury bolted up in Hale, could see the man was relentless. Well, maybe—

Suddenly Trent smiled. "Hale," he said slowly, "I've heard you're a fightin' man. I hope that ain't a lie. I'm callin' you now. We fight, man to man, right here in this barroom, no holds barred, an' if I win, you leave the nesters alone. If you win, we all leave!"

King Bill wheeled, his eyes bulging. "You challenge *me*? You dirty-necked, nestin' renegade. No! I bargain with no man. You nesters get movin' or suffer the consequences."

"What's the matter, Bill?" Trent said slowly. "Afraid?"

For a long moment, there was deathly stillness in the room, while Hale's face grew darker and darker. Slowly then, he unbuckled his gunbelt. "You asked for it, nester," he sneered. "Now you get it."

He rushed. Trent had been watching, and as Hale rushed, he sidestepped quickly. Hale's rush missed, and Trent faced him, smiling.

"What's the matter, King? I'm right here!"

Hale rushed, and Trent stepped in with a left jab that split Hale's lips and showered him with blood. In a fury, Hale closed in and caught Trent with a powerful right swing that sent him staggering back on his heels. Blood staining his gray shirt, King Bill leaped at Trent, swinging with both hands. Trent crashed to the floor, rolled over, and got up. Another swing caught him, and he went down again, his head roaring with sound.

King Bill rushed in, aiming a vicious kick, but Trent rolled out of the way and scrambled up, groggy and hurt. Hale rushed, and Trent weaved inside of a swing and smashed a right and left to that massive body.

Hale grabbed Trent and hurled him into the bar with terrific power and then sprang close, swinging both fists to Trent's head. Trent slipped the first punch, but took the other one, and started to sag. King Bill set himself, a cold sneer on his face, and measured Trent with a left, aiming a ponderous right, but Trent pushed the left aside and smashed a wicked left uppercut to Hale's wind.

The bigger man gasped and missed a right, and Trent stabbed another left to the bleeding mouth. Hale landed a right and knocked Trent rolling on the floor. Somebody kicked him wickedly in the ribs as he rolled against the feet of the crowd, and he came up staggering as Hale closed in. Hurt, gasping with pain, Trent clinched desperately and hung on.

Hale tore him loose, smashed a left to his head that split his cheekbone wide open, and then smashed him on the jaw with a powerful right. Again Trent stabbed that left to the mouth, ducked under a right and bored in, slamming away with both hands at close quarters.

Hale grabbed him and threw him then and rushed upon him, but even as he jumped at him, Trent caught Hale with a toe in the pit of the stomach and pitched him over on his head and shoulders.

King Bill staggered up, visibly shaken. Then Trent walked in. His face was streaming blood and his head was buzzing, but he could see Hale's face weaving before him. He walked in, deliberately lanced that bleeding mouth with a left, and then crossed a right that ripped the flesh over Hale's eye.

Dunn started forward, and with an oath, Hale waved him back. He put up his hands and walked in, his face twisted with hatred. Trent let him come, feinted, and then dropped a right under the big man's heart. Hale staggered, and Trent walked in, stabbed another left into the blood-covered face, and smashed another right to the wind.

Then he stood there and began to swing. Hale was swinging too, but his power was gone. Trent bored in, his head clearing, and he slammed punch after punch into the face and body of the tottering rancher. He was getting his second wind now, although he was hurt, and blood dripped from his face to his shirt. He brushed Hale's hands aside and crossed a driving right to the chin. Hale's knees buckled, but before he could fall, Trent hit him twice more, left and right to the chin. Then Hale crashed to the ground.

In the instant of silence that followed the fall of the King, a voice rang out. "You all just hold to where you're standin' now. I ain't a-wantin' to shoot nobody, but sure as my name's Quince Hatfield, the one to make the first move dies!"

The long rifle stared through the open window at them, and on the next windowsill they saw another. Nobody in the room moved.

In three steps, Trent was out of the room. The buckskin was standing at the edge of the walk with the other horses. Swinging into the saddle, he wrenched the rifle from the boot and with two quick shots, sent the chandelier crashing to the floor, plunging the Mecca into darkness. Then, the Hatfields at his side, he raced the buckskin toward the edge of town. When they slowed down, a mile out of town, Quince looked at him, grinning in the moonlight.

"I reckon you all sure busted things wide open now!"

Trent nodded soberly. "I tried to make peace talk. When he wouldn't, I thought a good lickin' might show the townspeople the fight wasn't all on one side. We're goin' to need friends."

"You done a good job!" Jesse said. "Parson'll sure wish he'd been along. He always said what Hale needed was a good whuppin'. Well, he sho' nuff had it tonight!"

Nothing, Trent realized, had been solved by the fight. Taking to the brush, they used every stratagem to ward off pursuit, although they knew it was exceedingly doubtful if any pursuit would be started against three armed men who were skilled woodsmen. Following them in the dark would be impossible and scarcely wise.

Three hours later, they swung down at the Hatfield cabin. A tall young man with broad shoulders stepped out of the darkness.

"It's us, Saul," Jesse said, "an' Trent done whipped King Bill Hale with his fists!"

Saul Hatfield strode up, smiling. "I reckon Paw will sure like to hear that!"

"They gone to bed?"

"Uh-huh. Lijah was on guard till a few minutes back. He just turned in to catch hisself some sleep afore mornin'."

"O'Hara get here?" Quince asked softly.

"Yeah. Him an' Smithers an' Bartram are here. Havin' a big confab, come mornin'."

## Chapter VI
### *The Rallying Call*

The morning sun was lifting over the pines when the men gathered around the long table in the Hatfield home. Breakfast was over, and the women were at work. Trent sat quietly at the foot of the table, thoughtfully looking at the men around him. Yet even as he looked, he could not but wonder how many would be alive to enjoy the fruits of the victory, if victory it was to be.

The five Hatfields were all there. Big O'Hara was there, too, a huge man with great shoulders and mighty hands, a bull for strength and a good shot. Bartram, young, good-looking, and keen, would fight. He believed in what he was fighting for, and he had youth and energy enough to be looking forward to the struggle.

Smithers was middle-aged, quiet, a man who had lived a peaceful life, avoiding trouble, yet fearless. He was a small man, precise, and an excellent farmer, probably the best farmer of the lot.

Two more horsemen rode in while they were sitting down. Jackson Hight was a wild-horse hunter, former cowhand, and buffalo hunter; Steven Runyon was a former miner.

Parson Hatfield straightened up slowly. "I reckon this here meetin' better get started. Them Haleses ain't a-goin' to wait on us to get organized. I reckon they's a few things we got to do. We got to pick us a leader, an' we got to think of gettin' some food."

Trent spoke up. "Parson, if you'll let me have a word. We all better leave our places an' come here to yours. We better bring all the food an' horses we got up here."

"Leave our places?" Smithers objected. "Why, man, they'd burn us out if we aren't there to defend 'em. They'd ruin our crops."

"He's right," O'Hara said. "If we ain't on hand to defend 'em, they sure won't last long."

"Which of you feel qualified to stand off Hale's riders?" Trent asked dryly. "What man here could hold off ten or twenty men? I don't feel I could. I don't think the Parson could, alone. We've got to get together. Suppose they burn us out. We can build again, if we're alive to do it, an' we can band together and help each other build back. If you ain't alive, you ain't goin' to build very much!"

"Thet strikes me as bein' plumb sense," Hight said, leaning forward. "Looks to me like we got to sink or swim together. Hale's got too much power, an' we're too scattered. He ain't plannin' on us gettin' together. He's plannin' on wipin' us out one at a time. Together, we got us a chance."

"Maybe you're right," O'Hara said slowly. "Dick Moffitt didn't do very well alone."

"This place can be defended," Trent said. "Aside from my own place, this is the easiest to defend of them all. Then, the house is the biggest and strongest. If we have to fall back from the rocks, the house can hold out."

"What about a leader?" Bartram asked. "We'd better get that settled. How about you, Parson?"

"No." Parson drew himself up. "I'm right flattered, right pleased. But I ain't your man. I move we choose Trent, here."

There was a moment's silence, and then O'Hara spoke up. "I second that motion. Trent's good for me. He whipped old King Bill."

Runyon looked thoughtfully at Trent. "I don't know this gent," he said slowly. "I ain't got any objections to him. But how do we know he's our man? You've done a power of feudin', Parson. You should know this kind of fightin'."

"I do," Parson drawled. "But I ain't got the savvy Trent has. First, lemme say this here. I ain't been here all my life. I was a sharpshooter with the Confederate Army, an' later I rid with Jeb Stuart. Well, we was only whipped once, an' that was by a youngster of a Union officer. He whipped our socks off with half as many men—an' that officer was Trent here."

Trent's eyes turned slowly to Parson, who sat there staring at him, his eyes twinkling. "I reckon," Hatfield went on, "Trent is some surprised. I ain't said nothin' to him about knowin' him, specially when his name wasn't Trent, but I knowed him from the first time I seen him."

"That's good enough for me," Runyon said flatly. "You say he's got the savvy, I'll take your word for it."

Trent leaned over the table. "All right. All of you mount up and go home. Watch your trail carefully. When you get home, load up and get back. Those of you who can, ride together. Get back here with everything you want to save, but especially with all the grub you've got. But get back, and quick."

He got to his feet. "We're goin' to let Hale make the first move, but we're goin' to have a Hatfield watchin' the town. When Hale moves, we're goin' to move, too. We've got twelve men—"

"Twelve?" Smithers looked around. "I count cloven."

"Jackie Moffitt's the twelfth," Trent said quietly. "I gave him a Sharps. He's fourteen. Many of you at fourteen did a man's job. I'll stake my saddle that Jackie Moffitt will do his part. He can hit squirrels with that gun, an' a man's not so big. He'll do.

"Like I say, we've got twelve men. Six of them can hold this place. With the other six, or maybe with four, we'll strike back. I don't know how you feel, but I feel no man ever won a war by sittin' on his royal American tail, an' we're not a-goin' to."

"That's good talk," Smithers said quietly, "I'm not a warlike man, but I don't want to think of my place being burned when they go scot-free. I'm for striking back, but we've got to think of food."

"I've thought of that. Lije an' Saul Hatfield are goin' out today after some deer. They know where they are, an' neither of them is goin' to miss any shots. With the food we have, we can get by a few days. Then I'm goin' after some myself!"

"You?" O'Hara stated. "Where you figger on gettin' this grub?"

"Blazer." He looked down at his hands on the table and then looked up. "I'm not goin' to spend three days, either. I'm goin' through Smoky Desert!"

There was dead silence. Runyon leaned forward, starting to speak, but then he sat back shaking his head. It was Smithers who broke the silence.

"I'll go with you," he said quietly.

"But, man!" Hight protested. "There ain't no way through that desert, an' if there was—"

"The Indians used to go through," Trent said quietly, "and I think I know how. If it can be done, I could reach Blazer in a little over a day an' start back the same night."

He looked over at Jesse Hatfield. "You want to watch Cedar? I reckon you know how to Indian. Don't take any chances, but keep an eye on 'em. You take that chestnut of mine. He's a racer. You take that horse, an' when they move, you take the back trails for here."

Jesse Hatfield got up and slipped from the room. Then Trent said, "All right, start rolling. Get back here when you can."

He walked outside and saddled the buckskin. Jackie sauntered up, the Sharps in the hollow of his arm.

"Jackie," Trent said, "you get up there in the eye, an' keep a lookout on the Cedar trail." Mounting, he rode out of the hollow at a lope and swung into the trail toward his own cabin.

He knew what they were facing, but already in his mind the plan of campaign was taking shape. If they sat still, sooner or later they must be wiped out, and sooner or later his own men would lose heart. They must strike back. Hale must be made to learn that he could not win all the time, that he must lose, too.

All was quiet and green around the little cabin, and he rode up, swinging down. He stepped through, hurriedly put his grub into sacks, and hung it on a packhorse. Then he hesitated. Slowly, he walked across to the peg on the cupboard. For a long minute he looked at the guns hanging there. Then he reached up and took them down. He buckled them on, heavyhearted and feeling lost and empty.

It was sundown when he hazed his little band of carefully selected horses through the notch into the Hatfield hollow and, with Jackie's help, put them in the corral. All the men were back, and the women were working around, laughing, pleasant. They were true women of the West, and most of them had been through Indian fights before this.

Hight was the last one in. He came riding through the notch on a spent horse, his face drawn and hard.

"They burned me out!" he said hoarsely, sweat streaking his face. "They hit me just as I was a-packin'. I didn't get off with nothin'. I winged one of 'em, though!"

Even as he spoke, Smithers caught Trent's arm. "Look!" he urged, and pointed. In the sky they could see a red glow from reflected fire. "O'Hara's place," he said. "Maybe they got him, too."

"No." O'Hara walked up, scowling. "They didn't get me. I got here twenty minutes ago. They'll pay for this, the wolves."

Jesse Hatfield on the chestnut suddenly materialized in the gloom. "Two bunches ridin'," he said, "an' they aim to get here about sunup. I heard 'em talkin'."

Trent nodded. "Get some sleep, Jesse. You, too, Jackie. Parson, you an' Smithers better keep watch. Quince, I want you an' Bartram to ride with me."

"Where you all goin'?" Saul demanded.

"Why, Saul," Trent smiled in the darkness, "I reckon we're goin' to town after groceries. We're goin' to call on Leathers, an' we'll just load up while we're there. If he ain't willin', we may have to take him along anyway!"

"Count me in," Saul said. "I sure want to be in on that!"

"You'd better rest," Trent suggested. "You got three antelope today, you an' Lije."

"I reckon I ain't so wearied I'd miss that ride, Captain, if you all say I can go."

"We can use you."

Suddenly, there was a burst of flame to the south. "There goes my place," Smithers exclaimed bitterly. "I spent two years a-buildin' that place. Had some onions comin' up, too, an' a good crop of potatoes in."

Trent had started away, but he stopped and turned. "Smithers," he said quietly, "you'll dig those potatoes yourself. I promise you—if I have to wipe out the Hales personally so's you can do it."

Smithers stared after him as he walked away. "Y'know," he remarked thoughtfully to O'Hara, "I believe he would do it. O'Hara," he turned to look at the big Irishman, "maybe we can win this fight after all."

# Chapter VII
## Food for the Siege

Cedar Bluff lay dark and still when the four horsemen rode slowly down the path behind the town. Trent, peering through the darkness, studied the town carefully. Taking the trail might have been undue precaution, for there was small chance the road would be watched. There had been, of course, the possibility that some late puncher might have spotted them on the trail.

It was after three, and the Crystal Palace and the Mecca had closed their doors over an hour earlier. Trent reined in on the edge of the town and studied the situation. King Bill, secure in his power even after the beating he had taken, would never expect the nesters to approach the town. He would be expecting them to try the overland route to Blazer for supplies, and in his monumental conceit, he would never dream that they would come right to the heart of his domain.

"Bartram," Trent whispered, "you an' Saul take the packhorses behind the store. Keep 'em quiet. Don't try to get in or do anything. Just hold 'em there."

He turned to the older Hatfield. "Quince, we're goin' to get Leathers."

"Why not just bust in?" Saul protested. "Why bother with him? We can find what we need."

"No," Trent said flatly. "He's goin' to wait on us, an' we're goin' to pay him. We ain't thieves, an' we're goin' to stick to the legal way. I may hold him up an' bring him down there, but we're goin' to pay him, cash on the barrelhead, for everything we take."

Leaving their horses with the others behind the store, Trent took Quince and soft-footed it toward the storekeeper's home, about a hundred yards from the store. Walking along the dark street, Trent looked around from time to time to see Quince. The long, lean Hatfield, six foot three in his socks, could move like an Indian. Unless Trent had looked, he would never have dreamed there was another man so close.

Trent stopped by the garden gate. There was a faint scent of lilacs in the air, and of some other flowers. Gently, he pushed open the gate. It creaked on rusty hinges, and for an instant, they froze. All remained dark and still, so Trent moved on, and Quince deftly took the gate from him and eased it slowly shut.

The air was heavy with lilac now, and the smell of damp grass. Trent stopped at the edge of the shadow and motioned to Quince to stand by. Ever so gently, he lifted one foot and put it down on the first step. Lifting himself by the muscles of his leg, he put down the other foot. Carefully, inch by inch, he worked his way across the porch to the house.

Two people slept inside. Leathers and his wife. His wife was a fat, comfortable woman, one of those in the town who idolized King Bill Hale and held him up as an example of all the West should be and all a man should be. King Bill's swagger and his grandiose manner impressed her. He was, she was convinced, a great man.

Once, shortly after he had first come to Cedar, Trent had been in this house. He had come to get Leathers to buy supplies after the store had been closed. He remembered, vaguely, the layout of the rooms.

The door he was now opening gently opened into the kitchen. From it, there were two doors, one to a living room, rarely used, and one to the bedroom. In that bedroom, Leathers would be sleeping with his wife.

Once inside the kitchen he stood very still. He could hear the breathing of two people in the next room, the slow, heavy breathing of Elsa Leathers and the more jerky, erratic breathing of the store-keeper. The kitchen smelled faintly of onions and of homemade soap.

Drawing a large handkerchief from his pocket, he tied it across his face under his eyes. Then he slid his six-gun into his hand and tiptoed through the door into the bedroom. For a moment, Elsa Leathers's breathing caught, hesitated, and then went on. He heaved a sigh of relief. If she awakened, she was almost certain to start screaming.

Alongside the bed, he stooped and put the cold muzzle of his gun under the storekeeper's nose. Almost instantly, the man's eyes opened. Even in the darkness of the room, Trent could see them slowly turn upward toward him. He leaned down, almost breathing the words.

"Get up, quietly!"

Very carefully, Leathers eased out of bed. Trent gestured for him to put on his pants, and as the man drew them on, Trent watched him like a hawk. Then Trent gestured toward the door, and Leathers tiptoed outside.

"What's the matter?" he whispered, his voice hoarse and shaking. "What do you want me for?"

"Just a little matter of some groceries," Trent replied. "You open your store an' give us what we want, an' you won't have any trouble. Make one squawk an' I'll bend this gun over your noggin!"

"I ain't sayin' anythin'!" Leathers protested. He buckled his belt and hurried toward the store with Trent at his heels. Quince Hatfield sauntered along behind, stopping only to pluck a blue corn-flower and stick it in an empty buttonhole of his shirt.

Leathers fumbled for the lock on the door. "If my wife wakes up an' finds me gone, mister," he said grumpily, "I ain't responsible for what happens."

"Don't you worry about that," Trent assured him dryly, "you just fill this order an' don't make us any trouble!"

He motioned to Saul, who came forward. "As soon as you get four horses loaded, you let Bartram take 'em back to the trail an' hold 'em there. Then if anything happens he can take off with that much grub."

As fast as Leathers piled out the groceries, Saul and Quince hurried to carry them out to the horses. Trent stood by, gun in hand.

"You ain't goin' to get away with this!" Leathers stated, finally. "When Hale finds out, he's a-goin' to make somebody sweat!"

"Yeah," Trent said quietly, "maybe he will. From all I hear he'd better wait until he gets over one beatin' afore he starts huntin' another! An' while we're talkin', you better make up your mind, too. When this war is over, if Hale doesn't win, what d'you suppose happens to you?"

"Huh?" Leathers straightened, his face a shade whiter. "What d'you mean?"

"I mean, brother," Trent said harshly, "that you've taken sides in this fuss. An' if Hale loses, you're goin' out of town—but fast!"

"He ain't a-goin' to lose!" Leathers brought out a sack of flour and put it down on the floor. "Hale's got the money, an' he's got the men. Look what happened to Smithers's place today, an' O'Hara's. An' look what happened to—"

"To Dick Moffitt?" Trent's voice was cold. "That was murder!"

Quince stepped into the door. "Somebody's comin'!" he hissed. "Watch it!"

"Let 'em come in," Trent said softly, "but no shootin' unless they shoot first."

Trent thrust a gun against Leathers. "If they come in," he whispered, "you talk right, see? Answer any questions, but answer 'em like I tell you, because if there is any shootin', Elsa Leathers is goin' to be a widow, but quick."

Two men walked up to the door, and one tried the knob. Then as the door opened, he thrust his head in.

"Who's there?" he demanded.

"It's me," Leathers said, and as Trent prodded him with the gun barrel, "fixin' up an order that has to get out early."

The two men pushed on inside. "I never knew you to work this late, afore. Why, man, it must be nearly four o'clock."

"Right," Quince stepped up with a six-gun. "You hombres invited yourself to this party, now pick up them sacks an' cart 'em outside!"

"Huh?" The two men stared stupidly. "Why—?"

"Get movin'!" Quince snapped. "Get them sacks out there before I bend this over your head!" The man hesitated and then obeyed, and the other followed a moment later.

It was growing gray in the east when the orders were completed. Quickly, they tied up the two men while Leathers stood by. Then, at a motion from Trent, Saul grabbed Leathers and he was bound and gagged. Carrying him very carefully, Trent took him back into his cottage and placed him in bed, drawing the blankets over him. Elsa Leathers sighed heavily, and turned in her sleep. Trent stood very still, waiting. Then her breathing became even once more, and he tiptoed from the house.

Quince was standing in the shadow of the store, holding both horses. "They've started up the trail," he said. Then he grinned. "Gosh a' mighty, I'll bet old Leathers is some sore!"

"There'll be a chase, most likely," Trent said. "We'd better hang back a little in case."

Bartram was ahead, keeping the horses at a stiff trot. He was a tough, wiry young farmer and woodsman who had spent three years convoying wagon trains over the Overland Trail before he came south. He knew how to handle a pack train, and he showed it now.

Swinging the line of pack horses from the trail, he led them into the shallow water of Cedar Branch and walked them very rapidly through the water. Twice he stopped to give them a breather, but kept moving at a good pace, Saul riding behind the string, his long Kentucky rifle across his saddle.

"You pay Leathers?" Quince asked, riding close.

"Yeah," Trent nodded. "I stuck it down between him an' his wife after I put him in bed. He'll be some surprised!"

Using every trick they knew to camouflage their trail, they worked steadily back up into the hills. They were still five miles or more from the Hatfield place when they heard shots in the distance.

Quince reined in, his features sharpened. "Looks like they've done attacked the place," he said. "What d'you think, Trent? Should we leave this to Saul an' ride up there?"

Trent hesitated and then shook his head. "No. They can hold 'em for a while. We want to make sure this food is safe." Suddenly he reined in. "Somebody's comin' up our back trail. Go ahead, Saul. But don't run into the attackin' party."

Saul nodded grimly, and Trent, taking a quick look around, indicated a bunch of boulders above the trail. They rode up and swung down, and Quince gave an exclamation of satisfaction as he noted the deep arroyo behind the boulders—a good place for their horses and good for a getaway, if need be.

The horsemen were coming fast now. Lying behind the boulders, they could see the dust rising above them as they wound their way through the cedars and huge rocks that bordered the narrow trail. A hundred yards away they broke into the open.

"Dust 'em!" Trent said, and fired.

Their two rifles went off with the same sound and two puffs of dust went up in front of the nearest horse. The horse reared sharply and spun halfway around. Trent lowered his rifle to note the effect of their shots and then aimed high at the second horseman and saw his sombrero lift from his head and sail into the brush. The men wheeled and whipped their horses back into the brush.

Quince chuckled and bit off a chew. "That'll make 'em think a mite—say!" He nodded toward a nest of rocks on the other side. "What'll you bet one of them rannies ain't a-shinnyin' up into that nest of rocks about now?"

There was a notch in the rocks and a boulder beyond, not four feet beyond by the look of it. Quince Hatfield lifted his Kentucky rifle, took careful aim, and then fired.

There was a startled yell and then curses. Quince chuckled a little. "Dusted him with granite off that boulder," he said. "They won't hurry to get up there again."

Trent thought swiftly. If he took the arroyo and circled back, he could then get higher up on the mountain. With careful fire, he could still cover the open spot and so give Quince a chance to retreat while he held them. Swiftly, he told Hatfield. The big mountaineer nodded.

"Go ahead. They won't move none till you get there."

It took Trent ten minutes to work his way out of the arroyo and up the mountain. As distance went, he wasn't so far, being not more than four hundred yards away. He signaled his presence to Quince Hatfield by letting go with three shots into the shelter taken by their pursuers. From above, that shelter was scarcely more than concealment and not at all cover.

In a few minutes Quince joined him. They each let go with two shots and then, mounting, rode swiftly away, out of view of the men in the brush below.

"They'll be slow about showin' themselves, I reckon," Quince said, "so we'll be nigh to home afore they get nerve enough to move."

When they had ridden four miles, Quince reined in sharply. "Horses ahead," he advised. "Maybe they're ours."

Approaching cautiously, they saw Bartram with the eight packhorses. He was sitting with his rifle in his hands, watching the brush ahead. He glanced around at their approach and then with a wave of the hand, motioned them on.

"Firing up ahead. Saul's gone up. He'll be back pretty soon."

Low-voiced, Trent told him what had happened. Then as they talked they saw Saul Hatfield coming through the brush on foot. He walked up to them and caught his horse by the bridle.

"They got 'em stopped outside the cup," he said. "I think only one man of theirs is down. He's a-lyin' on his face in the open not far from the boulders where O'Hara is. There must be about a dozen of them, no more."

"Is there a way into the cup with these horses?" Trent asked.

Saul nodded. "Yeah, I reckon if they was busy over yonder for a few minutes we could run 'em all in."

"We'll make 'em busy, eh, Quince?" Trent suggested. "Bart, you an' Saul whip 'em in there fast as soon as we open up." He had reloaded his rifle, and the two turned their horses and started skirting the rocks to outflank the attackers.

Trent could see what had happened. The Hatfield place lay in a cuplike depression surrounded on three sides by high, rocky walls and on the other by scattered boulders. Through the cliffs, there were two ways of getting into the cup. One of these, now about to be attempted, lay partly across an open space before the cup was entered.

The attackers were mostly among the scattered boulders, but had been stopped and pinned down by O'Hara and someone else. Two men there could hold that ground against thirty. Obviously, some of the others were up in the cliffs above the cup, waiting for any attack.

Approaching as they were, Trent and Quince were coming down from the south toward the west end of the cup, where the scattered boulders lay. By working up close there, they could find and dislodge the attackers or at least keep them so busy the pack animals could get across the open to the cup.

About three acres of land lay in the bottom of the cup. There was a fine, cold spring, the barn, horse corrals, and adequate protection. The cliffs were ringed with scattered cedar and rocks, so men there could protect the approach to the boulder. However, if a rifleman got into those rocks on the edge of the cup, he could render movement in the cup impossible until he could be driven out. It was the weak spot of the stronghold.

When they had ridden several hundred yards the two men reined in and dismounted. Slipping through the cedars, Indian fashion, they soon came to the edge of the woods overlooking the valley of boulders. Not fifty yards away, two men lay behind boulders facing toward the Hatfield cup.

Trent lifted his Winchester and let go with three fast shots. One, aimed at the nearest man's feet, clipped a heel from his boot; the others threw dust in his face, and with a yell the fellow scrambled out of there. Trent followed him with two more shots, and the man tumbled into a gully and started to run.

The other man started to get up, and Quince Hatfield made him leap like a wild man with a well-placed shot that burned the inside of his leg. Scattering their shots, the two had the rest of the attackers scattering for better cover.

# Chapter VIII
## Cain Brockman Rides In

Parson Hatfield walked out to meet them as they rode in. He grinned through his yellowed handlebar mustache. "Well, I reckon we win the first round," he chuckled. "Sure was a sight to see them punchers dustin' out of there when you all opened up on 'em!"

"Who was the man we saw down?" Trent asked.

"Gunhand they called Indian Joe. A killer. He wouldn't stop comin', so O'Hara let him have it. Dead center."

They walked back to the cabin. "We got grub to keep us for a few days, but we got a passel of folks here," Parson said, squatting on his haunches, "an' I don't reckon you're goin' to be able to hit Cedar again."

Trent nodded agreement. "We've got to get to Blazer," he said. "There isn't any two ways about it. I wish I knew what they'd do now. If we had a couple of days' leeway—"

"You know anythin' about the celebration Hale's figurin' on down to Cedar? They's been talk about it. He's been there ten years, an' he figures that's reason to celebrate."

"What's happenin'?" Trent asked.

"Horse races, horseshoe pitchin', wrestlin', footraces, an' a prize fight. King Bill's bringing in a prizefighter. Big feller, they called him Tombull Turner."

Trent whistled. "Say, he is good! Big, too. He fought over in Abilene when I was there. A regular bruiser."

"That may keep 'em busy," Quince said. He had a big chunk of corn pone in his hand. "Maybe we'll get some time to get grub."

Trent got up. "Me, I'm goin' to sleep!" he said. "I'm fairly dead on my feet. You'd better, too," he added to Quince Hatfield.

It was growing dusk when Trent awakened. He rubbed his hand over his face and got to his feet. He had been dead tired, and no sooner had he lain down on the grass under the trees than he had fallen asleep.

Walking over to the spring he drew a bucket of water and plunged his head into it. Then he dried himself on a rough towel Sally handed him.

"Two more men came in," Sally told him. "Tot Wilson from down in the breaks by the box canyon, and Jody Miller, a neighbor of his."

Saul looked up as he walked into the house. "Wilson an' Miller were both burned out. They done killed Wilson's partner. Shot him down when he went out to rope him a horse."

"Hi." Miller looked up at Trent. "I've seen you afore."

"Could be." Trent looked away.

This was it. He could tell by the way Miller looked at him and said, "I'd have knowed you even if it wasn't for that hombre down to the Mecca."

"What hombre?" Trent demanded.

"Big feller, bigger'n you. He come in there about sundown yesterday, askin' about a man fittin' your description. Wants you pretty bad."

"Flat face? Deep scar over one eye?"

"That's him. Looks like he'd been in a lot of fights, bad ones."

"He was in one," Trent said dryly. "One was enough."

Cain Brockman!

Even before he'd heard from Lee Hall he had known this would come sooner or later. All that was almost two years behind him, but

Cain wasn't a man to forget. He had been one of the hard-riding, fast-shooting duo, the Brockman twins. In a fight at Cottonwood, down in the Live Oak country, Trent, then known by his real name, had killed Abel. Later, in a hand-to-hand fight, he had beaten Cain Brockman into a staggering, punch-drunk hulk.

Now Brockman was here. As if it weren't enough to have the fight with King Bill Hale on his hands!

Parson Hatfield was staring at Trent. Then he glanced at Miller. "You say you know this feller?" he gestured at Trent. "I'd like to, myself!"

"The name," Trent said slowly, "is Lance Kilkenny."

"Kilkenny!" Bartram dropped his plate. "You're Kilkenny."

"Uh-huh." He turned and walked outside and stood there with his hands on his hips, staring out toward the scattered boulders at the entrance to the Hatfield cup. He was Kilkenny. The name had come back again. He dropped his hands, and almost by magic the big guns leaped into them, and he stood there, staring at them. Slowly, thoughtfully, he replaced them.

Cain Brockman was here. The thought made him suddenly weary. It meant, sooner or later, that he must shoot it out with Cain. In his reluctance to fight the big man there was something more than his hatred of killing. He had whipped Cain Brockman with his hands; he had killed Abel. It should be enough.

If there was to be any killing—his thoughts skipped Dunn and Ravitz, and he found himself looking again into the blazing white eyes of a trim young man in buckskin, Cub Hale.

He shook his head to clear it and walked toward the spring. What would King Bill do next? He had whipped Hale. Knowing what he had done to the big man, he knew he would still be under cover. Also, Hale's pride would be hurt badly by his beating.

Also, it was not only that he had taken a licking. He had burned out a few helpless nesters, only to have those nesters band together and fight off his raiding party, and in the meantime they had ridden into his own town and taken a load of supplies, supplies he had refused them!

The power of any man is built largely on the belief of others in that power. To maintain leadership, he must win victories, and King Bill had been whipped and his plans had been thwarted. The answer to that seemed plain—King Bill must do something to retrieve his losses. But what would he do?

Despite the victories the nesters had won, King Bill was still in the driver's seat. He knew how many men they had. He knew about what supplies they had taken from the store, and he knew the number they had at the Hatfields' could not survive for long without more food.

Hale could, if he wished, withdraw all his men and just sit tight across the trail to Blazer and wait until the nesters had to move or starve. He might do that. Or he might strike again, and in greater force.

Kilkenny—it seemed strange to be thinking of himself as Kilkenny again, he had been Trent so long—ruled out the quick strike. By now Hale would know that the Hatfields were strongly entrenched.

The main trail to Blazer led through Cedar Bluff. There was a trail, only occasionally used, from the Hatfields' to the Blazer mountain trail, but Hale knew that, and would be covering it. There was a chance they might slip through. Yet even as he thought of that, he found himself thinking again of the vast crater that was the Smoky Desert. That was still a possibility.

O'Hara walked out to where he was standing under the trees. "Runyon an' Wilson want to try the mountain trail to Blazer," he told him. "What do you think?"

"I don't think much of it," Kilkenny said truthfully, "yet we've got to have grub."

"Parson told 'em what you said about Smoky Desert. Wilson says it can't be done. He said he done tried it."

Jackson Hight, Miller, and Wilson walked out. "We're all for tryin' the mountain trail," Wilson said. "I don't believe Hale will have it watched this far up. What do you say, Kilkenny?"

Kilkenny looked at his boot toe thoughtfully. They wanted to go, and they might get through. After all, his Smoky Desert seemed an impossible dream, and even more so to them than to him. "It's up to you," he said finally, "I won't send a man over that trail, but if you want to try it, go ahead."

It was almost midnight when the wagon pulled out of the cup. Miller was driving, with Wilson, Jackson Hight, and Lije Hatfield riding escort. Kilkenny was up to watch them go, and when the sound of the wagon died away, he returned to his pallet and turned in.

Twice during the night he awakened with a start to lie there listening in the stillness, his body tense, his mind fraught with worry, but despite his expectations, there were no sounds of shots, nothing.

When daybreak came he ate a hurried breakfast and swung into the saddle. He left the cup on a lope and followed the dim trail of the wagon. He followed it past the charred ruins of his own cabin and past those of Moffitt's cabin, yet as he neared the Blazer trail, he slowed down, walking the buckskin and stopping frequently to listen.

He could see by the tracks that Lije and Hight had been riding

ahead, scouting the way. Sometimes they were as much as a half
mile ahead, and he found several places where they had sat their
horses, waiting.

Suddenly, the hills seemed to fall away and he saw the dim trail
that led to Blazer, more than forty miles away. Such a short distance,
yet the trail was so bad that fifteen miles a day was considered good.

There was no sign of the wagon or of the men. There were no
tracks visible, and that in itself was a good thing. It meant that
someone, probably Lije, was remembering they must leave no trail.

He turned the buckskin then and rode back over the trail. He took
his time, and it was the middle of the afternoon before he reached
the ledge where he could look down into the awful haze that hung
over the Smoky Desert. Once, in his first trip up over this route, it
had been clearer below, and he had thought he saw a ruined wagon
far below.

Kilkenny found the place where he had stood that other day, for
long since he had marked the spot with a cairn of stones. Then
slowly and with great pains he began to seek. Time and again he was
turned back by sheer drops of hundreds of feet, and nowhere could
he find even the suggestion of a trail.

Four hours later, with long fingers of darkness reaching out from
the tall pines, he mounted the buckskin and started down toward the
cup. Jackson Hight could be correct. Possibly he was mistaken and
the Indians were wrong, and there was no trail down to the valley
below and across that wasteland. In his long search he had found
nothing.

Parson met him as he rode through the notch. Ma Hatfield had
come to the door and was shading her eyes toward him.

"They got through to the trail," Kilkenny said. "Maybe they'll
make it."

Sally was working over the fireplace when he walked inside.
Young Bartram was sitting close by, watching her. Kilkenny glanced
at them and smiled grimly. Sally caught his eye and flushed painfully, so he walked outside again and sat down against the house.

Quince had gone after deer into the high meadows, and Saul was
on guard. Runyon was sleeping on the grass under the trees, and
Jesse Hatfield was up on the cliffs somewhere. Kilkenny sat for a
long time against the house, and then he took his blankets over to
the grass, rolled up, and went to sleep.

Shortly after daybreak he roped a black horse from his string,
saddled up, and with a couple of sandwiches, headed back toward
the Smoky Desert. There must be a route. There had to be one.

When he reached the rim of the cliff again, he dismounted and
studied the terrain thoughtfully. He stood on a wide ledge that

thrust itself out into space. The desert below was partially obscured, as always, by clouds of dust or smoke, yet the rim itself was visible for some distance.

Actually, studying the rim, he could see that it bore less resemblance to the crater he had previously imagined than to a great sink. In fact, it looked as though some internal upheaval had caused the earth to subside at this point, breaking off the rock of the ledge and sinking the plateau several hundred feet.

For the most part the cliffs below the rim were jagged but almost sheer, yet at places the rim had caved away into steep rock slides that led, or seemed to lead, to the bottom. This great rift in the plateau led for miles, causing the trail to Blazer to swing in a wide semicircle to get around it. Actually, as best he could figure, Blazer was almost straight across from the ledge where he now stood.

Again he began to work with painstaking care along the rim. The Indians had said it could be crossed, that there was a way down, and Lance Kilkenny had lived in the West long enough to know that what the Indians said was usually right.

It was almost noon before he found the path. It was scarcely three feet wide, so he left his horse standing under the cedars and started walking. The path dipped through some gigantic slabs of ragged-edged rock and then ran out to the very edge of the cliff itself. When it seemed he was about to step right off into space, the path turned sharply to the right and ran along the face of the cliff.

He hesitated, taking off his hat and mopping his brow. The path led right along the face of the cliff, and at times it seemed almost broken away, but then it continued on. One thing he knew—this was useless for his purpose, for no man could take a horse, not even such a surefooted mountain horse as the buckskin, along this path. Yet he walked on.

The end was abrupt. He started to work his way around a thread of path that clung to the precipice, but when he could see around the corner, he saw the trail had ended. An hour of walking had brought him to a dead end.

Clinging to the rock, he looked slowly around. Then his eyes riveted. There, over three hundred feet below, on what even at this distance was obviously a trail, he could see a wagon wheel!

Leaning out with a precarious handhold on a root, he could distinguish the half-buried wagon from which the wheel had been broken. Of the rest of the trail, he could see nothing. It vanished from sight under the bulge of the cliff. He drew back, sweating.

The trail was there. The wagon was there. Obviously, someone, at some time, had taken a wagon or wagons over that trail. But where was the beginning? Had the shelf upon which it ran broken off and ruined the trail for use?

Taking a point of gray rock for a landmark he retraced his steps along the path. By the time he reached the buckskin again his feet hurt from walking over the rough rock in his riding boots, and he was tired, dead tired. He had walked about six miles, and that was an impossible distance to a horseman.

## Chapter IX
### *On Short Rations*

When he rode into the cup that night, Parson looked up from the rifle that he was cleaning. "Howdy, son! You look done up!"

Kilkenny nodded and stopped beside the older man. He was tired, and his shirt stuck to his back with sweat. For the first time he wondered if they would win. For the first time, he doubted. Without food they were helpless. They could neither escape nor resist. He doubted now if Hale would ever let them go, if he would ever give them any chance of escape.

They ate short rations that night. He knew there was still a good deal of food, yet fourteen men, if he included those who were gone, and six women had to eat there. And there were nine children. Yet there was no word of complaint, and only on the faces of those women who had men with the food wagon could he distinguish the thin gray lines of worry.

"Any sign from Hale?" he asked O'Hara.

The Irishman shook his head. "Not any. He's got men out in the rocks. They ain't tryin' to shoot nobody. Just a-watchin'. But they're there."

"I don't think he'll try anything now until after the celebration," Bartram said. "He's plannin' on makin' a lot of friends with that celebration. It means a lot to him, anyway."

Jesse Hatfield pushed back his torn felt hat. "I took me a ride today," he said. "Done slipped out through the brush. I got clean to Cedar without bein' seen. I edged up close to town, an' I could see a lot of workin' around.

"They got 'em a ring set up out in front of the livery stable near the horse corral. Ropes an' everythin'. Lots of talk around, an' the big wonder is who's goin' to fight Tombull Turner."

Kilkenny listened absently, not caring. His thoughts were back on that ragged rim, working along each notch and crevice, wondering where that road reached the top of the plateau.

"This here Dan Cooper was there, an' he done some talkin'. He looked powerful wise, an' he says Turner ain't been brought here by accident. He's been brought to whip one man—Kilkenny!"

"Did he say 'Kilkenny'?" Kilkenny looked around to ask. "Do they know who I am?"

"He said Trent," Jesse drawled. "I don't reckon they know."

Tombull Turner to beat him? Kilkenny remembered the bullet head, the knotted cauliflower ears, the flat nose and hard, battered face of the big bare-knuckle fighter. Tombull was a fighter. He was more; he was a brute. He was an American who had fought much in England, and against the best on both continents. He had even met Joe Goss and Paddy Ryan. While he, Kilkenny, was no prizefighter.

An idle rumor. It could be no more, for he was not in Cedar Bluff, nor was he likely to be. Studying the faces of the men around him, he could see what was on their minds. Despite their avoidance of the subject, he knew they were all thinking of the wagon on the road to Blazer.

The food was necessary, but four men were out there, four men they all knew, men who had shared their work, their trials, and even the long trip west from their lands in Kentucky, Pennsylvania, and Missouri. Lije Hatfield was gone, and knowing the family, Kilkenny knew that if he were killed no Hatfield would stop until all the Hales were dead or the Hatfields wiped out.

Knowing the route, he could picture the wagon rolling slowly along over the rocky road, horsemen to the front and rear, watching, hoping, fearing. They, too, if still alive and free, would have their worries. They would know that back here men and women were getting close to the end of their food supply, that those men and women were depending on them.

On the morning of the third day, Kilkenny mounted again and started for the rim. He saw Parson Hatfield staring after him, but the old man said nothing.

This time Kilkenny had a plan. He was going back where he had been the day before, and by some means, he was going down the face of the cliff to the wagon. Then he would backtrack. If there was no trail back, he would have to come up the cliff. Well, that was a bridge to be crossed later. Somewhere in that jumble of broken cliffs, great slabs of jagged rock, and towering shoulders of stone, there must be a trail down which that wagon had gone.

It was almost seven o'clock in the morning before he found himself, two ropes in his hands, at the tapering edge of the trail along the face of the cliff.

Lying flat, he peered over the edge. The rock on which he lay was a bulge that thrust out over the face of the cliff, and if he dropped over here he must use the rope purely as a safety precaution and

work down with his hands. There were cracks and knobs that could
be used. The depth below was sickening, but partially obscured by
the strange thickness of the air.

A gnarled cedar grew from the face of the rock, and he tested it for
strength. The thing seemed as immovable as the rocks themselves.
Making his first rope fast to the cedar, Kilkenny knotted the other
end in a bowline around himself. Then he turned himself around and
backed over the edge, feeling with his feet for a toehold.

For a time, he knew, he would be almost upside down like a fly on
a ceiling. Unless he could find handholds where he could get a good
grip and if necessary, hang by them, there was small chance of
making it. But there were, he had noticed, a number of roots,
probably of rock cedar, thrusting out through the rock below.

Forcing himself to think of nothing but the task at hand, he
lowered himself over the edge, and when he got the merest toehold,
he swung one hand down and felt around until he could grasp one of
the roots. Then he let go with his left hand and let himself down
until he was half upside down, clinging by a precarious toehold and
his grip on the root.

Finding another hold for his left hand, he took a firm grasp and
then pulled out his left toe and felt downward. He found a crack,
tested it with his toe, and then set the foot solidly. Carefully, he
released a handhold and lowered his hand to another root, lower
down. Then, sweating profusely, he lowered his weight to the lowest
foot.

He resolutely kept his thoughts away from the awful depths below. He had a chance, but a very slim one. Slowly and with great
care, he shifted himself down the bulging overhang. Every time he
moved a foot or hand his life seemed to end. He was, he knew,
wringing with perspiration, his breath was coming painfully, and he
swung himself precariously toward the sheer cliff below. Even that
great height of straight up and down cliff seemed a haven to this
bulge of the overhang.

Clinging to a huge root and pressing himself as tightly to the face
as he could, he turned his head right and then left, searching the
face of the bulge. There were handholds enough here. The roots of
the cedars that had grown on the ledge above thrust through the
bulge. Yet that very fact seemed to indicate that at some time in the
past huge chunks of rock had given way, leaving these roots exposed.
It had happened once, and it could happen again.

Far out in the blue sky a buzzard whirled in great, slow circles.
His fingers ached with gripping, and he lowered himself away from
the face of the cliff and looked down between his legs. A notch
showed in the rock, and he worked his toe loose and then lowered it
with care until he could test the notch. He tried it.

Solid. Slowly, carefully, he began to settle weight on the ball of his foot. There was a sudden sag beneath his foot and then a rattle of stones, and the notch gave way under him, forcing him to grip hard with his hands to catch the additional weight.

His right foot hung free. Carefully, he began to feel with his toe for another foothold. He found it, tried, and rested his weight again, and the stone took it. Slowly, he shifted hands again and then lowered himself down a little more.

Glancing down again, he found himself looking at a stretch of rock at least fifteen feet across that was absolutely smooth. No single crack or crevice showed, no projection of stone, no root. His muscles desperate with weariness, he stared, unbelieving—to come this far and fail.

Forcing himself to think, he studied the face of the cliff. There was, some twenty feet below and almost that far to the left, a gnarled and twisted rock cedar growing out of the mountainside. It was too far to the right, and there was no way of reaching it. Yet, as he stared, he could see that a crevice, deep enough for a good foothold, ran off at an angle from the cedar. If he could reach it—

But how?

There was a way. It hit him almost at once. If he released his grip on the roots, he would instantly swing free. As he had worked himself far to the right of the cedar to which his lariat was tied, his release would swing him far out from the cliff, and then as he swung back, for an instant he would be above the clump of cedar. On each succeeding swing he would fall shorter and shorter, until finally he was suspended in midair, hanging like a great pendulum from the cedar above.

Then all his efforts would be vain, for he would have to catch the rope over his head and go up it, hand over hand to the cedar above, and he would have failed. On the other hand, if he could release himself above the cedar, he would fall into it, and unless some sharp branch injured him, the chances were the limbs would cushion his fall.

He had his knife, and it was razor sharp. Even as these thoughts flitted through his mind, he was drawing the knife. Luckily, before leaving his horse he had tied a rawhide thong over each six-shooter, so his guns were secure. Yet the rope was rawhide and tough. Could he slash through at one blow?

The answer to that was simple. He had to. If he swung out over the void below on half or less of the strength of the lariat, there was small chance it would not break at the extreme end of the swing, and he would go shooting out over the deadly waste of the Smoky Desert to fall, and fall—over and over into that murky cloud that obscured the depths.

He let go and shoved hard with both feet and hands. His body swept out in a long swing over the breathtaking depths below. Then, hesitating but an instant as the rope tore at his sides, he swept back like a giant pendulum, rushing through the air toward the cliff! It shot toward him, and he raised his arm, and seeing the cedar below and ahead, he cut down with a mighty slash.

He felt himself come loose and then he was hurled forward at the cedar. He hit it, all doubled into a ball, heard a splintering crash, slipped through, and felt the branches tearing at his clothes like angry fingers. Then he brought up with a jolt and lay, trembling in every limb, clinging to the cedar.

How long he lay there, he did not know. Finally, he pulled himself together and crawled out of the tree and got his feet on the narrow foothold. He worked his way along until the ledge grew wide enough for him to walk. His breath was coming with more regularity now. He felt gingerly of his arms and body where the rawhide rope had burned him.

The path, if such it might be called, slanted steeply away from him, ending in some broken slabs. He stopped when he reached them. He was, at last, on the Smoky Desert.

# Chapter X
## *Land of Legendary Men*

Lance Kilkenny stood on a dusty desert floor littered with jagged slabs of rock, obviously fallen from the cliff above. There was no grass here, no cedar, nothing growing at all, not even a cactus.

Above him the dark, basalt cliff lifted toward the sky, towering and ugly. Looking off over the desert he could see only a few hundred yards, and then all became indistinct. The reason was obvious enough. The floor of the desert was dust, fine as flour, and even the lightest breeze lifted it into the air, where it hung for hours on end. A strong wind would fill the air so full of these particles as to make the air thick as a cloud, and the particles were largely silicate.

One thing he knew now. Crossing the Smoky Desert, even if there was a trail, would be a frightful job. Unfastening the thongs that had held his guns in place, he walked on slowly. It was still, only a little murmur from the wind among the rocks, and nothing else.

The cliff lifted on his right, and off to the left stretched the awful expanse of the desert, concealed behind that curtain of dust. He stepped over the dead and bleached bones of an ancient cedar, fallen from above, and rounded a short bend in the cliff.

As he walked, little puffs of dust lifted from his boot soles, and his mouth grew dry. Once, he stopped and carefully wiped his guns free of dust and then lowered them once more into the holsters.

Then he saw the white scar of the road, tracks of vehicles filled with fine white dust, and the rough, barely visible marks of what had been a fairly good road, dwindling away into the gray, dusty vagueness that was the desert. He looked up and saw the trail winding steeply up the cliff's face through a narrow draw.

Turning, he began to climb the trail. Several times he paused to roll boulders from the path. He was already thinking in terms of a wagon and a team. It could be done. That is, it could be done if there was still a way of getting a team onto this trail. That might be the catch. What lay at the end?

Sweat rolled down his face, making thin rivulets through the white dust. White dust clung to the hairs on the backs of his hands, and once when he stopped to remove his sombrero and wipe the sweat from his brow, he saw his hat was covered with a thin gray coat of it.

He looked ahead. He could see the road for no more than a hundred yards, but the cliff to his right was now growing more steep, and glancing down, he could see the trail was already far above the valley floor. He walked, making heavy work of it in his riding boots, sweat soaking his shirt under the film of gray dust, and the draw was narrowing.

The rock under the trail sloped steeply away into a dark, shadowy canyon now over two hundred feet down. He walked on, plodding wearily. For over an hour he walked, winding around and around to follow the curving walls of the canyon. Then he halted suddenly.

Ahead of him the trail ended. It ended and explained his difficulties in one instant. A gigantic pine, once perched upon the edge of the cliff, had given way, its roots evidently weakened by wind erosion. The tree had blown down and fallen across the trail. Pines had sprung up around it and around its roots until the trail was blocked by a dense thicket that gave no hint of the road that had once run beneath it.

Crawling over the pine, Kilkenny emerged from the thicket and walked back to his horse. Mounting, he rode slowly homeward, and as he rode he thought he had never been so utterly tired as he was now. But there was coolness in the breeze through the pines, and some of their piny fragrance seemed to get into his blood. He looked up, feeling better as he rode slowly along the grassy trail, through the mountain meadows and down through the columned trunks of the great old trees toward the Hatfield cup.

Yes, it was worth fighting for, worth fighting to keep what one had in this lonely land among the high peaks. It was such a country as a man would want, a country where a man could grow and could live, and where his sons could grow.

Even as he thought of that, Kilkenny found himself remembering Nita. King Bill Hale wanted her. Well, what would be more understandable? Certainly she was beautiful, the most beautiful woman in Cedar Valley and many other valleys. And what did she think? Hale had everything to offer: strength, position, wealth. She could reign like a queen at the Castle.

And Hale himself? He was a handsome man. Cold, but yet, what man ever sees another man as a woman sees him? The side of himself that a man shows to women is often much different from that seen by men.

Worry began to move through him like a drug. Nita nearby was one thing, but Nita belonging to someone else, that was another idea. He realized suddenly it was an idea he didn't like, not even a little bit. Especially, he did not want her to belong to the arrogant King Bill.

Hale wanted her, and regardless of what she thought, he could bring pressure to bear, if his own eloquence failed him. He was king in Cedar Valley. Her supplies came in over the road he controlled. He could close her business. He could even prevent her from leaving. He might. Jaime Brigo was the reason why he might not succeed. Brigo and himself, Kilkenny.

King Bill's lack of action disturbed him. Hale had been beaten in a fist fight. Knowing the arrogance of the man, Kilkenny knew he would never allow that to pass. He had refused them supplies, and they had come and taken them from under his nose.

Was Hale waiting to starve them? He knew how many they were. He knew the supplies they had were not enough to last long. And he held the trail to Blazer. Did he know of the trail through the Smoky Desert? Kilkenny doubted that. Even he did not know if it were passable. The chances were Hale had never even dreamed of such a thing. Aside from the Indian to whom he had talked, Kilkenny had heard no mention of it.

Saul Hatfield walked down from among the trees as he neared the cup. "Anything happen?" Kilkenny asked.

Saul shook his head, staring curiously at the dust-covered Kilkenny. "Nope. Not any. Jesse took him a ride down to town. They sure are gettin' set for that celebration. Expectin' a big crowd. They say Hale's invited some folks down from Santa Fe, some big muckymucks."

"From Santa Fe?" Kilkenny's eyes narrowed. That was a neat bit of politics, a good chance to entertain the officials and then tell them casually of the outlaws in the mountains, the men who had come in and tried to take away valuable land from King Bill.

Lance knew how persuasive such a man could be. And he would entertain like royalty, and these men would go away impressed. That King Bill didn't intend to strengthen his position very much would be foolhardy to imagine. Hale would know how to play politics, how to impress these men with his influence and the power of his wealth.

The audience would all be friendly, too. They would give the visiting officials the idea that all was well in Cedar Valley. Then, when the elimination of some outlaws hiding in the mountains was revealed, if it ever was, the officials would imagine it was merely that and never inquire as to the rightness or wrongness of Hale's actions.

In that moment, Kilkenny decided. He would go to Cedar Bluff for the celebration.

Yet, even as the thought occurred to him, he remembered the thick neck and beetling brow of Tombull Turner.

For the first time he began to think of the prizefighter. He had seen the man fight. He was a mountain of muscle, a man with a body of muscle and iron. His jaw was like a chunk of granite. His flat nose and beetling brow were fearsome.

Kilkenny rode down into the cup and swung from his horse. Parson walked slowly toward him, Jesse and O'Hara beside him. They stared at the dust on his clothes.

"Looks like you been places, son," Parson drawled.

"I have." Kilkenny removed the saddle and threw it on the rail. "I've been down into Smoky Desert."

"Smoky Desert?" O'Hara stepped forward. "You found a way?"

"Uh-huh. Take a little ax work to clear it."

"Could a wagon get across?"

Kilkenny shrugged, looking up at the big Irishman. "Your guess is as good as mine. I know I can get a wagon into the desert. I know there used to be a trail. I could see it. There's parts of a wagon down there. Somebody has been across. Where somebody else went, we'll go."

"How about gettin' out?" Parson drawled.

"That," Kilkenny admitted, "is the point. You put your finger right on the sore spot. Maybe there's a way, maybe there isn't. There was once. But I'm a-goin'. I'm goin' over, an' with luck I'll get back. We'll have to take water. We'll have to tie cloths over our faces and over the nostrils of the horses. Otherwise that dust will fix us for good."

"When you goin'?" Jesse demanded.

"Right soon. We got to make a try. If we could make it soon enough we might bring the others back that way. I'll start tomorrow."

"Leave us shorthanded," Parson suggested.

"It will." Kilkenny nodded agreement. He looked at the old mountaineer thoughtfully. "The trouble is, Hale has time, an' we haven't. I'm bankin' that he won't try anything until after the celebration. I think this is not only his tenth anniversary but a bit of politics to get friendly with them down at Santa Fe. He'll wait until he's solid with them before he cleans us out!"

"Maybe. Ain't nobody down to town goin' to tell our side of this. Not a soul," Hatfield agreed.

"There will be." Kilkenny stripped off his shirt and drew a bucket of water from the well. His powerful muscles ran like snakes beneath his tawny skin. "I'm goin' down."

"They'll kill you, man!" O'Hara declared. "They'd shoot you like a dog."

"No, not while those Santa Fe officials are there. I'll go. I hear they want me to fight Tombull Turner. Well, I'm goin' down an' fight him."

"What?" Runyon shouted. "That man's a killer. He's a ringer."

"I know." Kilkenny shrugged. "But I've seen him fight. Maybe I'm a dang fool, but I've got to get down there an' see those Santa Fe men. This is my chance."

"You think you can do any good against Hale?" Parson asked keenly. "He'll be winin' and dinin' them folks from Santa Fe. He won't let you go nowhere close to 'em."

"But they'll be at the fight," Kilkenny told him. "I'm countin' on that."

At daybreak the labor gang had reached the thicket of pines covering the entrance to the road. Axes in hand, they went to work. Other men began bucking the big fallen tree into sections to be snaked out of the way with ox teams.

Once, during a pause when he straightened his back from the saw, Quince looked over at Kilkenny. "They should be there today," he drawled slowly. "I sure hope they make it."

"Yeah." Lance straightened and rubbed his back. It had been a long time since he'd used a crosscut saw. "You know Blazer?"

"Uh-huh." Hatfield bit off a chew of tobacco. "Man there named Sodermann. Big an' fat. Mean as a wolf. He's Hale's man. Got a gunman with him name of Rye Pitkin."

"I know him. A two-bit rustler from the Pecos country. Fair hand with a six-gun."

"There's others, too. Ratcliff an' Gaddis are worst. We can expect trouble."

"We?" Kilkenny looked at him. "You volunteerin' for the trip?"

"Sure." Quince grinned at him. "I need me a change of air.

Gettin' old, a-settin' around. Reckon the bore of that Kentucky rifle needs a bit of cleanin', too."

They worked on until dark, and when they stopped, the road was open. O'Hara, who had done the work of two men with an ax, stood on the edge of the canyon in the dimming light and looked across that awful expanse toward the distance, red ridges touched now with light from a vanished sun. "It don't look good to me, Kilkenny," he said. "It sure don't look good."

The wagon was loaded with water—not heavily, but three good kegs of it. With Bartram on the driver's seat, they started. Kilkenny led the way down the steep trail, Quince behind him. He reined in once and watched the wagon trundle over the first stones and past the ruin of the great tree. Then he continued on. For better or worse, they were committed now.

## Chapter XI
### *The Road of Death*

He led the way slowly, stopping often, for it was slow going for the wagon. He watched it coming and watched the mules. They were good mules; Hale himself had no better. They would need to be good.

At the bottom of the road he swung down, and standing there with Quince Hatfield, he waited, listening to the strange, lonely sighing of the mysterious wind that flowed like a slow current through the dusty depths of the sink.

Bartram was a hand with mules. He brought the wagon up beside them, and Kilkenny indicated the mules. "Soak those cloths in water an' hang one over the nose of each of them. We better each wear a handkerchief over the nose and mouth, too."

He was riding the buckskin, and he got down and hung a cloth over the horse's nostrils, where it would stop part of the dust at least without impeding the breathing. Then they started on.

From here, it was guesswork. He had a compass, and before leaving the cliff top he had taken a sight on a distant peak. How closely the trail would hold to that course he did not know, or if any trail would be visible once they got out into the desert.

Walking the buckskin, he led off into the dust. The wind did not howl. It blew gently but steadily, and the dust filled the air. Much of it, he knew, was alkali. Behind him, Quince Hatfield rode a raw-boned roan bred to the desert.

Fifteen minutes after leaving the cliff, they were out of sight of it. Overhead the sky was only a lighter space dimly visible through a hanging curtain of dust. Dust arose in clouds from their walking horses and from the wagon, fine, powdery, stifling dust.

Over and around them the cloud closed in, thick and prickly when the dust settled on the flesh. Glancing at Quince during one interval, Kilkenny saw the man's face was covered with a film of dust; his eyelashes were thick with it; his hair was white.

When they had been going an hour, he reined in and dismounted. Taking a damp cloth, he sponged out the buckskin's nostrils and wiped off the horse's head and ears. Quince had drawn abreast and was doing likewise, and when the others came up, they worked over the mules.

The dust filled the air and drew a thick veil around them, as in a blizzard. Saul drew closer. "What if the wind comes up?" he asked.

Bartram's face was stern. "I've been thinking of that," he said. "If the wind comes up, in all of this, we're sunk."

"Where are we now?" Jackie asked, standing up on the wagon.

"We should have made about three or four miles. Maybe more, maybe less. We're right on our course so far."

They rested the mules. The wagon was heavy, even though it was not carrying a load now. The dust and sand in places were a couple of feet deep, but usually the wheels sank no more than six inches into the dust. The animals would all need rest, for the air was heavy with heat, and there was no coolness here in the sink. The dust made breathing an effort.

Kilkenny swung into the saddle and moved out. The flatness of the desert floor was broken now, and it began to slant away from them toward the middle. Kilkenny scowled thoughtfully, and rode more slowly. An hour later, they paused again. This time there was no talking. All of the men were feeling the frightful pressure of the heat, and glancing at the mules, Kilkenny could see they were breathing heavily. Streaks marred the thick whiteness of the dust on their bodies.

"We'll have to stop more often," he told Bartram, and the farmer nodded.

They rode on, and almost another hour had passed before the buckskin stopped suddenly. Lance touched him gently with a spur, but Buck would not move. Kilkenny swung down. Ahead of him, and he could see for no more than fifty feet, was an even, unbroken expanse of white. It was not even marred by the blackish upthrust of rock that had occasionally appeared along the back trail.

Quince rode up and stopped. "What's wrong?" he asked. Then he swung down and walked up.

"Don't know," Kilkenny said. "Buck won't go on, something wrong." He stepped forward and felt the earth suddenly turn to jelly under his feet. He gave a cry and tried to leap backward, but only tripped himself.

Quince helped him up. "Quicksand," he said, "an' the worst I ever see. Must be springs under."

The wagon drew up, and then Saul and Jackie. "Stay here," Lance told them. "I'll scout to the left."

"I'll go right," Quince suggested. "Might be a way around."

Kilkenny turned the buckskin and let him have his head. He walked at right angles to the course and then at Kilkenny's urging, tried the surface. It was still soggy. They pulled back and rode on. In a half hour he reined in. There was still no way around, and the edge of the quicksand seemed to be curving back toward him. Only the sagacity of Buck had kept them out of it. He rode back.

"Any luck?" he shouted as he saw Quince waiting with the wagon.

"Uh-huh. It ends back there about two mile. High ground, rocky."

They turned the wagon and started on once more. They would lose at least an hour more, perhaps two, in skirting the quicksand.

Hour after hour they struggled on. Weariness made their limbs leaden. The mules were beginning to weave a bit now, and Kilkenny found himself sagging in the saddle. His sweat-soaked shirt had become something very like cement with its heavy coating of white dust. They stopped oftener now, stopped for water and to sponge the nostrils of the mules and horses.

At times the trail led through acres upon acres of great, jagged black rocks that thrust up in long ledges that had to be skirted. All calculations on miles across were thrown out of kilter by this continual weaving back and forth across the desert. Time had ceased to matter, and they lived only for the quiet numbness of the halts.

All of them walked from time to time now. Time and again they had to get behind the wagon and push, or had to dig out rocks to roll them aside to clear the only possible trail.

The world had become a nightmare of choking, smothering, clinging dust particles, a nightmare of sticky heat and stifling dust-filled air. Even all thought of Hale was gone. They did not think of food or of family, but only of getting across, of getting out of this hell of choking white.

Kilkenny was no longer sure of the compass. Mineral deposits might have made it err. They might be wandering in circles. His only hope was that the ground seemed to rise now, seemed to be slanting upward. Choking, coughing, they moved on into the dust blizzard, hearing the lonely sough of the wind. Dazed with heat, dust, and weariness, they moved on. The mules were staggering now, and they moved only a few yards at a time.

The black upthrust of the cliff loomed at them suddenly, when all hope seemed gone. It loomed, black and sheer, yet here at the base the dust seemed a little less, a little thinner.

Kilkenny swung down and waited until the rest came up. "Well," he said hoarsely, "we're across. Now to get up."

They rested there under the cliff for a half hour, and then his own restlessness won over his weariness. He had never been able to stop short of a goal; there was something in him that always drove him on, regardless of weariness, trouble, or danger. It came to the surface now, and he lunged to his feet and started moving.

He had walked no more than a hundred yards when he found it. He stared at the incredible fact, that through all their weaving back and forth, they had held that close to their destination. The road looked rough, but it was a way up, and beyond the hills, but a little way now, lay Blazer.

It was dusk when they reached the top of the cliff and drew up under the pines. Digging a hole in the ground among some rocks, they built a fire in the bottom and warmed some food and made coffee. The hole concealed the flames, and using dry wood, they would make no smoke.

Kilkenny drank the strong black coffee and found his hand growing lax and his lids heavy. He got up, staggered to his blankets, and fell asleep. He slept like he was drugged until Saul Hatfield shook him from his slumber in the last hours of the night to take over the watch.

Lance got up and stretched. Then he walked over to the water casks, drew water, and bathed himself, washing the dust from his hair and ears. Stripping to the waist, he bathed his body in the cold water. Refreshed, he crossed to the black bulk of the rocks and seated himself.

In the darkness thoughts come easily. He sat there, his eyes open and staring restlessly from side to side, yet his thoughts wandering back to Cedar Bluff.

They wanted him to fight Tombull Turner. He had decided to take the fight. Sitting here in the darkness with the wind in the pines overhead, he could think clearly. It was their only chance of getting to the Santa Fe officials. He knew how men of all sorts and kinds admire a fighting man. The Santa Fe officials, especially if one of them was Halloran, would be no exception. He would be going into the fight as the underdog. Hale wanted him whipped, but King Bill's power was destroying his shrewdness.

Halloran, or whoever came, would know about Tombull. The man had been fighting, and winning, all through the West. Any man who went against him would be the underdog, and the underdog always has the crowd with him. Kilkenny knew there was scarcely a chance that he would do anything but take a beating, yet he believed he could stay in there long enough to make some impression. And between rounds—that would be his chance.

If ever, he would have a chance to talk then. King Bill would have his guests in ringside seats. He would be expecting a quick victory.

Coldly, Kilkenny appraised himself. Like all fighting men, he considered himself good. He had fought many times in the rough and tumble fistfights of the frontier. As a boy he had fought many times in school. During the days when he was in the East, he had taken instruction from the great Jem Mace, the English pugilist, who was one of the most clever of all bare-knuckle fighters. Mace was a shrewd fighter who used his head for something aside from a parking place for two thick ears.

King Bill did not know that Kilkenny had ever boxed. Neither would Tombull know that. Moreover, Kilkenny had for years lived a life in the open, a life that required hard physical condition and superb strength. He had those assets, and above all, he had his knowledge of Turner, whereas Turner knew nothing of him. Turner would be overconfident.

Nevertheless, in all honesty, Kilkenny could find little hope of victory. His one hope was to make a game fight of it, to win the sympathy and interest of the officials before he spoke to them, as he would.

He would rest when he returned to the cup. He would soak his hands in brine, and he would wear driving gloves in the ring. Some of the younger fighters were wearing skintight gloves now, and Mace had told him of their cutting ability.

There was no sound but the sound of the forest, and he relaxed, watching and awaiting the dawn. When it came, they ate a hurried breakfast. They were rested and felt better. Kilkenny cleaned his guns carefully, both pistols and his rifle. The others did likewise.

"Quince," Kilkenny said as he holstered his guns. "You know Blazer. What d'you think?"

Hatfield shrugged. "I reckon they won't be expectin' us from hereabouts. I been takin' some bearin's, an' I reckon we will come into town from the opposite side. We got us a good chance of gettin' in afore they know who we are."

"Good!" Kilkenny turned to Bartram. "You know the team. You stay by the wagon an' keep your gun handy. Stay on the ground where you can either mount up or take cover.

"Saul, you an' Jackie hustle the grub out to the wagon, an' Quince will stand by to cover you."

"How about you?" Bartram asked, looking up at him.

"I'm goin' to look around for sign of the other wagon. I want to know what happened to Lije an' them. They may be all right, but I want to know."

As they mounted up, he turned in his saddle. "Quince, you ride with me. Saul an' Jackie will bring up the rear."

They started out, and less than a mile from where they had come from the desert, they rode down into the trail to Blazer. As Quince Hatfield had suggested, they were coming in from the opposite side.

Two rows of ramshackle saloons, cheap dance halls, and stores made up the town of Blazer. These two rows faced each other across a river of dust that was called a street. The usual number of town loafers sat on benches in front of the Crossroads, the Temple of Chance, and the Wagon Wheel.

It was morning, and few horses stood at the hitching rail. There was a blood bay with a beautifully handworked saddle standing in front of the Crossroads, and two cow ponies stood three-legged before the Wagon Wheel.

## Chapter XII
### *In the Enemy's Lair*

Lance Kilkenny rode past the Perkins General Store and swung down in front of the Wagon Wheel. Bartram stopped the wagon parallel to the hitching rail and began to fill his pipe. His rifle leaned against the seat beside him.

Saul and Jackie walked into the store, and Quince leaned against the corner of the store and lighted a cigarette. His rifle lay in the wagon, but he wore a huge Walker Colt slung to his belt.

A horseman came down the trail and swung down in front of the Wagon Wheel and walked inside. Quince straightened and stared at him, and his eyes narrowed. The man was big and had red hair and a red beard. Kilkenny stared at the man, and then, as Quince motioned with his head, he idled over toward him.

"That hombre was wearin' an ivory-handled Colt with a chipped ivory on the right side," Hatfield said. His narrow face was empty and his eyes bitter.

"A chipped ivory butt?" Kilkenny frowned, and then suddenly his face paled. "Why, Jody Miller had a gun like that. An' Jody was with the first wagon."

"Uh-huh. I reckon," Hatfield said, "I better ask me a few questions."

"Wait," Kilkenny said. "I'm goin' in there. You keep your eyes open. Remember, we need the grub first. Meantime, I'll find out somethin'."

He turned and walked over to the Wagon Wheel and ambled inside. Two cowpokes sat at a table with the bartender and a man in a black coat, a huge man, enormously big and enormously fat. That, he decided, would be Sodermann.

The red-bearded man was leaning on the bar. "Come on, Shorty," he snapped. "Give us a drink! I'm dry."

"Take it easy, Gaddis," Shorty barked. He was a short, thickset man with an unshaven face. "I'll be with you in a minute."

Kilkenny leaned against the bar and looked around. It didn't look good. If the big man was Sodermann—and there was small chance of there being two such huge men in any western town—that placed Sodermann and Gaddis. The cowpokes might be mere cowhands, but they didn't look it. One of the men might be Ratcliff. And there was still Rye Pitkin. But he knew Rye, and the rustler was not present.

Judging by appearances, Shorty could be counted on to side Sodermann, and if that was Jody Miller's gun, it meant that the other wagon had been stopped, and the chances were that the men who accompanied it had been wiped out.

Slow rage began to mount in Kilkenny at the thought of those honest, sincere men, who asked only the right to work and build homes, being killed by such as these. He was suddenly conscious that Sodermann was watching him.

Shorty got up and sauntered behind the bar. "What'll you have?" he asked, leaning on the hardwood. His eyes slanted from Gaddis to Kilkenny.

"Rye," Gaddis said. He turned abruptly and gave Kilkenny a cool glance, a glance that suddenly quickened as he noticed the dusty clothing and the tied-down guns. He stared at Kilkenny's face, but Lance had his hat brim low, and this man had never seen him before, anyway.

"Make mine rye, too," Kilkenny said. He turned his head and looked at Sodermann. "You drinkin'?"

"Maybe." The fat man got up, and he moved his huge bulk with astonishing lightness. Kilkenny's eyes sharpened. This man could move. "Maybe I will. I always likes to know who I'm drinkin' with, howsoever."

"Not so particular where I come from," Kilkenny said softly. "A drink's a drink."

"I reckon." Sodermann nodded affably. "You appear to be a stranger hereabouts. I reckon every man who wears a gun like you wear yours knows Doc Sodermann."

"I've heard the name." Kilkenny let his eyes drift to the table. One of the men was sitting up straight rolling a smoke, the other idly riffling the cards. Either could draw fast. Red Gaddis had turned to face them.

\*     \*     \*

The whole setup was too obviously ready to spring. He was going to have to relax them a little. He would have to relieve this tension.

"Heard there might be a job up this way for a man," he said slowly, "an' I could use a job up here where it's quiet."

"Away from the law, you mean?" Sodermann laughed until he shook all over. Kilkenny noticed there was no laughter in his eyes.

"Uh-huh. Away from everythin'."

"We got law here. King Bill Hale runs this country."

"Heard of him."

"You hear a lot," Gaddis suggested. His eyes were mean.

"Yeah." Kilkenny turned a little and let his green eyes stare from under his hatbrim at the red-headed man. "Yeah, I make it my business to hear a lot."

"Maybe you hear too much!" Gaddis snapped.

"You want to show me how much?" Kilkenny's voice was level. He spoke coolly, yet he was sure there would be no shooting here, yet. He was wondering if Sodermann knew Hatfield was outside beside the window.

Gaddis stepped away from the bar, and his jaw jutted. "Why, I think you're—!"

"Stop it!" Sodermann's voice was suddenly charged with anger. "You're too anxious for trouble, Gaddis. Someday you'll get yourself killed."

Gaddis relaxed slowly, his eyes ugly. Yet, watching the man, Kilkenny could sense a certain relief in him also. Gaddis was a killer, but not a gunman in the sense that he was highly skilled. He was a paid killer, a murderer, the sort of man who would drygulch men around a wagon. And he wore a chipped gun.

"Your friend's right proddy," Kilkenny said softly. "He must have a killin' urge."

"Forget it," Sodermann said jovially. "He's all right. Just likes to fight, that's all!"

Kilkenny stared at Gaddis. "Seems like you should be somebody I know," he drawled slowly, "I don't recognize that face, but I do know you. But then, I never remember a face, anyway. I got my own methods of knowin' a man. I look at the only thing that's important to me!"

"What's that?" Sodermann asked. He was studying Kilkenny, curiosity in his eyes and some puzzlement.

"I always remember a man's gun. Each gun has its own special look, or maybe it's the way a man wears a gun. Take that one now, with that chipped ivory on the side of the butt. A man wouldn't forget a gun like that in a hurry."

Gaddis stiffened, and his face turned gray. Then the tip of his tongue touched his lips. Before he could speak, Sodermann looked straight into Kilkenny's eyes.

"An' where would you see that gun?"

"In Santa Fe," Kilkenny drawled, remembering that Miller had once lived there. "It was hangin' to a man they said was comin' west to farm. His name was Jody Miller."

"You talk too much!" Gaddis snarled, his face white and his lips thin.

"It was in Santa Fe." Kilkenny was adding a touch now that he hoped would worry Sodermann. Only a word, yet sometimes—

"Miller stopped off in Santa Fe to see some folks at the fort there an' to talk to Halloran an' Wallace. Seems they was old friends of his."

Sodermann's face sharpened, and he turned. His raised hand made Gaddis draw back a little.

"You're talkin' a lot, stranger," he said smoothly. "You say this Miller knowed Halloran an' Wallace?"

"Uh-huh." Kilkenny motioned to Shorty to refill his glass. "Seems he knowed them back East. One of 'em married a sister of his, or somethin'. I heard 'em talkin' in a saloon once. Heard Halloran say he was comin' out here to visit Miller."

Kilkenny glanced at Gaddis, his face expressionless. "I reckon you'll be plumb glad to see him, Miller. It's mighty nice to have an official, big man like that, for a friend."

Lance could have laughed if he hadn't known what he knew now, that the wagon had been waylaid and that Miller was probably dead. There would be no other reason for Gaddis looking as he did. The man was obviously afraid. Sodermann was staring keen-eyed, yet there was uncertainty in the big man. When that uncertainty ended, there would be danger, Kilkenny knew.

"Funny," Kilkenny said softly, "I don't remember Miller havin' red hair. Seemed to me it was black. That's what it was. Black."

"It was yel—!" Gaddis began.

"Yellow. That's right. It *was* yellow. Strange, I couldn't remember that. But you, stranger, you've got Jody Miller's gun. How d'you explain that?"

Suddenly, the door behind Kilkenny opened. He felt the flesh along the back of his neck tighten. He dared not turn. He had been deliberately baiting them, hoping for more information, yet baiting them, too. Now, suddenly, there was a man behind him.

Sodermann seemed to make up his mind. Assurance returned to him, and he spoke low, almost amused. "Why, howdy, Rye! I reckon you should come in an' meet our friend, here. Says he recognizes this gun Red's a-wearin'."

Rye Pitkin walked past Kilkenny and then turned.

His jaw dropped as though he had seen a ghost, and he made an involuntary step backward, his face slowly going white. "You!" he gasped. "You!"

"Why, yes," Kilkenny said. "It's me, Pitkin. Long ways from the Pecos country, isn't it? An' a sight further from the Brazos. Now, Pitkin, I'll tell you somethin'. I'm not real anxious to kill anybody right here an' now. If I start shootin', two of you are goin' to die.

"That'll be you, Rye, and Sodermann here. I couldn't miss him. An' if I am still shootin', as I will be, I'm goin' to take care of Gaddis next. Gaddis because he killed Jody Miller. But that comes later. Right now I'm leavin', an' right now you better impress it on your friends that reachin' for an iron won't do any good."

He stepped back toward the door, and his eyes shifted under the hatbrim from one face to the other. Sodermann's eyes were narrowed. Pitkin's obvious fear put doubt in the big man. Who was the stranger? Red Gaddis shifted toward the center of the room, his eyes watchful.

Rye stiffened as Red moved. "Don't, Red! That's Kilkenny!"

Gaddis stopped, and his face turned blank with mingled astonishment and fear. Then glass tinkled from the front of the room, and a long Kentucky rifle barrel slid into the room. Kilkenny stepped back to the door.

"Now if you hombres are smart, you'll just hole up here for the time bein'. We don't want trouble, but we may have it!"

He stepped through the door and glanced quickly up and down the street. Bartram was on the wagon seat, his rifle across his knees. Jackie Moffitt was standing by his horse, his rifle in his hands, and Saul was across the street. Kilkenny smiled in narrow-eyed apprehension. They were fighters, these men.

"Start the wagon," he said, "down the Cedar trail. Jackie, stay with Bartram."

He walked out and swung into the saddle and then slid a rifle from the boot. "All right, slide!"

He wheeled the buckskin and whipped down the street. A shot rang out from behind him, and he twisted to look. Saul was mounted, but Quince had turned and thrown up his rifle. He fired. A man staggered from the shelter of the Wagon Wheel and spilled on his face in the dust. The next instant there was a fusillade of shots from the Wagon Wheel and nearby buildings. The gunmen had slid out the back way and were getting into action.

Kilkenny reined in behind the last building and swung to the ground. Then, with careful fire, he covered the Hatfields as they raced up the street to join him.

Quince was smiling, his eyes hard. "That was Red Gaddis," he said coolly. "He won't take no more dead men's guns."

"Give the wagon a start," Kilkenny said. "We three are going to make some buzzard bait! We have to come back to this town, and we might as well let them know what the score is."

Every time a head moved, one of them fired. While they stayed where they were, no man dared enter that street, and no man dared try the back way in this direction.

Leaving the two Hatfields, Kilkenny sprinted down behind the buildings toward the Wagon Wheel. The men there were killers. He did not know what had happened to the other wagon, but he meant to find out. It was his reason for taking the Blazer trail. He was hoping they might not all be dead. At least, he could bury those that were.

## Chapter XIII
### Ambush Toll

The rear door of the saloon was open, and there was no one in sight. He stood behind the next building and watched for an instant. He wanted Pitkin or Ratcliff. He would get nothing from Sodermann unless the fat man elected to tell him.

Several old boards lay on the ground behind the saloon, dry and parched. On a sudden inspiration, he moved swiftly from the shelter of the building and holstering his gun, hurriedly piled them together. Then, using a piece of old sacking and some parched grass, he lit the fire.

It was away from the buildings, but the wind would blow the smoke into the saloon. He hoped they would think he was burning them out, the last thing he wanted to do, as they needed the town as a supply base.

As the boards caught fire, he stepped back quickly.

There was a startled exclamation as the fire began to crackle and wood smoke blew in the back of the saloon. A second later a man stepped to the door, thrust his head out, and then stared at the fire. He seemed puzzled. Out of sight, Kilkenny waited.

Then the man stepped out and kicked the boards apart.

"All right!" Kilkenny snapped. "Don't move!"

It was Ratcliff, and the man froze. "What's up, Kilkenny? I never done nothin' to you."

"Start this way, walk careful, an' watch your hands."

Ratcliff was a weasel-faced man with shifty eyes. He started mov-

ing, but shot a glance at the doorway. He held his hands wide.
When he was six feet away, Kilkenny stopped him.

"All right, talk. I want to know what happened to that other
wagon."

Ratcliff sneered. "You think I'll tell? Guess again. You don't dare
shoot. If you do, they'll be out, but fast."

With one quick step, Kilkenny grabbed the man by the throat and
slammed him back against the building. Then he lifted the pistol.

"Want a pistol-whipping, man?" he asked harshly. "If I start on
you, you'll never look the same again!"

"Leave me be," Ratcliff pleaded, his face yellow. "I'll talk."

"Get at it then."

"They done loaded up with grub. We let 'em get out of town.
Then Sodermann ambushed 'em. Had about six men, I think."

"Who was killed?"

"We lost a man. We got Miller an' Tot Wilson in the first blast. It
was Hatfield got our man. Nailed him dead center between the
eyes."

"What happened to Hatfield an' Hight?"

"They got Hight. I seen him go down. He was shot two, maybe
three times. We got Hatfield, too. But he got up, an' he dragged
Hight into some rocks. We couldn't get to 'em."

"Then what?"

A voice roared from the saloon. It was Sodermann. "Ratcliff! What
in time are you doin' out there?"

"Answer me!" Kilkenny snapped. "Then what?"

"Sodermann said it'd serve 'em right. Leave 'em there to die with
two men to see they didn't move out of them rocks. They been there
two days now."

"On the Blazer trail?"

"Yeah, almost to the turnoff to the peaks."

With a swift movement, Kilkenny flipped Ratcliff's pistol from its
holster. "All right, get goin'!" he snapped.

With a dive, Ratcliff started for the saloon door. And just at that
instant, Sodermann thrust his huge bulk into the open space. He
glimpsed Kilkenny as he released Ratcliff, and with a swift motion,
palmed his gun and fired.

He fired from the hip, and he wasn't a good hip shot. His first
bullet caught Ratcliff square in the chest, and the weasel-faced rider
stopped dead still and then dropped. Kilkenny's gun swept up, and
spraddle-legged in the open, he fired.

Sodermann's gun went off at the same instant, but Kilkenny's
bullet hit him right above the belt buckle in the middle of that vast
expanse. The blow staggered Sodermann, and his bullet clipped

slivers from the building above Kilkenny's head and whined angrily away into the grass back of the saloon.

The big man looked sick, and then suddenly his knees gave way and he toppled face downward upon the steps. The pistol fell from fingers that had lost their life, and rattled on the boards below.

Kilkenny walked toward the saloon, keeping his gun in his hand. Stepping up beside the door, he saw Rye Pitkin and the short bartender, rifles in hand, crouched by the front window.

"Drop 'em!" Kilkenny snapped. He stepped quickly inside. "Unbuckle your belts and let those guns down—quick!"

Surprised into helplessness, the men did as they were told. "Rye, I've given you a break before. I'm givin' you one again. The same for Shorty. You two mount and ride. If I ever see either of you again, I'll kill you. I'll be back to Blazer, an' you be doggone sure you aren't here."

Backing them away, he scooped up the guns and then backed out the door. He hurried to the corner where the Hatfields waited. Quince was chewing on a straw. He looked at the weapons, grinned a little, and started for his horse.

"Lije may be alive," Kilkenny told him. Then he explained quickly.

Quince narrowed his eyes. "You won't be needin' us," he said. "We'll ride on."

"Go ahead," Kilkenny said, "an' luck with you."

With a rush of hoofs, Saul and Quince Hatfield swept off down the trail. Kilkenny watched them go. The Hatfields were hard to kill. Lije might be alive. It was like him to have thought of Hight, even when wounded. Those lean, wiry men were tough. He might still be alive.

He rode up to the wagon and saw Bartram's face flush with relief. Jackie was riding beside the wagon, his old Sharps ready. His face was boyishly stern.

"What is it?" Bartram asked. "What happened?"

"We've won another round," Kilkenny said. "We can come to Blazer for supplies now. . . ."

Dust devils danced over the desert, and the mules plodded slowly along the trail. The wagon rumbled and bumped over the stones in the road, and Bartram dozed on the wagon seat.

To the left the mountains lifted in rocky slopes with many upthrust edges of jagged rock. To the right the ground sloped away toward Cedar Branch, which lay miles away beyond the intervening sagebrush and mesquite.

Jackie Moffitt rode silently, looking from time to time at Kilkenny. Lance knew the youngster was dying to ask him about what had happened in Blazer, and he was just as loath to speak of it. He could understand the youngster's curiosity.

He moved the buckskin over alongside the boy. "Trouble back there, Jack," he said after a minute. "Men killed back there."

"Who was it? Did you kill 'em?" Jackie asked eagerly.

"One. I had to, Jack. Didn't want to. Nobody ever likes to kill a man unless there's something wrong with him. I had to get news out of somebody. I got it from Ratcliff and then turned him loose, but in tryin' to get me, Sodermann shot him. Then I shot Sodermann."

"What about the others?"

"Let 'em go. I told Pitkin an' Shorty to get out of the country. I think they'll go."

"We asked 'em in the store, but they was scared. They wouldn't talk, nohow. Saul, he asked 'em. They was afraid. But they was right nice with us."

They rode on through the heat. Occasionally they stopped to rest the mules. It was slower this way, as the road was longer, but there was no dust, and they had to come this way to make sure about Lije and the others.

Again and again Kilkenny found his thoughts reverting to Nita. How was she faring with Hale? Would she marry him? The thought came to him with a pang. He was in love with Nita. He had admitted that to himself long before this, but he knew too well what it would mean to be the wife of a gunman, a man who never knew when he might go down to dusty death in a lead-spattered street.

A man couldn't think only of himself. A few men seemed to be able to leave it all behind, but they were few. Of course, he could go east, but his whole life had been lived in the West, and he had no source of income in the East. He had been a gambler at times and had done well, but it was nothing to build a life upon.

His thoughts moved ahead to the Hatfields. What would they find? Would the men left behind have murdered the wounded Lije? Had Hight been dead? How many more would die before this war was settled? Why did one man see fit to push this bloody fight upon men who wanted only peace and time to till their fields? Why should one man desire power so much? There was enough in the world for all to have a quiet, comfortable living, and what more could a man desire?

The wagon rumbled over the rocks, and he lifted his eyes and let them idle over the heat-waved distance. After the fire and blood there would be peace, and men could come to this land and settle these hills. Perhaps someday there would be water, and then grass would grow where now there were only cacti and sagebrush.

Cicadas whined and sang in the mesquite until the sound became almost the voice of the wastelands.

They camped that night in a hollow in the hills and pushed on at dawn toward the joining of the trails. The country was rockier now. The distance closed in, pushing the mountains nearer, and there was less breeze. The air was dead and still.

Jackie traded places with Bartram and handled the mules. Bartram rode on ahead, riding carefully. Kilkenny watched him go, liking the easy way the farmer rode, and liking his cleancut honesty.

It was morning of the third day when Kilkenny saw a horseman drawing near. He recognized him even before he came up with him. It was Saul.

"Found 'em," Saul said briefly, "both alive. Hight's plumb riddled. Lije was hit three times, one time pretty bad. They was holed up in some rocks, more dead than alive."

"Anybody around?"

"Yeah. One man. He was dead. Lije must've got him, bad off as he was. The other took out. Lije'll live. We Hatfields are tough."

When they reached the cluster of rocks, they pulled the wagon close. Quince had both men stretched out and had rigged a shelter from the sun. Kilkenny knelt over the men. That Hight was breathing was a marvel, though all his wounds showed signs of care. Lije, wounded as he was, had cared for the other man. His wounds had been bathed and crudely bandaged. His lips seemed moist, and he had evidently not lacked for water.

Lije Hatfield was grimly conscious. There was an unrelenting look in his eyes, enough to show them that Lije meant to face death, if need be, as sternly and fearlessly as he faced life and danger.

His lips were dry and parched. Even the water that Quince had given him failed to reduce the ravages brought on by several days of thirst. Obviously, from the condition of the two men, Lije had been giving the little water they had to Jackson Hight.

The two men were lifted carefully and placed in the wagon, with groceries piled around them and sacks and blankets beneath them. Another blanket was placed over two barrels to form a crude awning over their faces. Then, with Bartram handling the mules, they started once more.

## Chapter XIV
## *"I'm A-Goin' to Kill Bill Hale!"*

It was quiet in the Hatfield cup when the little group rode in. The Hatfield women did not cry. They gathered around, and they watched when the two men were lifted from the wagon and carried within.

Parson waited, grim-faced, for Kilkenny. "That's two more, Kilkenny. Two more good men gone, an' two that are like to die! I'm tellin' you, man, I'm a-goin' to kill Bill Hale!"

"Not now. Wait." Kilkenny kicked a toe into the dust. "Any more trouble here?"

"Smithers ain't come back."

"Where'd he go?"

"To look at his crop. He sets great store by that crop. Says he'll be back to harvest it."

"When did he leave?"

"Yesterday mornin'. Shouldn't keep him that long, noways. I reckon he might hole up in the hills somewhere."

Talking slowly, Lance recounted all that had transpired. He told of the bitter crossing of the Smoky Desert, of the fight at Blazer, and of the death of Gaddis and the others.

"We can cross the desert anytime unless the wind is blowin' strong," he concluded. "They can't bottle us up. It's a miserable trip, an' if a man was to try it an' get caught in a windstorm, there's a good chance you'd never hear of him again. The same if he got into that quicksand."

"I knowed that Gaddis was a bad one. Glad he's gone. The same for Sodermann."

"There's something else," Kilkenny suggested after a minute. "We've proved we could get across, an' we slipped by their guards comin' back by the Blazer trail, but it won't take them much time to figure what happened. They may try comin' in our back door by that way."

Parson nodded shrewdly. "I was thinkin' of that. We'll have to be careful."

When morning came and Lance rolled out of his blankets, he looked quickly at the house. Then he saw Saul. The tall, lean boy was walking away from the house, and he looked sick and old. They saw each other at almost the same instant.

"Saul?" Kilkenny said. "Is—?"

"He's dead. Lijah's dead."

Kilkenny turned away, and for the first time something like despair welled up inside of him. One of the Hatfields had died. It seemed as though something of the mountains themselves had gone, for there was in those lean, hardheaded, rawboned men something that lived on despite everything. And Lije had died.

O'Hara came out to him later, and the big Irishman's face was sullen and ugly. "An' that doc down to Cedar. We sneaked in an' tried to get him to come. He wouldn't come, an' he set up a squall when we tried to take him. We was lucky to get away."

"We'll remember that," Kilkenny said quietly. "We can't use a doctor who won't come when he's called, not in this country."

Parson looked at him thoughtfully and then he looked away. "Lance, you ever think maybe we won't win? That maybe they'll wipe us out? Suppose you can't talk to them Santa Fe men? Supposin' if you do, they won't listen?"

Kilkenny looked down at the ground, and then slowly he lifted his head. "There's a man behind this, Parson," he said slowly, "a man who's gone mad with power cravin'. His son's a-drivin' him. Parson, I've seen men murdered because they wanted homes. There was no harm in Jody Miller, nor in Tot Wilson. They were hardworkin' men an' honest ones. Lije, well, he was a fine boy, a real man, too. He had strength, courage, an' all that it takes to make a man.

"There at the last, when they were holed up in the rocks, he cared for Hight when he must've been near dead himself. He must've had to drag himself to Hight's side, he must've had to force himself to forget his own pain.

"Those men are dead, an' they are dead because of one man, maybe two. Maybe I'm wrong, Parson, but if all else fails, I'm ridin' to Cedar, an' I'll kill those two men!"

"An' I'll go with you!" Parson stated flatly. His old face was grim and hard. "Lije was my son, he—"

"No, Parson, you can't go with me. You'll have to stay here, keep this bunch together, an' see they make the most of their land. I want homes in these high meadows, Parson. Homes, an' kids around 'em, an' cattle walkin' peaceful in the evenin'.

"No, it'll be my job down there. We all, we who live by the gun, we all die in the end. It's better for me to go alone an' then live or die by what happens then. At least, it'll be in a good cause."

He lay in the shade of a huge Norway pine, resting and thinking of what lay ahead of him, thinking of the fight with Tombull Turner. Lying there with his eyes shut, he could hear the sound of the shovels as Runyon and Jesse Hatfield dug a grave for Lije. In his mind he was taking himself back to the times when he had seen Turner fight. He was remembering, not the battered men who went down before Turner, but every move the big man made.

No man was without a fault. Kilkenny had been taught well. He knew how he must plan, and he ran over and over in his mind the way the big man held his hands, the way his feet moved when he advanced or retreated, the way they moved when he punched, and what Turner did when hit with a left or right.

Each fighter develops habits. A certain method of stopping or countering a punch is easy for him, so he uses that method most, even though he may know others. A smooth boxer, walking out into the ring and expecting a long fight, will feel out an opponent, find how he uses a left, how he blocks one. Then he knows what to do.

If he lasted in this fight, Kilkenny knew, he would last only because of brains, only because he could think faster, better, and more effectively than Turner or those who handled him.

Yet again and again as he lay there thinking, his mind reverted to Nita Riordan. The dark, voluptuous beauty of the Irish and Spanish girl at the Crystal Palace was continually in his mind. There was something else, too. In the back of his mind loomed the huge, ominous Cain Brockman.

On that desperate day back in Cottonwood, in the Live Oak country, he had killed Abel, and Cain had been thrown from his rearing horse and knocked unconscious. Later, in the Trail House, he had slugged it out and whipped Cain in a bitter knock-down-and-drag-out fistfight. Cain had sworn to kill him. And Cain Brockman was in Cedar Bluff.

When night came, Kilkenny threw a saddle on a slim, black horse and rode out of the cup. He was going to see Nita. Even as he rode, he admitted to himself there was little reason to see her except that he wanted to. He had no right to take chances with his life when it could mean so much to the cause he was aiding, yet he had to see Nita. Also, he could find out what Hale was doing, what he was planning.

He rode swiftly, and the black horse was eager for the trail. It wasn't Buck, but the horse was fast, with speed to spare.

It was late when he rode down to the edge of Cedar Bluff, and his thoughts went back to Leathers, aroused out of a sound sleep and made to put up groceries, and to Dan Cooper, the tough cowhand and gunman who had watched Leathers's store. Cooper was a good man on the wrong side. Leathers was a man who would be on any winning side, one of the little men who think only of immediate profits and who try to ride with the powers that be. Well, the payoff for Leathers was coming.

Leaving his horse in the shadows of the trees beyond the Crystal Palace, Kilkenny moved up into the shadows of the stable, and his eyes watched the Palace for a long time. Finally he moved, ghost-like, across the open space back of the gambling hall. Tiptoeing along the wall, he came to the door he sought. Carefully, he tried the knob. It was locked.

Ahead of him a curtain blew through an open window, waving a little and then sagging back as the momentary breeze died. He paused beneath the window, listening. Inside he could hear the steady rise and fall of a man's breathing. It was the only way in. Hesitating only a minute, he put his foot through the open window and stepped inside.

Almost at once there was a black shadow of movement, and a forearm slipped across his throat in a stranglehold. Then that forearm crushed back into his throat with tremendous power. Setting the muscles in his neck, he strained forward, agonizing pain shooting through the growing blackness in his brain. He surged forward and felt the man's feet lift from the floor. Then suddenly, the hold relaxed, and he felt a hand slide down to his gun and then to the other gun. Then he was released.

"Brigo!" he said.

"Sí, Señor," Brigo answered in a whisper. "I did not know. But only one man is so powerful as you. When you lifted me, I knew it must be you. Then I felt your guns, and I know them well."

"The señorita is here?"

"Sí." Brigo was silent for a moment. "Señor, I fear for her. This Hale, he wants her very much! Also, the Cub of the bear. He wants her. I fear for her. One day they will come to take her."

Kilkenny could sense the worry in the big man's voice. "But you, Brigo?"

He could almost see the Yaqui shrug. "I see the two hombres, Dunn an' Ravitz. They watch me always. Soon they will try to kill me. The señorita says I must not go out to kill them, but soon I must."

"Wait, if you can," Kilkenny said. "Then act as you must. If you feel the time has come, do not wait for the señorita to say. You do not kill heedlessly. If there is no other way, you are to judge."

"Gracias, Señor," Brigo said simply. "If you will come with me?"

Kilkenny followed him through the darkness down the hall to another door, and there Brigo tapped gently. Almost at once, he heard Nita's voice. "Jaime?"

"Sí. The señor is here."

The door opened quickly, and Brigo vanished into the darkness as Kilkenny stepped in. Nita closed the door. Her long dark hair fell about her shoulders. In the vague light he could see the clinging of her nightgown, the rise and fall of her bosom beneath the thin material.

"Kilkenny, what is it?" Her voice was low, and something in its timbre made his muscles tremble. It required all the strength that was in him not to take her in his arms.

"I had to see you. You are all right?"

"Sí. For now. He has given me until after the celebration to make up my mind. After that, I shall have to marry him or run."

"That celebration," he said bitterly, "is the cornerstone of everything now." Briefly, dispassionately, he told her of all that had happened. Of the trip across the Smoky Desert, of the deaths of Miller, Wilson, and Lije Hatfield, and then of the death of Sodermann and the others of Hale's men.

"Does he know of that yet?" he asked.

"I doubt it. He told me there had been an attempt to get food over the Blazer trail and that the men who made it had been wiped out. I don't think he knew more than that."

"I am going to fight Turner," he said.

She caught her breath suddenly. "Oh, no! Kilkenny, he is a brute! I have seen him around the Palace. So huge. And so strong. I have seen him bend silver dollars in his fingers. I have seen him squat beside a table, take the edge in his teeth, and lift it clear off the floor."

"I know, but I must fight him. It is my only chance to get close to Halloran." He explained quickly. "If we can just let them know that we aren't outlaws! If they could only realize what is happening here, that these are good men, trying only to establish homes! To fight him is my only chance."

"I heard you would. Brigo told me the word had come that you would fight him."

"What did Brigo say?" Kilkenny suddenly found he was very anxious to know. The big Yaqui had an instinct for judging the fighting abilities of men. Powerful, fierce, and ruthless himself, he knew fighting men, and he had been long in lands where men lived by courage and strength.

"He says you will win." She said it simply. "I cannot see how anyone could defeat that man, but Brigo is sure. He has made bets. And he is the only one who dares to bet against Turner."

"Nita, if there's a chance, say something to Halloran."

"There won't be. Hale will see to that. But if there is, I surely will."

"Nita, when the fight is over, I'll come for you. I'm going to take you away from this. Will you go?"

"Need you ask?" She smiled up at him in the dimness. "You know I will go, Kilkenny. Wherever you go I will go, Kilkenny. I made my choice long ago."

Kilkenny slipped from the house and returned to his horse. The black stood patiently, and when Lance touched his bridle, he jerked up his head and was ready to go. Yet when he reached the turn, Lance swung the black horse down the street of Cedar Bluff.

Walking the horse, he rode slowly up to the ring. It had been set up in an open space near the corrals. Seats had been placed around, with several rows close to the ringside. That would be where King Bill would sit with his friends. The emperor would watch the gladiators. Kilkenny smiled wryly.

A light footstep sounded at the side of the ring, and Kilkenny's gun leaped from its holster. "Don't move!" he whispered sharply.

"It's all right, Kilkenny." The man stepped closer, his hands held wide. "It's Dan Cooper."

"So you know I'm Kilkenny?"

Cooper chuckled.

"Yeah, I recognized your face that first day, but couldn't tie it to a name. It came to me just now. Hale will be wild when he hears."

"You're a good man, Cooper," Kilkenny said suddenly. "Why stay on the wrong side?"

"Is the winnin' side the wrong side? Not for me it ain't. I ain't sayin' as to who's right in this squabble, but for a gunhand, the winnin' side is the right one."

"No conscience, Cooper?" Kilkenny questioned, trying to see the other man's eyes through the darkness. "Dick Moffitt was a good man. So were Jody Miller, Tot Wilson, an' Lije Hatfield."

"Then Lije died?" Cooper's voice quickened. "That's not good, for you or us. The Hales, they don't think much of the Hatfields. I do. I know 'em. The Hales will have to kill every last Hatfield now or die themselves. I know them."

"You could have tried a shot at me, Cooper," Kilkenny suggested.

"Me?" Cooper laughed lightly. "I'm not the kind, Kilkenny. Not in the dark, without a warnin'. I ain't so anxious to get you, anyway. I'd be the hombre that killed Kilkenny, an' that's like settin' yourself up in a shootin' gallery. Anyway, I want to see the fight."

"The fight?"

"Between you and Tombull. That should be good." Cooper leaned against the platform of the ring. "Between the two of us, I ain't envyin' you none. That hombre's poison. He ain't human. Eats food enough for three men. Still," Cooper shoved his hat back on his head, "you sure took King Bill, an' he was some shakes of a scrapper."

Cooper straightened up. "Y'know, Kilkenny, just two men in town are bettin' on you."

"Two?"

"Uh-huh. One's that Yaqui gunman, Brigo. The other's Cain Brockman."

"Cain Brockman?" Kilkenny was startled.

"Yeah. He says he's goin' to kill you, but he says you can whip

Turner first. He told Turner to his face that you was the best man. Turner was sure mad."

Dan Cooper hitched up his belt. "Almost time for my relief. If I was you, I'd take out. The next hombre might not be so anxious to see a good fight that he'd pass up five thousand dollars."

"You mean there's money on my head?" Kilkenny asked.

"Yeah. Five thousand. Dead or alive." Cooper shrugged. "Cub didn't like the idea of the reward. He figures you're staked out for him."

"Okay, Dan. Enjoyed the confab."

"Thanks. Listen, make that fight worth the money, will you? An' by the way—watch Cub Hale. He's poison mean and faster than a strikin' rattler!"

Kilkenny rode out of town and took to the hills. The route he took homeward was not the same as that by which he had approached the town. Long ago he had learned it was very foolhardy to retrace one's steps. He bedded down about daylight and slept until early afternoon.

So Cain Brockman was betting on him. For a long time, Kilkenny sat in speculation. He lived over again that bitter, bloody afternoon in the Trail House when he had whipped the huge Cain. It had seemed that great bulk was impervious to anything in the shape of a human fist. Yet he had brought him down, had beaten him into helplessness.

Parson and Quince strolled over and sat down. Their faces were grave. It was like these men to hide their grief, yet he knew that under the emotionless faces of the men there was a feeling of family and unity stronger than any he had ever known. These men loved each other and lived for each other.

"Kilkenny, you set on fightin' this Turner?" Parson inquired.

"Yes, I am," Kilkenny said quietly. "It's our big chance. It is more than a chance to talk to Halloran, too. It's a chance to hit Hale another wallop."

"To hurt him, you got to beat Turner," Quince said, staring at Kilkenny. "You got to win."

"That's right," Kilkenny agreed. "So I'm goin' in to win. I've changed my mind about some things. I was figurin' just on stayin' in there long enough to talk to the officials from Santa Fe, but now I am goin' in there to win.

"If I win, I make friends. People will like to see Hale beat again. Halloran is an Irishman, an' an Irishman loves a good fighter. Well, I got to win."

They were silent for a few minutes and Parson chewed on a straw. Then he looked up from under his bushy gray eyebrows.

"It ain't the fight what worries me. If the good Lord wants you to win, you'll win. What bothers me is after—win or lose, what happens then? Think Hale will let you go?"

Kilkenny smiled grimly. "He will, or there'll be blood on the streets of Cedar. Hale blood!"

## Chapter XV
### *The Chips Are Down*

The crowds had started coming to Cedar by daylight. The miners had come, drifting over for the rodeo and the fight. The gold camps had been abandoned for the day, as there was rarely any celebration for them, rarely any relief from the loneliness and the endless masculinity of the gold camps.

The cowhands from the Hale Ranch were around in force. The bars were doing a rushing business even before noon, and the streets were jammed with people.

Kilkenny rode into town on the buckskin when the sun was high. For over an hour he had been lying on a hillside above the town, watching the movement. It was almost certain that King Bill would avoid trouble today. There were too many visitors, too many people who were beyond his control. He would be on his good behavior today, making an impression as the upright citizen and free-handed giver of celebrations.

A rider under a flag of truce had appeared in the cup the evening before with an invitation to Kilkenny and the actual challenge for the fight. Word of Kilkenny's willingness for the fight had seeped into town by the grapevine several days before, so no tricks were needed. Kilkenny was to report to a man named John Bartlett, at the Crystal Palace.

Kilkenny, accompanied by Parson Hatfield and Steve Runyon, rode down to the Palace and dismounted. Quince Hatfield and O'Hara had already arrived in town, and they moved up outside the Palace and loafed where they could watch the horses. Only a few of the Hale riders actually knew them by sight.

Pushing open the batwing doors, Kilkenny stepped inside, Parson at his elbow. The place was crowded, and all the games were going full blast. Kilkenny's quick eyes swept the place. Jaime Brigo was in his usual chair across the room, and their eyes met. Then Kilkenny located Price Dixon. He was dealing cards at a nearby table.

There was a warning in Dixon's eyes, and then Price made an almost imperceptible gesture of his head. Turning his eyes, Kilkenny felt a little chill go over him. Cain Brockman was standing at the bar, and Cain was watching him.

Slowly, as though subtly aware of the tension in the room, eyes began to lift. As if by instinct they went from the tall, broad-shouldered man with the bronzed face, clad completely in black, to the towering bruiser in the checked shirt and the worn levis.

Then, his hands hanging carelessly at his sides, his flat-brimmed hat tipped just a little, Kilkenny started across the room toward Cain Brockman. A deadly hush fell over the room. Cain had turned, his wide unshaven face still marked by the scars of his former battle with Kilkenny, marked with scars he would carry to his grave.

Through narrow eyes the big man looked at Kilkenny, watching his slow steps across the floor, the studied ease, the grace of the man in black, the two big guns at his hips. Unseen, Nita Riordan had come to the door of her room, and eyes wide, she watched Kilkenny walk slowly among the tables and pause before Cain Brockman.

For a minute the two men looked at each other. Then Kilkenny spoke. "I hear you've come to town to kill me, Cain," he said quietly. Yet in the deathly hush of the room his voice carried to each corner.

"Well, I've another fight on my hands, with Tombull Turner. If we shoot it out, I'm going to kill you, but you're a good man with a gun, and I reckon I'll catch some lead. Fighting Tombull is going to be enough without carrying a crawful of lead when I do it. So how about a truce until afterward?"

For an instant, Cain hesitated. In the small gray eyes, chill and cold, there came a little light of reluctant admiration. He straightened.

"I reckon I can wait," Cain drawled harshly. "Let it never be said that Cain Brockman broke up a good fight!"

"Thanks." Abruptly, Kilkenny turned away, turning his back full on Cain Brockman, and with the same slow walk crossed the room to Price Dixon. A big red-headed man stood at the table near Price.

As he walked up to the table, the batwing doors pushed open and four men walked in. Kilkenny noticed them and felt the flash of recognition of danger go over him. It was King Bill Hale, Cub Hale, and the gold-dust twins, Dunn and Ravitz.

Ignoring them, Kilkenny walked up to the red-headed man. "You're John Bartlett?" he asked. "I'm Kilkenny."

"Glad to meet you." Bartlett thrust out a huge hand. "How'd you know me?"

"Saw you in Abilene. Again in New Orleans."

"Then you've seen Turner fight?" Bartlett demanded keenly. He glanced up and down Kilkenny with a quick, practiced eye.

"Yes. I've seen him fight."

"An' you're not afraid? He's a bruiser. He nearly killed Tom Hanlon."

Kilkenny smiled. "An' who was Tom Hanlon? A big chunk of beef so slow he couldn't get out of his own way. I see nothing in Turner to fear."

"You'll actually fight him then?" Bartlett was incredulous.

"Fight him?" Kilkenny asked. "Fight him? I'm going to whip him!"

"That's the way to talk!" A big, black-bearded miner burst out. "I'm sick of this big bull of a Turner struttin' around. My money goes on Kilkenny."

"Mine, too," another miner said. "I'd rather he was a miner, but I'll even bet on a cowhand if he can fight."

Kilkenny turned and looked at the miner, and then he grinned. "Friend," he said, "I've swung a single jack for many a day and tried a pan on half the creeks in Arizona."

Bartlett leaned forward. "This fight is for a prize of one thousand dollars in gold, put up by King Hale. However, if you want to make a side bet—?"

"I do," Kilkenny said. He unbuttoned his shirt and took out a packet of bills. "Five thousand dollars of it."

"Five thousand?" Bartlett swallowed and saw Hale frown. "I don't think we can cover it."

"What?" Kilkenny looked up, and his eyes met those of King Bill. "I understood that Hale was offering three to one, and no takers. That's the money I want. Some of that three to one that Bill Hale is offering."

"Three to one?" Hale demanded. "Why, I never—" The astonishment in his voice was plain enough, but Kilkenny knew he had him, and every move was calculated to win the crowd, not for himself, but for the men he represented. To back down would mean loss of prestige to Hale; to declare he knew of no three-to-one offer would make many believe he had welshed on his bet. And if Kilkenny won, Hale would never dare order him killed because all would think it was revenge for losing the bet. And if Kilkenny lost, it would still put Hale in a bad light if he were suddenly murdered.

"What's the matter, Hale?" Kilkenny demanded sharply, and his voice rang loud in the crowded room. "Are you backing down? Have you decided the man who whipped you on your own ground can whip Turner, too? Didn't you bring Tombull Turner here to whip me or to force me to back down?

"I'm calling you, Hale. Put up or shut up! I'm betting five thousand against your fifteen thousand that I win. I'm betting all I own, aside from that little claim you're trying to take away from me, against a mere fifteen thousand. Are you backing down?"

"No, by the Lord Harry, I'm not!" Hale's face was purple with anger. "I'm not going to let any fence-crawling nester throw money in my face. I'm covering you."

Kilkenny smiled slowly. "Looks like an interesting afternoon," he said cheerfully. Then he turned and walked slowly from the room, conscious that at every step he took, the white cold eyes of Cub Hale followed him, their hatred almost a tangible thing.

When they got outside, Parson stared at him. "You sure made King Bill look bad in there. You made some friends."

"You mean, *we* made friends," Kilkenny said quietly. "That's the point. We've got to make friends, we've got to get the sympathy of these miners and the outside people Hale can't touch. If we can get enough of them, we've got a fighting chance. Hale can't get too raw. There's law in this country now, an' he can win only so long as he can make what he's doin' seem right.

"If it stopped right here, an' he got me killed or took my land, a lot of people would be asking questions. They'll remember what I said. You see, Parson, we're little people buckin' a powerful an' wealthy man. That makes us the underdogs.

"I'm the smaller man in this fight, too. I'm a cowhand and a miner fightin' a trained prizefighter with my fists. A good part of that crowd is goin' to be with me for that reason, even some of Hale's cowhands."

It was midafternoon when Kilkenny walked down to the ring. The corral fence was covered with cowhands and miners, and the intervening space was filled with them. They were crowded along roofs and in every bit of space. Scanning the crowd, Kilkenny's eyes glinted. The miners were out in strength, and with them had come a number of gamblers, cowhands from outside the valley, and a few odds and ends of trappers.

The cluster of seats near the ring was empty, and two men guarded them. Kilkenny walked down to the ringside and stripped to the waist. He slipped off his boots and pulled on a pair of Indian moccasins that fitted snugly.

There was a roar from the crowd, and he saw Tombull Turner leaving the back door of Leathers's store and striding toward the ring, wrapped in a blanket. As he climbed through the ropes and walked to his corner, King Bill Hale, Cub Hale, and two men in store clothes left the Mecca and started toward the ring. Behind them walked Dunn and Ravitz.

Then, escorted by Jaime Brigo, Nita Riordan left the Palace and walked slowly through the crowd toward the ring. She was beautifully dressed, in the very latest of fashion, and carried her chin high. Men drew aside to let her pass, and those along the way she walked removed their hats.

Nita Riordan had proved to Cedar Bluff that a woman could run a gambling joint and still remain a lady. Not one word had ever been said against her character. Even the most skeptical had been convinced, both by her own ladylike manner and by the ever-watchful presence of Brigo.

Price Dixon walked down to Kilkenny's corner. He hesitated and then stepped forward. "I've had some experience as a handler," he said simply, "if you'll trust a gambling man."

Kilkenny looked at him and then smiled. "Why, I reckon we're all gambling men after a fashion, sir. I'd be proud to have you."

He glanced around quickly. John Bartlett was to referee, and the big red-headed man was already in the ring. Parson Hatfield, wearing a huge Walker Colt, lounged behind Kilkenny's corner. Runyon was a short distance away, and near him was Quince Hatfield. O'Hara was to work in Kilkenny's corner also.

## Chapter XVI
### Test of Battle

Kilkenny climbed quickly into the ring and slipped off the coat he had hung around his shoulders. He heard a low murmur from the crowd. He knew they were sizing him up.

Tombull Turner was the larger by thirty pounds. He was taller, broader, and thicker, a huge man with a round, bullet head set on a powerful neck and mighty shoulders. His biceps and forearms were heavy with muscle, and the deltoid development on the ends of his shoulders was large. His stomach was flat and solid, his legs columns of strength.

Kilkenny was lean. His shoulders were broad and had the strength of years of living in the open, working, fighting, and struggling. His stomach was flat and corded with muscle and his shoulders splendidly muscled, yet beside the bigger man, he appeared much smaller.

Actually, he weighed two hundred pounds. Yet scarcely a man present, if asked to guess his weight, would have made it more than one hundred and eighty.

Bartlett walked to the center of the ring and raised a huge hand. "The rules is no punches below the belt. Hit as long as they have one hand free. No gouging or biting allowed. Holding and hitting is fair. When a man falls, is thrown, or is knocked to the floor, the round ends. The fight is to a finish." He strode back, glancing with piercing eyes from Turner to Kilkenny.

The call of time was made, and the two men came forward to the scratch. Instantly, Tombull rushed, swinging with both hands. Kilkenny weaved inside and smashed hard with a right and left to the body.

Then Turner grabbed him and attempted to hurl him to the floor, but Kilkenny twisted himself loose and struck with a lightninglike left to the bigger man's mouth.

Turner set himself and swung a left that caught Kilkenny in the chest and knocked him back against the ropes. The crowd let out a roar, but unhurt, Kilkenny slipped away from Turner's charge and landed twice to the ribs. The big man closed in, feinted a left, and caught Kilkenny with a wicked overhand right that hit him on the temple.

Groggy, Kilkenny staggered into the ropes, and Turner charged like a bull and struck twice, left and right, to Kilkenny's head. Lance clinched and hung on tight. Then, slipping a heel behind Turner's ankle, he tripped him up and threw him hard to the canvas!

He walked to his corner, seeing through a mist. They doused him with water, and at the call of time he came out slowly until almost up to the scratch. Then he lunged forward and landed with a hard left to the side of the neck. Tombull took it flat-footed and walked in, apparently unhurt. Kilkenny evaded a right and then lashed back with both hands, staggering the big man again.

Turner lunged forward, hitting Kilkenny with a short right, and then, slipping Kilkenny's left, he grabbed him and threw him to the floor. The third round opened with both men coming out fast, and walking right together they began to slug. Then Kilkenny blocked Turner's left and hit him in the body with a right. They broke free, and circling, Kilkenny got a look at the two men sitting with Hale.

One was Halloran. The other was a leaner, taller man. Lance evaded a rush and then clipped Turner with a right. He had been doing well, but he was no fool. Turner was a fighter, and the big man had not been trying yet, was just getting warmed up now. He was quite sure Tombull was under orders to beat him, to pound him badly, but to keep him in the ring as long as possible. Hale was to have his revenge, his bloodletting.

Tombull Turner moved in, landing a powerful left to the head and then a right to the body. Kilkenny circled away from Turner's heavy-hitting right. Turner bored in, striving to get his hands on the lighter man and to get his fists where he could hit better. He liked to use short punches when standing close. Kilkenny slid away, stabbed a long left to Turner's mouth, feinted, and when Tombull swung his right, stepped in and smashed both hands to the body.

For all the effect the punches had he might have been hitting a huge drum. Turner rushed, crowding Kilkenny against the ropes, where he launched a storm of crashing, battering blows. One fist caught Kilkenny over the eye, and another crashed into the pit of his stomach. Then a clubbing right hit Kilkenny on the kidney. He staggered away, and Turner, his big fists poised, crowded closer.

He swung for the head, and Kilkenny ducked the right but caught a chopping blow from the left that started blood flowing from a cut over one eye. Kilkenny backed away, and Turner rushed and floored Kilkenny with a smashing right.

Dixon worked over the eye rapidly and skillfully. Kilkenny found time to be surprised at his skill. "Watch that right," O'Hara said. "It's bad."

Kilkenny moved up to scratch and then sidestepped just in time to miss Turner's bull rush. He stepped in and stabbed a left to the head, and then Tombull got in close and hurled him to the canvas again.

Taking the rest on the stool, Kilkenny relaxed. Then at the call, he came to the scratch again, and suddenly, leaping in, he smashed two rocking punches to Turner's jaw. The bigger man staggered, and before he could recover, Kilkenny stepped in, stabbed a hard left to the mouth, and then hooked a powerful right to the body. Turner tried to get his feet under him, but Kilkenny was relentless. He smashed a left to the mouth and a right to the body and then landed both hands to the body as Turner hit the ropes.

Tombull braced himself and, summoning his tremendous strength, bulled in close, literally hurled Kilkenny across the ring, and then followed with a rush. The crowd was on its feet now. Kilkenny feinted and then smashed a powerful right to the ribs. Turner tried a left, and pushing it aside, Kilkenny stepped in with a wicked left uppercut to the wind. Turner staggered.

The crowd was on its feet now, yelling for Kilkenny. He shook Turner with a right, but Tombull set himself and threw a mighty right that caught Kilkenny coming in and flattened him on the canvas.

When he got to his corner, he could see the crowd was excited. He was badly shaken, but not dazed by the blow. Suddenly, he was on his feet, and before anyone could realize what was happening, he had stepped across to the ringside where Hale sat with the two officials.

"Gentlemen," he said swiftly, "I've little time. I am fighting here today because it is the only way I could get to speak to you. I am one of a dozen nesters who have filed on claims among the peaks, claims from which Hale is unlawfully trying to drive us. One man has been cruelly murdered—"

The call of time interrupted. He wheeled to see Tombull charging, and he slid away along the ropes. Then Turner hit him and he staggered, but Turner lunged close, unwilling to let him fall. Shoving him back against the ropes, Turner shoved a left to his chin and then clubbed a powerful right.

Blasting pain seared across Kilkenny's brain. He saw that right go up again and knew he could never survive another such punch. With all his strength, he jerked away. Turner intended to kill him now.

In a daze, he could see Hale was on his feet, as were the officials. Cub Hale had a hand on his gun, and Parson Hatfield was facing him across the ring. Then Kilkenny jerked loose.

But Turner was on him like a madman, clubbing, striking with all his mighty strength, trying to batter Kilkenny into helplessness before the round ended. The crowd was in a mighty uproar, and in a haze of pain and waning consciousness, Kilkenny saw Steve Runyon had slipped behind Cub Hale and had a gun on him.

Somebody was shouting outside the ring, and then Turner hit him again and he broke away from Tombull and crashed to the canvas.

O'Hara carried him bodily to his corner, where Dixon worked over him like mad. The call of time came, and Kilkenny staggered to his feet and had taken but one step toward the mark when Tombull hit him like a hurricane, sweeping him back into the ropes with a whirlwind of staggering, pounding, battering blows. Weaving, swaying, slipping and ducking punches, Kilkenny tried to weather the storm.

Somehow he slipped under a right to the head and got in close. Spreading his legs wide, he began to slug both hands into the big man's body. The crowd had gone mad now, but he was berserk. The huge man was fighting like a madman, eager for the kill, and Kilkenny was suddenly lost to everything but the battering fury of the fight and the lust to put the big man down and to keep him down.

Slipping a left, he smashed a wicked right to the ribs and then another and another. Driving in, he refused to let Turner get set and smashed him with punch after punch. Turner threw him off, but he leaped in again, got Tombull's head in chancery with a crude head-lock, and proceeded to batter blow after blow into the big man's face before Turner did a back somersault to break free and end the round.

Panting, gasping for every breath when each stabbed like a knife, Kilkenny swung to the ropes. "We've been refused food in Cedar!" Kilkenny shouted hoarsely at the officials. "We sent a wagon to Blazer, and three men were waylaid and killed. On a second attempt, we succeeded in getting a little, but only after a pitched battle."

The call of time came and he wheeled. Turner was on him with a rush, his face bloody and wild. Kilkenny set himself and struck hard with a left that smashed Turner's nose and then with a wicked right that rocked Turner to his heels. Faster than the big man, he carried less weight and was tiring less rapidly. Also, the pounding of his body blows had weakened the bigger man.

*     *     *

Close in, they began to slug, but here, too, despite Turner's massive strength, Kilkenny was the better man. He was faster, and he was beating the big man to the punch. Smashing a wicked left to the chin, Kilkenny stepped in and hooked both hands hard to the body. Then he brought up an uppercut that ripped a gash across Turner's face. Before Tombull could get set, Kilkenny drove after him with a smashing volley of hooks and swings that had the big man reeling.

Everyone was yelling now, yelling like madmen, but Turner was gone. Kilkenny was on him like a panther. He drove him into the ropes and, holding him there, struck the big man three times in the face. Then Tombull broke loose and swung a right that Kilkenny took in his stride. He smashed Turner back on his heels with a right of his own.

The big man started to fall, and Kilkenny whipped both hands to his face with cracking force! Turner went down, rolled over, and lay still.

In an instant, Kilkenny was across the ring. Grabbing his guns, he strapped them on. His fists were battered and swollen, but he could still hold a gun. He caught a quick glimpse of Nita and saw Brigo was hurrying her from the crowd. Parson and Quincy Hatfield closed in beside him, guns drawn.

"I'll have to go with you," Dixon said. "If I stay now they'll kill me."

"Come on," Kilkenny said grimly. "We can use you."

Backing after them, Runyon kept Cub Hale at the end of his gun. The younger Hale's face was white. Then as the Hale cowhands began to gather, a mob of miners surged between them.

"Go ahead," a big miner shouted. "We'll stand by you."

Kilkenny smiled suddenly, and swinging away from his men he walked directly toward the crowding cowhands. Muttering sullenly, they broke ahead of him, and he strode up to King Bill Hale. The big rancher was pale, and his eyes were cold as ice and bitter. Halloran stood behind him, and the tall, cool-eyed man stood nearby.

"I will take my fifteen thousand dollars now," Kilkenny said quietly.

His face sullen and stiff, Hale counted out the money and thrust it at him. Kilkenny turned then, bowed slightly to Halloran and the other man, and said quietly:

"What I have told you here, gentlemen, is true. I wish you would investigate the claims of Hale to our land, and our own filings upon that land."

Turning, he walked back to the miners, mounted, and rode off with the Hatfields, O'Hara, and Runyon close about him.

"We'll have to move fast!" Kilkenny said. "What happens will happen quick now!"

"What can he do now?" Runyon asked. "We got our story across."

"Supposin' when they come back to investigate, there aren't any of us left?" Kilkenny demanded. "What could anybody do about that? There'd be no witnesses, an' even if they asked a lot of questions it wouldn't do us any good. The big fight will come now."

They rode hard and fast, sticking to little-known trails through the brush. They threaded the bottom of a twisted, broken canyon and curled along a path that led along the sloping shoulder of a rocky hill among the cedars.

Kilkenny rode with his rifle across the saddle in front of him and with one hand always ready to swing it up. He was under no misapprehension about King Bill. The man had been defeated again, and he would be frantic now. His ego was being sadly battered, and to prove to himself that he was still the power in the Cedar Valley country he must wipe this trouble from the earth.

He would have lost much. Knowing the man, and knowing the white lightning that lay beneath the surface of Cub Hale, he knew the older man must more than once have cautioned the slower, surer method. Now Cub would be ranting for a shootout. Kilkenny knew he had gauged that young man correctly. He was spoiled. The son of a man of power, he had ridden wild and free and had grown more arrogant by the year, taking what he wanted and killing those who thwarted him.

Dunn and Ravitz would be with him, he knew. That trio was poison itself. He was no fool. He believed he could beat Hale. Yet he had no illusions about beating all three. There was, of course, the chance of catching them off side as he had caught the Brockmans that day in Cottonwood. The Brockmans! Like a flash he remembered Cain. The big man was free to come gunning for him now!

## Chapter XVII
### *Fight in the Gorge*

Winding around a saddle trail leading into a deep gorge, they came out on the sandy bottom, and he speeded their movement to a rapid trot. Despite himself, he was worried. At the cup, there were only Jesse and Saul Hatfield, Bartram, and Jackie Moffitt. Suppose Hale had taken that moment to sweep down upon them and shoot it out? With luck, the defenders might hold the cup, but if the breaks went against them—

He turned his horse up a steep slope toward the pines. Ahead of him, suddenly, there was a rifle shot—just one. It sounded loud and clear in the canyon, yet he heard no bullet. As if by command, the little cavalcade spread out and rode up through the trees. It was Kilkenny who swept around a clump of scrub pine and saw several men scrambling for their horses. He reined in and dropped to the ground.

A rifle shot chunked into the trunk of the pine beside him, but he fired. One of the riders dropped his rifle and grabbed for the saddle horn, and then they swept into the trees. He got off three carefully spaced shots, heard Runyon, off to his left, opening up, and then, further along, Parson himself.

He wheeled the buckskin and rode the yellow horse toward the canyon, yelling his name as he swept into the cup. What he saw sent his face white with fear! Jesse Hatfield lay sprawled full length on the hard-packed ground of the cup, a slow curl of blood trickling from under his arm, a bloody gash on his head.

As he reined in alongside Jesse, the door of the house burst open and Jackie Moffitt came running out. "They hit us about two hours ago!" Jackie said excitedly. "They nicked Bart, too!"

Kilkenny dropped to his knees beside Hatfield and turned him gently. One bullet had grazed his scalp; another had gone through his chest, high up. He looked at the wound and the bubbling froth on the man's lips, and his lips tightened.

Price Dixon swung down beside him. Kneeling over Hatfield, he examined the wound. Kilkenny's eyes narrowed as he saw the gambler's fingers working over him with almost professional skill. He quickly cut away the cloth and examined the wound.

"We'll have to get him inside," he said gravely. "I've got to operate."

"Operate?" Parson Hatfield stared at him. "You a doc?"

Dixon smiled wryly. "I was once," he said. "Maybe I still am."

Ma Hatfield came to the door bearing a rifle. Then putting it down she turned and walked back inside, and when they brought the wounded man in, a bed was ready for him. Her long, thin-cheeked face was grave, and only her eyes showed pain and shock. She worked swiftly and without hysteria. Sally Crane was working over a wound in Bartram's arm, her own face white.

Kilkenny motioned to Parson and stepped outside. "I've got to go back tonight an' get Nita," he said quietly. "I'll go alone."

"You better take help. There's enough of us now to hold this place. You'll have you a fight down to Cedar. An' don't forget Cain Brockman."

"I won't. By night I can make it, I think. This is all comin' to a head now, Parson. They can't wait now. We've called their hand an' raised 'em. They never figured on me talkin'. They never figured on me winnin' that fight."

"All right," Parson said, "we'll stand by." He looked down at the

ground a moment. "I reckon," he said slowly, "we've done a good
day's work. I got me a man back on the trail, too. Jackie says Jesse
got one up on the rim. A couple more nicked. That's goin' to spoil
their appetite for fightin', an' spoil it a heap!"

"Yeah," Kilkenny agreed. "I'm ridin' at sundown, Parson."

Yet it was after sundown before he got started. Jesse Hatfield was
in a bad way. Price Dixon had taken a compact packet of tools from
his saddlebags, and his operation had been quick and skilled. His
gambler's work had kept his hands well, and he showed it now.
Kilkenny glanced at him, curiosity in his eyes. At one time this man
had been a fine surgeon.

He was never surprised. In the West you found strange men—
noblemen from Europe, wanderers from fine old families, veterans
of several wars, schoolboys, and boys who had grown up along the
cattle trails. Doctors, lawyers, men of brilliance, and men with none,
all had thronged west, looking for what the romantic called adven-
ture and the experienced knew was trouble, or looking for a new
home, for a change, or escaping from something.

Price Dixon was one of these. The man was observant, shrewd,
and cultured. He and Kilkenny had known each other from the first,
not as men who came from the same life, but men who came from
the same stratum of society. They were men of the lost legion, the
kind who always must move.

Despite his lack of practice, Dixon's moves were sure and his
hands skilled. He removed the bullet from dangerously near the
spine. When he finished he washed his hands and looked up at
Parson.

"He'll live, with rest and treatment. Beef broth, that's what he
needs now, to build strength in him."

Parson grinned behind his gray mustache. "He'll get it," he said
dryly. "He'll get it as long as King Bill Hale has a steer on the
range."

Sally Crane caught Kilkenny as he was saddling the little gray
horse he was riding that night. She hurried up to him and then
stopped suddenly and stood there, shifting her feet from side to side.
Kilkenny turned and looked at her curiously from under his flat-
brimmed hat.

"What's the trouble, Sally?"

"I wanted to ask—" she hesitated, and he could sense her shyness.
"Do you think I'm old enough to marry?"

"To marry?" He stopped, startled. "Why, I don't know, Sally.
How old are you?"

"I'm sixteen, most nigh seventeen."

"That's young," he conceded, "but I've heard Ma Hatfield say she was just sixteen when she married, an' down in Kentucky and Virginia many a girl marries at that age. Why?"

"I reckon I want to marry," Sally said shyly. "Ma Hatfield said I should ask you. Said you was Daddy Moffitt's friend, an' you was sort've my guardian."

"Me?" He was thunderstruck. "Well, I reckon I never thought of it that way. Who wants to marry you, Sally?"

"It's Bart."

"You love him?" he asked. He suddenly felt strangely old, and yet, looking at the young girl standing there so shyly, he felt more than ever before the vast loneliness there was in him, and also a strange tenderness such as he had never known before.

"Yes." Her voice was shy, but he could sense the excitement in her, and the happiness.

"Well, Sally," he said slowly, "I reckon I'm as much a guardian as you've got now. I think if you love Bartram an' he loves you, that's all that's needed. I know him. He's a fine, brave, serious young fellow who's goin' to do right well as soon as this trouble clears up. Yes, I reckon you can marry him."

She was gone, running.

For a few minutes he stood there, one foot in the stirrup. Then he swung his leg over the gray horse and shook his head in astonishment.

"That's one thing, Lance," he told himself, "you never expected to happen to you!"

But as he turned the horse into the pines, he remembered the Hatfields digging the grave for their brother. Men died, men were married, and the fighting and living and working went on. So it would always go. Lije Hatfield was gone, Miller and Wilson were gone, and Jesse Hatfield lay near to death in the cabin in the cup.

Yet Sally was to marry Tom Bartram, and they were to build a home. Yes, this was the country, and these were its people. They had the strength to live, the strength to endure. In such a country men would be born, men who loved liberty and would ever fight to preserve it.

The little gray was as surefooted as a mountain goat. Even the long-legged yellow horse could walk no more silently, no more skillfully than this little mountain horse. He talked to it in a low whisper and watched the ears flick backward with intelligence. This was a good horse.

Yet when he reached the edge of Cedar Bluff, he reined in sharply. Something was wrong. There was a vague smell of smoke in the air, and an atmosphere of uneasiness seemed to hang over the town. He looked down, studying the place. Something was wrong. Something had changed. It was not only the emptiness left after a crowd is gone, it was something else, something that made him uneasy.

He moved the gray horse forward slowly, keeping to sandy places where the horse would make no sound. The black bulk of a building loomed before him, and he rode up beside it and swung down. The smell of wood smoke was stronger. Then he peered around the corner of the building. Where the Mecca had stood was only a heap of charred ruins.

Hale's place—burned! He scowled, trying to imagine what could have happened. An accident? It could be, yet something warned him it was not that, and more, that the town wasn't asleep.

Keeping to the side of the buildings, he walked forward a little. There was a faint light in Bert Leathers's store. The Crystal Palace was dark. He went back to the gray horse and carefully skirting the troubled area, came in from behind the building and then swung down.

A man loomed ahead of him, a huge bulk of man. His heart seemed to stop, and he froze against the building. It was Cain Brockman!

Watching, Kilkenny saw him moving with incredible stealth, slip to the side of the Crystal Palace, work for an instant at the door, and then disappear inside.

Like a ghost, Kilkenny crossed the alley and went in the door fast. There he flattened against the wall. He could hear the big man ahead of him, but only his breathing. Stealthily, he crept after.

What could Brockman be doing here? Was he after Nita? Or hoping to find him? He crept along, closed a door after him, and lost Brockman in the stillness. Then suddenly a candle gleamed, and another. The first person he saw was Nita. She was standing there, in riding costume, staring at him.

"You've come, Lance?" she said softly. "Then it was you I heard?"

"No," he spoke softly, "it wasn't me. Cain Brockman's here."

A shadow moved against the curtain at the far side of the big room, and Cain Brockman stepped into the open.

"Yeah," he said softly, "I'm here."

He continued to move, coming around the card tables until he stood near, scarcely a dozen feet away. The curtains were drawn on all the windows, thick drapes that kept all light within. If he lived to be a thousand, Lance Kilkenny would never forget that room.

It was large and rectangular. Along one side ran the bar; the rest, except for the small dance floor where they stood now, was littered with tables and chairs. Here and there were fallen chips, cards, cigarette butts, and glasses.

A balcony surrounded the room on three sides, a balcony with curtained booths. Only the candles flickered in the great room, candles that burned brightly but with a wavering uncertain light. The girl held her candles—Nita Riordan, with her dark hair gathered against the nape of her neck, her eyes unusually large in the dimness.

Opposite Kilkenny stood the bulk of Cain Brockman. His big black hat was shoved back on his huge head. His thick neck descended into powerful shoulders, and the checkered shirt was open to expose a hairy chest. Crossed gun belts and big pistols completed the picture, guns that hung just beneath the open hands.

Cain stood there, his flat face oily and unshaven in the vague light, his stance wide, his feet in their riding boots seeming unusually small.

"Yeah," Cain repeated. "I'm here."

Kilkenny drew a deep breath. Suddenly a wave of hopelessness spread over him. He could kill this man. He knew it. Yet why kill him? Cain Brockman had come looking for him, had come because it was the code of the life he had lived and because the one anchor he had, his brother Abel, had pulled loose.

Suddenly, Kilkenny saw Cain Brockman as he had never seen him before, as a big man, simple and earnest, a man who had drifted along the darker trails because of some accident of fate, and whose one tie, his brother, had been cut loose. He saw him now as big, helpless, and rather lost. To kill Kilkenny was his only purpose in life—

Abruptly, Kilkenny dropped his hands away from his guns. "Cain," he said, "I'm not going to shoot it out with you. I'm not going to kill you. I'm not even goin' to try. Cain, there's no sense in you an' me shootin' it out. Not a mite."

"What d'you mean?" The big man's brow was furrowed, his eyes narrowed with thought as he tried to decide what deception was in this.

"I don't want to kill you, Cain. You an' your brother teamed up with the wrong crowd in Texas. Because of that, I had to kill him. You looked for me, an' I had to fight you an' whip you. I didn't want to then, an' I don't now.

"Cain, I owe somethin' to those people up there, the Hatfields an' the rest. They want homes out here. I've got a reason to fight for them. If I kill, it'll be for that. If I die, it'll be to keep their land for them. There's nothin' to gain for you or me by shootin' it out. Suppose you kill me? What will you do then?"

Cain hesitated, staring, puzzled.

"Why, ride out of here. And go back to Texas."

"An' then?"

"Go to ridin', I guess."

"Maybe, for a while. Then some hombre'll come along an' you'll rustle a few cows. Then you'll rob a stage, an' one time they'll get you like they got Sam Bass. You'll get shot down or you'll hang.

"I'm not goin' to shoot you, Cain. An' you're too good a man to draw iron on a man who won't shoot! You're a good man, Cain. Just a good man on the wrong trail. You've got too much good stuff in you to die the way you'll die."

Cain Brockman stared at him, and in the flickering candlelight, Kilkenny waited. He was afraid for the first time, afraid his words would fail and the big man would go for his gun. He didn't want to kill him, and he knew that his own gunman's instinct would make him draw if Cain went for a gun.

Cain Brockman stood stock-still in the center of the room, and then he lifted a hand to his face and pawed at his grizzled chin.

"Well, I'll be—" he muttered. "I'll be eternally—"

He shook his head, turned unsteadily, and lurched into the darkness toward the door.

## Chapter XVIII
### Disaster Stalks

Kilkenny stepped back and wiped the sweat from his brow. Nita crossed the room to him, her face radiant with relief.

"Oh, Lance!" she exclaimed. "That was wonderful! Wonderful!"

Kilkenny grinned dazedly. "It was awful—just plain awful."

He glanced around. "What's happened here? Where's Brigo?"

"He's in my room, Lance," Nita said quickly. "I was going to tell you, but Brockman came. He's hurt, very badly."

"Brigo? Hurt?" It seemed impossible. "What happened?"

"It was those two gunmen of Hale's. Cub sent them here after me. Brigo met them right here, and they shot it out. He killed both Dunn and Ravitz, but he was hit three times, once through the body."

"What happened to the Mecca? What happened in town?"

"That was before Dunn and Ravitz came. Some miners were in the Mecca, and they were all drinking. A miner had some words with a Hale gunman about the fight and about the nesters. The miner spoke very loudly, and I guess he said what he thought about Hale.

"The gunman reached for a gun, and the miner hit him with a bottle, and it was awful. It was a regular battle. Miners against the Hale hands, and it was bloody and terrible.

"Some of the Hale riders liked your fight and your attitude, and they had quit. The miners drove the others out of the Mecca and burned it to the ground. Then the miners and the Hale riders fought all up and down the streets. But no one was killed. Nobody used a gun then. I guess all of them were afraid what might happen."

"And the miners?" Kilkenny asked quickly.

"They mounted up and got into wagons and rode out of town on the way back to their claims. It was like a ghost town then. Nobody stirred on the streets. They are littered with bottles, broken windows, and clubs. Then everything was quiet until Dunn and Ravitz came."

"What about Hale? King Bill, I mean?"

"We've only heard rumors. Some of the cowhands who quit stopped by here to get drinks. They said that Hale acts like a man who'd lost his mind. He had been here after the fight, before he went home. He asked me to marry him, and I refused. He said he would take me, and I told him Brigo would kill him if he tried. Then he went away. It was afterward that Cub sent the gunmen for me. He wanted me for himself.

"Something has happened to Hale. He doesn't even look like the same man. You won fifteen thousand dollars from him, and he paid you. He lost money to the miners, too, and to Cain Brockman. It hit him hard. He's a man who has always won, always had things his own way. He isn't used to being thwarted, isn't used to adversity, and he can't take it.

"Then before he left, Halloran told him he would have to let the law decide about the nesters, and Hale declared that he was the law. Halloran told him he would find out he was not and that if he had ordered the killing of Dick Moffitt, he would hang."

"And then?"

"He seemed broken. He just seemed to go to pieces. I think he had ruled here these past ten years and that he actually believed he was king, that he had the power and that nothing could win against him. Everything had gone just as he wanted until you came along."

"You mean," Kilkenny said dryly, "until he tried to turn some good Americans out of their homes."

"Well, anyway, you'd managed to get food from here right under his nose. Then when the attempt along the Blazer trail was tried, and he practically wiped your men out, he was supremely confident. But his attack on the cup failed.

"What really did it all was your defeat of Turner, and at the moment when he had finished paying off, he was told for the first time of the death of Sodermann at Blazer.

"Then some of the cowhands who quit took the opportunity to drive off almost a thousand head of cattle. These defeats and what Halloran told him have completely demoralized the man."

"What about Cub?"

"He's wild. He hated you, and he was furious that some of the men quit. He doesn't care about Halloran, for he's completely law-less. He's taken a dozen of the toughest men and gone after the stolen cattle."

"Good! That means we have time." Kilkenny took her by the arms. "Nita, you can't stay here. He might just come back. You must go to the cup and send Price Dixon down here. He can do something for Brigo. Tell him to get here as fast as he can. And you'll be safe there."

"But you?" Nita protested.

He smiled gently and put his hand on her head. "Don't worry about me, Nita. I've lived this way for years. I'll do what I can for Jaime. But hurry."

She hesitated only an instant. Then, suddenly on tiptoe, she kissed him lightly on the lips and turned toward the door.

"Just take my horse," he said. "It'll be quicker. The little gray. Give him his head and he'll go right back to the cup. I got him from Parson Hatfield."

Nita was gone.

Kilkenny turned swiftly and took a quick look around the darkened room. Then he walked through the door and over to the bed where Brigo lay.

The big Yaqui was asleep. He was breathing deeply, and his face was pale. When Kilkenny laid a hand on his brow, it was hot to the touch. Yet he was resting and was better left alone.

Kilkenny walked back into the main room and checked his guns by the candles. Then he got Brigo's guns, reloaded them, and hunted around. He found two more rifles, a double-barrelled shotgun and many shells, and two more pistols. He loaded them all and placed the pistols in a neat row on the bar. One he thrust into his waist-band, leaving his own guns in their holsters.

Then he doused the candles and sat down in Brigo's chair by the door. It would be a long time until morning.

Twice during the long hours he got up and paced restlessly about the great room, staring out into the vague dimness of the night at the ghostly street. It was deathly still. Once, something struck a bottle, and he was out of his chair, gun in hand. But when he tiptoed to the window, he saw it was merely a lonely burro wandering aimlessly in the dead street.

Toward morning he slept a little, only restlessly and in snatches, every nerve alert for trouble or some sound that would warn of danger. When it was growing gray in the street, he went in to look at the wounded man. Brigo had opened his eyes and was lying there. He looked feverish. Kilkenny changed the dressing on the wound after bathing it and then checked the two flesh wounds.

"Señor? Is it bad?" Brigo asked, turning his big black eyes toward Kilkenny.

"Not very. You lie still. Dixon is coming down."

"Dixon?" Brigo was puzzled.

"Yeah, he used to be a doctor. Good, too."

"A strange man." Sudden alarm came into Brigo's eyes. "And the señorita?"

"I sent her to the cup, to the Hatfields. She'll be safe there."

"*Bueno.* Cub, he has not come?"

"No. You'd better rest and lay off the talk. Don't worry if they come. I've got plenty of guns."

He put the water bucket close by the bed, and a tin cup on the table. Then he went out into the saloon.

In the gray light of dawn it looked garish and tawdry. Empty glasses lay about, and scattered poker chips. Idly, he began to straighten things up a little. Then, after making a round of the windows, he went to the kitchen and started a fire. Then he put on water for coffee.

Cub Hale would come. It might take him a few hours or a few days to find the herd. He might grow impatient and return here first. He would believe Nita was still here, and his gunmen had not returned.

Or he might send some men. Nita would not go over the trail as fast as he or the Hatfields. If all was well at the cup, the earliest Price could get here would be midday.

No one moved in the street. The gray dawn made it look strange and lonely in its emptiness. Somewhere, behind one of the houses, he heard the squeaking of a pump handle and then the clatter of a tin pail. His eyelids drooped and he felt very tired. He shook himself awake and walked to the kitchen. The water was ready, so he made coffee, strong and black.

Brigo was awake when he came in and the big man took the coffee gratefully. "*Bueno,*" he said.

Kilkenny noticed the man had somehow managed to reach his gun belt and had his guns on the table.

"Any pain?" he asked.

Brigo shrugged, and after a look at him, Kilkenny walked out. Out in the main room of the saloon, he looked thoughtfully around. Then he searched until he found a hammer and nails. Getting some loose lumber from the back room, he nailed boards over the windows, leaving only a narrow space as a loophole from which each side of the building might be observed. Then he prepared breakfast.

The work on breakfast showed him how dangerously short of food they were. He thrust his head in the door and saw Brigo's eyes open.

"We're short of grub an' might have to stand a siege. I'm goin' down to Leathers's store."

The street was empty when he peered out of the door. He took a step out onto the porch. One would have thought the town was deserted. There was no sound now. Even the squeaky pump was still. He stepped down into the street and walked along slowly, little puffs of dust rising at every step. Then he went up on the boardwalk. There was still no sign of life.

The door to Leathers's store was closed. He rattled the knob, and there was no response. Without further hesitation he put his shoulder to the door, picked up on the knob and shoved. It held, but then he set himself and lunged. The lock burst and the door swung inward. Almost instantly, Leathers appeared from the back of the store.

"Here!" he exclaimed angrily. "You can't do this!"

"When I rattled the door you should have opened it," Kilkenny said quietly. "I need some supplies."

"I told you once I couldn't sell to you," Leathers protested.

Kilkenny looked at him with disgust. "You're a yellowbelly, Leathers," he said quietly. "Why did you ever come west? You're built for a neat little civilized community where you can knuckle under to authority and crawl every time somebody looks at you. We don't like that in the West."

He picked up a slab of bacon and thrust it into a sack, and then he began piling more groceries into the burlap sack, until it was full. He took out some money and dropped it on the counter. He turned then to go. Leathers stood watching him angrily.

"Hale will get you for this," he snapped out.

Kilkenny turned patiently. "Leathers, you're a fool. Can't you realize that Hale is finished? That whole setup is finished—and you sided with them, so you're finished.

"You're the kind that always has to bow to authority. You think money is everything and power is everything. You've spent your life living in the shadow and cringing before bigger men. A good part of it's due to that sanctimonious wife of yours. If King Bill smiled at her she walked in a daze for hours. It's because she's a snob and you're a weakling.

"Take a tip from me. Take what cash you've got, load up some supplies, and get out of here—but fast."

"An' leave my store?" Leathers wailed. "What do you mean?"

"What I say." Kilkenny's voice was harsh. "There's going to be some doin's in this town before another day. Hale's riders are comin' back, an' Cub Hale will be leadin' 'em. You know how much respect he has for property or anythin'. If he doesn't clear you out, the Hatfields will. There's no place for you in Cedar anymore. We want to build from the ground up here, an' we want men who'll fight for what they believe. You won't, an' you were against us, so get out!"

He walked back down the silent street, went into the saloon and stored his grub. Despite himself, he was worried. The morning was early yet, and he was expecting some of the Hale riders, and soon. The longer he waited, the more worried he became.

Brigo needed medical attention, and Doc Pollard, the Hale hench-man, had gone to the Hale ranch. He was little better than useless, anyway.

Seated at a table he riffled the cards, and the sound was loud in the room. No one moved in the deserted street, and he played silently, smoking endless cigarettes and waiting.

Again and again his thoughts returned to Nita. After all, should he wait? Supposing he was killed eventually? Why not have a little happiness first? He knew without asking that she was the girl for him, and he knew she would marry him in an instant and be completely happy to live in a house built among the high peaks.

She was lovely, tender, thoughtful. A man could ask no more of any woman than she had for the giving. Yet he remembered the faces of other gunmen's wives when word came that their men had died. He remembered their faces when their men went down into the streets, when they waited through every lonely hour, never sure whether he would come back or not.

Bartram had Sally Crane. He remembered her sweet, youthful face, flushed with happiness. It made him feel old and lonely.

He slipped his guns out and checked them once more.

Then he took up the cards and shuffled them again. Suddenly an idea came to him. He got up and went to the back door, took a quick look around, and slipped out to the stable. There were still horses there.

He had a hunch he might need them, and saddled two.

Then he went back inside and closed the door.

The place was deathly still and the air close and hot. It felt like a storm was impending. He brushed the sweat from his brow and crossed to have a look at Brigo. The big man was sleeping, but his face was flushed and feverish. He looked bad.

He glanced out the door at the empty street. Clouds were build-ing up around the peaks. If it rained, it was going to make it tough to move Jaime Brigo. Thunder rumbled like a whimper of far-off trum-pets and then deeper like a rolling of gigantic casks along the floor of a cavern. He walked back inside and sat down.

## Chapter XIX
### *This Is the Test*

They came down the dusty street at high noon, a tight little cavalcade of men expecting no trouble. They rode as tired men ride, for there was dust on their horses and dust on their clothing and dust on their wide-brimmed hats. It was only their guns that had no dust.

There was no humor in them, for they were men for whom killing was the order of business. The softer members of the Hale outfit were gone. These were the pick of the tough, gun-handy crew.

Lee Wright was in the lead, riding a blood bay. At his right and a bit behind, was Jeff Nebel, and a bit behind him were gunslick Tandy Wade and Kurt Wilde. There were ten in all, ten tough, gun-belted men riding into Cedar Bluff when the sun was high.

Dunn and Ravitz had not returned. What that meant, they could not know, nor did they care. They had come to get a woman, and if Dunn and Ravitz had decided to keep her, these men would take her away. If those two had failed in their mission, they were to take her from the protection of Brigo. They had their orders and they knew what to do.

Near Leathers's store the group broke, and three men rode on down to the Crystal Palace. Lee Wright, big, hard-faced and cruel, was in the lead. With him were Kurt Wilde and Tandy Wade.

His eyes slanting up the street at the scattering men, Kilkenny let the three come on. When they reined in and were about to swing down, Kilkenny stopped them.

"Hold it!" he said sharply. "What do you want, Wright?"

Wright froze and then settled back in the saddle. "Who is that?" he demanded, peering to see under the darkness of the sheet-metal awning and into the vagueness of the doorway.

"It's Kilkenny," he said. "What do you want?"

"We've come for that woman. Cub wants her," Wright said harshly. "What are you doin' here?"

"Me?" Kilkenny chuckled quietly. His eyes were cold and watchful. He knew these men were uncertain. They hadn't expected him. Now they did not know what the situation was. How many men were inside? Was Brigo there? The Hatfields? Kilkenny knew their lack of knowledge was half his strength. "Why, I've been waitin' for you boys to show up! Wanted to tell you that I'd slope, if I were you. The Hales are through."

"Are they?" Wright's eyes swept the building. Those boarded windows bothered him. "We came after the woman. We'll get her."

Kilkenny began building a smoke. "With only ten men? It ain't enough, Wright." He touched his tongue to the paper. "You're a fightin' man, Wright. Ever try to take a place like this with no more men than you got?"

"You're bluffin'!" Wright said. "You're alone."

Kilkenny chuckled. "You reckon I'd come down here alone? Or that the Hatfields would let me? They are right careful of me, Wright."

"Where are they?" Wright declared. "You—" The words died on his lips as there was a tinkle of glass from down the building. Wright looked, and Kilkenny saw his face darken. It could mean but one thing. Brigo had gotten out of bed and thrust a rifle through the window at the right moment.

But how long could he stand there? The man was weak— Kilkenny laughed. "Well, you can start comin' any time you want, Wright, but a lot of you boys are goin' to die for nothin'. If you think Hale can pay off now, you're wrong."

Kurt Wilde had been sitting quietly. Now he exploded suddenly. "To hell with this! Let's go in there!" He jumped his horse to one side and grabbed for his gun.

Kilkenny's hand swept down, and his gun was barking before it reached belt high. The first shot cut the rearing horse's bridle at the bit and whined off into the street. The second took Wilde in the shoulder and knocked him sprawling into the dust.

At the same instant, Brigo fired, and Tandy Wade's horse backed up suddenly and went down. Wade leaped clear and sprinted with Lee Wright for the shelter of the nearest building. From up the street, there was a volley of shots, but Kilkenny was safely inside.

With one quick look, he dodged away from the door and ran to Brigo in the other room. The big man's face was deathly pale, and his movements had started his wounds bleeding.

"Lie down, damn it!" Kilkenny commanded. "You did your part. You fooled 'em. Now lie down!"

"No, Señor, not when you fight."

"I can hold 'em now. Lie down an' rest till I need you. When they rush, I'll need help."

Brigo hesitated and then sank back on the bed. From where he lay he could see through a crack in the boards without moving. Lance grabbed a box of shells and dropped them on the bed beside him and handed him another rifle. Then he went back and made a round of the loopholes. He fired from one, skipped one, and fired from the next. He made the rounds, hunting for targets, but trying to keep the shots mixed so they would be in doubt.

Wilde was getting up. Kilkenny watched him, letting him go. Suddenly the man wheeled and blasted at the door, and Brigo, lying on his bed, drilled him through the chest!

"One down!" Kilkenny told himself, "an' nine to go!"

He was under no illusions. They could trade shots for a while, and he could fool Wright and the Hale riders for a few hours, perhaps. But they were much too shrewd to be fooled for long. Sooner or later they would guess, and then under cover of an attack from one direction, they would drive from the other, and the whole thing would end in a wicked red-laced blasting inside the Palace.

Kilkenny found a good place near a window where he could watch up the street toward Leathers's store. The dusty street was empty. He waited, and suddenly he saw a man slip around the corner of the store and dart for the door. He fired quickly, twice.

The first shot hit the man about waist high, but on the outside and probably near his holster. He staggered, and Kilkenny fired again and saw the fellow go to one knee. He crawled through the door. The first shot had not been a disabling one, he was sure, but the second, when he aimed at the thigh, had brought the man down.

He got up restlessly and started for the back of the saloon. There was no movement, but when he moved to the door, a bullet clipped the doorjamb right over his head, and had he not been crouched, it would probably have been dead center. No chance to get to the horses then, not by day, anyway. The afternoon wore on, and there were only occasional shots.

They came with a rush finally.

It had been quiet. Then suddenly a volley blasted at the back of the store. Taking a chance, Kilkenny rushed to the front just in time to see a half dozen men charging across the street. He dropped his rifle, whipped out both guns, and leaped into the doorway.

His first shot was dead center, a bullet fired from the hip that hit the Hale man and knocked him rolling. His guns roaring and blasting, he smelled the acrid smell of gunpowder, felt a red-hot whip laid across his cheek, and knew he'd been grazed. Then he blasted again, felt a gun go empty, and still triggering the first gun, jerked out his belt gun and opened up again.

They fell back, and he saw two men were down. He knew neither of them. His cheekbone was burning like fire and he lifted a hand. It came away bloody. He sopped the wound with his handkerchief and then dropped it and began reloading his guns. This time he brought the shotgun up to the door and stuffed his pockets with shotgun shells. The waiting was what got a man. He didn't want to wait. He wanted to go out there.

There was no firing now. The attacking party was down to seven, and one of those was wounded. They would hesitate a little now. And he still had the shotgun. That was his payoff weapon. He knew what it would do to a man and hated to use it. At close range a shotgun wouldn't just make a wound. It would blast a man in two.

He showed himself at a window and got no action. He could hear loud voices in the Leathers store. There was some kind of an argument. After all, what had they to gain? Suddenly, Kilkenny had an idea. He wheeled and went into the bedroom. Brigo was lying on the bed, breathing hoarsely. He looked terrible.

"Lie still an' watch," Kilkenny said. "I'm goin' out."

"Out?" Brigo's eyes fired. "You after them?"

"Sí. With this." He touched the shotgun. "They are all in Leathers's store. I'm goin' to settle this once an' for all."

He went to the door. For a long time he studied the terrain. He was worried. Price Dixon should be here by now. The Hale men probably knew he had joined Kilkenny and the Hatfields, so if he came back they would shoot him. And if Jaime Brigo was to live he would need Dixon's attention.

Kilkenny waited. The sun was making a shadow under the awning, even if not much of a one. He eased outside, listening to the loud voices, and then he left the porch with a rush.

There was no shot. He got to the side of Leathers's store. From here it was four good steps to the door, and there was no window to pass. He stepped up on the porch, knowing that if they had a man across the street he was a gone gosling.

He took another step and waited. Inside, the voices continued, and he could hear Lee Wright's voice above all the others. "Cub'll pay off, all right. If he don't, we can always take some cows ourselves!"

"Blazes!" somebody said disgustedly. "I don't want any cows! I want money! An'," he added, "I want out of this with a whole skin!"

"Personally," a voice drawled, "I don't see no percentage in gettin' a hide full of lead because some other hombre wants a woman. I'll admit that Riordan gal is somethin' to look at, but I think if she wanted to have a Hale, she'd take one. I think the gal's crazy for this Kilkenny, an' for my money she's got the best of the lot."

"What's it to you, Tandy?" Wright demanded. "Hale's got the money. He pays us. Besides, that Kilkenny figgers he's too durned good."

Tandy laughed. "Why, Lee, I reckon if you'd go out there an' tell him you wanted a shootout, he'd give it to you."

"Say!" Wright jumped to his feet. "That's it! That's the way we'll get him. I'll go out and challenge him. Then when he comes out, pour it into him."

There was a moment of silence, but Kilkenny was just outside the screened door now. "Lee, that sure is a polecat's idea. You know durned well I wouldn't have no part of that. I'm a fightin' man, not a murderer."

"Tandy Wade, someday you'll—!" Wright began, angrily.

"Suppose," Kilkenny said, "that I take over from here?"

Wright froze, his mouth open, his face slowly turning white. Only Tandy turned, and he turned very slowly, keeping his hands wide. He looked at the double-barrelled shotgun for just an instant.

"Well, Kilkenny," he said softly, "I reckon that shotgun calls my hand."

"Shotgun?" Wright gasped. Kilkenny let him turn. He knew how ugly a double-barrelled shotgun can seem when seen at close quarters.

"Buckshot in it, too," Kilkenny said lazily. "I might not be able to get more'n four or five of you hombres. Might be even one or two, but I'm sure goin' to get them good. Who wants a hot taste of buckshot?"

Wright backed up, licking his lips. He didn't want any trouble now. You could see it in his eyes that he knew that shotgun was meant for him, and he didn't want any part of it.

"Leathers!" Kilkenny's voice cracked like a whiplash. "Come around here and get their guns. Slap their shirts, too. I don't want any sneak guns."

The storekeeper, his face dead white, came around and began lifting the guns, and no one said a word. When the guns were collected and all laid at Kilkenny's feet, he stood there for a moment looking at the men.

"Wright, you wanted to trick me an' kill me. Didn't you?"

Lee Wright's eyes were wide and dark in the sickly moon of his face. "I talked too much," he said, tight-lipped, "I wouldn't of had nerve enough for that."

"Well—"

There was a sudden rattle of horses' hoofs in the street, and Kilkenny saw Lee Wright's eyes brighten, but as he looked at Kilkenny his face went sick.

"Careful, Lee!" Kilkenny said quietly. "Don't get uneasy. If I go, you go with me."

"I ain't movin'," Wright said hoarsely. "For heaven's sake, don't shoot!"

# Chapter XX
## *The Last Menace*

Now the horses were walking. They stopped before the Crystal Palace. Kilkenny dared not turn. He dared not look. Putting a toe behind the stack of guns, he pushed them back. Then, still keeping his eyes on the men, he dragged them back further. Then he waited.

Sweat came out on his forehead, and he felt his mouth go dry.

They could slip up and come in. They could just walk up. And he dared not turn, or one of these men would leap and have a gun. His only way out was to go out fighting.

Looking at the men before him, he could see what was in their minds. Their faces were gray and sick. A shotgun wasn't an easy way to die, and once that gun started blasting, there was no telling who would get it. And Kilkenny, with an empty shotgun, was still closer to the guns on the floor than they were.

The flesh seemed to crawl on the back of Kilkenny's neck, and he saw Wright's tongue feeling his dry lips. Only Tandy Wade seemed relaxed. The tension was only in his eyes. Any moment now might turn this room into a bloody bit of hell. The shotgun was going to—

A door slammed at the Crystal Palace.

Had Brigo passed out? There was no sound, but Kilkenny knew someone was crossing the dusty space between the buildings. He was drawing closer now. The sound of a foot on the boardwalk made them all jump. Suddenly Leathers slipped to the floor in a dead faint. Tandy looked down, amusedly, and then lifted his eyes as a board creaked.

Any moment now. When that door opened, if a friendly voice didn't speak—

The door creaked just a little. That was only when it opened wide. Kilkenny remembered that door. He had eased through a crack himself. He lifted the shotgun slightly, his own face gray.

Suddenly he knew that if this was Cub Hale he would turn this store into a shambles. He, Kilkenny, was going to go out taking a bloody dozen with him. He had these guns, and if the first shot didn't get him he wasn't going alone. He clicked back the hammers.

"No!" He didn't know who spoke. "No, Kilkenny! My God, no!"

These men who could stand a shootout with perfect composure were frightened and pale at the gaping muzzles of the shotgun.

"Kilkenny?" The voice was behind him, and it was Parson Hatfield.

"Yeah, Parson. I got me a few restless hombres here."

Hatfield came in, and behind him were Bartram and Steve Runyon. "Where's Cub?" Parson demanded sharply.

"He cut off for the ranch. He figured Dunn would have the girl there."

"We didn't find him," Parson said. "He must've stopped off on the way. Hale shot hisself."

"He did?" Kilkenny turned. "What happened at the place?"

"She was plumb deserted," Runyon offered. "Not a soul around. Looks as if they all deserted like rats from a sinkin' ship. He was all alone, an' when he seen us comin', he shot hisself."

"What happened then?" Kilkenny asked.

"We set fire to the place. Too big for any honest rancher. It's burnin' now."

"What happens to us?" Tandy demanded.

Kilkenny looked at them for a minute, but before he could speak, Parson spoke up. "We want Jeff Nebel an' Lee Wright. They done murdered Miller, Wilson, an' Lije. They got Smithers, too. Jeff Nebel killed him. An' they was in on the killin' of Dick Moffitt. We got a rope for 'em!"

"Take them, then," Kilkenny said. He looked at Tandy Wade. "You're too good a man to run with this owlhoot crowd, Wade. You better change your ways before they get a rope on you. Get goin'!"

Wade looked at him. "Thanks, man," he said. "It's more'n I deserve."

"You," Kilkenny said to the others, "ride! If you ever come into this country again we'll hang you."

They scrambled for the door. The Hatfields were already gone with Wright and Nebel. Kilkenny turned away and looked at Leathers, who had recovered from his faint. "You got twenty-four hours," he said quietly. "Take what you can an' get out of here. Don't come back."

He walked out of the store into the dusty street. A man was coming down the street on a rangy sorrel horse. He looked and then looked again. It was Dan Cooper. A short distance behind him, another man rounded the corner. It was Cain Brockman. They rode straight on until they came up to Kilkenny.

Cooper reined in and began to roll a smoke. "Looks like I backed the wrong horse," he said slowly. "What's the deal? Got a rope for me? Or do I draw a ticket out of here?"

"What do you want?" Kilkenny demanded sharply. He had his thumbs in his belt, watching the two men.

"Well," Dan said, looking up at Kilkenny, "we talked it over. We both won money on your fight, an' we sort've had an idea we'd like to join you all an' take up some claims ourselves."

"Right pretty places up in them meadows," Cain suggested. He sat his horse, looking at Kilkenny.

For a long minute Kilkenny looked from one to the other. "Sure," he said finally. "You might find a good place up near mine, Cain. And the Moffitt place is empty now."

He turned and walked back to the Palace. He had forgotten Brigo. Yet when he entered the place, his worry left him. Price Dixon had come, and Nita had returned with him. She met Kilkenny at the door.

"He's asleep," she whispered. "Dixon got the bullet out, and he's going to be all right."

"Good." Kilkenny looked at the girl, and then he took her in his arms. He drew her close and her lips melted into his, and for a long time they stood there holding each other.

"Oh, Lance," she whispered, "don't let me go. Keep me now. It's been so long, and I've been so lonely."

"Sure," he said quietly, "I'll keep you now. I don't want to let you go—ever!"

Slowly, in the days that followed, the town came back to itself. Widows of two of the nesters moved into the Leathers's house and took over the store. Kilkenny and Bartram helped them get things arranged and get started. The ruins of the Mecca were cleared away. Van Hawkins, a former actor from San Francisco, came in and bought the Crystal Palace from Nita. Kilkenny started to build a bigger, more comfortable house on the site of the old one that the Hales had burned for him.

Yet, over it all, there was restlessness and uneasiness. Kilkenny talked much with Nita in the evenings and saw the dark circles under her eyes. She was sleeping little, he knew.

The Hatfields carried their guns all the time, and Steve Runyon came and went with a pistol strapped on. It was because of Cub Hale. No one ever mentioned his name, yet his shadow lay over them all. He had vanished mysteriously, leaving no trace, nothing to tell them of where he had gone, what he planned to do, or when he would return.

Then one day Saul Hatfield rode up to Kilkenny's claim. He leaned on the saddle horn and looked down at Lance.

"How's things?" he asked. "Seems you're doin' right well with the house."

"Yeah," Kilkenny admitted. "It's goin' up." He looked up at Saul. "How's your dad?"

"Right pert."

"Jesse goin' to dig those potatoes of Smithers's?"

"I reckon."

"He'd like it. He was a savin' man." Kilkenny straightened and their eyes met. "What's on your mind, Saul?"

"I was ridin' this mornin', down on the branch," Saul said thoughtfully. "Seen some tracks where a horse crossed the stream. I was right curious. I followed him a ways. Found some white hairs on the brush."

Cub Hale always rode a white horse. An albino, it was.

"I see." Kilkenny rubbed his jaw. "Which way was he headin'?"

"Sort of circlin'. Sizin' up the town, like."

Kilkenny nodded. "I reckon I better go down to Cedar," he said thoughtfully. "I want to stick around town awhile."

"Sure." Saul looked at him. "A body could follow them tracks," he suggested. "It was a plain trail."

"Dangerous. He's a bad one. Maybe later. We'll see."

Kilkenny mounted the long-legged yellow horse and headed for town. Cub Hale was mean. He wasn't going to leave. It wasn't in him to leave. He was a man who had to kill, even if he died in the process. Kilkenny had known that. He knew that some of the men believed Cub had lit out and left the country. He had never believed that. Cub was prowling, licking his wounds, waiting. And the hate in him was building up.

Kilkenny rode the yellow buckskin to the little cottage where Nita Riordan and Sally Crane were living together while Sally prepared for her wedding with Bartram. Nita came to the door, her sewing in her hand.

"Lance," she said quickly, "is it—?"

"He's close by." He swung down from the horse. "I reckon you've got a guest for dinner."

Sitting by the window with a book, he glanced occasionally down the street. He saw two Hatfields ride in—Quince and Saul. They dismounted at the store, and then Steve Runyon rode in and, after him, Cain Brockman.

Brockman rode right on to the Palace, dismounted, and went in for a drink. Then he came out and loafed on a bench by the door. He was wearing two guns.

The room was bright and cheery, with curtains at the windows and china plates. Nita came in, drying her hands on an apron, and called him to lunch. He took a last look down the street and then got up and walked in to the table. Sally's face was flushed and she looked very pretty, yet he had eyes only for Nita.

He had never seen her so lovely as now. Her face looked softer and prettier than he had ever seen it. She was happy, too, radiantly happy. Even the news of the nearness of Cub Hale had not been able to wipe it from her face.

Bartram came in and joined them. He grinned at Kilkenny. "Not often a man gets a chance to try his wife's cooking as much as I have before he marries her!" he chuckled. "I'll say this for her, she can sure make biscuits!"

"I didn't make them!" Sally protested. "Nita did!"

"Nita?" Kilkenny looked up, smiling. "I didn't know you could cook!"

There was a low call from the door. "Kilkenny?" It was Cain Brockman. "He's comin'. Shall I take him?"

"No." Kilkenny touched his mouth with a napkin and drew back from the table. "It's my job."

His eyes met Nita's across the table. "Don't pour my coffee," he said quietly. "I like it hot."

He turned and walked to the door. Far down the street he could see Cub Hale. He was on foot, and his hat was gone, his yellow hair blowing in the wind. He was walking straight up the center of the street, looking straight ahead.

Kilkenny stepped down off the porch. The roses were blooming, and their scent was strong in his nostrils. He could smell the rich odor of fresh earth in the sunlight, and somewhere a magpie shrieked. He opened the gate and stepping out, closed it carefully behind him. Then he began to walk.

He took his time. There was no hurry. There was never any hurry at a time like this. Everything always seemed to move by slow motion, until suddenly it was over and you wondered how it all could have happened. Saul Hatfield was standing on the steps, his rifle in the hollow of his arm. He and Quince were just there in case he failed.

Failed? Kilkenny smiled. He had never failed. Yet, they all failed soon or late. There was always a time when they were too slow, when their guns hung or missed fire. The dust smelled hot, and in the distance thunder rumbled. Then a few scattered drops fell. Odd, he hadn't even been aware it was clouding up.

Little puffs of dust lifted from his boots when he walked. He could see Cub more clearly now. He was unshaven, and his face was scratched by brush. His fancy buckskin jacket was gone. Only the guns were the same, and the white eyes, eyes that seemed to burn.

Suddenly, Hale stopped, and when he stopped, Kilkenny stopped too. He stood there perfectly relaxed, waiting. Cub's face was white, dead. Only his eyes seemed alive, and that burning white light was in them.

"I'm goin' to kill you!" he said, his voice sharp and strained.

It was all wrong. Kilkenny felt no tension, no alertness. He was just standing there, and in him suddenly there welled up a tremendous feeling of pity. Why couldn't they ever learn? There was nothing in a gun but death.

Something flickered in those white, blazing eyes, and Kilkenny, standing perfectly erect, slapped the butt of his gun with his palm. The gun leaped up, settled into a rocklike grip, and then bucked in his hand, once, twice.

The gun before him flowered with flame, and something stabbed, white hot, low down on his right side. The gun flowered again, but the stabbing flame wasted itself in the dust and Cub's knees buckled and there was a spot of blood on his chest, right over the heart.

He fell face down and then straightened his legs, and there was silence in the long dusty street of Cedar Bluff.

Kilkenny thumbed shells into his gun, holstered it, and then turned. Steadily, quietly, looking straight ahead, he walked back up the hill toward the cottage. It was just a little hill, but it suddenly seemed steep. He walked on, and then he could see Nita opening the gate and running toward him.

He stopped then and waited. There was a burning in his side, and he felt something wet against his leg. He looked down, puzzled, and when he looked, he fell, flat on his face in the dust.

Then Nita was turning him over, and her face was white. He tried to sit up, but they pushed him down. Cain Brockman came over, and with Saul Hatfield they carried him up the hill. It was only a few steps, and it had seemed so far.

He was still conscious when Price Dixon came in.

Dixon made a brief examination and then shrugged.

"He's all right. The bullet went into his side, slid off a rib, and narrowly missed his spine. But it's nothing that we can't fix up. Shock, mostly—and bleeding."

Later, Nita came in. She looked at him and smiled. "Shall I put the coffee on now?" she asked lightly. Her eyes were large and dark.

"Let Sally put it on," he said gently. "You stay here."

# AUTHOR'S NOTE
## The Trail to Peach Meadow Canyon

*Peach trees have been found growing in several of the canyons branching off from the Grand Canyon; they were probably planted by somebody at some time in the past. I ventured into a box canyon in Arizona at one time, a place enclosed by high cliffs with some sixty acres of fairly level ground in the bottom, a good stand of grass, and about three dozen peach and apricot trees, all old and in bad need of pruning. There was also a half dugout built of logs against the side of a low mound, and a stream about two feet wide running diagonally across the bottom of the canyon.*

*Somebody had enjoyed a small corner of paradise here, probably for many years. There was an old corral, and my suspicion was that he had kept burros rather than horses.*

*Not far from Mooney Falls in the Grand Canyon, there are iron ladders spiked to the walls to enable one to climb further down.*

# THE TRAIL TO PEACH MEADOW CANYON

## I

**W**inter snows were melting in the forests of the Kaibab, and the red-and-orange hue of the thousand-foot Vermilion Cliffs was streaked with the dampness of melting frost. Deer were feeding in the forest glades among the stands of ponderosa and fir, and the trout were leaping in the streams. Where sunlight trailed through the webbed overhang of the leaves, the water danced and sparkled.

Five deer were feeding on the grass along a mountain stream back of Finger Butte, their coats mottled by the light and shadow of the sun shining through the trees.

A vague something moved in the woods behind them, and the five-pronged buck lifted his regal head and stared curiously about. He turned his nose into the wind, reading it cautiously. But his trust was betrayal, for the movement was downwind of him.

The movement came again, and a young man stepped from concealment behind a huge fir not twenty feet from the nearest deer. He was straight and tall in gray, fringed buckskins, and he wore no hat. His hair was thick, black, and wavy, growing full over the temples, and his face was lean and brown. Smiling, he walked toward the deer with quick, lithe strides, and had taken three full steps before some tiny sound betrayed him.

The buck's head came up and swung around, and then with a startled snort it sprang away, the others following.

Mike Bastian stood grinning, his hands on his hips.

"Well, what do you think now, Roundy?" he called. "Could your Apache beat that? I could have touched him if I had jumped after him!"

Rance Roundy came out of the trees—a lean, wiry old man with a gray mustache and blue eyes that were still bright with an alert awareness.

291

"No, I'll be darned if any Apache ever lived as could beat that!" he chortled. "Not a mite of it! An' I never seen the day I could beat it, either. You're a caution, Mike, you sure are. I'm glad you're not sneakin' up after *my* hair!" He drew his pipe from his pocket and started stoking it with tobacco. "We're goin' back to Toadstool Canyon, Mike. Your dad sent for us."

Bastian looked up quickly. "Is there trouble, is that it?"

"No, only he wants to talk with you. Maybe"—Roundy was cautious—"he figures it's time you went out on a job. On one of those rides."

"I think that's it," Mike nodded. "He said in the spring, and it's about time for the first ride. I wonder where they'll go this time."

"No tellin'. The deal will be well planned, though. That dad of yours would have made a fine general, Mike. He's got the head for it, he sure has. Never forgets a thing, that one."

"You've been with him a long time, haven't you?"

"Sure—since before he found you. I knowed him in Mexico in the war, and that was longer ago than I like to think. I was a boy then, my own self.

"Son," Roundy said suddenly, "look!"

He tossed a huge pinecone into the air, a big one at least nine inches long.

With a flash of movement, Mike Bastian palmed his gun, and almost as soon as it hit his hand it belched flame—and again. The second shot spattered the cone into a bunch of flying brown chips.

"Not bad!" Roundy nodded. "You still shoot too quick, though. You got to get over that, Mike. Sometimes, one shot is all you'll ever get."

Side by side the two walked through the trees, the earth spongy with a thick blanket of pine needles. Roundy was not as tall as Mike, but he walked with the long, springy stride of the woodsman. He smoked in silence for some distance, and then he spoke up.

"Mike, if Ben's ready for you to go out, what will you do?"

For two steps, Bastian said nothing. Then he spoke slowly. "Why, go, I guess. What else?"

"You're sure? You're sure you want to be an outlaw?"

"That's what I was raised for, isn't it?" There was some bitterness in Mike's voice. "Somebody to take over what Ben Curry started?"

"Yeah, that's what you were raised for, all right. But this you want to remember, Mike, it's your life. Ben Curry, for all his power, can't live it for you. Moreover, times have changed since Ben and me rode into this country. It ain't free and wild like it was, because folks are comin' in, settlin' it up, makin' homes. Gettin' away won't be so easy, and your pards will change, too. In fact, they have already changed.

"When Ben and me come into this country," Roundy continued, "it was every man for himself. More than one harum-scarum fella, who was otherwise all right, got himself the name of an outlaw. Nobody figured much about it, then. We rustled cows, but so did half the big ranchers of the West. And if a cowpoke got hard up and stopped a stage, nobody made much fuss unless he killed somebody. They figured it was just high spirits. But the last few years, it ain't like that no more. And it ain't only that the country is growin' up—it's partly Ben Curry himself."

"You mean he's grown too big?" Mike put in.

"What else? Why, your dad controls more land than there is in New York State! Got it right under his thumb! And he's feared over half the West by those who know about him, although not many do.

"Outside of this country around us, nobody ain't seen Ben Curry in years, not leastwise to know him. But they've heard his name, and they know that somewhere an outlaw lives who rules a gang of almost a thousand men. That he robs and rustles where he will, and nobody has nerve enough to chase him.

"He's been smart, just plenty smart," old Roundy went on. "Men ride out and they meet at a given point. The whole job is planned in every detail; it's rehearsed, and then they pull it and scatter and meet again here. For a long time folks laid it to driftin' cowpunchers or to gangs passin' through. The way he's set up, one of the gangs he sends out might pull somethin' anywhere from San Antone to Los Angeles, or from Canada to Mexico, although usually he handles it close around.

"He's been the brains, all right, but don't ever forget it was those guns of his that kept things in line. Lately, he hasn't used his guns. Kerb Perrin and Rigger Molina or some of their boys handle the discipline. He's become too big, Ben Curry has. He's like a king, and the king isn't getting any younger. How do you suppose Perrin will take it when he hears about you takin' over? You think he'll like it?"

"I don't imagine he will," Mike replied thoughtfully. "He's probably done some figuring of his own."

"You bet he has! So has Molina, and neither of them will stop short of murder to get what they want. Your dad still has them buffaloed, I think, but that isn't going to matter when the showdown comes. And I think it's here!"

"You do?" Mike said, surprise in his voice.

"Yeah, I sure do!" Roundy hesitated. "You know, Mike, I never told you this, but Ben Curry has a family."

"A family?" Despite himself, Mike Bastian was startled.

"Yes, he has a wife and two daughters, and they don't have any idea he's an outlaw. They live down near Tucson somewhere. Occasionally, they come to a ranch he owns in Red Wall Canyon, a ranch supposedly owned by Voyle Ragan. He visits them there."

"Does anybody else know this?"

"Not a soul. And don't you be tellin' anybody. You see, Ben always wanted a son, and he never had one. When your real dad was killed down in Mesilla, he took you along with him, and later he told me he was going to raise you to take over whatever he left. That was a long time ago, and since then he's spent a sight of time and money on you.

"You can track like an Apache," Roundy said, looking at the tall lad beside him. "In the woods you're a ghost, and I doubt if old Ben Curry himself can throw a gun any faster than you. I'd say you could ride anything that wore hair, and what you don't know about cards, dice, and roulette wheels ain't in it. You can handle a knife and fight with your fists, and you can open anything a man ever made in the way of safes and locks. Along with that, you've had a good education, and you could take care of yourself in any company. I don't reckon there ever was a boy had the kind of education you got, and I think Ben's ready to retire."

"You mean, to join his wife and daughters?" Mike questioned.

"That's it. He's gettin' no younger, and he wants it easy-like for the last years. He was always scared of only one thing, and he had a lot of it as a youngster. That's poverty. Well, he's made his pile and now he wants to step out. Still and all, he knows he can't get out alive unless he leaves somebody behind him that's strong enough and smart enough to keep things under control. That's where you come in."

"Why don't he let Perrin have it?"

"Mike, you know Perrin. He's dangerous, that one. He's poison mean and power crazy. He'd have gone off the deep end a long time ago if it wasn't for Ben Curry. And Rigger Molina is kill crazy. He would have killed fifty men if it hadn't been that he knew Ben Curry would kill him when he got back. No, neither of them could handle this outfit. The whole shebang would go to pieces in ninety days if they had it."

Mike Bastian walked along in silence. There was little that was new in what Roundy was saying, but he was faintly curious as to the old man's purpose. The pair had been much together, and they knew each other as few men ever did. They had gone through storm and hunger and thirst together, living in the desert, mountains, and forest, only rarely returning to the rendezvous in Toadstool Canyon.

Roundy had a purpose in his talking, and Bastian waited, listening. Yet even as he walked he was conscious of everything that went on around him. A quail had moved back into the tall grass near the stream, and there was a squirrel up ahead in the crotch of a tree. Not far back a gray wolf had crossed the path only minutes ahead of them.

It was as Roundy had said. Mike was a woodsman, and the thought of taking over the outlaw band filled him with unease. Always, he had been aware this time would come, that he had been schooled for it. But before, it had seemed remote and far off. Now, suddenly, it was at hand, it was facing him.

"Mike," Roundy went on, "the country is growin' up. Last spring some of our raids raised merry hell, and some of the boys had a bad time gettin' away. When they start again, there will be trouble and lots of it. Another thing, folks don't look at an outlaw like they used to. He isn't just a wild young cowhand full of liquor, nor a fellow who needs a poke, nor somebody buildin' a spread of his own. Now, he'll be like a wolf, with every man huntin' him. Before you decide to go into this, you think it over, make up your own mind.

"You know Ben Curry, and I know you like him. Well, you should! Nevertheless, Ben had no right to raise you for an outlaw. He went his way of his own free will, and if he saw it that way, that was his own doin'. But no man has a right to say to another, 'This you must do; this you must be.' No man has a right to train another, startin' before he has a chance to make up his mind, and school him in any particular way."

The old man stopped to relight his pipe, and Mike kept a silence, would let Roundy talk out what seemed to bother him.

"I think every man should have the right to decide his own destiny, insofar as he can," Roundy said, continuing his trend of thought. "That goes for you, Mike, and you've got the decision ahead of you. I don't know which you'll do. But if you decide to step out of this gang, then I don't relish bein' around when it happens, for old Ben will be fit to be tied.

"Right now, you're an honest man. You're clean as a whistle. Once you become an outlaw, a lot of things will change. You'll have to kill, too—don't forget that. It's one thing to kill in defense of your home, your family, or your country. It's another thing when you kill for money or for power."

"You think I'd have to kill Perrin and Molina?" Mike Bastian asked.

"If they didn't get you first!" Roundy spat. "Don't forget this, Mike, you're fast. You're one of the finest and, aside from Ben Curry, probably the finest shot I ever saw. But that ain't shootin' at a man who's shootin' at you. There's a powerful lot of difference, as you'll see!

"Take Billy the Kid, this Lincoln County gunman we hear about. Frank and George Coe, Dick Brewer, Jesse Evans—any one of them can shoot as good as him. The difference is that the part down inside

of him where the nerves should be was left out. When he starts
shootin' and when he's bein' shot at, he's like ice! Kerb Perrin's that
way, too. Perrin's the cold type, steady as a rock. Rigger Molina's
another kind of cat—he explodes all over the place. He's white-hot,
but he's deadly as a rattler."

Mike was listening intently as Roundy continued his description:

"Five of them cornered him one time at a stage station out of
Julesburg. When the shootin' was over, four of them were down and
the fifth was holdin' a gun-shot arm. Molina, he rode off under his
own power. He's a shaggy wolf, that one! Wild and uncurried and
big as a bear!"

Far more than Roundy realized did Mike Bastian know the facts
about Ben Curry's empire of crime. For three years now, Curry had
been leading his foster son through all the intricate maze of his
planning. There were spies and agents in nearly every town in the
Southwest, and small groups of outlaws quartered here and there on
ranches who could be called upon for help at a moment's notice.

Also, there were ranches where fresh horses could be had, and
changes of clothing, and where the horses the band had ridden could
be lost. At Toadstool Canyon were less than two hundred of the total
number of outlaws, and many of those, while living under Curry's
protection, were not of his band.

Also, the point Roundy raised had been in Mike's mind, festering
there, an abscess of doubt and dismay. The Ben Curry he knew was
a huge, kindly man, even if grim and forbidding at times. He had
taken the homeless boy and given him kindness and care, had,
indeed, trained him as a son. Today, however, was the first inkling
Mike had of the existence of that other family. Ben Curry had
planned and acted with shrewdness and care.

Mike Bastian had a decision to make, a decision that would change
his entire life, whether for better or worse.

Here in the country around the Vermilion Cliffs was the only
world he knew. Beyond it? Well, he supposed he could punch cows.
He was trained to do many things, and probably there were jobs
awaiting such a man as himself.

He could become a gambler, but he had seen and known a good
many gamblers and did not relish the idea. Somewhere beyond this
wilderness was a larger, newer, wealthier land—a land where honest
men lived and reared their families.

## II

In the massive stone house at the head of Toadstool Canyon, so called because of the gigantic toadstool-like stone near the entrance, Ben Curry leaned his great weight back in his chair and stared broodingly out the door over the valley below.

His big face was blunt and unlined as rock, but the shock of hair above his leonine face was turning to gray. He was growing old. Even spring did not bring the old fire to his veins again, and it had been long since he had ridden out on one of the jobs he planned so shrewdly. It was time he quit.

Yet this man who had made decisions sharply and quickly was for the first time in his life, uncertain. For six years he had ruled supreme in this remote corner north of the Colorado. For twenty years he had been an outlaw, and for fifteen of those twenty years he had ruled a gang that had grown and extended its ramifications until it was an empire in itself.

Six years ago he had moved to this remote country and created the stronghold where he now lived. Across the southern limit rolled the Colorado River, with its long canyons and maze of rocky wilderness, a bar to any pursuit from the country south of the river, where he operated.

As far as other men were concerned, only at Lee's Ferry was there a crossing, and in a cabin nearby, his men watched it night and day. In fact there were two more crossings—one that the gang used in going to and from their raids, and the other known only to himself. It was his ace in the hole, even if not his only one.

One law of the gang, never transgressed, was that there was to be no lawless activity in the Mormon country to the north of them. The Mormons and the Indians were left strictly alone and were their friends. So were the few ranchers who lived in the area. These few traded at the stores run by the gang, buying their supplies closer to home and at cheaper prices than they could have managed elsewhere.

Ben Curry had never quite made up his mind about Kerb Perrin. He knew that Perrin was growing restive, that he was aware that Curry was aging and was eager for the power of leadership. Yet the one factor Curry couldn't be certain about was whether Perrin would stand for the taking over of the band by Mike Bastian.

Well, Mike had been well trained; it would be his problem. Ben smiled grimly. He was the old bull of the herd, and Perrin was pawing the dirt, but what would he say when a young bull stepped in? One who had not won his spurs with the gang?

That was why Curry had sent for him, for it was time Mike be groomed for leadership, time he moved out on his first job. And he

had just the one. It was big, it was sudden, and it was dramatic. It
would have an excellent effect on the gang if it was brought off
smoothly, and he was going to let Mike plan the whole job himself.

There was a sharp knock outside, and Curry smiled a little, recog-
nizing it.

"Come in!" he bellowed.

He watched Perrin stride into the room with his quick, nervous
steps, his eyes scanning the room.

"Chief," Perrin said, "the boys are gettin' restless. It's spring, you
know, and most of them are broke. Have you got anything in mind?"

"Sure, several things. But one that's good and tough! Struck me it
might be a good one to break the kid in on."

"Oh?" Perrin's eyes veiled. "You mean he'll go along?"

"No, I'm going to let him run it. The whole show. It will be good
for him."

Kerb Perrin absorbed that. For the first time, he felt worry. For
the first time, an element of doubt entered his mind. He had
wondered before about Bastian and what his part would be in all
this.

For years, Perrin had looked forward to the time when he could
take over. He knew there would be trouble with Rigger Molina, but
he had thought that phase of it out. He knew he could handle it. But
what if Curry was planning to jump young Bastian into leadership?

Quick, hot passion surged through Perrin, and when he looked
up, it was all he could do to keep his voice calm.

"You think that's wise?" he questioned. "How will the boys feel
about goin' out with a green kid?"

"He knows what to do," Curry said. "They'll find he's smart as any
of them, and he knows plenty. This is a big job, and a tough one."

"Who goes with him?"

"Maybe I'll let him pick them," Curry said thoughtfully. "Good
practice for him."

"What's the job?" Perrin asked, voice sullen.

"The gold train!"

Perrin's fingers tightened, digging into his palms. This was the job
*he* wanted! The shipment from the mines! It would be enormous,
rich beyond anything they had done!

Months before, in talking of this job, he had laid out his plan for it
before Curry. But it had been vetoed. He had recommended the
killing of every man jack of them, and burial of them all, so the train
would vanish completely.

"You sound like Molina," Curry had said, chuckling. "Too bloody!"

"Dead men don't talk!" he had replied grimly.

"That will be tough for the kid," Perrin said now, slowly. "Mighty tough!"

Yet, even as he spoke he was thinking of something else. He was thinking of the effect of this upon the men of the outfit. He knew many of them liked Mike Bastian, and more than one of them had helped train him. In a way, many of the older men were as proud of Mike as if he had been their own son. If he stepped out now and brought off this job, he would acquire power and prestige in the gang equal to Perrin's own.

Fury engulfed Perrin. Curry had no right to do this to him! Sidetracking him for an untried kid. Shoving Bastian down all their throats!

Suddenly, the rage died, and in its place came resolution. It was time he acted on his own. He would swing his own job, the one he had had in mind for so long, and that would counteract the effect of the gold-train steal. Moreover, he would be throwing the challenge into Ben Curry's teeth, for he would plan this job without consulting him. If there was going to be a struggle for leadership, it could begin here and now.

"He'll handle the job all right," Curry said confidently. "He has been trained, and he has the mind for it. He plans well. I hadn't spoken of it before, but I asked his advice on a few things without letting him know why, and he always came through with the right answers."

Kerb Perrin left the stone house filled with burning resentment but also something of triumph. At last, after years of taking orders, he was going on his own. Yet the still, small voice of fear was in him, too. What would Ben Curry do?

The thought made him quail. He had seen the cold fury of Curry when it was aroused, and he had seen him use a gun. He himself was fast, but was he as fast as Ben Curry? In his heart, he doubted it. He dismissed the thought, although storing it in his mind. Something would have to be done about Ben Curry. . . .

Mike Bastian stood before Ben Curry's table, and the two men stared at each other.

Ben Curry, the old outlaw chief, was huge, bearlike, and mighty, his eyes fierce yet glowing with a kindly light now, and something of pride, too. Facing him, tall and lithe, his shoulders broad and mighty, was Mike Bastian, child of the frontier, grown to manhood and trained in every art of the wilds, every dishonest practice in the books, every skill with weapons. Yet educated, too, a man who could conduct himself well in any company.

"You take four men and look over the ground yourself, Mike," Ben Curry was saying. "I want you to plan this one. The gold train leaves the mines on the twentieth. There will be five wagons, the gold distributed among them, although there won't be a lot of it as far as quantity is concerned. That gold train will be worth roughly five hundred thousand dollars.

"When that job is done," he continued, "I'm going to step down and leave you in command. You knew I was planning that. I'm old, and I want to live quietly for a while, and this outfit takes a strong hand to run it. Think you can handle it?"

"I think so," Mike Bastian said softly.

"I think so, too. Watch Perrin—he's the snaky one. Rigger is dangerous, but whatever he does will be out in the open. Not so Perrin. He's a conniver. He never got far with me because I was always one jump ahead of him. And I still am!"

The old man was silent for a few minutes as he stared out the window.

"Mike," he said then, doubt entering his voice, "maybe I've done wrong. I meant to raise you the way I have. I ain't so sure what is right and wrong, and never was. Never gave it much thought, though.

"When I come west it was dog eat dog, and your teeth had to be big. I got knocked down and kicked around some, and then I started taking big bites myself. I organized, and then I got bigger. In all these years nobody has ever touched me. If *you've* got a strong hand, you can do the same. Sometimes you'll have to buy men, sometimes you'll have to frighten them, and sometimes you'll have to kill."

He shook his head as if clearing it of memories past, and then glanced up.

"Who will you take with you?" he asked. "I mean, in scouting this layout."

Ben Curry waited, for it was judgment of men that Bastian would need most. It pleased him that Mike did not hesitate.

"Roundy, Doc Sawyer, Colley, and Garlin."

Curry glanced at him, his eyes hard and curious. "Why?"

"Roundy has an eye for terrain like no man in this world," Mike said. "He says mine's as good, but I'll take him along to verify or correct my judgment. Doc Sawyer is completely honest. If he thinks I'm wrong, he'll say so. As for Colley and Garlin, they are two of the best men in the whole outfit. They will be pleased that I ask their help, which puts them on my side in a measure, and they can see how I work."

Curry nodded. "Smart—and you're right. Colley and Garlin are two of the best men, and absolutely fearless." He smiled a little. "If you have trouble with Perrin or Molina, it won't hurt to have them on your side."

*       *       *

Despite himself, Mike Bastian was excited. He was twenty-two years old and by frontier standards had been a man for several years. But in all that time, aside from a few trips into the Mormon country and one to Salt Lake, he had never been out of the maze of canyons and mountains north of the Colorado.

Roundy led the way, for the trail was an old one to him. They were taking the secret route south used by the gang on their raids, and as they rode toward it, Mike stared at the country. He was always astonished by its ruggedness.

Snow still lay in some of the darker places of the forest, but as they neared the canyon the high cliffs towered even higher and the trail dipped down through a narrow gorge of rock. Countless centuries of erosion had carved the rock into grotesque figures resembling those of men and animals, colored with shades of brown, pink, gray and red, and tapering off into a pale yellow. There were shadowed pools among the rocks, some from snow water and others from natural springs, and there were scattered clumps of oak and piñon.

In the bottom of the gorge the sun did not penetrate except at high noon and there the trail wound along between great jumbled heaps of boulders, cracked and broken from their fall off the higher cliffs.

Mike Bastian followed Roundy, who rode hump shouldered on a ragged, gray horse that seemed as old as he himself but also as surefooted and mountainwise. Mike was wearing a black hat now, but his same buckskins. He had substituted boots for the moccasins he usually wore, although they reposed in his saddlebags, ready at hand.

Behind them rode Doc Sawyer, his lean, saturnine face quiet, his eyes faintly curious and interested as he scanned the massive walls of the canyon. Tubby Colley was short and thick chested, and very confident—a hard-jawed man who had been a first-rate ranch foreman before he shot two men and hit the outlaw trail.

Tex Garlin was tall, rangy, and quiet. He was a Texan, and little else was known of his background, although it was said he could carve a dozen notches on his guns if he had wished.

Suddenly, Roundy turned the gray horse and rode abruptly at the face of the cliff, but when he came close up, the sand and boulders broke and a path showed along the under-scoured rock. Following this for several hundred yards, they found a canyon that cut back into the cliff itself and then turned to head toward the river.

The roar of the Colorado, high with spring freshets, was loud in their ears before they reached it. Finally they came out on a sandy bank littered with driftwood.

Nearby was a small cabin and a plot of garden. The door of the house opened, and a tall old man came out.

"Howdy!" he said. "I been expectin' somebody." His shrewd old eyes glanced from face to face and then hesitated at sight of Mike. "Ain't seen you before," he said pointedly.

"It's all right, Bill," Roundy said. "This is Mike Bastian."

"Ben Curry's boy?" Bill stared. "I heard a sight of you, son. I sure have! Can you shoot like they say?"

Mike flushed. "I don't know what they say," he said, grinning. "But I'll bet a lot of money I can hit the side of that mountain if it holds still."

Garlin stared at him thoughtfully, and Colley smiled a little.

"Don't take no funnin' from him," Roundy said. "That boy can shoot!"

"Let's see some shootin', son," Bill suggested. "I always did like to see a man who could shoot."

Bastian shook his head. "There's no reason for shootin'," he protested. "A man's a fool to shoot unless he's got cause. Ben Curry always told me never to draw a gun unless I meant to use it."

"Go ahead," Colley said. "Show him."

Old Bill pointed. "See that black stick end juttin' up over there? It's about fifty, maybe sixty, paces. Can you hit it?"

"You mean that one?" Mike palmed his gun and fired, and the black stick pulverized.

It was a movement so smooth and practiced that no one of the men even guessed he had intended to shoot. Garlin's jaws stopped their calm chewing, and he stared with his mouth open for as long as it took to draw a breath. Then he glanced at Colley.

"Wonder what Kerb would say to that?" he said, astonished. "This kid can shoot!"

"Yeah," Colley agreed, "but the stick didn't have a gun!"

Old Bill worked the ferry out of a cave under the cliff and freighted them across the swollen river in one hair-raising trip. With the river behind, they wound up through the rocks and started south.

### III

The mining and cow town of Weaver was backed up near a large hill on the banks of a small creek. Colley and Garlin rode into the place at sundown, and an hour later Doc Sawyer and Roundy rode in.

Garlin and Colley were leaning on the bar having a drink, and they ignored the newcomers. Mike Bastian followed not long afterward and walked to the bar alone.

All the others in the saloon were Mexicans, except for three tough-looking white men lounging against the bar nearby. They glanced at Mike and his buckskins, and one of them whispered something to the others, at which they all laughed.

Doc Sawyer was sitting in a poker game, and his eyes lifted. Mike leaned nonchalantly against the bar, avoiding the stares of the three toughs who stood near him. One of them moved over closer.

"Hi, stranger!" he said. "That's a right purty suit you got. Where could I get one like it?"

Garlin looked up and his face stiffened. He nudged Colley. "Look!" Garlin said quickly. "Corbus and Fletcher! An' trouble huntin'! We'd better get into this!"

Colley shook his head. "No. Let's see what the kid does."

Mike looked around, his expression mild. "You want a suit like this?" he inquired of the stranger. His eyes were innocent, but he could see the sort of man he had to deal with. These three were toughs, and dangerous. "Most any Navajo could make one for you."

"Just like that?" Corbus sneered.

He was drinking and in a nagging, quarrelsome mood. Mike looked altogether too neat for his taste.

"Sure! Just like this," Mike agreed. "But I don't know what you'd want with it, though. This suit would be pretty big for you to fill."

"Huh?" Corbus's face flamed. Then his mouth tightened. "You gettin' smart with me, kid?"

"No." Mike Bastian turned, and his voice cracked like a whip in the suddenly silent room. "Neither am I being hurrahed by any lamebrained, liquor-guzzling saddle tramp! You made a remark about my suit, and I answered it. Now, you can have a drink on me, all three of you, and I'm suggesting you drink up." His voice suddenly became soft. "I want you to drink up because I want to be very, very sure we're friends, see?"

Corbus stared at Bastian, a cold hint of danger filtering through the normal stubbornness of his brain. Something told him this was perilous going, yet he was stubborn, too stubborn. He smiled slowly. "Kid," he drawled, "supposin' I don't want to drink with no tenderfoot brat?"

Corbus never saw what happened. His brain warned him as Mike's left hand moved, but he never saw the right. The left stabbed his lips and the right cracked on the angle of his jaw, and he lifted from his feet and hit the floor on his shoulder blades, out cold.

Fletcher and the third tough stared from Corbus to Mike. Bastian was not smiling. "You boys want to drink?" he asked. "Or do we go on from here?"

Fletcher stared at him. "What if a man drawed a gun instead of usin' his fists?" he demanded.

"I'd kill him," Bastian replied quietly.

Fletcher blinked. "I reckon you would," he agreed. He turned and said, "Let's have a drink. That Boot Hill out there's already got twenty graves in it."

Garlin glanced at Colley, his eyebrows lifted. Colley shrugged.

"I wonder what Corbus will do when he gets up?" he said.

Garlin chuckled. "Nothin' today. He won't be feelin' like it!"

Colley nodded. "Reckon you're right, an' I reckon the old man raised him a wildcat! I can hardly wait to see Kerb Perrin's face when we tell him."

"You reckon," Garlin asked, "that what we heard is true? That Ben Curry figures to put this youngster into his place when he steps out?"

"Yep, that's the talk," Colley answered.

"Well, maybe he's got it. We'll sure know before this trip is over."

Noise of the stagecoach rolling down the street drifted into the saloon, and Mike Bastian strolled outside and started toward the stage station. The passengers were getting down to stretch their legs and to eat. Three of them were women.

One of them noticed Mike standing there and walked toward him. She was a pale, pretty girl with large gray eyes.

"How much farther to Red Wall Canyon?" she inquired.

Mike Bastian stiffened. "Why, not far. That is, you'll make it by morning if you stick with the stage. There is a cross-country way if you had you a buckboard, though."

"Could you tell us where we could hire one? My mother is not feeling well."

He stepped down off the boardwalk and headed toward the livery stable with her. As they drew alongside the stage, Mike looked up. An older woman and a girl were standing near the stage, but he was scarcely aware of anything but the girl. Her hair was blondish, but darker than that of the girl who walked beside him, and her eyes, too, were gray. There the resemblance ended, for where this girl beside him was quiet and sweet, the other was vivid.

She looked at him, and their eyes met. He swept off his hat. The girl beside him spoke.

"This is my mother, Mrs. Ragan, and my sister, Drusilla." She looked up at him quickly. "My name is Juliana."

Mike bowed. He had eyes only for Drusilla, who was staring at him.

"I am Mike Bastian," he said.

"He said he could hire us a rig to drive across country to Red Wall Canyon," Juliana explained. "It will be quicker that way."

"Yes," Mike agreed, "much quicker. I'll see what I can do. Just where in Red Wall did you wish to go?"

"To Voyle Ragan's ranch," Drusilla said. "The V Bar."

He had turned away, but he stopped in midstride.

"Did you say . . . Voyle Ragan's?"

"Yes. Is there anything wrong?" Drusilla stared at him. "What's the matter?"

He regained his composure swiftly. "Nothing. Only, I'd heard the name, and"—he smiled—"I sort of wanted to know for sure, so if I came calling."

Juliana laughed. "Why, of course! We'd be glad to see you."

He walked swiftly away. These, then, were Ben Curry's daughters! That older woman would be his wife! He was their foster brother, yet obviously his name had meant nothing to them. Neither, he reflected, would their names have meant anything to him, nor the destination, had it not been for what Roundy had told him only the previous day.

Drusilla, her name was. His heart pounded at the memory of her, and he glanced back through the gathering dusk at the three women standing there by the stage station.

Hiring the rig was a matter of minutes. He liked the look of the driver, a lean man, tall and white-haired. "No danger on that road this time of year," the driver said. "I can have them there in no time by takin' the canyon road."

Drusilla was waiting for him when Mike walked back.

"Did you find one?" she asked, and then listened to his explanation and thanked him.

"Would it be all right with you," Mike said, "if I call at the V Bar?"

She looked at him, her face grave, but a dancing light in her eyes. "Why, my sister invited you, did she not?"

"Yes, but I'd like you to invite me, too."

"I?" She studied him for a minute. "Of course, we'd be glad to see you. My mother likes visitors as well as Julie and I, so won't you ask her, too?"

"I'll take the invitation from you and your sister as being enough." He grinned. "If I ask your mother, I might have to ask your father!"

"Father isn't with us!" she laughed. "We'll see him at Ragan's. He's a rancher somewhere way up north in the wilds. His name is Ben Ragan. Have you heard of him?"

"Seems to me I have," he admitted, "but I wouldn't say for sure."

After they had gone Mike wandered around and stopped in the saloon, after another short talk with a man at the livery stable. Listening and asking an occasional question, he gathered the information he wanted on the gold shipment. Even as he asked the questions, it seemed somehow fantastic that he, of all people, should be planning such a thing.

Never before had he thought of it seriously, but now he did. And it was not only because the thought went against his own grain, but because he was thinking of Drusilla Ragan.

What a girl she was! He sobered suddenly. Yet, for all of that, she was the daughter of an outlaw. Did she know it? From her question, he doubted it very much.

Doc Sawyer cashed in his chips and left the poker game to join Mike at the bar.

"The twentieth, all right," he said softly. "And five of them are going to carry shotguns. There will be twelve guards in all, which looks mighty tough. The big fellow at the poker table is one of the guards, and all of them are picked men."

Staring at his drink, Mike puzzled over his problem. What Roundy had said was of course true. This was a turning point for him. He was still an honest man, yet when he stepped over the boundary it would make a difference. It might make a lot of difference to a girl like Dru Ragan, for instance.

The fact that her father also was an outlaw would make little difference. Listening to Sawyer made him wonder. Why had such a man, brilliant, intelligent, and well educated, ever become a criminal?

Sawyer was a gambler and a very skillful one, yet he was a doctor, too, and a fine surgeon. His education was as good as study and money could make it, and it had been under his guidance that Mike Bastian had studied.

"Doc," he said suddenly, "whatever made you ride a crooked trail?"

Sawyer glanced at him suddenly, a new expression in his eyes. "What do you mean, Mike? Do you have doubts?"

"Doubts? That seems to be all I do have these last few days."

"I wondered about that," Doc said. "You have been so quiet that I never doubted but what you were perfectly willing to go on with Ben Curry's plans for you. It means power and money, Mike—all a man could want. If it is doubt about the future for outlaws that disturbs you, don't let it. From now on it will be political connections and bribes, but with the money you'll have to work with, that should be easy."

"It should be," Mike said slowly. "Only maybe—just maybe—I don't want to."

"Conscience rears its ugly head!" Sawyer smiled ironically. "Can it be that Ben Curry's instructions have fallen on fallow ground? What started this sudden feeling? The approach of a problem? Fear?" Doc had turned toward Mike and was staring at him with aroused interest. "Or," he added, "is there a woman? A girl?"

"Would that be so strange?"

"Strange? But no! I've wondered it hasn't happened before, but then you've lived like a recluse these past years. Who is she?"

"It doesn't matter," Mike answered. "I was thinking of this before I saw her. Wondering what I should do."

"Don't ask me," Sawyer said. "I made a mess of my own life. Partly a woman and partly the desire for what I thought was easy money. Well, there's no such a thing as easy money, but I found that out too late. You make your own decision. What was it Matthew Arnold said? I think you learned the quotation."

" 'No man can save his brother's soul, or pay his brother's debt.' "

"Right! So you save your own and pay your own. There's one thing to remember, Mike. No matter which way you go, there will be killing. If you take over Ben Curry's job, you'll have to kill Perrin and Molina, if you can. And you may have to kill them, and even Ben Curry, if you step out."

"Not Dad," Mike said.

"Don't be sure. It isn't only what he thinks that matters, Mike. No man is a complete ruler or dictator. His name is only the symbol. He is the mouthpiece for the wishes of his followers, and as long as he expresses those wishes, he leads them. When he fails, he falls. Ben Curry is the boss not only because he has power in him, but also because he has organization, because he has made them money, because he has offered them safety. If you left, there would be a chink in the armor. No outlaw ever trusts another outlaw who turns honest, for he always fears betrayal."

Bastian tossed off his drink. "Let's check with Roundy. He's been on the prowl."

Roundy came to them hastily. "We've got to get out of town, quick!" he said. "Ducrow and Fernandez just blew in, and they are drunk and raisin' the devil. Both of them are talkin', too, and if they see us they will spill everything!"

"All right." Mike straightened. "Get our horses. Get theirs, too. We'll take them with us."

Garlin and Colley had come to the bar. Garlin shook his head. "Ducrow's poison mean when he's drunk, and Fernandez sides him in everything," Garlin informed. "When Ducrow gets drunk he always pops off too much! The boss forbade him weeks ago to come down here."

"He's a pal of Perrin's," Colley said, "so he thinks he can get away with it."

"Here they come now!" Roundy exclaimed.

"All right—drift!" Bastian ordered. "Make it quick with the horses."

## IV

Saloon doors slammed open, and the two men came in. One look, and Mike could see there was cause for worry. Tom Ducrow was drunk and ugly, and behind him was Snake Fernandez. They were an unpleasant pair, and they had made their share of trouble in Ben Curry's organization, though always protected by Perrin.

Bastian started forward, but he had scarcely taken a step when Ducrow saw him.

"There he is!" he bellowed loudly. "The pet! The boss's pet!" He stared around at the people in the barroom. "You know who this man is? He's—"

"Ducrow!" Mike snapped. "Shut up and go home. Now!"

"Look who's givin' orders!" Ducrow sneered. "Gettin' big for your britches, ain't you?"

"Your horses will be outside in a minute," Mike said. "Get on them and start back, fast!"

"Suppose," Ducrow sneered, "you make me!"

Mike had been moving toward him, and now with a pantherlike leap he was beside the outlaw and with a quick slash from his pistol barrel, floored him.

With an oath, Snake Fernandez reached for a gun, and Mike had no choice. He shot him in the shoulder. Fernandez staggered, the gun dropping from his fingers. Mouthing curses, he reached for his left-hand gun.

But even as he reached, Garlin—who had stayed behind when the others went for the horses—stepped up behind him. Jerking the gun from the man's holster, he spun him about and shoved him through the door.

Mike pulled the groggy Ducrow to his feet and pushed him outside after Fernandez.

A big man got up hastily from the back of the room. Mike took one quick glimpse at the star on his chest.

"What goes on here?" the sheriff demanded.

"Nothing at all," Mike said affably. "Just a couple of the boys from our ranch feeling their oats a little. We'll take them out and off your hands."

The sheriff stared from Mike to Doc Sawyer and Colley, who had just come through the door.

"Who are you?" he demanded. "I don't believe I know you hombres."

"That's right, sir, you don't," Mike said. "We're from the Mogollons, riding back after driving some cattle through to California. It was a rough trip, and this liquor here got to a couple of the boys."

The sheriff hesitated, looking sharply from one to the other.

"*You* may be a cowhand," he said, "but *that* hombre"—he pointed to Sawyer—"looks like a gambler!"

Mike chuckled. "That's a joke on you, boy!" he said to Doc. Then he turned back to the sheriff. "He's a doctor, sir, and quite a good one. A friend of my boss's."

A gray-haired man got up and strolled alongside the sheriff. His eyes were alive with suspicion.

"From the Mogollons?" he queried. "That's where I'm from. Who did you say your boss was?"

Doc Sawyer felt his scalp tighten, but Mike smiled.

"Jack McCardle," he said, "of the Flying M. We aren't his regular hands, just a bunch passing through. Doc, here, he being an old friend of Jack's, handled the sale of the beef."

The sheriff looked around.

"That right, Joe?" he asked the gray-haired man. "There's a Flying M over there?"

"Yes, there is." Joe was obviously puzzled. "Good man, too, but I had no idea he was shipping beef!"

The sheriff studied Bastian thoughtfully. "Guess you're all right," he said finally. "But you sure don't *talk* like a cowhand."

"As a matter of fact," Mike said, swallowing hard, "I was studying for the ministry, but my interests began to lead me in more profane directions, so I am afraid I backslid. It seems," he said gravely, "that a leaning toward poker isn't conducive to the correct manner in the pulpit!"

"I should say not!" the sheriff chuckled. "All right, son, you take your pardners with you. Let 'em sleep it off."

Mike turned, and his men followed him. Ducrow and Fernandez had disappeared. They rode swiftly out of town and took the trail for Toadstool Canyon. It wasn't until they were several miles on the road that Sawyer glanced at Mike.

"You'll do," he said. "I was never so sure of a fight in my life!"

"That's right, Boss!" Garlin said. "I was bettin' we'd have to shoot our way out of town! You sure smooth talked 'em. Never heard it done prettier!"

"Sure did," Colley agreed. "I don't envy you havin' Ducrow an' Fernandez for enemies, though."

Kerb Perrin and Rigger Molina were both in conference with Ben Curry when Mike Bastian came up the stone steps and through the door. They both looked up sharply.

"Perrin," Bastian said, "what were Ducrow and Fernandez doing in Weaver?"

"In Weaver?" Perrin straightened up slowly, nettled by Mike's tone, but puzzled, too.

"Yes, in Weaver! We nearly had to shoot our way out of town because of them. They were down there, drunk and talking too much. When I told them to get on their horses and go home, they made trouble."

Kerb Perrin was on dangerous ground. He well knew how harsh Ben Curry was about talkative outlaws, and while he had no idea what the two were doing in Weaver, he knew they were troublemakers. He also knew they were supporters of his. Ben Curry knew it, and so did Rigger Molina.

"They made trouble?" Perrin questioned now. "How?"

"Ducrow started to tell who I was."

"What happened?"

Mike was aware that Ben Curry had tipped back in his chair and was watching him with interest.

"I knocked him down with a pistol barrel," he said.

"You *what*?" Perrin stared. Ducrow was a bad man to tangle with. "What about Fernandez?"

"He tried to draw on me, and I put a bullet in his shoulder."

"You should've killed him," Molina said. "You'll have to, sooner or later."

Kerb Perrin was stumped. He had not expected this, or that Mike Bastian was capable of handling such a situation. He was suddenly aware that Doc Sawyer had come into the room.

Bastian faced Ben Curry. "We got what we went after," he said, "but another bad break like Ducrow and Fernandez, and we'd walk into a trap!"

"There won't be another!" Curry said harshly.

When Mike had gone out, Doc Sawyer looked at Ben Curry and smiled.

"You should have seen him and heard him," he said as Molina and Perrin were leaving. "It would have done your heart good! He had a run-in with Corbus and Fletcher, too. Knocked Corbus out with a punch and backed Fletcher down. Oh, he'll do, that boy of yours, he'll do! The way he talked that sheriff out of it was one of the smoothest things I've seen!"

Ben Curry nodded with satisfaction. "I knew it! I knew he had it!"

Doc Sawyer smiled, and looked up at the chief from under his sunburned eyebrows. "He met a girl, too."

"A girl? Good for him! It's about time!"

"This was a very particular girl, Chief," Sawyer continued. "I thought you'd like to know. If I'm any judge of men, he fell for her and fell hard. And I'm not so sure it didn't happen both ways. He told me something about it, but I had already seen for myself."

Something in Sawyer's tone made Curry sit up a little.

"Who was the girl?" he demanded.

"A girl who came in on the stage." Doc spoke carefully, avoiding Curry's eyes now. "He got the girl and her family a rig to drive them out to a ranch. Out to the V Bar."

Ben Curry's face went white. So Doc knew! It was in every line of him, every tone of his voice. The one thing he had tried to keep secret, the thing known only to himself and Roundy, was known to Doc! And to how many others?

"The girl's name," Doc continued, "was Drusilla Ragan. She's a beautiful girl."

"Well, I won't have it!" Curry said in a strained voice.

Doc Sawyer looked up, faintly curious. "You mean the foster son you raised isn't good enough for your daughter?"

"Don't say that word here!" Curry snapped, his face hard. "Who knows besides you?"

"Nobody of whom I am aware," Doc said with a shrug. "I only know by accident. You will remember the time you were laid up with that bullet wound. You were delirious, and that's why I took care of you myself—because you talked too much."

Doc lighted his pipe. "They made a nice-looking pair," he said. "And I think she invited him to Red Wall Canyon."

"He won't go! I won't have any of this crowd going there!"

"Chief, that boy's what you made him, but he's not an outlaw yet," Doc said, puffing contentedly on his pipe. "He could be, and he might be, but if he does become one the crime will lie on your shoulders."

Curry shook himself and stared out the window.

"I said it, Chief, the boy has it in him," Sawyer went on. "You should have seen him throw that gun on Fernandez. The kid's fast as lightning! He thinks, too. If he takes over this gang, he'll run this country like you never ran it. I say, *if.*"

"He'll do it," Curry said confidently, "you know he will. He always does what I tell him."

Doc chuckled. "He may, and again he may not. Mike Bastian has a mind of his own, and he's doing some thinking. He may decide he doesn't want to take over. What will you do then?"

"Nobody has ever quit this gang. Nobody ever will!"

"You'd order him killed?"

Ben Curry hesitated. This was something he had never dreamed of. Something— "He'll do what he's told!" he repeated, but he was no longer sure.

A tiny voice of doubt was arising within him, a voice that made him remember the Mike Bastian who was a quiet, determined little boy who would not cry, a boy who listened and obeyed. Yet now Curry knew, and admitted it for the first time, that Mike Bastian always had a mind of his own.

Never before had the thought occurred to him that Mike might disobey, that he might refuse. And if he did, what then? It was a rule of the outlaw pack that no man could leave it and live. It was a rule essential to their security. A few had tried, and their bodies now lay in Boot Hill. But Mike, his son? No, not Mike!

Within him, there was a deeper knowledge, an awareness that here his interests and those of the pack would divide. Even if he said no, they would say yes.

"Who would kill him, Chief? Kerb Perrin? Rigger Molina? You?" Doc Sawyer shook his head slowly. "You *might* be able to do it, maybe one of the others, but I doubt it. You've created the man who may destroy you, Chief, unless you join him."

Long after Doc Sawyer was gone, Ben Curry sat there staring out over the shadowed valley. He was getting old. For the first time he was beginning to doubt his rightness, beginning to wonder if he had not wronged Mike Bastian.

And what of Mike and Dru, his beloved, gray-eyed daughter? The girl with dash and spirit? But why not? Slowly, he thought over Mike Bastian's life. Where was the boy wrong? Where was he unfitted for Dru? By the teachings given him on his, Curry's, own suggestion? His own order? Or was there yet time?

Ben Curry heaved himself to his feet and began to pace the carpeted floor. He would have to decide. He would have to make up his mind, for a man's life and future lay in his hands, to make or break.

What if Dru wanted him anyway, outlaw or not? Ben Curry stopped and stared into the fireplace. If it had been Julie now, he might forbid it. But Dru? He chuckled. She would laugh at him. Dru had too much of his own nature, and she had a mind of her own.

Mike Bastian was restless the day after the excitement in Weaver. He rolled out of his bunk and walked out on the terrace. Only he and Doc Sawyer slept in the stone house where Ben Curry lived. Roundy was down in town with the rest of them, but tonight Mike wanted to walk, to think.

There had been a thrill of excitement in outtalking the sheriff, in facing down Fletcher, in flattening Corbus. And there had been more of it in facing Ducrow and Fernandez. Yet, was that what he wanted? Or did he want something more stable, more worthwhile? The something he might find with Drusilla Ragan?

Already, he had won a place with the gang. He knew the story would be all over the outlaw camp now.

Walking slowly down the street of the settlement, he turned at right angles and drifted down a side road. He wanted to get away from things for a little while, to think things out. He turned again and stared back into the pines, and then he heard a voice coming from a nearby house. The words halted him.

". . . at Red Wall." Mike heard the ending.

Swiftly, he glided to the house and flattened against the side. Kerb Perrin was speaking:

"It's a cinch, and we'll do it on our own without anybody's say-so. There's about two thousand cattle in the herd, and I've got a buyer for them. We can hit the place just about sunup. Right now, they have only four hands on the place, but about the first of next month they will start hiring. It's now or not at all."

"How many men will we take?" That was Ducrow speaking.

"A dozen. That will keep the divvy large enough, and they can swing it. Hell, that Ragan ranch is easy! The boss won't hear about it until too late, and the chances are he will never guess it was us."

"I wouldn't want him to," Fernandez said.

"To hell with him!" Ducrow was irritated. "I'd like a crack at that Bastian again."

"Stick with me," Perrin said, "and I'll set him up for you. Curry is about to turn things over to him. Well, we'll beat him to it."

"You said there were girls?" Ducrow suggested.

"There's Curry's two girls and a couple of Mexican girls who work there. One older woman. I want one of those girls myself—the youngest of the Ragan sisters. What happens to the others is none of my business."

Mike Bastian's hand dropped to his gun, and his lips tightened. The tone of Perrin's voice filled him with fury, and Ducrow was as bad.

"What happens if Curry does find out?" Ducrow demanded.

"What would happen?" Perrin said fiercely. "I'll kill him like I've wanted to all these years! I've hated that man like I never hated anyone in my life!"

"What about that Bastian?" Ducrow demanded.

Perrin laughed. "That's your problem! If you and Fernandez can't figure to handle him, then I don't know you."

"He knocked out Corbus, too," Ducrow said. "We might get him to throw in with us, if this crowd is all afraid of old Ben Curry."

"I ain't so sure about him my own self," said another voice, which Mike placed as belonging to an outlaw named Bayless. "He may not be so young anymore, but he's hell on wheels with a gun!"

"Forget him!" Perrin snapped. Then: "You three, and Clatt, Panelli, Monson, Kiefer and a few others, will go with us. All good men. There's a lot of dissatisfaction, anyway. Molina wants to raid the

Mormons. They've a lot of rich stock, and there's no reason why we can't sell it south of the river and the other stock north of it. We can get rich!"

# V

Mike Bastian waited no longer, but eased away from the wall. He was tempted to wait for Perrin and brace him when he came out. His first thought was to go to Ben Curry; but he might betray his interest in Drusilla, and the time was not yet ripe for that. What would her father say if he found the foster son he had raised to be an outlaw was in love with his daughter?

It was foolish to think of it, yet he couldn't help it. There was time between now and the twentieth for him to get back to Red Wall and see her.

A new thought occurred to him. Ben Curry would know the girls and their mother were here and would be going to see them! That would be his chance to learn of Ben's secret pass to the riverbank and how he crossed the Colorado.

Recalling other trips, Bastian knew the route must be a much quicker one than any he knew of, and was probably farther west and south, toward the canyon country. Already he was eager to see the girl again, and all he could think of was her trim figure, the laughter in her eyes, the soft curve of her lips.

There were other things to be considered. If there was as much unrest in the gang as Perrin said, things might be nearing a definite break. Certainly, outlaws were not the men to stand hitched for long, and Ben Curry had commanded them for longer than anyone would believe. Their loyalty was due partly to the returns from their ventures under his guidance, and partly to fear of his far-reaching power. But he was growing old, and there were those among them who feared he was losing his grip.

Mike felt a sudden urge to saddle his horse and be gone, to get away from all this potential cruelty, the conniving and hatred that lay dormant here, or was seething and ready to explode. He could ride out now by the Kaibab trail through the forest, skirt the mountains, and find his own way through the canyon. It was a question whether he could escape, whether Ben Curry would let him go.

To run now meant to abandon all hope of seeing Dru again, and Mike knew he could not do that.

Returning to his quarters in the big stone house, he stopped in front of a mirror. With deadly, flashing speed, he began to practice quick draws of his guns. Each night he did this twenty times as swiftly as his darting hands could move.

Finally he sat down on his bed thinking. Roundy first, and today Doc Sawyer. Each seemed to be hoping he would throw up the sponge and escape this outlaw life before it was too late. Doc said it was his life, but was it?

There was a light tap on the door. Gun in hand, he reached for the latch. Roundy stepped in. He glanced at the gun.

"Gettin' scary, Mike?" he queried. "Things are happenin'!"

"I know."

Mike went on to explain what he had overheard, and Roundy's face turned serious. "Mike, did you ever hear of Dave Lenaker?"

Bastian looked up. "You mean the Colorado gunman?"

"That's the one. He's headed this way. Ben Curry just got word that Lenaker's on his way to take over the Curry gang!"

"I thought he was one of Curry's ablest lieutenants?"

Roundy shrugged. "He was, Mike, but the word has gone out that the old man is losing his grip, and outlaws are quick to sense a thing like that. Lenaker never had any use for Perrin, and he's most likely afraid that Perrin will climb into the saddle. Dave Lenaker's a holy terror, too."

"Does Dad Curry know?" Mike said.

"Yeah. He's some wrought up, too," Roundy answered. "He was figurin' on bein' away for a few days, one of those trips he takes to Red Wall. Now he can't go."

Morning came cool and clear. Mike Bastian could feel disaster in the air, and he dressed hurriedly and headed for the bunkhouse. Few of the men were eating, and those few were silent. He knew they were all aware of impending change. He was finishing his coffee when Kerb Perrin came in.

Instantly, Mike was on guard. Perrin walked with a strut, and his eyes were bright and confident. He glanced at Bastian, faintly amused, and then sat down at the table and began to eat.

Roundy came in, and then Doc Sawyer. Mike dallied over his coffee, and a few minutes later was rewarded by seeing Ducrow come in with Kiefer, followed in a few minutes by Rocky Clatt, Monson and Panelli.

Suddenly, with the cup half to his mouth, Mike recalled with a shock that this was the group Perrin planned to use on his raid on the Ragan ranch! That could mean the raid would come off today!

He looked up to see Roundy suddenly push back his chair and leave his breakfast unfinished. The old woodsman hurried outside and vanished.

Mike put down his own cup and got up. Then he stopped, motionless. The hard muzzle of a gun was prodding him in the back, and a voice was saying, "Don't move!"

The voice was that of Fernandez, and Mike saw Perrin smiling.

"Sorry to surprise you, Bastian," Perrin said. "But with Lenaker on the road we had to move fast. By the time he gets here I'll be in the saddle. Some of the boys wanted to kill you, but I figured you'd be a good talkin' point with the old man. He'd be a hard kernel to dig out of that stone shell of his without you. But with you for an argument, he'll come out, all right!"

"Have you gone crazy, Perrin? You can't get away with this!"

"I am, though. You see, Rigger Molina left this morning with ten of his boys to work a little job they heard of. In fact, they are on their way to knock over the gold train."

"The gold train?" Bastian exclaimed. "Why, that was *my* job! He doesn't even know the plan made for it. Or the information I got."

Perrin smiled triumphantly. "I traded with him. I told him to give me a free hand here, and he could have the gold train. I neglected to tell him about the twelve guards riding with it, or the number with shotguns. In fact, I told him only five guards would be along. I think that will take care of Rigger for me."

Perrin turned abruptly. "Take his guns and tie his hands behind his back, then shove him out into the street. I want the old man to see him."

"What about him?" Kiefer demanded, pointing a gun at Doc Sawyer.

"Leave him alone. We may need a doctor, and he knows where his bread is buttered."

Confused and angry, Mike Bastian was shoved out into the warm - morning sun, then jerked around to face up the canyon toward the stone house.

Suddenly, fierce triumph came over him. Perrin would have a time getting the old man out of that place. The sunlight was shining down the road from over the house, full into their faces. The only approach to the house was up thirty steps of stone, overlooked by an upper window of the house. From that window and the doorway, the entire settlement could be commanded by an expert rifleman.

Ben Curry had thought of everything. The front and back doors of every building in the settlement could be commanded easily from his stronghold.

Perrin crouched behind a pile of sandbags hastily thrown up near the door of the store.

"Come on down, Curry!" he shouted. "Give yourself up or we'll kill Bastian!"

There was no answer from up the hill. Mike felt cold and sick in his stomach. Wind touched his hair and blew a strand down over his face. He stared up at the stone house and could see no movement, hear no response.

"Come on out!" Perrin roared again. "We know you're there! Come out or we'll kill your son!"

Still no reply.

"He don't hear you," Clatt said. "Maybe he's still asleep. Let's rush the place."

"You rush it," Kiefer said. "Let me watch!"

Despite his helplessness, Mike felt a sudden glow of satisfaction. Old Ben Curry was a wily fighter. He knew that once he showed himself or spoke, their threat would take force. It was useless to kill Bastian unless they knew Curry was watching them.

Perrin had been so sure Curry would come out rather than sacrifice Mike, and now they were not even sure he was hearing them! Nor, Mike knew suddenly, was anybody sure Ben would come out even if they did warn him Mike would be killed.

"Come on out!" Perrin roared. "Give yourself up and we'll give you and Bastian each a horse and a half mile start! Otherwise, you both die! We've got dynamite!"

Mike chuckled. Dynamite wasn't going to do them much good. There was no way to get close to that stone house, backed up against the mountain as it was.

"Perrin," he said, "you've played the fool. Curry doesn't care whether I live or die. He won't come out of there, and there's no way you can get at him. All he's got to do is sit tight and wait until Dave Lenaker gets here. He will make a deal with Dave then, and where will you be?"

"Shut up!" Perrin bellowed. But for the first time he seemed to be aware that his plan was not working. "He'll come out, all right!"

"Let's open fire on the place," Ducrow suggested. "Or rush it like Clatt suggested!"

"Hell!" Kiefer was disgusted. "Let's take what we can lay hands on and get out! There's two thousand head of cattle down in those bottoms. Rigger's gone and Lenaker ain't here yet, so let's take what we can an' get out."

"Take pennies when there's millions up there in that stone house?" Perrin demanded. His face swelled in anger and the veins stood out on his forehead. "That strong room has gold in it! Stacks of money! I know it's there. With all that at hand, would you run off with a few cattle?"

Kiefer was silent but unconvinced.

Standing in the dusty street, Mike looked up at the stone house. All the loyalty and love he felt for the old man up there in that house came back with a rush. Whatever he was, good or bad, he owed to Ben Curry. Perhaps Curry had reared him for a life of crime, for outlawry, but to Ben Curry it was not a bad life. He lived like a feudal lord and had respect for no law he did not make himself.

Wrong he might be, but he had given the man that was Mike Bastian a start. Suddenly, Mike knew that he could never have been an outlaw, that it was not in him to steal and rob and kill. But that did not mean he could be unloyal to the old man who had reared him and given him a home when he had none.

He was suddenly, fiercely proud of the old man up there alone. Like a cornered grizzly, he would fight to the death. He, Mike Bastian, might die here in the street, but he hoped old Ben Curry would stay in his stone shell and defeat them all.

Kerb Perrin was stumped. He had made his plan quickly when he'd heard Dave Lenaker was on his way here, for he knew that if Lenaker arrived it might well turn into a bloody four-cornered fight. But with Molina out of the way, he might take over from Ben Curry before Lenaker arrived, and kill Lenaker and the men he brought with him in an ambush.

He had been sure that Ben Curry would reply, that he might give himself up or at least show himself, and Perrin had a sniper concealed to pick him off if he moved into the open. That he would get nothing but silence, he could not believe.

Mike Bastian stood alone in the center of the street. There was simply nothing he could do. At any moment Perrin might decide to have him killed where he stood. With his hands tied behind him, he was helpless. Mike wondered what had happened to Roundy? The old mountain man had risen suddenly from the table and vanished. Could he be in league with Perrin?

That was impossible. Roundy had always been Ben Curry's friend and had never liked anything about Kerb Perrin.

"All right," Perrin said suddenly, "we'll hold Bastian. He's still a good argument. Some men will stay here, and the rest of us will make that raid on the Ragan outfit. I've an idea that when we come back, Curry will be ready to talk business."

# VI

Bastian was led back from the street and thrown into a room in the rear of the store. There his feet were tied and he was left in darkness.

His mind was in a turmoil. If Perrin's men hit the ranch now they would take Drusilla and Juliana! He well knew how swiftly they would strike and how helpless any ordinary ranch would be against them. And here he was tied hand and foot, helpless to do anything!

He heaved his body around and fought the ropes that bound him, until sweat streamed from his body. Even then, with his wrists torn by his struggles against the rawhide thongs that made him fast, he did not stop. There was nothing to aid him—no nail, no sharp corner, nothing at all.

The room was built of thin boards nailed to two-by-fours. He rolled himself around until he could get his back against the boards, trying to remember where the nails were. Bracing himself as best he could, he pushed his back against the wall. He bumped against it until his back was sore. But with no effect.

Outside, all was still. Whether they had gone, he did not know. Yet if Perrin had not gone on his raid, he would be soon leaving. However, if he, Mike, could escape and find Curry's private route across the river, he might beat them to it.

He wondered where Doc Sawyer was. Perhaps he was afraid of what Perrin might do if he tried to help. Where was Roundy?

Just when he had all but given up, he had an idea—a solution so simple that he cursed himself for not thinking of it before. Mike rolled over and got up on his knees and reached back with his bound hands for his spurs. Fortunately, he was wearing boots instead of the moccasins he wore in the woods. By wedging one spur against the other, he succeeded in holding the rowel almost immovable, and then he began to chafe the rawhide with the prongs of the rowel.

Desperately he sawed, until every muscle was crying for relief. As he stopped he heard the rattle of horses' hoofs. They were just going! Then he had a fighting chance if he could get free and get his hands on a gun!

He knew he was making headway, for he could feel the notch he had already cut in the rawhide. Suddenly footsteps sounded outside. Fearful whoever was there would guess what he was doing, Mike rolled over on his side.

The door opened and Snake Fernandez came in, and in his hand he held a knife. His shoulder was bandaged crudely but tightly, and the knife was held in his left hand. He came in and closed the door.

Mike stared, horror mounting within him. Perrin was gone, and Snake Fernandez was moving toward him, smiling wickedly.

"You think you shoot Pablo Fernandez, eh?" the outlaw said, leering. "Now, we see who shoots! I am going to cut you to little pieces! I am going to cut you very slowly!"

Bastian lay on his shoulder and stared at Fernandez. There was murder in the outlaw's eyes, and all the savagery in him was coming to the fore. The man stooped over him and pricked him with the knife. Clamping his jaws, Mike held himself tense.

Rage mounted in the man. He leaned closer. "You do not jump, eh? I make you jump!"

He stabbed down hard with the knife, and Mike whipped over on his shoulder blades and kicked out wickedly with his bound feet. The movement caught the killer by surprise. Mike's feet hit him in the knees and knocked him rolling. With a lunge, Mike rolled over and jerked at the ropes that bound him.

Something snapped, and he jerked again. Like a cat the killer was on his feet now, circling warily. Desperately, Mike pulled at the ropes, turning on his shoulders to keep his feet toward Fernandez. Suddenly, he rolled over and hurled himself at the Mexican's legs, but Fernandez jerked back and stabbed.

Mike felt a sliver of pain run along his arms, and then he rolled to his feet and jerked wildly at the thongs. His hands came loose suddenly and he hurled himself at Fernandez's legs, grabbing one ankle.

Fernandez came down hard, and Bastian jerked at the leg and then scrambled to get at him. One hand grasped the man's wrist, the other his throat. With all the power that was in him, Mike shut down on both hands.

Fernandez fought like an injured wildcat, but Mike's strength was too great. Gripping the throat with his left hand, Mike slammed the Mexican's head against the floor again and again, his throttling grip freezing tighter and tighter.

The outlaw's face went dark with blood, and his struggles grew weaker. Mike let go of his throat hold suddenly and slugged him three times on the chin with his fist.

Jerking the knife from the unconscious man's hand, Mike slashed at the thongs that bound his ankles. He got to his feet shakily. Glancing down at the sprawled-out Fernandez, he hesitated. The man was not wearing a gun, but must have had one. It could be outside the door. Easing to the door, Mike opened it a crack.

The street was deserted as far as he could see. His hands felt awkward from their long constraint, and he worked his fingers to loosen them up. There was no gun in sight, so he pushed the door wider. Fernandez's gun belts hung over the chair on the end of the porch.

He had taken two steps toward them when a man stepped out of the bunkhouse. The fellow had a toothpick lifted to his lips, but when he saw Mike Bastian he let out a yelp of surprise and went for his gun.

It was scarcely fifteen paces and Mike threw the knife under-handed, pitching it point first off the palm of his hand. It flashed in the sun as the fellow's gun came up. Then Mike could see the haft protruding from the man's middle section.

The fellow screamed and, dropping the gun, clutched at the knife hilt in an agony of fear. His breath came in horrid gasps that Mike

could hear as he grabbed Fernandez's guns and belted them on.
Then he lunged for the mess hall, where his own guns had been
taken from him. Shoving open the door, he sprang inside, gun in
hand.

Then he froze. Doc Sawyer was standing there smiling, and Doc
had a shotgun on four of Perrin's men. He looked up with relief.

"I was hoping you would escape!" he said. "I didn't want to kill
these men and didn't know how to go about tying them up by
myself."

Mike caught up his own guns, removed Fernandez's gun belts,
and strapped his own on. Then he shoved the outlaw's guns inside
the waistband of his pants.

"Down on the floor," he ordered. "I'll tie them, and fast!"

It was the work of only a few minutes to have the four outlaws
bound hand and foot. He gathered up their guns.

"Where's Roundy?" he asked.

"I haven't seen him since he left here," Doc said. "I've been
wondering."

"Let's go up to the house. We'll get Ben Curry, and then we'll
have things under control in a hurry."

Together, they went out the back door and walked swiftly down
the line of buildings. Mike took off his hat and sailed it into the
brush, knowing he could be seen from the stone house and hoping
that Ben Curry would recognize him. Sawyer was excited, but trying
to appear calm. He had been a gambler, and while handy with guns,
was not a man accustomed to violence. Always before, he had been a
bystander rather than an active participant.

Side by side, gambling against a shot from someone below, they
went up the stone stairs.

There was no sound from within the house. They walked into the
wide living room and glanced around. There was no sign of anyone.
Then Mike saw a broken box of rifle shells.

"He's been around here!" he said. Then he looked up and shouted,
"Dad!"

A muffled cry reached them, and Mike was out of the room and up
another staircase. He entered the room at the top and then froze in
his tracks. Sawyer was behind him, now.

This was the fortress room, a heavy-walled stone room that had
water trickling from a spring in the wall of the cliff and running down
a stone trough and out through a pipe. There was food stored here,
and plenty of ammunition.

The door was heavy and could be locked and barred from within.
The walls of this room were all of four feet thick, and nothing short of
dynamite could have blasted a way in.

This was Ben Curry's last resort, and he was here now. But he was sprawled on the floor, his face contorted with pain.

"Broke my leg!" he panted. "Too heavy! Tried to move too . . . fast! Slipped on the steps, dragged myself up here!" He looked up at Mike. "Good for you, son! I was afraid they had killed you. You got away by yourself?"

"Yes, Dad."

Sawyer had dropped to his knees, and now he looked up.

"This is a bad break, Mike," he said. "He won't be able to move."

"Get me on a bed where I can see out of that window." Ben Curry's strength seemed to flow back with his son's presence. "I'll stand them off. You and me, Mike, we can do it!"

"Dad," Mike said. "I can't stay. I've got to go."

Ben Curry's face went gray with shock; then slowly the blood flowed back into it. Bastian dropped down beside him.

"Dad, I know where Perrin's going. He's gone to make a raid on the Ragan ranch. He wants the cattle and the women."

The old man lunged so mightily that Sawyer cried out and tried to push him back. Before he could speak, Mike said:

"Dad, you must tell me about the secret crossing of the Colorado that you know. I must beat them to the ranch."

Ben Curry's expression changed to one of vast relief and then quick calculation. He nodded.

"You could do it, but it'll take tall riding!" Quickly, he outlined the route, and then added, "Now listen! At the river there's an old Navajo. He keeps some horses for me, and he has six of the finest animals ever bred. You cross that river and get a horse from him. He knows about you."

Mike got up. "Make him comfortable, Doc. Do all you can."

Sawyer stared at Mike. "What about Dave Lenaker? He'll kill us all!"

"I'll take care of Lenaker!" Curry flared. "I'm not dead by a danged sight! I'll show that renegade where he heads in. The moment he comes up that street, I'm going to kill him!" He looked at Mike again. "Son, maybe I've done wrong to raise you like I have, but if you kill Kerb Perrin or Lenaker you would be doing the West a favor. If I don't get Dave Lenaker, you may have to. So remember this, *watch his left hand!*"

Mike ran down the steps and stopped in his room to grab his .44 Winchester. It was the work of a minute to throw a saddle on a horse, and then he hit the trail. Ben Curry and Doc Sawyer could, if necessary, last for days in the fortresslike room—unless, somehow, dynamite was pitched into the window. He would have to get to the Ragan ranch and then get back here as soon as possible.

Mike Bastian left the stable and wheeled the gray he was riding into the long winding trail through the stands of ponderosa and fir. The horse was in fine fettle and ready for the trail, and he let it out. His mind was leaping over the trail, turning each bend, trying to see how it must lay.

This was all new country to him, for he was heading southwest now into the wild, unknown region toward the great canyons of the Colorado, a region he had never traversed and, except for old Ben Curry, perhaps never crossed by any except Indians.

How hard the trail would be on the horse, Mike could not guess, but he knew he must ride fast and keep going. His route was the shorter, but Kerb Perrin had a lead on him and would be hurrying to make his strike and return.

Patches of snow still hid themselves around the roots of the brush and in the hollows under the end of some giant deadfall. The air was crisp and chill, but growing warmer, and by afternoon it would be hot in the sunlight. The wind of riding whipped his black hair. He ran the horse down a long path bedded deep with pine needles and then turned at a blazed tree and went out across the arid top of a plateau.

This was the strange land he loved, the fiery, heat-blasted land of the sun. Riding along the crest of a long ridge, he looked out over a long valley dotted with mesquite and sagebrush. Black dots of cattle grazing offered the only life beyond the lonely, lazy swing of a high-soaring buzzard.

He saw the white rock he had been told to look for and turned the free-running horse into a cleft that led downward. They moved slowly here, for it was a steep slide down the side of the mesa and out on the long roll of the hill above the valley.

Time and time again Mike's hand patted his guns, as if to reassure himself they were there. His thoughts leaped ahead, trying to fore-see what would happen. Would he arrive only to find the buildings burned and the girls gone?

He knew only that he must get there first, that he must face them, and that at all costs he must kill Kerb Perrin and Ducrow. Without them the others might run, might not choose to fight it out. Mike had an idea that without Perrin, they would scatter to the four winds.

Swinging along the hillside, he took a trail that led again to a plateau top and ran off through the sage, heading for the smoky-blue distance of the canyon.

# VII

Mike's mind lost track of time and distance, leaping ahead to the river and the crossing, and beyond it to Ragan's V Bar ranch. Down steep trails through the great, broken cliffs heaped high with the piled-up stone of ages, and down through the wild, weird jumble of boulders, and across the flat toplands that smelled of sage and piñon, he kept the horse moving.

Then suddenly he was once more in the forests of the Kaibab. The dark pines closed around him, and he rode on in the vast stillness of virgin timber, the miles falling behind, the trail growing dim before him.

Then suddenly the forest split aside and he was on the rim of the canyon—an awful blue immensity yawning before him that made him draw the gray to a halt in gasping wonder. Far out over that vast, misty blue rose islands of red sandstone, islands that were laced and crossed by bands of purple and yellow. The sunset was gleaming on the vast plateaus and buttes and peaks with a ruddy glow, fading into the opaques of the deeper canyon.

The gray was beaten and weary now. Mike turned the horse toward a break in the plateau and rode down it, giving the animal its head. They came out upon a narrow trail that hung above a vast gorge, its bottom lost in the darkness of gathering dusk. The gray stumbled on, seeming to know its day was almost done.

Dozing in the saddle, almost two hours later Mike Bastian felt the horse come to a halt. He jerked his head up and opened his eyes. He could feel the dampness of a deep canyon and could hear the thundering roar of the mighty river as it charged through the rock-walled slit. In front of him was a square of light.

"Halloo, the house!" he called.

He swung down as the door opened.

"Who's there?" a voice cried out.

"Mike Bastian!" he said, moving toward the house with long, swinging strides. "For Ben Curry!"

The man backed into the house. He was an ancient Navajo, but his eyes were keen and sharp.

"I want a horse," Mike said.

"You can't cross the river tonight." The Navajo spoke English well. "It is impossible!"

"There'll be a moon later," Mike answered. "When it comes up, I'm going across."

The Indian looked at him and then shrugged.

"Then eat," he said. "You'll need it."

"There are horses?"

"Horses?" The Navajo chuckled. "The best a man ever saw! Do you suppose Ben Curry would have horses here that were not the best? But they are on the other side of the stream, and safe enough. My brother is with them."

Mike slumped into a seat. "Take care of my horse, will you? I've most killed him."

When the Indian was gone, Mike slumped over on the table, burying his head in his arms. In a moment he was asleep, dreaming wild dreams of a mad race over a strange misty-blue land with great crimson islands, riding a splendid black horse and carrying a girl in his arms. He awakened with a start. The old Indian was sitting by the fireplace, and he looked up.

"You'd better eat," he said. "The moon is rising."

They went out together, walking down the path to the water's edge. As the moon shone down into the canyon, Mike stared at the tumbling stream in consternation. Nothing living could swim in that water! It would be impossible.

"How do you cross?" he demanded. "No horse could swim that! And a boat wouldn't get fifty feet before it would be dashed to pieces!"

The Indian chuckled. "That isn't the way we cross it. You are right in saying no boat could cross here, for there is no landing over there, and the canyon is so narrow that the water piles up back of the narrows and comes down with a great rush."

Mike looked at him again. "You talk like an educated man," he said. "I don't understand."

The Navajo shrugged. "I was for ten years with a missionary, and after I traveled with him as an interpreter he took me back to the States, where I stayed with him for two years. Then I lived in Santa Fe."

He was leading the way up a steep path that skirted the cliff but was wide enough to walk comfortably. Opposite them, the rock wall of the canyon lifted and the waters of the tumbling river roared down through the narrow chasm.

"Ben Curry does things well, as you shall see," the guide said. "It took him two years of effort to get this bridge built."

Mike stared. "Across there?"

"Yes. A bridge for a man with courage. It is a rope bridge, made fast to iron rings sunk in the rock."

Mike Bastian walked on the rocky ledge at the edge of the trail and looked out across the gorge. In the pale moonlight he could see two slim threads trailing across the canyon high above the tumbling water. Just two ropes, and one of them four feet above the other.

"You mean," he said, "that Ben Curry crossed on *that*?"

"He did. I have seen him cross that bridge a dozen times, at least."

"Have you crossed it?"

The Navajo shrugged. "Why should I? The other side is the same as this, is it not? There is nothing over there that I want."

Mike looked at the slender strands, and then he took hold of the upper rope and tentatively put a foot on the lower one. Slowly, carefully, he eased out above the raging waters. One slip and he would be gone, for no man could hope to live in those angry flood waters. He slid his foot along, then the other, advancing his hand-holds as he moved. Little by little, he worked his way across the canyon.

He was trembling when he got his feet in the rocky cavern on the opposite side and so relieved to be safely across that he scarcely was aware of the old Indian who sat there awaiting him.

The Navajo got up and without a word started down the trail. He quickly led Mike to a cabin built in the opening of a dry branch canyon, and tethered before the door of the cabin was a huge bay stallion.

Waving at the Indian, Mike swung into the saddle, and the bay turned, taking to the trail as if eager to be off.

Would Perrin travel at night? Mike doubted it, but it was possible, so he kept moving himself. The trail led steadily upward, winding finally out of the canyon to the plateau.

The bay stallion seemed to know the trail; it was probable that Curry had used this horse himself. It was a splendid animal, big and very fast. Letting the horse have his head, Mike felt the animal gather his legs under him. Then he broke into a long, swinging lope that literally ate up the space. How long the horse could hold the speed he did not know, but it was a good start.

It was at least a ten-hour ride to the Ragan V Bar ranch.

The country was rugged and wild. Several times, startled deer broke and ran before him, and there were many rabbits. Dawn was breaking faintly in the east now, and shortly after daybreak he stopped near a pool of melted snow water and made coffee. Then he remounted the rested stallion and raced on.

Drusilla Ragan brushed her hair thoughtfully and then pinned it up. Outside, she could hear her mother moving about and the Mexican girls who helped around the house whenever they were visiting. Julie was up, she knew, and had been up for hours. She was outside talking to that blond cowhand from New Mexico, the one Voyle Ragan had hired to break horses.

Suddenly she heard Julie's footsteps, and then the door opened.

"Aren't you ready yet?" Julie asked. "I'm famished!"

"I'll be along in a minute." Then as Julie turned to go: "What did you think of him, Julie—that cowboy who got the buckboard for us? Wasn't he the handsomest thing?"

"Oh, you mean that Mike Bastian?" Julie said. "I was wondering why you were mooning around in here. Usually you're the first one up. Yes, I expect he is good-looking. But did you see the way he looked when you mentioned Uncle Voyle? He acted so strange!"

"I wonder if Uncle Voyle knows anything about him? Let's ask!"

"You ask," Julie replied, laughing. "He's *your* problem!"

Voyle Ragan was a tall man, but lean and without Ben Curry's weight. He was already seated at the table when they came in, and Dru was no sooner in her seat than she put her question. Voyle's face became a mask.

"Mike Bastian?" he said thoughtfully. "I don't know. Where'd you meet him?"

The girls explained, and he nodded.

"In Weaver?" Voyle Ragan knew about the gold train, and his eyes narrowed. "I think I know who he is, but I never saw him that I heard of. You probably won't see him again, because most of those riders from up in the strip stay there most of the time. They are a wild bunch."

"On the way down here," Julie said, "the man who drove was telling us that outlaws live up there."

"Could be. It's wild enough." Voyle Ragan lifted his head, listening. For a moment he had believed he heard horses. But it was too soon for Ben to be coming. If anyone else came, he would have to get rid of them, and quickly.

He heard the sound again, and then he saw the cavalcade of horsemen riding into the yard. Voyle came to his feet abruptly.

"Stay here!" he snapped.

His immediate thought was of a posse, and then he saw Kerb Perrin. He had seen Perrin many times, although Perrin had never met him. Slowly, he moved up to the door, uncertain of his course. These were Ben's men, but Ben had always told him that none of them was aware that he owned this ranch or that Voyle was his brother.

"Howdy!" Voyle said. "What can I do for you?"

Kerb Perrin swung down from his horse. Behind him Monson, Ducrow and Kiefer were getting down.

"You can make as little trouble as you know how," Perrin said, his eyes gleaming. "All you got to do is stay out of the way. Where's the girls? We want them, and we want your cattle."

"What is this?" Voyle demanded. He wasn't wearing a gun; it was hanging from a clothes tree in the next room. "You men can't get away with anything here!"

Perrin's face was ugly as he strode toward the door. "That's what *you* think!" he sneered.

The tall old man blocked his way, and Perrin shoved him aside. Perrin had seen the startled faces of the girls inside and knew the men behind him were spreading out.

Ragan swung suddenly, and his fist struck Perrin in the mouth. The gunman staggered, and his face went white with fury.

A Mexican started from the corral toward the house, and Ducrow wheeled, firing from the hip. The man cried out and sprawled over on the hard-packed earth, moaning out his agony.

Perrin had drawn back slowly, his face ugly with rage, a slow trickling of blood from his lips. "For that, I'll kill you!" he snarled at Ragan.

"Not yet, Perrin!"

The voice had a cold ring of challenge, and Kerb Perrin went numb with shock. He turned slowly, to see Mike Bastian standing at the corner of the corral.

## VIII

Kerb Perrin was profoundly shocked. He had left Bastian a prisoner at Toadstool Canyon. Since he was free now, it could mean that Ben Curry was back in the saddle. It could mean a lot of things. An idea came with startling clarity to him. He had to kill Mike Bastian, and kill him now!

"You men have made fools of yourselves!" Bastian's voice was harsh. He stood there in his gray buckskins, his feet a little apart, his black hair rippled by the wind. "Ben Curry's not through! And this place is under his protection. He sent me to stop you, and stop you I shall! Now, any of you who don't want to fight Ben Curry, get out while the getting is good!"

"Stay where you are!" Perrin snapped. "I'll settle with you, Bastian— Right now!"

His hand darted down in the sweeping, lightning-fast draw for which he was noted. His lips curled in sneering contempt. Yet, as his gun lifted, he saw flame blossom from a gun in Bastian's hand, and a hard object slugged him. Perplexed and disturbed, he took a step backward. Whatever had hit him had knocked his gun out of line. He turned it toward Bastian again. The gun in Mike's hand blasted a second time, and a third.

Perrin could not seem to get his own gun leveled. His mind wouldn't function right, and he felt a strangeness in his stomach. His legs— Suddenly he was on his knees. He tried to get up and saw a dark pool forming near his knees. He must have slipped, he must have— That was blood.

It was *his* blood!

From far off he heard shouts, then a scream, then the pound of horses' hoofs. Then the thunder of those hoofs seemed to sweep through his brain and he was lying face down in the dirt. And then he knew: Mike Bastian had beaten him to the draw. Mike Bastian had shot him three times. Mike Bastian had killed him!

He started to scream a protest—and then he just lay there on his face, his cheek against the bloody ground, his mouth half open.

Kerb Perrin was dead.

In the instant that Perrin had reached for his gun, Ducrow had suddenly cut and ran toward the corner of the house. Kiefer, seeing his leader gunned down, then made a wild grab for his own weapon. The old man in the doorway killed him with a hastily caught-up rifle.

The others broke for their horses. Mike rushed after them and got off one more shot as they raced out of the yard. It was then he heard the scream, and whirled.

Ducrow had acted with suddenness. He had come to the ranch for women, and women he intended to have. Even as Bastian was killing Perrin, he rushed for the house. Darting around the corner where two saddle horses were waiting, he was just in time to see Juliana, horrified at the killing, run back into her bedroom. The bedroom window opened beside Ducrow, and the outlaw reached through and grabbed her.

Julie went numb with horror. Ducrow threw her across Perrin's saddle, and with a piggin string, which he always carried from his days as a cowhand, he jerked her ankles together under the horse's belly.

Instantly, he was astride the other horse. Julie screamed then. Wheeling, he struck her across the mouth with a backhand blow. He caught up the bridle of her horse and drove in spurs to his own mount, and they went out of the ranch yard at a dead run.

Mike hesitated only an instant when he heard Julie scream and then ran for the corner of the house. By the time he rounded the corner, gun in hand, the two horses were streaking into the piñons. In the dust, he could only catch a glimpse of the riders. He turned and walked back.

That had been a woman's scream, but Dru was in the doorway and he had seen her. Only then did he recall Julie. He sprinted for the doorway.

"Where's Julie?" he shouted to Drusilla. "Look through the house!"

He glanced around quickly. Kerb Perrin, mouth agape, lay dead on the hard earth of the ranch yard. Kiefer lay near the body of the

Mexican Ducrow had killed. The whole raid had been a matter of no more than two or three minutes.

Voyle Ragan dashed from the house. "Julie's gone!" he yelled hoarsely. "I'll get a horse!"

Bastian caught his arm. His own dark face was tense and his eyes wide.

"You'll stay here!" he said harshly. "Take care of the women and the ranch. I'll go after Julie."

Dru ran from the house. "She's gone, Mike, she's gone! They have her!"

Mike walked rapidly to his horse, thumbing shells into his gun. Dru Ragan started to mount another horse.

"You go back to the house!" he ordered.

Dru's chin came up. In that moment she reminded him of Ben Curry.

"She's my sister!" Dru cried. "When we find her, she may need a woman's care!"

"All right," Mike said, "but you'll have to do some riding!"

He wheeled the big bay around. The horse Dru had mounted was one of Ben Curry's beautiful horses, bred not only for speed but for staying power.

Mike's mind leaped ahead. Would Ducrow get back with the rest of them? Would he join Monson and Clatt? If he did, it was going to be a problem. Ducrow was a handy man with a six-gun, and tackling the three of them, or more if they were all together, would be nothing less than suicide.

He held the bay horse's pace down. He had taken a swift glance at the hoofmarks of the horses he was trailing and knew them both.

Would Ducrow head back for Toadstool Canyon? Bastian considered that as he rode, and decided he would not. Ducrow did not know that Julie was Ben Curry's daughter. But from what Mike had said, Ducrow had cause to believe that Ben was back in the saddle again. And men who went off on rebel raids were not lightly handled by Curry. Besides, he would want, if possible, to keep the girl for himself.

Mike had been taught by Roundy that there was more to trailing a man than following his tracks, for you trailed him down the devious paths of the mind as well. He tried to put himself in Ducrow's place.

The man could not have much food, yet on his many outlaw forays he must have learned the country and would know where there was water. Also, there were many ranch hangouts of the outlaws that Ducrow would know. He would probably go to one of them. Remembering the maps that Ben Curry had shown him and made him study, Mike knew the locations of all those places.

The trail turned suddenly off through the chaparral, and Mike turned to follow. Drusilla had said nothing since they started. Once he glanced at her. Even now, with her face dusty and tear streaked, she was lovely. Her eyes were fastened on the trail, and he noted with a little thrill of satisfaction that she had brought her rifle along.

Dru certainly was her father's daughter, and a fit companion for any man.

Bastian turned his attention to the trail. Despite the small lead he had, Ducrow had vanished. That taught Mike something of the nature of the man he was tracing; his years of outlawry had taught him how to disappear when need be. The method was simple. Turning off into the thicker desert growth, he had ridden down into a sandy wash.

Here, because of the deep sand and the tracks of horses and cattle, tracking was a problem and it took Mike several minutes to decide whether Ducrow had gone up or down the wash. Then he caught a hoofprint and they were off, winding up the sandy wash. Yet Mike knew they would not be in that sand for long. Ducrow would wish to save his horses' strength.

True enough, the trail soon turned out. From then on, it was a nightmare. Ducrow ran off in a straightaway and then turned at right angles, weaving about in the sandy desert. Several times he had stopped to brush out portions of his trail, but Roundy had not spent years training Mike Bastian in vain. He hung to the trail like a bloodhound.

Dru, riding behind him, saw him get off and walk, saw him pick up sign where she could see nothing.

Hours passed, and the day slowly drew toward an end. Dru, her face pale, realized night would come before they found her sister. She was about to speak, when Mike looked at her.

"You wanted to come," he said, "so you'll have to take the consequences. I'm not stopping because of darkness."

"How can you trail them?"

"I can't," he shrugged. "But I think I know where they are going. We'll take a chance."

Darkness closed around them. Mike's shirt stuck to his body with sweat, and a chill wind of the higher plateaus blew down through the trees. He rode on, his face grim and his body weary with long hours in the saddle. The big bay kept on, seemingly unhurt by the long hours of riding. Time and again he patted the big horse, and Dru could hear him talking to it in a low voice. Suddenly at the edge of a clearing, he reined in.

"Dru," he said, "there's a ranch ahead. It's an outlaw hangout. There may be one or more men there. Ducrow may be there. I am going up to find out."

"I'll come too," the girl said impulsively.

"You'll stay here!" His voice was flat. "When I whistle, then you come. Bring my horse along."

He swung down and, slipping off his boots, pulled on his moccasins. Then he went forward into the darkness. Alone, she watched him vanish toward the dark bulk of the buildings. Suddenly a light came on—too soon for him to have arrived.

Mike weaved his way through sage and mesquite to the corral and worked his way along the bars. Horses were there, but it was too dark to make them out. One of them stood near, and he put his hand through the bars, touching the horse's flank. It was damp with sweat.

His face tightened.

The horse stepped away, snorting. As if waiting for just that sound, a light went on in the house, a lamp had been lighted. By that time Mike was at the side of the house, flattened against the wall, peering in.

He saw a heavy, square-faced man with a pistol in his hand. The man put the gun under a towel on the table and then began pacing around the room, waiting. Mike smiled grimly, walked around the house, and stepped up on the porch. In his moccasins, he made no sound. He opened the door suddenly and stepped into the room.


# IX


Obviously the man had been waiting for the sound of boots or horses, or the jingle of spurs. Even a knock. Mike Bastian's sudden appearance startled him, and he straightened up from the table, his hand near the towel that covered the gun.

Bastian closed the door behind him. The man stared at the black-haired young man who faced him, stared with puckered brow. This man didn't look like a sheriff to him. Not those tied-down guns or that gray buckskin stained with travel, and no hat.

"You're Walt Sutton," Mike snapped. "Get your hands off that table before I blow you wide open! Get 'em off!"

He drew his gun and jammed the muzzle into Sutton's stomach with such force that it doubled the man up.

Then he swept the towel from the gun on the table.

"You fool!" he said sharply. "If you'd tried that, I'd have killed you!"

Sutton staggered back, his face gray. He had never even seen Mike's hand move.

"Who are you?" he gasped, struggling to get his wind back.

"I'm Mike Bastian, Ben Curry's foster son. He owns this ranch.

He set you up here and gave you stock to get started with. Now you double-cross him! Where's Ducrow?"

Sutton swallowed. "I ain't seen him!" he protested.

"You're a liar, Sutton! His horses are out in that corral. I could pistol-whip you, but I'm not going to. You're going to tell me where he is, and now—or I'm going to start shooting!"

Walt Sutton was unhappy. He knew Ducrow as one of Ben Curry's men who had come here before for fresh horses. He had never seen this man who called himself Mike Bastian, yet so far as he knew, no one but Curry himself had ever known the true facts about his ranch. If this man was lying, how could he know?

"Listen, mister," he protested, "I don't want no trouble—least of all with old Ben. He did set me up here. Sure, I seen Ducrow, but he told me the law was after him."

"Do I look like the law?" Mike snapped. "He's kidnapped the daughter of a friend of Curry's, niece of Voyle Ragan. I've got to find him."

"Kidnapped Voyle's niece? Gosh, mister, I wondered why he wanted two saddle horses!"

Mike whistled sharply. "Where'd he go?" he demanded then.

"Darned if I know," Sutton answered. "He come in here maybe an hour ago, wanted two saddle horses and a packhorse loaded with grub. He took two canteens then and lit out."

Drusilla appeared now in the doorway, and Walt Sutton's eyes went to her.

"I know you," he said. "You're one of Voyle Ragan's nieces."

"She is," Mike said. "Ducrow kidnapped the other one. I'm going to find him. Get us some grub, but fast!"

Mike paced restlessly while Sutton filled a pack and strapped it behind the saddle of one of the fresh horses he furnished them. The horses were some of those left at the ranch by Ben Curry's orders and were good.

"No packhorses," Mike had said. "We're traveling fast."

Now, he turned to Sutton again. "You got any idea where Ducrow might be going?"

"Well"—Sutton licked his lips—"he'd kill me if he knowed I said anything, but he did say something about Peach Meadow Canyon."

"Peach Meadow?" Bastian stared at Sutton. The canyon was almost a legend in the Coconino country. "What did he ask you?"

"If I knowed the trail in there, an' if it was passable."

"What did you say?"

Sutton shrugged. "Well, I've heard tell of that there canyon ever since I been in this country, an' ain't seen no part of it. I've looked, all right. Who wouldn't look, if all they say is true?"

When they were about to mount their horses, Mike turned to the girl and put his hand on her arm.

"Dru," he said, "it's going to be rough, so if you want to go back, say so."

"I wouldn't think of it!" she said firmly.

"Well, I won't say I'm sorry, because I'm not. I'll sure like having you beside me. In fact"—he hesitated and then went on—"it will be nice having you."

That was not what he had started to say, and Dru knew it. She looked at Mike for a moment, her eyes soft. He was tired now, and she could see how drawn his face was. She knew only a little of the ride he had made to reach them before Perrin's outlaws came.

When they were in the saddle, Mike explained a little of what he had in mind. "I doubt Ducrow will stop for anything now," he said. "There isn't a good hiding place within miles, so he'll head right for the canyon country. He may actually know something about Peach Meadow Canyon. If he does, he knows a perfect hideaway. Outlaws often stumble across places in their getaways that a man couldn't find if he looked for it in years."

"What is Peach Meadow Canyon?" Dru asked.

"It's supposed to be over near the river in one of the deep canyons that branch off from the Colorado. According to the story, a fellow found the place years ago, but the Spanish had been there before him, and the Indians before them. There are said to be old Indian ruins in the place, but no way to get into it from the plateau. The Indians found a way through some caves in the Coconino sandstone, and the Spanish are supposed to have reached it by boat.

"Anyway," he continued, "this prospector who found it said the climate was tropical, or almost. That it was in a branch canyon, that there was fresh water and a nice meadow. Somebody had planted some fruit trees, and when he went back he took a lot of peach pits and was supposed to have planted an orchard.

"Nobody ever saw him or it again," Mike went on, "so the place exists only on his say-so. The Indians alive now swear they never heard of it. Ducrow might be trying to throw us off, or he might honestly know something."

For several miles the trail was a simple thing. They were riding down the floor of a high-walled canyon from which there was no escape. Nevertheless, from time to time Bastian stopped and examined the sandy floor with matches. Always the tracks were there and going straight down the canyon.

This was new country to Mike. He knew the altitude was gradually lessening and believed they would soon emerge on the desert plateau that ran toward the canyon and finally lost itself on the edge of the pine forest.

When they had traveled about seven miles, the canyon ended abruptly and they emerged in a long valley. Mike reined in and swung down.

"Like it or not," he said, "here's where we stop. We can't have a fire, because from here it could be seen for miles. We don't want Ducrow to believe we stopped."

Mike spread his poncho on the sand and handed Dru a blanket. She was feeling the chill and gathered it close around her.

"Aren't you cold?" she said suddenly. "If we sat close together we could share the blanket."

He hesitated and then sat down alongside her and pulled the blanket across his shoulders, grateful for the warmth. Leaning back against the rock, warmed by their proximity and the blanket, they dozed a little.

Mike had loosened the girths and ground hitched the horses. He wasn't worried about them straying off.

When the sky was just faintly gray, he opened his eyes. Dru's head was on his shoulder and she was sleeping. He could feel the rise and fall of her breathing against his body. He glanced down at her face, amazed that this could happen to him—that he, Mike Bastian, foster son of an outlaw, could be sitting alone in the desert, with this girl sleeping on his shoulder!

Some movement of his must have awakened her, for her breath caught, and then she looked up. He could see the sleepy smile in her eyes and on her mouth.

"I was tired!" She whispered the words and made no effort to move her head from his shoulder. "You've nice shoulders," she said. "If we were riding anywhere else, I'd not want to move at all."

"Nor I." He glanced at the stars. "We'd better get up. I think we can chance a very small fire and a quick cup of coffee."

While he was breaking dried mesquite and greasewood, Dru got the pack open and dug out the coffee and some bread. There was no time for anything else.

The fire made but little light, shielded by the rocks and kept very small, and there was less glow now because of the grayness of the sky. They ate quickly.

When they were in the saddle again, he turned down the trail left by the two saddle horses and the packhorse he was following. Sign was dim, but could be followed without dismounting. Dawn broke, and the sky turned red and gold, then blue. The sun lifted and began to take some of the chill from their muscles.

The trail crossed the valley, skirting an alkali lake, and then dipped into the rocky wilderness that preceded the pine forest. He could find no signs of a camp. Julie, who lacked the fire and also the strength of Dru, must be almost dead with weariness, for Ducrow was not stopping. Certainly, the man had more than a possible destination before him. In fact, the farther they rode, the more confident Mike was that the outlaw knew exactly where he was headed.

The pines closed around them, and the trail became more difficult to follow. It was slow going, and much of it Mike Bastian walked. Suddenly he stopped, scowling.

The trail, faint as it had been, had vanished into thin air!

"Stay where you are," he told Dru. "I've got to look around a bit."

Mike studied the ground carefully. Then he walked back to the last tracks he had seen. Their own tracks did not cover them, as he had avoided riding over them in case he needed to examine the hoofprints once more.

Slowly, Mike paced back and forth over the pine needles. Then he stopped and studied the surrounding timber very carefully. It seemed to be absolutely uniform in appearance. Avoiding the trail ahead, he left the girl and circled into the woods, describing a slow circle around the horses.

There were no tracks.

He stopped, his brow furrowed. It was impossible to lose them after following so far—yet they were gone, and they had left no trail. He walked back to the horses again, and Dru stared at him, her eyes wide.

"Wait a minute," he said as she began to speak. "I want to think."

He studied, inch by inch, the woods on his left, the trail ahead, and then the trail on his right. Nothing offered a clue. The tracks of three horses had simply vanished as though the animals and their riders had been swallowed into space.

On the left the pines stood thick, and back inside the woods the brush was so dense as to allow no means of passing through it. That was out, then. He had studied that brush and had walked through those woods, and if a horseman did turn that way there would be no place to go.

The trail ahead was trackless, so it had to be on the right. Mike turned and walked again to the woods on his right. He inched over the ground, yet there was nothing, no track, no indication that anything heavier than a rabbit had passed that way. It was impossible, yet it had happened.

"Could they have backtracked?" Dru asked suddenly. "Over their same trail?"

Mike shook his head. "There were no tracks," he said, "but those going ahead, I think—" He stopped dead still and then swore. "I'm a fool! A darned fool!" He grinned at her. "Lend me your hat."

Puzzled, she removed her sombrero and handed it to him. He turned and using the hat for a fan, began to wave it over the ground to let the wind disturb the surface needles. Patiently, he worked over the area around the last tracks seen, and then to the woods on both sides of the trail. Suddenly, he stopped.

"Got it," he said. "Here they are!"

Dru ran to him. He pointed to a track, then several more.

"Ducrow was smart," Mike explained. "He turned at right angles and rode across the open space, and then turned back down the way he had come, riding over on the far side. Then he dismounted and, coming back, gathered pine needles from somewhere back in the brush and came along here, pressing the earth down and scattering the needles to make it seem there had been no tracks at all!"

Mounting again, they started back, and from time to time he dismounted to examine the trail. Suddenly the tracks turned off into thick woods. Leading their horses, they followed.

"Move as quietly as you can," Mike said softly. "We may be close, now. Or he may wait and try to ambush us."

"You think he knows we're following him?" Dru asked.

"Sure! And he knows I'm a tracker. He'll use every trick in the books, now."

For a while, the trail was not difficult to follow, and they rode again. Mike Bastian could not take his mind from the girl who rode with him. What would she think when she discovered her father was an outlaw—that he was the mysterious leader of the outlaws?

# X

Pine trees thinned out, and before them was the vast blue and misty distance of the canyon. Mike slid to the ground and walked slowly forward on moccasined feet. There were a few scattered pines and the cracked and splintered rim of the canyon, breaking sharply off to fall away into the vast depths. Carefully, he scouted the edge of the canyon, and when he saw the trail he stopped flat-footed and stared, his heart in his mouth.

Had they gone down *there*? He knelt on the rock. Yes, there was the scar of a horse's hoof. He walked out a little farther, looking down.

The cliff fell away for hundreds of feet without even a hump in the wall. Then, just a little farther along, he saw the trail. It was a rocky ledge scarcely three feet wide that ran steeply down the side of the rock from the canyon's rim. On the left the wall, on the right the vast, astonishing emptiness of the canyon.

Thoughtfully, he walked back and explained.

"All right, Mike," Dru nodded. "If you're ready, I am."

He hesitated to bring the horses, but decided it would be the best thing. He drew his rifle from the saddle scabbard and jacked a shell into the chamber.

Dru looked at him, steady-eyed. "Mike, maybe he'll be waiting for us," she said. "We may get shot. Especially you."

Bastian nodded. "That could be," he agreed.

She came toward him. "Mike, who are you? What are you? Uncle Voyle seemed to know you, or about you, and that outlaw, Perrin. He knew you. Then I heard you say Ben Curry had sent you to stop them from raiding the ranch. Are you an outlaw, Mike?"

For as long as a man might have counted a slow ten, Mike stared out over the canyon, trying to make up his mind. Now, at this stage, there was only one thing he could say.

"No, Dru, not exactly, but I was raised by an outlaw," he explained. "Ben Curry brought me up like his own son, with the idea that I would take over the gang when he stepped out."

"You lived with them in their hideout?"

"When I wasn't out in the woods." He nodded. "Ben Curry had me taught everything—how to shoot, to track, to ride, even to open safes and locks."

"What's he like, this Ben Curry?" Dru asked.

"He's quite a man!" Mike Bastian said, smiling. "When he started outlawing, everybody was rustling a few cows, and he just went a step further and robbed banks and stages, or planned the robberies and directed them. I don't expect he really figured himself bad. He might have done a lot of other things, for he has brains. But he killed a man—and then in getting away, he killed another. The first one was justified. The second one— Well, he was in a hurry."

"Are you apologizing for him?" Dru said quickly. "After all, he was an outlaw and a killer."

He glanced at her. "He was, yes. And I am not making any apologies for him, nor would he want them. He's a man who always stood on his own two feet. Maybe he was wrong but there were the circumstances. And he was mighty good to me. I didn't have a home, no place to go, and he took me in and treated me right."

"Was he a big man, Mike? A big old man?"

He did not look her way. She knew, then?

"In many ways," he said, "he is one of the biggest men I know. We'd better get started."

\*     \*     \*

It was like stepping off into space, yet the horses took it calmly enough. They were mountain bred and would go anywhere as long as they could get a foothold on something.

The red maw of the canyon gaped to receive them, and they went down, following the narrow, switchback trail that seemed to be leading them into the very center of the earth.

It was late afternoon before they started down, and now the shadows began to creep up the canyon walls, reaching with ghostly fingers for the vanished sunlight. Overhead the red blazed with the setting sun's reflection and seemed to be hurling arrows of flame back into the sky. The depths of the canyon seemed chill after the sun on the plateau, and Mike walked warily, always a little ahead of the horse he was leading.

Dru was riding, and when he glanced back once, she smiled brightly at him, keeping her eyes averted from the awful depths below.

Mike had no flair for making love, for his knowledge of women was slight. He wished now that he knew more of their ways, knew the things to say that would appeal to a girl.

A long time later they reached the bottom, and far away on their right they could hear the river rushing through the canyon. Mike knelt and striking a match, he studied the trail. The tracks turned back into a long canyon that led back from the river.

He got into the saddle then, his rifle across his saddle, and rode forward.

At the end, it was simple. The long chase had led to a quiet meadow, and he could smell the grass before he reached it, could hear the babble of a small stream. The canyon walls flared wide, and he saw, not far away, the faint sparkle of a fire.

Dru came alongside him. "Is . . . that them?" she asked, low voiced.

"It couldn't be anyone else." Her hand was on his arm and he put his own hand over it. "I've got to go up there alone, Dru. I'll have to kill him, you know."

"Yes," she said, simply, "but don't *you* be killed!"

He started to ride forward, and she caught his arm.

"Mike, why have you done all this?" she asked. "She isn't your sister."

"No." He looked very serious in the vague light. "She's yours."

He turned his head and spoke to the horse. The animal started forward.

When, shortly, he stopped the mount, he heard a sound nearby. Dru Ragan was close behind him.

"Dru," he whispered, "you've *got* to stay back! Hold my horse. I'm going up on foot."

He left her like that and walked steadily forward. Even before he got to the fire, he could see them. The girl, her head slumped over on her arms, half dead with weariness, and Ducrow bending over the fire. From time to time Ducrow glanced at the girl. Finally, he reached over and cuffed her on the head.

"Come on, get some of this coffee into you!" he growled. "This is where we stay—in Peach Meadow Canyon. Might as well give up seein' that sister of yours, because you're my woman now!" He sneered. "Monson and them, they ran like scared foxes! No bottom to them. I come for a woman, and I got one!"

"Why don't you let me go?" Juliana protested. "My father will pay you well. He has lots of money."

"Your pa?" Ducrow stared at her. "I thought Voyle Ragan was your uncle?"

"He is. I mean Ben Ragan. He ranches up north of the canyon."

"North of the canyon?" Ducrow laughed. "Not unless he's a Mormon, he don't. What's he look like, this pa of yours?"

"He's a great big man, with iron-gray hair, a heavy jaw—" She stopped, staring at Ducrow. "What's the matter with you?"

Ducrow got slowly to his feet. "Your pa—Ben Ragan? A big man with gray hair, an' maybe a scar on his jaw—that him?"

"Oh, yes! Take me to him! He'll pay you well!"

Suddenly, Ducrow let out a guffaw of laughter. He slapped his leg and bellowed. "Man, oh, man! Is that a good one! You're Ben Curry's daughter! Why, that old—" He sobered. "What did you call him? Ragan? Why, honey, that old man of yours is the biggest outlaw in the world! Or was until today! Well, of all the—"

"You've laughed enough, Ducrow!"

As Mike Bastian spoke, he stepped to the edge of the firelight. "You leave a tough trail, but I followed it."

Ducrow turned, half crouching, his cruel eyes glaring at Bastian.

"Roundy was right," he snarled. "You could track a snake across a flat rock! Well, now that you're here, what are you goin' to do?"

"That depends on you, Ducrow. You can drop your guns, and I'll take you in for a trial. Or you can shoot it out."

"Drop my guns?" Ducrow chuckled. "You'd actually take me in, too! You're too soft, Bastian. You'd never make the boss man old Ben Curry was. He would never even of said yes or no; he would have seen me and gone to blastin'! You got a sight to learn, youngster. Too bad you ain't goin' to live long enough to learn it."

Ducrow lifted one hand carelessly and wiped it across the tobacco-stained stubble of his beard. His right hand swept down for his gun even as his left touched his face. His gun came up, spouting flame.

Mike Bastian palmed his gun and momentarily held it rigid. Then he fired.

Ducrow winced like he had been slugged in the chest, and then he lifted on his tiptoes. His gun came level again.

"You're . . . fast!" he gasped. "Devilish fast!"

He fired, and then Mike triggered his gun once more. The second shot spun Ducrow around and he fell, face down, at the edge of the fire.

Dru came running, her rifle in her hand, but when she saw Mike still standing, she dropped the rifle and ran to him.

"Oh, Mike!" she sobbed. "I was so frightened! I thought you were killed!"

Julie started to rise and then fell headlong in a faint. Dru rushed to her side.

Mike Bastian absently thumbed shells into his gun and stared down at the fallen man. He had killed a third man. Suddenly, and profoundly, he wished with all his heart he would never have to kill another.

He holstered his weapon and, gathering up the dead man, carried him away from the fire. He would bury him here, in Peach Meadow Canyon.

# XI

Sunlight lay upon the empty street of the settlement in Toadstool Canyon when Mike Bastian, his rifle crosswise on his saddle, rode slowly into the lower end of the town.

Beside him, sitting straight in her saddle, rode Dru Ragan. Julie had stayed at the ranch, but Dru had flatly refused. Ben Curry was her father, and she was going to him, outlaw camp or not.

If Dave Lenaker had arrived, Mike thought, he was quiet enough, for there was no sound. No horses stood at the hitch rails, and the doors of the saloon were wide open.

Something fluttered on the ground, and Mike looked at it quickly. It was a torn bit of cloth on a man's body. The man was a stranger. Dru noticed it and her face paled.

His rifle at ready, Mike rode on, eyes shifting from side to side. A man's wrist lay in sight across a window sill, his pistol on the porch outside. There was blood on the stoop of another house.

"There's been a fight," Mike said, "and a bad one. You'd better get set for the worst."

Dru said nothing, but her mouth held firm. At the last building, the mess hall, a man lay dead in a doorway. They rode on and then drew up at the foot of the stone steps and dismounted. Mike shoved his rifle back in the saddle scabbard and loosened his six-guns.

"Let's go!" he said.

The wide veranda was empty and still, but when he stepped into the huge living room, he stopped in amazement, five men sat about a table playing cards.

Ben Curry's head came up and he waved at them.

"Come on in, Mike!" he called. "Who's that with you? Dru, by all that's holy!"

Doc Sawyer, Roundy, Garlin, and Colley were there. Garlin's head was bandaged, and Colley had one foot stretched out stiff and straight, as did Ben Curry. But all were smiling.

Dru ran to her father and fell on her knees beside him.

"Oh, Dad!" she cried. "We were so scared!"

"What happened here?" Mike demanded. "Don't sit there grinning! Did Dave Lenaker come?"

"He sure did, and what do you think?" Doc said. "It was Rigger Molina got him! Rigger got to Weaver and found out Perrin had double-crossed him before he ever pulled the job. He discovered that Perrin had lied about the guards, so he rushed back. When he found out that Ben was crippled and that Kerb Perrin had run out, he waited for Lenaker himself.

"He was wonderful, Mike," Doc continued. "I never saw anything like it! He paced the veranda out there like a bear in a cage, swearing and waiting for Lenaker. Muttered, 'Leave you in the lurch, will they? I'll show 'em! Lenaker thinks he can gun you down because you're gettin' old, does he? Well, killer I may be, but I can kill him!' And he did, Mike. They shot it out in the street down there. Dave Lenaker, as slim and tall as you, and that great bear of a Molina.

"Lenaker beat him to the draw," Doc went on. "He got two bullets into the Rigger, but Molina wouldn't go down. He stood there spraddle-legged in the street and shot until both guns were empty. Lenaker kept shooting and must have hit Molina five times, but when he went down, Rigger walked over to him and spat in his face. 'That for double-crossers!' he said. He was magnificent!"

"They fooled me, Mike," Roundy said. "I seen trouble a-comin' an' figured I'd better get to old Ben. I never figured they'd slip in behind you like they done. Then the news of Lenaker comin' got me. I knowed him an' was afraid of him, so I figured to save Ben Curry I'd get down the road and dry-gulch him. Never killed a gunslinger like him in my life, Mike, but I was sure aimin' to! But he got by me on another trail. After Molina killed Lenaker, his boys and some of them from here started after the gold they'd figured was in this house."

"Doc here," Garlin said, "is some fighter! I didn't know he had it in him."

"Roundy, Doc, Garlin, an' me," Colley said, "we sided Ben Curry. It was a swell scrap while it lasted. Garlin got one through his scalp, and I got two bullets in the leg. Aside from that, we came out all right."

Briefly, then, Mike explained all that had transpired, how he had killed Perrin and then had trailed Ducrow to Peach Meadow Canyon and the fight there.

"Where's the gang?" he demanded now. "All gone?"

"All the live ones." Ben Curry nodded grimly. "There's a few won't go anywhere. Funny, the only man who ever fooled me was Rigger Molina. I never knew the man was that loyal, yet he stood by me when I was in no shape to fight Lenaker. Took that fight right off my hands. He soaked up lead like a sponge soaks water!"

Ben Curry looked quickly at Dru. "So you know you're the daughter of an outlaw? Well, I'm sorry, Dru. I never aimed for you to know. I was gettin' shet of this business and planned to settle down on a ranch with your mother and live out the rest of my days plumb peaceful."

"Why don't you?" Dru demanded.

He looked at her, his admiring eyes taking in her slim, well-rounded figure. "You reckon she'll have me?" he asked. "She looked a sight like you when she was younger, Dru."

"Of course, she'll have you! She doesn't know—or didn't know until Julie told her. But I think she guessed. *I* knew. I saw you talking with some men once, and later heard they were outlaws, and then I began hearing about Ben Curry."

Curry looked thoughtfully from Dru to Mike.

"Is there something between you two? Or am I an old fool?"

Mike flushed and kept his eyes away from Dru.

"He's a fine man, Dru," Doc Sawyer said. "And well educated, if I do say so—who taught him all he knows."

"All he knows!" Roundy stared at Doc with contempt. "Book larnin'! Where would that gal be but for what I told him? How to read sign, how to foller a trail? Where would she be?"

Mike took Dru out to the veranda then.

"I can read sign, all right," he said, "but I'm no hand at reading the trail to a woman's heart. You would have to help me, Dru."

She laughed softly, and her eyes were bright as she slipped her arm through his. "Why, Mike, you've been blazing a trail over and back and up again, ever since I met you in the street at Weaver!"

Suddenly, she sobered. "Mike, let's get some cattle and go back to

Peach Meadow Canyon. You said you could make a better trail in, and it would be a wonderful place! Just you and I and—"

"Sure," he said. "In Peach Meadow Canyon."

Roundy craned his head toward the door and then he chuckled.

"That youngster," he said. "He may not know all the trails, but he sure gets where he's goin'. He sure does!"